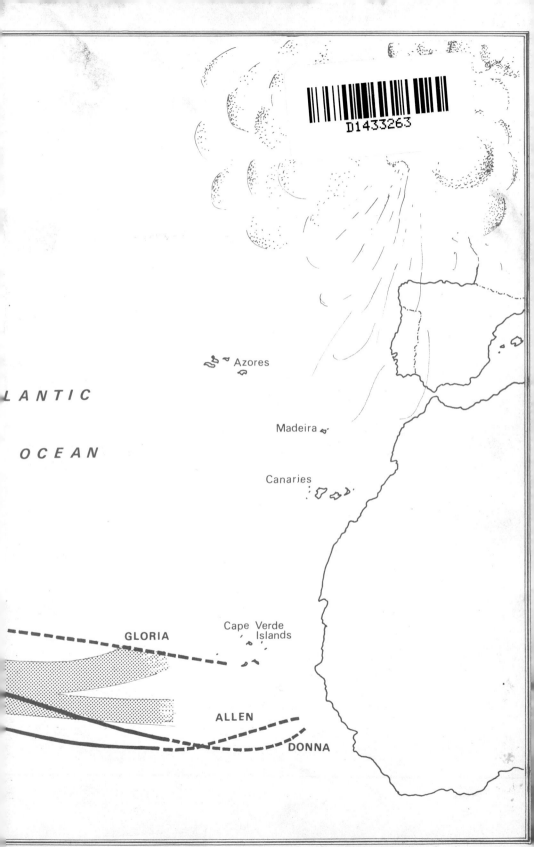

ATLANTIC

OCEAN

Azores

Madeira

Canaries

Cape Verde
Islands

GLORIA

ALLEN

DONNA

HER NAME WILL BE FAITH

Max Marlow

HER NAME WILL BE FAITH

NEW ENGLISH LIBRARY

British Library Cataloguing in Publication Data

Marlow, Max
  Her name will be Faith.
  I. Title
  813'.54[F]

ISBN 0-450-48548-x

Published by New English Library,
a hardcover imprint of Hodder and Stoughton,
a division of Hodder and Stoughton Ltd,
Mill Road, Dunton Green, Sevenoaks, Kent TN13 2YE
Editorial Office: 47 Bedford Square, London WC1B 3DP

Photoset by Rowland Phototypesetting Ltd,
Bury St Edmunds, Suffolk

Printed in Great Britain by St Edmundsbury Press Ltd,
Bury St Edmunds, Suffolk

This is a novel. The characters are invented and are not intended to depict real persons, living or dead.
The events related have not yet happened.

TABLE OF EVENTS

May – The beginning?
May – The last week
Thursday 1 June
June – The first two weeks
June – The last two weeks
July – The second week
July – The third week
July – The fourth week
Monday 24 July
Tuesday 25 July
Wednesday 26 July
Thursday 27 July
Friday 28 July
Saturday 29 July – Pre-dawn
Saturday 29 July – Early morning
Saturday 29 July – Mid-morning
Saturday 29 July – Afternoon
Saturday 29 July – Evening and after
May – The end?

CHARACTERS

THE DONNELLYS
Josephine (Jo), Englishwoman on editorial staff of *Profiles* magazine
Michael, junior, her husband, partner in the New York stockbroking firm of Donnelly and Son
Owen Michael, their son
Tamsin, their daughter
Michael, senior (Big Mike), Michael's father and senior partner in Donnelly and Son
Barbara (Babs), his wife
Belle Garr, their elder daughter
Lawson Garr, son-in-law, real estate agent in Nassau, Bahamas
Marcia, their younger daughter, an artist
Benny, her fiancé
Dale, their younger son
Florence Bennett, Jo Donnelly's housekeeper

NATIONAL AMERICAN BROADCASTING SYSTEM
J. Calthrop White, President and chief shareholder
Kiley, Executive Vice-President
Richard Connors, chief weather forecaster
Julian Summers, his assistant
Jayme, his secretary
Dave, newsreader
Rod Kimmelman, reporter
Maisie, switchboard operator
Joe Murray, J. Calthrop White's chauffeur

HURRICANE TRACKING TEAM
Dr Eisener, official at the United States Hurricane Tracking Center, Coral Gables, Florida
Captain Mark Hammond, United States Navy, seconded to the Weather Bureau
Bob Landry, his co-pilot
Mackenzie, his navigator

THE ROBSON FAMILY
 Neal, friend of the Donnellys
 Margaret (Meg), his wife
 James, their son
 Suzanne, their daughter

MICHAEL DONNELLY'S YACHT CREW
 Larry Simmons
 Pete Albicete
 Mark Godwin
 Jon Tremayne
 Sam Davenport
 Sally, Sam's wife (not in crew)
 Beth, Larry's wife (not in crew)

ON ELEUTHERA
 Melba, the Donnellys' cook
 Josh, her husband, their gardener
 Goodson, their nephew
 Christabel, airline agent

JO DONNELLY'S INTERVIEWEES
 Washington Jones, janitor at the junior Donnellys' New York apartment
   building
   Celestine, his wife
   Patsy, their daughter
 Lila Vail, widow from Florida, now living in New York with Tootsie,
   her widowed sister
   Dai Evans, their neighbour
 Nancy Duval, Joe's hairdresser
   Bill, her husband
   Ernest, his brother
 Alfred Muldoon, a New York cab driver
 Stuart Alloan, a drop-out
   Garcia, a criminal fugitive, his friend

NEW YORK POLICE DEPARTMENT
 Commissioner Grundy
 Assistant Commissioner McGrath
 Captain Harmon
 Captain Wright
 Captain Jonsson
 Captain Luther

* * *

Characters

Bert, Florence Bennett's husband
Ed Kowicz, Managing Editor of *Profiles*
Gordon, a Florida weather forecaster
Bill Naseby, Mayor of New York
Mitch, his assistant
Seth Hatton, President of the Hunt National Bank
The President of the United States.

'Tropical cyclones are the most energetic and destructive of all weather systems.'

The Times Atlas of the Oceans

MAY

The Beginning?

WEDNESDAY 24 MAY

The Atlantic

The big amphibian was alone in the sky. Four hundred miles due east of Puerto Rico, Captain Mark Hammond looked down on fleecy white clouds, and, where they had drifted apart, on to the surging blue of the North Atlantic Ocean.

It was a sight with which he was thoroughly familiar. Since his secondment to the Weather Service a year earlier, he had flown out here at least once a week, looking, watching . . . May was traditionally the quietest month of the year, weatherwise, but there had been major storms in May before. And now the month was drawing to a close; next Thursday would mark the official beginning of the hurricane season. If there was a Tropical Storm about, it was his duty to find it, and let the boffins determine its potential, long before it could approach land.

Dr Eisener was at his shoulder. "You can take her down now, Mark."

Mark's long thin neck moved as he nodded; his neck matched both his body, which seemed to be coiled even in the spacious flight deck, and his face, in which a long nose and pointed chin gave him a certain resemblance to a cigar-store Indian. A Californian, he had volunteered for a spell in the Weather Service to see how the other half of the country lived, and often wished he had stayed at home: Miami to him was like a poor man's San Francisco . . . and California had been hit by three hurricanes last year: Florida, protected by the natural breakwaters of Cuba and the Bahamas, by none at all.

He gave the signal to his co-pilot, and the aircraft began to sink through the clouds. If she wore navy colours, she was still the very latest in flying laboratories, only a few hundred hours old, with sensors protruding from her roof and wings and belly to record every possible aspect of the atmosphere in which she found herself . . . and her true commander was Eisener, surrounded back in the main cabin by his staff and their various computers and radars; if the satellites whirling high in space above their heads were photographing every cloud over the ocean, it was Eisener who was going to add the fine print for the nation's busy weather forecasters.

Mark certainly didn't wish a major storm on anyone. But as discovering such an event was, at the moment, his sole reason for existing, he hoped one day to justify that existence. There hadn't been a truly major storm, a Category Four hurricane, for instance, in the North Atlantic since before he had been born. So Category Three storms, of which Gloria back in 1985 remained the most famous, could do a whole lot of damage – it was still the possibility of a really big one which fascinated everyone connected with Atlantic weather. One was about due.

The aircraft sank lower and lower. The clouds were above them now, the dark blue of the ocean below them coming closer every second. There was clearly very little wind; only the occasional wave flopped into a whitecap, dissolving in a splodge of foam; even the trade wind was in a May-like mood.

Now Mark was skimming the surface of the sea, the huge turbos throttled back almost to stalling point as he allowed Eisener to suck sea water into his tanks. Although it was calm enough to splash down without difficulty – and get up again – if he had to, this was always the most tense part of the patrol; he breathed a sigh of relief when Eisener's voice came through the intercom, "Okay, Mark, take her up."

The engines increased power, the plane rose like a bird, and a moment later was through the clouds.

"Home, I think," Eisener said, coming up to the flight deck.

"Anything?" Mark asked.

"Why, yes. Something."

Mark turned his head in surprise. "Today? It all looks pretty good to me."

"It all is pretty good," Eisener agreed. "Save for the water temperature. I have a reading of 27° Centigrade."

"At the end of May?"

"Interesting, isn't it? Especially when we add it to all those other readings."

"Yeah, Doctor," Mark said. "Goddamned interesting."

The aircraft droned back over Puerto Rico and Haiti, gaining height to fly across the serrated mountains of Communist Cuba, then dipping lower again as the tiny Bahamian islands came into view – splashes of green against the pale colours of the immense sandbank on which they rested – before landing at Key West soon after six. Mark went straight to the public telephone after debriefing, dialled a New York number. "Hi," he said, "Richard about?" He waited, drumming a finger on the glass wall of the booth.

"Connors," said the voice on the end of the line.

"Mark."

"Hi, old buddy. Something for me?" Richard Connors' drawl was suddenly animated.

"Could be. How does a water temperature of 27° Centigrade in mid-Atlantic grab you."

"On 24 May?"

"That's what the man says. And let me give you some more." He listed numbers, slowly, giving his friend time to write them down. "Yeah," Connors said, thoughtfully. "Yeah. Thanks a million, Mark. You coming north any time?"

"I've a furlough next month. You got an apartment yet?"

"Maybe. We're talking terms this afternoon. There'll be a bed in the lounge."

"So I'll see you. Guess what. Or who, I saw the other day. Pam."

"Great," Connors said without enthusiasm. "How's she doing?"

"Looks pretty good to me. Tall, tanned . . ."

"And terrific," Connors agreed, and sighed. He could picture her in front of him. But her predilection for sun, sand, and sea, and the beach-bums who went with those things, had been the prime reason for his divorce. Without which, he thought grimly, he would never have left Florida . . . not even to be on nationwide television. "Next time, give her my regards. And Mark . . . keep me up to date on those water temperatures, eh?"

"You got it," Mark said, and hung up.

MAY

The Last Week

THURSDAY 25 MAY

National American Broadcasting Service Offices, Fifth Avenue

"I have Connors outside, JC," Kiley said.

J. Calthrop White grunted as he perused the financial pages of the *New York Times*, and Kiley twisted his fingers together. He might be network manager, but the company president was a difficult man to work for, or with. J. Calthrop White was a short, thin man, whose energy belied his shock of white hair, and whose irascibility made a nonsense of his puckish features; his more junior employees were wont to refer to him as Jesus Christ, and his more senior staff sometimes supposed that he also might have mistaken his initials.

"Who's Richard Connors?" he asked.

"The new forecaster, JC," Kiley explained.

"From Florida," White remarked, still studying his paper.

"Well, from California, actually, JC," Kiley said nervously. "But he worked in Florida, yes. For three years."

"So what decided you to bring him up here, for Chrissake?"

"Well, JC . . ." Kiley's fingers were tying themselves in knots. "Down in Miami he was big. He's got it all. Looks, personality, charm, knowhow . . . and an almost prescient way of forecasting the weather. He was getting seventy plus letters a week down with WJQT. I reckon he'll make an impact on the ratings up here."

"Weather forecasters make impacts?"

"Everyone watches the weather, JC; it's right after the News. Give them a face they like watching, a guy who sounds like he knows what he's talking about, and they just start watching one particular channel to listen to that guy again."

J. Calthrop White at last raised his head. "How much?" he asked.

Kiley knew that although his boss was thinking of the ratings, he wasn't actually referring to them. "Well, I had to go a little over the odds," he said.

"How much?" White repeated.

"Well, seventy-five."

White leaned back in his chair. "Kiley, you are paying some shavetail

9

beachbum as much as a cabinet minister to tell me it's gonna rain tomorrow? Jesus Christ!"

"He's good," Kiley said. "And it's only a one-year contract, renewable."

"He had better be good," White said. "Show him in."

Kiley almost ran to the door. "Mr White can see you now, Richard."

He held the door ajar, and Richard Connors entered the big office which looked down the length of Fifth Avenue from the top floor of the National American Broadcasting Service building. White looked him up and down. The new weather forecaster was six feet three inches tall, and had an undeniably handsome face except for the broken nose which had mended slightly off the straight, but this in turn gave him an attractively macho appearance. His shoulders were good and it was easy to tell he was fit. He also exuded confidence. These were all characteristics which J. Calthrop White personally disliked in other men, as he possessed none of them himself. Except confidence.

"Footballer, eh?" he inquired.

"Why, yes, Mr White," Connors agreed. "UCLA."

"I hate football," White informed him. "Kiley tells me you can forecast the weather."

"That's my job, Mr White," Connors said, refusing to be overawed.

"So tell me what sort of a summer we're gonna have."

Kiley was back to his finger twisting; he knew that JC never joked, and would remember whatever he was told.

"It'll be hot," Connors said.

"Yeah? That's easy. It's goddamned hot already."

"It'll be hotter," Connors insisted. "And there'll be more hurricane activity than usual."

"Now, how the hell can you tell that?"

"Because the ocean is much warmer than is usual at this time of year, Mr White. Warm water spawns tropical storms."

"Richard is an expert on hurricanes, JC," Kiley put in, eagerly.

"We don't have hurricanes in New York," White pointed out. "You're not in Florida now. Have a good day."

Kiley was waggling his eyebrows, and Connors nodded. "Thank you, Mr White," he said, and left the office.

"Seventy five thousand," White remarked, and pressed his buzzer. "Alice, get me Mike Donnelly."

"Senior, or junior, JC?"

"For Chrissake, when I want to talk to some kid I'll tell you," JC growled and released the switch to glare at Kiley. "Seventy-five thousand." He pointed. "He'd better be as good as you say, Kiley."

The phone buzzed. "I have Mr Donnelly senior, Mr White."

Calthrop White arranged his features into a smile, as if hoping thereby to influence his voice. "Mike, you old son of a gun. How's it going? . . . Yeah, damned hot. How's the boy? . . . Already? I thought the yacht racing season didn't start until June? . . . Is that a fact. Mike, I want to float a stock issue." This time he had to listen somewhat longer before he could speak again. "Oh, sure, sure," he said at last. "I read my papers. But this has to be, Mike. There's a franchise coming up in England this autumn . . . I reckon 125 million will do it . . . Sure, Mike, sure. I can swing my board, and my stockholders. For Chrissake, most of them are relatives anyway. Listen, why don't you come over and talk about it . . . Sure, bring Michael if you want, whenever he can spare the time from playing with his little boat. But make it soon . . . It has to be this summer, Mike . . . Sure, sure, but in my book, nothing is impossible if you really get to it. You come on over. Love to Babs and the kids." He replaced the phone, leaned back in his chair, gazed at Kiley. "Goddamned Irish shit," he remarked. "Can't be done, he says. What the hell is a stockbroker for, Kiley? You tell me that. Racing goddamned little yachts up and down the coast?"

FRIDAY 26 MAY

West Bay Street, Nassau, Bahamas

The automobile lights flickered under Lawson Garr's hand, and the roll-over garage door lifted to allow the sleek white Cadillac to slide into place beside Belle's Lotus. They could hear the kitchen phone bleeping as the key turned in the lock, and Belle threw her purse on to the counter, kicking off her high heels as she grabbed the receiver. Blonde and statuesquely beautiful – she took after her mother, Barbara Donnelly – she moved with an elegant grace even after several cocktails. "One of your clients," she said, passing the phone to her husband and grabbing her purse and shoes back again.

"Okay, I'll be right behind you." Lawson sat on a stool, pulling a pad open towards him. "Good evening, Lawson Garr here. Can I help you?" Tall, bronzed and athletic, he was the perfect mate for the American girl, at least physically; the attraction had been instant and mutual, parent-proof even if it meant Belle being married to a Limey ex-colonial and exiled two thousand miles from Bognor, Connecticut. That Belle shared Lawson's extravagant tastes, which made them a very unstable couple, financially – real estate in Nassau had not exactly boomed since Independence – was a more serious cause of worry to Mike and Babs

Donnelly. But Lawson worked as hard as he played. "Why, hello, Mr McKinley," he said. "Nice to hear from you . . ."

Liar, Belle thought, as she closed the bedroom door. Who the hell wants to hear from a client at 11.40 at night? Goddamn it, some people have no consideration . . . shit, what an evening! Why the hell did Lawson find it necessary to entertain so much? The people tonight had been gross. Fat, moronic slobs. How the hell did crumbs like that come to have money enough for a $400,000 holiday home, anyway?

She put her dress on a hanger and threw her undies into the clothes hamper before smoothing cleansing milk over her face; the weather was unnaturally warm for the time of year and she was a mess of sweat – but she was too tired even to shower. Lawson was ages, and she was nearly asleep when he came in, but one look at his face brought her bolt upright in bed. "Sweetheart? What is it? You look as if you've just fallen off the Empire State."

"I think I just did!" He sat beside her. "That was McKinley."

"I heard," Belle said. Fabian McKinley was one of the wealthiest men in the Bahamas. He owned land everywhere, and in particular, from her point of view, he owned most of Dolphin Point, the headland on Eleuthera – the most north-easterly of the Bahamian islands – where the elder Donnellys had a holiday home; he was not the ideal neighbour. "What's on his mind now? Josh been pinching his limes again?"

Josh was the Donnelly caretaker.

Lawson might not have heard her. "He wants to sell," he said.

Belle sat up. "Not Dolphin Point?"

"Every goddamned acre. Forty-two."

"But why?"

"Search me. It's not my business to ask."

"But he wants *you* to handle the sale?"

"Exclusive for three months. Because I know the area, he says. The asking price is one million US dollars."

"Oh, boy," Belle said. "Maybe he's not such a crumb after all. A million . . . you'll get twenty thousand, Lawson. Oh, boy. We'll be able to keep the boat." Suddenly she was anxious. "Do you think you can find a buyer? A million is a lot of loot."

"Listen, doll," Lawson said. "McKinley may only want a million, and that is in line with current prices, sure – for undeveloped land. But I am damned sure that I could triple that, by splitting it up into lots, laying water and electricity, having plans drawn up, maybe even starting building."

"You mean . . ." Belle frowned at him. "Develop it yourself?"

"Why not?"

"Two reasons. One, as you've been appointed sole agent, it wouldn't be ethical. Two, we don't have a million dollars; last time I checked the account we didn't even have a million cents."

"Granted. But your old man does. Or could raise it."

Belle's frown deepened. "Big Mike?"

"Why not? Don't he and your brother claim to be the biggest stock-brokers on Wall Street?"

"Not the biggest. Only the best. And that's open to opinion. Anyway, stockbrokers handle a lot of money. They don't necessarily keep it."

"Are you going to tell me that your dad couldn't lay hands on a million dollars if he had to?"

"Maybe. But he doesn't have to."

"Even if it means a quick million profit. One for him, one for us. Fifty-fifty. A million dollars, Belle. God, think what we could do with that! Pay off the mortgage, get those bills off our back, keep the boat . . . hell, we could buy a new boat. You know what I've always wanted? A Hatteras. Goddamn, a 42-foot Hatteras . . . they're the tops."

Belle allowed herself to dream for a moment. Then she said, "But would it be legal?"

"What can possibly be illegal about it? McKinley wants to sell, I find him a buyer. That's what I'm paid to do."

"Yes, but you know you can get more out of the land than he does. And you're going to take that profit. I mean, it sounds a bit like insider dealing to me. Shouldn't you be telling McKinley all of this?"

Lawson leaned forward and kissed her on the nose. "McKinley isn't a good listener. And who's to know? The land goes on the market, and some rich Connecticut stockbroker snaps it up."

"Who just happens to be your father-in-law."

"So I told him it's worth it. There's nothing illegal in that. It's my business, for God's sake. And a million dollars, Belle. Just think of it. A million dollars!"

Belle thought of it. "But what about Neal Robson? Now he's actually bought down here . . ."

"Forget it," Lawson said. "This has to be kept strictly in the family. Anyway, Robson wants his set-up kept a secret until he can tell your folks in the grand manner. Silly twit."

Belle nodded her agreement. "Think Dad'll go for it?" she asked.

"I'll be on the phone to him first thing tomorrow morning," Lawson promised.

"This morning, you mean," Belle yawned.

SATURDAY 27 MAY

Newport, Rhode Island

The sky was clear blue, just a little hazy with afternoon heat, and the water flat calm; the bridge was perfectly mirrored as the Mercedes sedan crossed the river to Newport after the four-hour drive up from New York.

Josephine Donnelly hadn't even paused to drop off the bags at the country cottage she and her husband maintained in Bognor, Connecticut; she'd do that on her way back to Pinewoods, her parents-in-law's house: she was in a hurry to welcome Michael home from the first race of the season – and try not to think about the rest of the summer, when she would hardly see him at all.

A short, slender English girl in her early thirties, Jo Donnelly wore her wavy dark-brown hair cut very short, leaving her crisp, handsome features exposed and compelling.

Her children sat together in the back, where they would distract her least by their constant wrangling; Owen Michael was ten, and Tamsin eight. Now they bubbled with excitement as they rolled into the yacht owners' car park near *Esmeralda*'s usual berth; she had no sooner braked than they were tumbling out to race along the pontoons.

Jo followed more slowly, running her fingers through her windswept hair, her grey-brown eyes searching the close-packed yachts. She wore slacks and a loose shirt and sandals, and still attracted glances from the various crews. She had a slim waist and breasts that filled her B-cup bras well, but her stomach muscles were flabby – and little wonder; it was years since she had played any serious tennis or squash, and in fact she had found little time for any sort of exercise since returning to full-time journalism.

And now her own heart was beating pleasantly; Michael might only have been away a few days, but it was the first race of the season, and even if she dreaded and resented the next twenty weeks, he was a compellingly attractive man. And not only because he was her husband. All the Donnellys were compellingly attractive, from Big Mike and Babs, through their so beautiful daughters, Belle and Marcia, to their so macho sons, Michael junior and Dale. The family bubbled, in a way her own had never done – her father had been an officer in the British army and had believed it weakness to reveal emotion of any kind. Which was probably why she had been instantly attracted to the handsome American boy doing a year at Cambridge when she was up reading English Literature.

She sighed, as she spotted the 40-foot yawl; it had all been so different, then.

Owen Michael had seen the yawl too. "There's Dad!" he shouted.

Michael Donnelly, junior, tall and powerfully built, waved to them, and hurried across the intervening decks. He jumped on to the pontoon and swept the kids up into his arms . . . then turned to Jo. She slid her hands round his back, feeling the warmth through his shirt. His arms hugged her, as his mouth found hers: whenever they kissed she felt dizzy with happiness.

"How did it go?" she asked, pulling her head back.

"Fucking awful," he replied. "We had a failure."

"Oh, no! In this weather? What happened?"

"A rigging screw went. Must have been faulty from the start. And it wasn't flat calm all the way. There was a squall night before last. Quite a heavy one. Hell, *Esmeralda* can take it, so we weren't bothered, then there was this sudden twang and the whole shitting boat shook, with wire flying all over the place. We damned near lost the mast."

"So you retired?"

"Yeah. What a way to start the season."

"You'll get it right. Where's your car? Can you leave now? Your folks are expecting us for dinner."

"It's at Sam's place. But there's no way I can come now."

"Oh, but . . ."

"Listen, Angelface. We only just got in. There's one hell of a lot of work to be done. And Sam of course had to go hustling off because Sally has a party tonight. So I have to put the ship to bed. And replace that screw and harden up the rigging; we sound like a banjo out of control in any breeze at all." He was helping them across the other yachts as he spoke, and Owen Michael was hurrying ahead to gain the deck. "Mark Godwin is giving me a hand. You remember Mark, Jo?"

The boy emerged from the companion hatch. "Hi, Mrs Donnelly."

"Is there so much to be done?" Jo asked. "I mean, you don't race again for a fortnight."

"Now, Angelface, you know the drill; the ship comes first." Michael saw her disappointment, and kissed her nose. "Listen, I will try to get down tonight, but tell Babs not to wait dinner for me."

"Oh, Daddy, we want to have you with us tonight," Tamsin begged.

"Yeah, Dad. Say, why don't you come with us now, and we'll all come and help you fix her up tomorrow," Owen Michael offered. "I thought we could have a little catching practice before dinner."

"No way," Michael said. "Work first, play after." He bent and kissed the top of Tamsin's head. "You hustle along now, and look after your Mommy."

The dismal trio walked back along the pontoon in single file, and Owen Michael kicked viciously at a pebble as they neared the car, sending it skipping across another pontoon on to a boat's deck.

"Owen Michael! Stop that." Jo shook his arm.

"Leave me alone, can't you!"

His mother said no more; she could understand his resenting being rated second to a piece of plastic. But then her pleasure at seeing Michael had also quickly dissipated into resentment. Even after ten years of marriage and living in New England she had not been able fully to accustom herself to the way Americans used obscenities as part of their everyday speech. But it was his attitude which was so shattering. Work before play, she thought bitterly. The fact was that he loved *Esmeralda* more than any of his family. And this was only the beginning of the season; for the next twenty weeks she was going to be the ultimate grass widow – even golfers at least came home for dinner. And it happened every year. What right did Michael have to abandon her and the children every summer for his yacht racing? Why should she always have to play the dual parent role? He never did. She felt like kicking a stone or two herself.

SATURDAY 27 MAY

Bognor, Connecticut

The square, white-painted, wooden-faced house stood tall and imposing, fifty feet behind a white rail fence bordering the sidewalk in the small rural Connecticut town. By New England standards it was very old, having been built in 1832, and from the moment that Big Mike and Barbara Donnelly bought it in 1971 they had taken endless pains to furnish it in its authentic period style. There were stained-glass panels on the inner door of the lobby, and beautifully laid tiles on the lobby and hall floors. Mouldings on the door and window frames were faithfully copied throughout and Babs had spent months poring over books and magazines and haunting retail outlets before selecting the correct wallpapers for each room. The owners of every used-furniture saleroom knew her face well, and Big Mike had laughed repeatedly when, on returning home from his New York office, he was proudly shown some decrepit chair or worm-eaten table, the result of Babs' – his wife's nickname to all the family – latest successful expedition. The little town boasted an expert upholsterer and restorer, who gladly joined in Babs' enthusiasm for ancient furniture, not least due to its profitability. The dining-room and sitting-room at Pinewoods were charming and immaculate from the gilt mirrors over the carved wood fire-surrounds and mantelpieces, fire baskets and brass-knobbed irons, and the panelled, interior folding window shutters, to the wood-framed settee, prim armchairs, dainty round coffee tables, and polished dining-table with its English silver candelabra, overlooked by oil paintings of sea scenes.

Big Mike genuinely admired the finished results, and was happy to show off the house to visiting friends, but his favourite room nevertheless was the big family kitchen in which they now sat watching the News. Authenticity was all very well in the other rooms, but it had been partially abandoned here. The tile-topped units, the cupboards, dishwasher, icebox and freezer were white-wood fronted, and the matching wall cupboards had leaded glass doors to display china and crystal. The bowed window ledges behind the kitchen sink and fitted dining area were filled with potted plants and flowers. Pictures and hand-painted plates hung on the walls beneath a collection of polished copper pans, and every size and shape of wicker shopping basket imaginable. Free-standing in one corner was an antique but highly efficient wood-burning stove, prettily painted enamel panels set in the dull grey metal sides. Next to it were two very comfortable armchairs. Big Mike was sitting in one now, shoulders hunched, greying black hair scattered thinly across his head, while Babs, tall and still blondely attractive, prepared vegetables.

Dale Donnelly breezed in, wearing shorts, throwing his tennis racket on to a chair. "Hi! Anything I can do to help, Babs? What's for dinner?"

"Sure. Empty the trash can. The Robsons and roast rib-eye." Babs tilted her face to receive her son's kiss of greeting.

"Who else?"

"Michael and Jo. James and Suzanne will probably come too, but Jason is away."

"Ugh!" Dale groaned; he was a languid young man who drifted from job to job, resolutely refusing to join his elder brother in the Wall Street firm. This lack of drive bothered his parents as much as the hash he enjoyed so much. "I suppose I'll have to entertain them."

"What's the problem? They're nice kids." Big Mike lit a cigarette and fiddled with the remote control panel.

"James is a wimp. He agrees with everything I say."

His father looked at him through a cloud of smoke. "Yeah? Well, in that case he's gotta be a wimp."

Dale grinned. "Okay. Okay."

"Suzanne's sweet," Babs said.

"Are you putting me on?"

"No, I'm serious." His mother turned away from the sink. "She's very shy and nervous, but she does try . . ."

"Too hard. And I think she has something going for me. She follows me around like a tame dog, rolling her contact lenses and saying, 'Yes, Dale,' and 'No, Dale,' and 'Can I fix you a cup of coffee, Dale.'"

"You've made your point; the girl's obviously a nut. Now shut up and listen to the news." Mike commanded more volume and concentrated on the Washington reporter's latest political scandal.

The door opened and Jo hurried in, following by Owen Michael and Tamsin. "Hi, Babs. Hi Dad. Dale." She kissed each in turn and laid a big bunch of mixed flowers on the counter.

"Hey, aren't those beautiful! Where did you get them?" Babs asked.

"I just picked them from your garden," Jo admitted.

Babs laughed. "I'll get you a vase and you can arrange them for me. Hi, Owen Michael. Have you got a kiss for your grandmother? And you, Tamsin? Where's Michael?"

"Oh . . . er . . . he sends his apologies. He's had to stay in Newport a while longer because he's got problems with the boat, but he hopes to join us later." Jo smiled brightly, but her mother-in-law detected the shadow in her eyes, and her heart sank. She was very aware of Jo's disappointment – and her own.

"They nearly lost the mast," Owen Michael announced.

"Holy shit!" Big Mike remarked, ignoring his wife's frown of disapproval. "How the hell did they manage that?"

"I'm sure Michael will tell you all about it when he gets here." Jo finished her flower arranging and Babs removed her frilled apron to join the men, immediately switching off the set.

"Hey," Big Mike protested. "What did you do that for?"

"Neal and Meg are due here in half an hour. You haven't opened the wine yet. And those pants are filthy. Anyway, you don't usually watch NABS."

"Yeah? Well I wanted to see this new whizz-kid weatherman they've got."

"Oh, Richard Connors," Jo said.

"That's the guy. You remember watching him last year when we were in Eleuthera, Babs. He was with WJQT in Miami then. Big, good-looking guy."

"I remember," Babs said. "He seemed to know what he was talking about. What's he doing in New York?"

"Working for NABS," Mike told her, with heavy patience.

"I'm to interview him next week," Jo said.

"Is that a fact?" Big Mike switched on the set again. "Shit! We've missed him. I didn't know he was that famous."

"NABS is working on it. Seems their manager, Kiley, called Ed and suggested it."

"Well, you·can watch him tomorrow," Babs said. "He can't tell us anything about the weather tonight we can't find out for ourselves by looking out of the window. Come on, Mike, be a doll." She blew him a kiss as she passed his chair and he grabbed her and sat her on his knee.

"Say, will you old folks cut this horsing around and attend to your visitors?"

"Marcia!" Babs jumped up and ran to the door to greet her younger daughter. "How are you, sweetheart?"

"To what do we owe this honour?" Big Mike held out a hand and pulled her down for a kiss.

"New York is hot and sticky, so we thought we'd drive up and beg dinner and a bed for the night."

"We?"

"There's someone I want you to meet. He's parking the car."

Big Mike and Babs exchanged glances; Marcia went through young men like a dose of salts – but everyone was *the* man, for as long as he lasted.

"Now," Marcia said. "What's for dinner?"

"The Robsons," her father announced.

"Oh, hell. Look, we can go . . ."

"No, you cannot," Babs said. "You're staying right here. I've set the table but we can easily place two more chairs." She opened the crockery cupboard.

"Here, let me." Marcia took the plates from her.

"You really only need to set one more. I doubt if Michael will be here much before ten," Jo pointed out.

Marcia glanced at her, one eyebrow raised as she identified both the irritation and the probable cause, but said nothing. What was there to say? In her opinion, if Michael wanted to fix the boat before coming home to see his parents – so what? Did that give Jo the right to look so pissed off? Why didn't she do her own thing, while he did his?

"Mommy, can I stay up until Daddy comes?" Tamsin asked.

"Depends on what time he comes and how sleepy you are," Jo called from behind the kitchen door. They'd had a long day and were both tired.

It was a bit rough on the kids, though. Marcia thought back to her own childhood and the weekends with Big Mike and Babs. At the time she hadn't always wanted to go sailing, or skiing, depending on the season, and would have preferred more time for sketching and painting. She had been thankful for boarding school and then college to take her away from what she had called 'cloying family'. Only recently had she begun to appreciate all the loving and caring her parents had offered their young family. She was always keen, nowadays, to find excuses to 'come home'. And tonight was extra special. When she heard the knock on the door she ran to open it, and pull the dark young man proudly into the room. "This is Benny," she announced.

"They're late," Jo observed, glancing at her watch.

"They're always late," Dale retorted. "They've never been on time for anything in their lives."

They were referring to the Robsons, but Babs was quite pleased about her guests' lack of punctuality on this occasion; it had given the family a chance to get to know Benny. And appreciate him. He was quiet and good-humoured, and he certainly seemed to worship Marcia – which was reciprocated. How grand it would be if Marcia could finally settle down . . . but Benny was also an art student, so it didn't look likely to happen for a while yet.

Nor would he gain a good idea of his possible future mother-in-law if his first dinner at Pinewoods was spoiled, especially with Marcia carrying on about the spaghetti Bolognaise Benny's mother made. But just as Babs was despairing, there was a 'cooee' from the front of the house. "Hope we're not la-ate?" Margaret Robson's head appeared round the kitchen door.

"Not more than usual." Big Mike left his chair to kiss her.

"Oh, good." She hugged Babs. "I was so worried, and kept nagging Neal. Jason couldn't make it, Babs; he sends his regards, and apologies." Jason was the eldest of her two sons. "James is just shunting the car around that great big Mercedes in the yard. Whose is it . . . ? Oh, yours, Josephine," she said as Jo came down the stairs. "My dear, how nice to see you. Is Michael still racing?"

"He's in Newport." Jo determined not to get irritated; Margaret Robson was the only person in the world who still insisted on calling her Josephine. "He had to . . ."

"Well, never mind. Where are those lovely kids of yours?"

"In bed. I've just kissed them good night."

"Not ill, I hope?"

"No, Meg, not ill," Babs interrupted. "Just sleepy. It's nearly nine, and . . ."

"No! Is it? We are late. I knew it. Neal! We are late. I told you . . ."

"Never mind, Meg." Mike handed her a gin and Martini. "Get yourself outside that and we'll go eat."

Meg was Babs' total opposite. Slim – skinny, Mike called her – nervous and excitable, she exuded energy and tensions. Her black hair would have been grey without help, but her blue eyes were as lively as they had been thirty years before. Meg worried about everything. She loved her children, and worried for them; loved her husband, worried about him. Her home, business, elderly mother, tomorrow's lunch . . . everything was of vital importance and a big problem.

Neal adored her. Not much taller, smooth, smiling features belying his white hair, he was one of those quiet, calm, confident men who make nervous women feel safe. Meg felt safe, most times. Except when he'd gotten some idea, some project in mind, like now. She knew he was dying to tell his friends about it, but he was waiting until they were all assembled.

James and Suzanne, the two younger Robson children, came in. "Hi, everybody." They gave a general greeting. "Hi, Dale," Suzanne added softly.

"Oh, hi there, Suzanne. How're you doing?"

"Okay, I guess." She sidled over to the bench around the breakfast table where he was sitting and parked herself on the end,.trapping him. She was plump and curvy with an uncooked pastry complexion, but her eyes were gentle and smiling and everyone knew her for a sweetheart.

Dale made a big effort to talk about subjects which might interest her, knowing he'd regret it later when she'd had a drink or two. She'd never needed much encouragement.

Jo and Marcia helped Babs to carry the serving dishes through to the antique sideboard in the dining-room where Big Mike sharpened the carving knife and set about the meat. When everyone had a heaped plate in front of them and Mike had said grace, Neal Robson rose to his feet. "Before we eat," he said, "I have something to say."

"Make it brief," Mike recommended; he and Neal had been in the army in Korea together.

Neal grinned at him. "We have done it," he said.

They stared at him.

"Bought that place in Eleuthera," he explained. "The one you've been trying to talk me into for years."

"Well, son of a gun," Mike said. "I never thought you'd go through with it."

"I'm so scared," Meg squealed. "I think it's a crazy idea."

"You'll love it," Babs told her. "Oh, I am so pleased. We'll be down there together . . . oh, the swimming, and the snorkelling . . ."

"And the diving," Dale added.

"And the sun," Jo put in.

"We'll be down in July, as usual," Mike said. "When are you planning on getting there?"

"Well," Neal said. "We rather thought we'd go down next month. According to your Lawson, that house hasn't been lived in for ten years."

"At least that," Mike agreed.

"It'll be full of crawly bugs," Dale grinned.

"Ooh!" Meg shrilled.

"Dale!" Babs remonstrated. "All you have to do, Meg dear, is shut the place up and have it fumigated."

"Yeah, but there's a lot to do to it," Neal said.

"Oh, I'm so scared," Meg said again.

"What about?" Mike inquired.

"Well, snakes, and . . ."

"There are no dangerous snakes in the Bahamas," Mike declared.

"But some of them are so big."

"Chicken snakes," Mike said reassuringly. "They won't trouble you."

"But what about things like hurricanes?" Meg squeaked.

"Hurricanes? They're no hassle."

"Oh, but when one reads the newspapers . . ."

"You don't want to believe everything you read in the newspapers," Mike announced. "We had a hurricane down there. Three years ago."

"Well," Babs said. "I don't think it was actually a hurricane. Didn't they call it a tropical depression, or something?"

"It was a hurricane," Mike said firmly. "Don't you remember that wind howling?"

"And the rain," Marcia said, squeezing Benny's hand. "So much got in we had to sleep in the lounge."

"It must have been awful, but awful. Weren't you terrified?" Meg asked.

The Donnellys exchanged glances.

"I'll confess I was a bit worried at first, but providing one is sensible and takes the proper precautions, like boarding up the windows, why . . ." Mike spread his hands expansively. "It's a doddle."

"Read three books by candlelight," Dale said.

"You read through a hurricane?" James Robson was aghast.

"Sure. Not easy, mind you, because the candle flame kept blowing out."

Marcia kicked him under the table but the Robsons didn't realise they were being roasted.

"Believe me," Mike declared. "Hurricanes aren't all they're cracked up to be."

"Then how come people die in them?" James wanted to know. "They do, you know."

"Oh, sure they do. When they're living in some shanty town in Haiti and the whole house comes down on them. It shouldn't ever happen to a proper building."

"Anyway," Dale said, "hurricanes hardly ever hit the same place again for years and years. So Eleuthera has got to be the safest place in the Bahamas for a long time to come."

"I think you're talking about lightning," Marcia objected. "So how come the house gets struck by lightning every year?"

"You get struck by lightning?" Meg gasped.

"Does no more damage than that storm," Mike asserted.

Jo remained silent as the conversation continued. Perhaps she was just irritated with Michael, but the whole family was being a bit over the top tonight. She could remember that storm. It certainly hadn't been a hurricane; the winds had never risen above 50 mph. Yet it had been terrifying, out on Dolphin Point, with the waves crashing on the rocks on one side and rolling up the beach on the other, and the wind howling, and the trees bending, and the rain teeming down as the thunder and lightning had been continuous. They had all been scared, not least Big Mike; she had been more afraid for the children than herself, had first really felt the bitterness that she should be there, coping, while Michael was racing *Esmeralda* in the relatively calm waters off Bermuda. But in fact no real damage had been done, although Mike was gradually increasing the wind strength every time he talked about it. She wondered what his reaction would be to a real hurricane.

"Hello there!" The front door opened and Michael stalked in. "Not too late for some food, I hope?"

"Mike!" His father leapt up and seized his hand; he was the only person allowed to call his eldest son by the diminutive, as Michael Donnelly junior was determined to grow away from his Irish roots. "Jo says you had trouble."

"Defective gear." He kissed Babs, blew one at his wife. "Kids in bed?"

"Yes," she said.

The rest of the party were already on their dessert, but Mike provided his son with a plate of roast beef, and the conversation became concerned with yachts and racing. Mike could hardly wait for the meal to end. As soon as they left the table, he pushed Michael into the little study. "Boy, am I glad you're back."

Michael raised his eyebrows. "Problems?"

"You have got to be kidding. Calthrop White wants to float a stock issue."

"So?"

"By August."

Michael sat down and lit a cigarette. "He has to be nuts."

"I told him. But he has to have it going. He's trying to buy some British TV station. Seems the franchise comes up in the fall and he reckons he can get it for $125 million."

"What the hell does he want another network for?"

"He's ambitious, I guess. So there's work to be done. He's our best customer."

"But, Dad . . ."

"Okay, okay. It shouldn't interfere with the racing. I'm letting Palmer handle most of the work on it. Now let me give you the big one."

Michael raised his eyebrows. "Bigger than that?"

Mike winked. "For us, maybe. I had a phone call from Lawson this morning. Let me tell you what he has in mind."

Michael listened, pulling his chin. "Sure it's not one of his get-rich-quick schemes?"

"Sure it is. But this one could just work."

"A million bucks? Can we raise that?"

"Could be. What do you think?"

"A million bucks," Michael said again. "Holy shit, Dad, that wouldn't be too bad. You talked to Babs?"

"I haven't talked to anyone except you. But if you're for it . . ."

Michael Donnelly considered a moment longer, then stretched out his hand. "Count me in. But . . . just let's keep it amongst ourselves for the time being, eh?"

MONDAY 29 MAY

National American Broadcasting Service Offices, Fifth Avenue

"Another week," Julian Summers remarked, slumping into his chair which faced that of his new senior, Richard Connors, in the weather room. "Had a good weekend?"

"I hung wallpaper," Richard told him, continuing to study the various items on his desk. "Ever heard of something called *Profiles*?"

"It's a magazine."

"So I gather."

"Quite up-market," Julian told him. "It's a monthly, does in-depth studies of prominent people. All over the country, all over the world. From politicians to pop stars. Why?"

"They seem to want to do me."

"You? Great balls of fire. You'll be famous."

Richard gave him an old-fashioned look. "Some female named Donnelly. Seems she has an appointment for Thursday. Shit!"

"Don't you like females named Donnelly?" Julian asked, innocently.

"I don't like females named anything, right this minute," Richard told him. "But Kiley says I have to see her. Says it'll please JC. You seen these, Julian?"

Julian got up to lean over his shoulder. "Water temperatures?"

"All Mark can get us."

"Say, is it legal, for him to feed you all that data?"

Richard grinned. "Maybe it isn't. We were at school together, then college. Heck, we played on the same team. So we're buddies."

"And so he keeps you one jump ahead of the other guys. Those look kind of high for May."

"They are, goddamned high for May. And look at the pattern. From mid-Atlantic right across into the Caribbean and then up into the

Bahamas and the Gulf Stream. Twenty-fours and fives and sixes, and out there, twenty-seven. But see that one?"

"Twenty-two."

"That's right. You know where that is?"

"Tell me."

"That was taken at the Ambrose Lightship." He pointed. "Not thirty miles east of New York Harbour."

"So it's gonna be one hot summer."

"Yeah," Richard said. "You know what sea temperature is needed to cause a hurricane?"

"Nope."

"26½° Centigrade. So there's probably one spawning in mid-Atlantic right this minute."

"So what's new? Tomorrow is the first of June: the official beginning of the hurricane season."

"Sure. We've had hurricanes on 1 June before," Richard agreed. "But they have to have warm water, so that this time of year they fizzle when they get up here, or even off the Bahamas. But here we are, at the beginning of June, and there's warm water everywhere. We could have 27° plus up here in another month if the weather holds as it is. That means the whole goddamned ocean is going to be hurricane-ripe by July."

"So the guys in Florida are going to be busy. Thank God it's nothing to do with us."

"You reckon? What about Hurricane Gloria in 1985? Didn't she just about knock on your door, up here?"

"She was a freak," Julian pointed out. "And she missed. Just."

"All hurricanes are freaks of nature, Julian," Richard told him. "And they all hit somewhere, some time."

Julian frowned. "You really reckon a hurricane could hit New York? Christ, that'd be something."

"Yeah," Richard said. "Yeah, it could happen. Just let's keep an eye on those water temperatures."

Thursday 1 June

Park Avenue – Morning

Sunlight flooded the bedroom, and Jo yawned and stretched, smiling as she touched the sleeping form beside her. They had been out to dinner the previous night, and he would probably sleep for a while yet. They had had a lot of fun.

She rolled out of bed, pulled on her dressing gown, cleaned her teeth and brushed her hair, and began to get the world moving. The apartment, thirty-eight floors up, was light and airy, with a plate-glass picture window in the lounge giving a panoramic view over the city and the East River. Jo had worked hard at her ambition to create a smart, modern home with a cosy, lived-in atmosphere; even the family room had style, despite the haphazard piles of yachting books and journals, children's games and Nana's bean-bag bed. Nana awoke as soon as her mistress did, and for all her age and rheumatism there was a bout of energetic tail-wagging before she grabbed Jo's hand, gently, and led her into the kitchen to stand, significantly, before a certain cupboard.

"You reckon it's milkbone time, do you?" Jo laughed and took a bone-shaped biscuit from its box. Nana accepted it daintily, and carried it away to her bean bag.

Florence had already arrived, and was making coffee, while Jo got the children out of bed, to wash their faces and get dressed for school. Florence Bennett had worked for Jo since Owen Michael's appearance was imminent. From being a nurse whole-time she had developed into a nanny-cum-housekeeper when the children started school. A large, red-faced woman of Scottish descent, married to a fishmonger named Bert, whom she loved dearly but who was half her size, she was a total treasure. Jo sometimes felt that Florence kept the entire junior Donnelly household sane.

This morning, as usual, Florence would walk the children to school. Jo had ideas about sending them to boarding school when they were a little older – she even dreamed of Owen Michael going to an English public school – but it was a touchy subject at the moment, like so many.

The children sat down to breakfast and she returned to her bedroom, to discover Michael sitting up and scratching his head. "Shit," he remarked. "That's exactly what I feel like. Must've been the olives."

Jo mixed up a glass of Alka-Seltzer, handed it to him.

"Um." He sighed. "Meet me at the Club at 11.30, will you?"

"Eh?" About to step into the shower, she turned in surprise.

"I'm taking an out-of-towner to lunch, and he's got his wife with him. So I reckon it'd be good to make up a foursome; he's quite well heeled. I've booked a table at the Four Seasons, but we'll have a drink at the Club first."

"I'm sorry." Jo shook her head. "I can't."

"Eh?" It was his turn to be surprised.

"I can't meet you at eleven. I have an appointment at 11.15."

"Cancel it."

"Now you know I can't do that, Michael. It's an interview. You should have told me sooner."

"I didn't goddam well know until yesterday."

"And you never thought to tell me last night. I'm sorry, but this interview was set up by the magazine. Tell you what, though: I might be able to join you at the restaurant at about one . . ."

"Fucking hell," he said. "What's the good of that? Do you think I want these people to know my wife works for a living?"

Jo sighed. Her going back to work had always been one of the several bones of contention between them; Michael felt she should just sit at home being a mother and twiddle her thumbs until he required her for some purpose or other.

"Okay," she said. "Then I won't come to the restaurant."

She stood beneath the shower, allowing the water to bounce off her flesh, and opened her eyes as the stall door was jerked wide. One look at his face told her that he was in one of his moods. He had them from time to time, fits of depression when his mind descended into some private black hell, and when he would seize on any controversial aspect of their relationship as a reason to quarrel. Often enough it was their different religions. Michael was not a serious Catholic – none of the Donnellys were, although they went to confession and attended mass from time to time – and although she, as an Anglican, had had to agree that the children would be brought up in the Roman faith, the point was never belaboured – when he was in a good mood. But too often, when he lost his temper, criticism of the way she was educating Owen Michael and Tamsin would be hurled at her. Thus usually she preferred it when he carried on about her job – but this morning there was an added bite to his aggression.

"You are one hell of a wife," he declared. "Talk about supporting your husband. Listen. I am your husband, right? You are my wife, right? And a selfish bitch who just wants to do her own thing. Now I want you to come to the Club and then out to lunch, and you are goddamned well going to do it, right?"

He was shouting, and she prayed the children couldn't hear, because suddenly she was angry too, and wanted to shout back. She had made sufficient allowance for his tantrums in the past, knowing all the time that they were caused by little things, little failures, little blows to the ego. Just as this one, she knew, was a residue of his unfortunate first race of the season. He had been waiting for an opportunity to sound off, let himself go – with her, as usual, as the target.

She exploded as she pushed him aside and reached for her towel. "You dare!" she snapped. "Selfish? You bloody bastard. You have the right to take off on your fucking plastic bathtub every goddamned weekend and you accuse me of being selfish for trying to do a job of work?"

"You . . ."

"No, you!" She jabbed a forefinger at his chest. "You are the most selfish, irresponsible, self-opinionated bastard who was ever born. You never wanted a wife and children; you just wanted ornaments to show off when the occasion arose, and someone to organise your home – for in case you ever need to use it." She paused, gasping for breath.

"Have you finished?" Michael asked, eyes narrowed, his face flushed with anger. "Well, then, this is the only possible answer to that sewage," and he swung his arm, the flat of his hand hitting the side of her face and sending her reeling across the bathroom to cannon into the wall.

The stinging blow brought moisture to her eyes – but she wasn't crying: she was too angry. She had fallen on to the toilet seat. Now she got up, wrapped herself in her dressing-gown. "The usual answer from a brainless fool." She went into the bedroom and began to dress. "Not the first time you've hit me, is it, Michael? But I promise you it will be the last." She tucked her blouse into her skirt, brushed her hair, and picked up her purse; make-up could wait until she was in the car. "I am going straight to my attorney."

"Now, Jo . . ."

"I have nothing more to say, at the moment. My next communication with you will be through Tom Wilson's office." She left him standing there, open-mouthed, and closed the door quietly behind her. "I'll drop the children off today, Florence," she said.

All three of them gazed at her, apprehensively. They had heard the raised voices, and her cheek was still red from the blow. But not a word was said, even on the drive to school. She kissed them both. "See you this afternoon," she said. "We'll do something together, shall we?"

Was she already preparing for a love tug over the kids? She couldn't be sure.

Tom Wilson was not in his office; he was in court. "Would you like to make an appointment, Mrs Donnelly?" the receptionist asked.

Jo had been in two minds whether actually to come and see him or not. The anger in which she had made her threat to Michael had cooled sufficiently for her to wonder what she was going to tell Tom. He was an old friend. He and his wife dined with Michael and herself from time to time, and the previous January they had all gone skiing in Vermont. Was she going to tell him she wanted to split with Michael? No, that was stupid; she didn't want to break up her marriage – she still hoped to make it work. But she did want to frighten Michael, make him realise that she wasn't taking any more of his impossible behaviour. Just telling him had got her nowhere.

The woman behind the desk was looking at her, probably knowing damned well what was in her mind, having seen innumerable other women standing there, vacillating . . .

"Er . . . I guess I'll leave it just now. I'll call him sometime. It's not important," she smiled.

Ed Kowicz, Managing Editor of *Profiles*, peered at her. "You don't look so good. That a bruise?"

Ed had hawkish eyes, and could see the discolouration even through the pancake she had applied. "I walked into a door."

"Happens all the time," he agreed. "You ready to take on Connors?"

"Of course I am. Are we supposed to wrestle?"

"He's something of a lady killer, I hear. But he knows his job. He's also an expert on tropical storms, I believe. And the hurricane season down south has just opened. Could be an angle."

"Why, yes," Jo agreed. Like everyone who holidayed in Florida or the Bahamas she was always happy to talk about hurricanes. But not everyone holidayed in Florida or the Bahamas. "Do you reckon anyone in New York is interested in hurricanes?"

"Why not, after Gloria's near miss? Anyway, everyone is interested in hurricanes, even if they don't ever expect to be hit by one. Besides, we don't only sell *Profiles* in New York, you know. It's a good angle. But don't let him snow you."

"Let me tell you something," Jo said. "Right this minute there isn't a man in the world could snow me, Ed. Not even you."

NATIONAL AMERICAN BROADCASTING SERVICE
OFFICES, FIFTH AVENUE

Mid-Morning

Manhattan shimmered. Even on the shaded side of the street heat bounced off the walls and up from the sidewalk. A few sensible matrons held parasols over their heads, but even they mopped their faces and gasped for breath. Traffic fumes hung in the streets without a whisper of breeze to shift them, and the sunny side of the street was almost deserted as pedestrians avoided the blistering solar rays.

Jo stumbled as she walked down Fifth Avenue, and tugged impatiently to free the heel of her sandal from the melted tar on the sidewalk, then sighed with relief as she passed through the doors into the air-conditioned cool of the NABS building. She had never been here before; she had interviewed a good many TV personalities, but always in hotel lobbies or at their homes. Now she was shown into a small waiting-room and left to herself for some fifteen minutes, which did not improve her mood. But finally Richard Connors appeared.

If he was flattered to have been selected for a prestigious interview, he didn't show it. Nor did he help matters by his opening remark: "Now, what can I do for you, Miss . . . er . . . ?"

Jo felt herself bristling, but controlled the retort on the tip of her tongue, smiled sweetly, and said, "My name is Josephine Donnelly, Mr Connors, and I would like you to talk about yourself." With which request she thought he would be happy to comply; she'd met this type before, smooth, suave, sophisticated, too damned good-looking for real, and boy, was he arrogant. "Do you mind if I tape our conversation?" She produced a small recorder from her purse.

"As a matter of fact I do," Connors said. "I find those things terribly inhibiting. Can't you make notes to assist your memory?"

It was an awful let down, after watching the handsome, charming face on TV. She managed a crooked smile as she put the gadget back and withdrew a notebook instead. "You're quite sure this won't paralyse you as well?"

His head jerked up; he really looked at her for the first time, and slowly his mouth widened into an apologetic smile. "Of course not. I'm sorry if I sounded rude. I guess my mind just wasn't in gear. So . . ." he leaned back in his chair. "What about me do you wish to know?"

Another act, she decided, as though he had just pressed an 'on with the charm' button, and again had to suppress her irritation with his artificiality. Not that she wasn't used to it. Most interviewees were stiff and artificial at first – it was her job to break through that barrier and reach the real person – but she hadn't expected it of Richard Connors. "You've come to NABS from WJQT in Miami, right? Have you always lived there?" A usual type of opening question.

"No. I was born in San Francisco. My father was a pharmacist there."

"What made you move to Florida?"

"I answered the advert for a weatherman, got the job. Simple as that."

"I really meant, what made you go in for forecasting? I . . ." she bit her lip, because he was grinning again. No doubt it had been suggested to him before that, with his looks and background, he could have done much better for himself. "I would say you were an athlete, once upon a time."

This time his grin was more genuine, and even a trifle cynical. "I played football, once upon a time. But never up to draft standard. And a guy has to major in something. I was always interested in TV – since I was a kid in short pants. And also an older cousin of mine was dead keen on sailing – and therefore weather. He'd take me out sometimes as crew – dead boring slopping about waiting for wind, but he was always looking at the sky and forecasting what was coming . . . and I guess I got involved myself." He paused to grin at her doubting smile. "Being a forecaster gets to be quite fun, you know. There are a lot of spin-offs, like doing commentaries from helicopters and getting involved in local organisations: you'd be surprised how many people in this country are really interested in the weather, even if they don't talk about it all the time as they do in England. You get to meet a hell of a lot of interesting folk."

"And presumably forecasting is a rung on the ladder up," she suggested.

Another grin. "To becoming a TV personality? You'd better believe it. I don't intend to stay in forecasting forever."

She realised she had found the real Richard Connors, a man just trying to work his way into his true place in society, the same as anyone else. She made notes on his college football career, his first job interviews, and his varied progress before moving into the world of television. But when she came to his personal life, his mood suddenly changed. "I shouldn't think that will interest anyone," he said.

"You couldn't be more wrong," she protested. "That's what it's all about."

He glanced at her ring finger. "Sorry, Mrs Donnelly. My private life stays private."

They stared at each other, and she realised that he meant what he said. Which left her projected article in tatters. She might as well get up and leave and scrap the idea right now. Then she remembered what Ed had told her. "Then talk to me about the job," she said. "Weather forecasting. And hurricanes," she added.

He frowned at her. "Hurricanes? You interested in hurricanes?"

"Sure I am. My parents-in-law have a holiday home in Eleuthera."

"Is that a fact? Say, would you really like to see how it all works?"

"Yes, I would." She followed him down endless corridors, past open office doors where typewriters rattled, computers bleeped, and coffee dispensers were in constant use.

"Would you like a coffee?" he asked.

"Not right now, thanks." She had never tasted anything drinkable from one of those machines.

The studio was like any other television centre, somewhat bare except for the various backdrops against which Richard would stand while making his forecasts, and a large and elaborate desk behind which he sat as each programme commenced, and dominated by the three cameras, presently unattended.

The control room was far more interesting. Richard introduced her to the news and weather programme director, who, even now, was sitting gazing through a soundproof glass wall at three rows of screens showing various pictures, from newsreels and interviews to plain tuning screens. The unit in front of his chair was solid with dials, knobs and switches, microphones and telephones.

"This is where all the mistakes are made," Richard said solemnly. "As when the anchorman introduces the President's state visit to France and you're shown a college quarterback haring down the pitch."

"Or the met man is left pressing his control button for his next chart and absolutely nothing happens," the director cut in, laughing.

Richard's office, on the other hand, was a relaxed place of comfortable furniture, just untidy enough, with piles of paper and reports scattered about, to look lived in. He showed Jo to a very comfortable armchair, seated himself behind his desk, introduced and dismissed his pretty secretary – she had been filing – and then smiled at her. "Now?"

"Well, tell me something about your job. How do you forecast weather?"

"You observe," he said. "There is really nothing much more to it than that. Anyone can forecast weather, and as I'm sure you know, most people do, constantly. However, the accuracy of the forecast does depend on the number of observations you can get hold of, which rather puts looking out of the window every morning at the bottom of the list. It also depends on the interpretation you put on what you see and learn; that last part can be pure experience, but it helps if you've been taught something about meteorology. For instance, a hundred years ago it was difficult to forecast the weather more than twenty-four hours ahead, because then it really was a matter of how much you could see from your window, and relating that to your barometer. The barometer is one of the most important of weather forecasting instruments, providing, that is . . ." he grinned. "That it's an accurate barometer."

"Why is a barometer so important?"

"Because it records the atmospheric pressure around you."

"But why is pressure important? I thought we were all under pressure? About 15 lbs per square inch of our bodies. Correct?"

"Correct. But that isn't to say pressure is uniform all over the world. Or even all over the state. The variations, thought of in terms of pressure per square inch of the human body, may not amount to much, although if you think about it, just before a storm, for instance, when it's all hot and muggy, everyone feels out of sorts. That's caused simply by a lowering of the pressure. The important thing, from a meteorologist's point of view, is that pressure controls the flow of wind. Wind flows from high pressure areas to low pressure areas, or down the pressure gradients, as we call them, just as water runs downhill. Actually, winds flow *round* centres of pressure, but always downhill. In the northern hemisphere, it does so in an anti-clockwise direction if it's a low pressure system, a depression, and a clockwise direction if it's a high pressure cell, an anti-cyclone. South of the equator, the reverse obtains. But a glance at the isobar lines always tells you the direction of the wind, and just about how strong."

"What's an isobar?"

"Very simply, it is a line drawn, as a result of reported barometric observations, through all the places on the earth's surface which have the same pressure at the same time. This is the most important duty of a weather observer, reporting quickly and accurately on the exact conditions wherever he is. In addition to recording the actual cloud formations and precipitations and temperature, all of which are necessary to the forecaster, he will record the barometric pressure. Here in the States we use inches, but in the rest of the world pressure is recorded in millibars. Then, when all those observations are received, the forecaster – or nowadays, the computer – joins all the lines of equal pressure together, making up what we call a synoptic chart."

"And that tells you what the weather is going to do?"

"Sure. Obviously, if Station A, five hundred miles away, reports heavy cloud and rain at, say, 8.00 am in the morning, and Station B, three hundred miles away, reports blue skies at that hour, and then at ten o'clock Station A reports clearing skies and Station B increasing cloud, you can assume a rain storm is approaching from A to B. If at ten o'clock Station A still reports cloud and rain, when it is also being reported from Station B, then it is obviously a pretty big storm system. That's pure observation. But the isobars tell us what wind speeds to expect. When the different lines are well spaced, a shallow gradient, we know the wind flow will be light. When the lines appear close packed, a steep gradient, strong winds are indicated. This is very important to ships at sea, which may be travelling down a pressure gradient themselves. It is an axiom, for instance, that if a ship's barometer drops as much as three millibars in any hour, the crew should prepare for a gale. In the sub-tropics, where there is very little pressure movement at all, a drop of three millibars in one hour can very well indicate a hurricane in the vicinity. But nowadays, of course, we have many more sophisticated ways of telling the weather . . ."

Jo was fascinated. Not only by the subject itself, which she had never really considered in any depth before, but by the total knowledge and expertise which flowed from the man. He *was* an expert. As well as being one of the most attractive men she had ever met. But that was dangerous thinking in her present state of mind.

"So," he was saying, "back in the days when radio was first developed, and as accurate weather forecasts became important to shipping, and sport, and of course aviation, and folks realised that long-range forecasting could even save lives, a whole series of these weather reporting stations I was talking about were set up. There were even ships at sea, whose business was to maintain a certain position and do nothing but report on the weather. So a regular series of observations could be obtained from very far away, and an idea of what was happening there fitted into an overall picture of what the weather was doing everywhere else, in what direction and how fast the systems were moving, what wind strengths could be anticipated, etcetera. But of course those are all virtually obsolete now. Since the Hitler War, radar has been developed to such an extent that we can look hundreds of miles out to sea, and in the last thirty years or so we've had the spread of satellite observation. From a satellite you can look across several hundred miles of weather at a glance. Take that picture, for instance . . ." he indicated the huge framed photograph hanging on the wall above his head.

Jo did indeed look at it. She had noticed it when she first sat down, and had intended to bring it into the conversation as soon as she could. It was an enlarged photograph of the Gulf of Mexico, taken from a great distance up, in the centre of which was a pile of white, rather like a large scoop of whipped cream dropped on to the cardboard, although the cream was clearly rotating in an anti-clockwise direction, while in the centre there was drilled a neat little blue hole. "That's a hurricane," she said. "The hole is the eye."

"The first hurricane of 1977," he agreed. "Named Anita. Now there you have the entire dimensions of the system on one photo. The outer clouds, those things which look like rocks, are over Brownsville, Texas. The hurricane force winds, the edge of that thick white cloud, are hitting the Mexican coast, around Yucatan. And of course the size of the system, and the speed at which it is travelling, is monitored from minute to minute."

"Gosh," she said. "That looks absolutely terrifying. Have you ever been in one of those?"

He grinned. "Nope. Nothing like that. Anita was a big storm. She carried sustained winds, for a little while, of 150 miles an hour, which made her a Category Four storm, and in fact, damned near a Category Five. She didn't make it, but in terms of wind speed she was the biggest storm in the Atlantic area for twenty years."

"Gosh," she said again, and paused. "May I ask you a $64,000 question?"

"Sure."

"Well, you have just convinced me how accurate all your observations and tracking systems are. That being so, how come the forecasts you hear are so often wrong?"

He held up a forefinger. "Not wrong. They are sometimes inaccurate as to timing, and sometimes the weather does quite unpredictable things. I'm afraid not the most sophisticated apparatus in the world can guarantee a system will do what it should do, by all the rules. There *are* certain rules on which we can rely, as I have outlined. If you have a low-pressure area in the northern hemisphere, the winds will rotate around it in an anti-clockwise direction. There is no possibility of them doing otherwise. Just as winds will always flow from high pressure to low; they will never blow *up* a pressure gradient. And tides rise and fall in approximately twelve-hour cycles, no matter what the weather may be doing. These are natural laws. But a weather system is its own boss. For instance, we might track a system all the way from its beginning, off, say, the West Coast of Africa, around Cape Verde, and for seven consecutive days it may travel due west at 15 knots. Now, we can say with absolute certainty that there is bad weather coming. And after seven days we might be tempted to say that in twenty-four hours from now the storm centre is going to be 360 nautical miles due west of its present position. But at any moment, without warning, it may change course, increase speed, decrease speed, or stop altogether. We do know that there are rivers of air in the atmosphere, along which storm systems flow like driftwood in a water river. We also know that tropical storms spawn, and can only flourish, over warm water. But we can still never be absolutely certain what they are going to do next. And incidentally, if you are going to use any of this, be sure you point up the difference between the speed at which the system may be travelling, and the wind speeds it is generating. A lot of people make the mistake of thinking that the faster a hurricane is travelling the more dangerous it is, whatever the wind speeds circulating round the eye happen to be. That is quite wrong. In fact, in most cases, the reverse is true. Hurricane winds are generated by heat, not by speed. Therefore, the slower a hurricane is travelling, the more time, for instance, it spends over warm water, the stronger the winds round the centre are likely to be. Equally, the faster a system is travelling, the faster it will hit you and be on its way again."

"Yes," she said. "I think I have it. Gosh . . ." she looked at her watch. "I have taken up an awful amount of your time. Really, I could sit here and talk to you forever, but . . ."

"I haven't told you about hurricanes yet," he pointed out.

"Well, maybe . . ."

"We can talk about them over lunch," he told her.

Jo was taken by surprise. She hadn't had a chance to analyse what she felt about this man, and it was necessary to feel something about him if she was going to write about him. And if she had often lunched with other interviewees, it had never been on a day quite like this, when she should have been supporting Michael at the Four Seasons . . . and if not, munching a sandwich at the office. But she only hesitated for a moment before accepting – she wanted to feel she could get some of her own back for that slap this morning.

"I can recommend the pizzas here," Richard told her, across the red-chequered tablecloth.

"I love good pizza," she said. "Pepperoni, please. And a salad."

"Make that two," he told the waiter. "And will you bring us a bottle of Frascati right away, please?"

"Si, signor." The boy departed, and returned to uncork and pour the pale Italian wine.

"I don't like spirits at midday unless I know I can ziz it off after lunch." Richard raised his glass. "Hope you enjoy this."

Jo sipped, and nodded. "It's lovely. Very light and refreshing."

He watched her, as he had throughout the interview. She fascinated him – probably because she was the greatest possible contrast to Pam, in every way, so relaxed and friendly on the one hand, and yet so correct on the other, reserved in her speech and gestures: the idea of her ever rolling around with a beachbum was impossible. "Are you English?" he asked suddenly.

"Heavens! Do I still have an accent?" She laughed and nodded. "Yes, I am."

"I can't say you have too much of an accent, but it's the way you talk, and sit, and your clothes . . . they look English."

"They are."

"And happily married, I would say."

Jo shrugged. "Isn't everyone?"

"No," Richard said briefly. "Tell me about yours."

Between mouthfuls of pizza, Jo told him a little about herself, how she and her husband had met, her career, surprised by the number of his questions, wanting to believe his apparent interest was genuine. "Now tell me what went wrong with yours?" she asked. And he knew her question was genuine, more than a mere attempt to gain copy for her article.

"I guess she wanted to live one way, and I another."

"I'm sorry. Are you divorced?"

He nodded.

"Would that be why you left Florida?"

"I left Florida because NABS offered me twice as much as I was getting there." Then he gave a crooked grin. "Don't you believe it: I was running like hell."

They gazed at each other for several moments, then she swallowed her last mouthful. "That was lovely."

"Dessert? Coffee? They do a great cappuccino."

"I really should be getting back."

"But we haven't talked about hurricanes, yet."

"Heavens! We haven't, have we? Well, perhaps, if you do recommend the cappuccino . . ."

Richard signalled the waiter.

"So," she said. "Can you tell me, as simply as possible, what a hurricane actually is?"

"Well, as simply as possible, it is a depression which has gotten out of hand. Depressions are caused by warm air rising, which warm air will always do: think of the steam from your kettle. Nature, as you know, abhors a vacuum, so when warm air rises, cold air rushes in to replace it. Even well up in the north it can do this at quite a speed, but being cold air the whole system tends to collapse fairly quickly. In the sub-tropics, when the water temperature heats up, the air starts to rise, and is replaced by only slightly cooler air. Thus this new air isn't cold enough to quash the system; it merely heats up and rises itself. So we have a continual spiral of rising air, which, if the other conditions are right, just gets faster and faster, like a top gaining speed instead of losing it. You could think of a hurricane as a gigantic tornado or waterspout, only they can be hundreds of miles across. And of course they are generating winds of Force Twelve and up."

"Why do you say Force Twelve? What does that mean?"

He grinned at her as he stirred coffee. "I think you know that one."

"Maybe I do, but tell me anyway. So I can quote you."

"Well, it's just a reference system invented by a British admiral named Beaufort about 150 years ago. So it's called the Beaufort Scale. It divides up wind speeds into readily recognisable categories. For instance, zero on the scale is flat calm. Force Three is a light breeze, say 12 knots: that's when you would get your first whitecaps at sea, and your first tree moving on land. Small trees, anyway. Force Five is a pretty good breeze, and when you have Force Six, which is around 25 knots, you have spray flying and big trees whipping to and fro. It's the sort of wind you'd have difficulty walking against. After that you get into storm territory. Force Eight is a gale, around 35 knots. That can be pretty serious at sea, at least to small craft. Yachts have to reef and that sort of thing. Then Force Ten is a storm, 50 knots. Now that really is something. You have big waves, twenty or thirty feet from trough to crest. Even good-sized ships can get into trouble in that type of situation. And on land you have some trees coming down, and chimney pots and that sort of thing."

"And Force Twelve is a hurricane." Jo gazed at him over the rim of her coffee cup. "How strong is that?"

"64 knots, or 75 miles per hour."

"And that's dangerous to everybody."

"It's dangerous. But 75 miles an hour is only what we call a Category One storm, and its damage effect, in hurricane terms, is minimal."

"That's right," she said. "Back at the studio you mentioned that Anita was Category Four. How strong is that?"

"That is strong," he said. "You see, although all winds of more than 75 miles per hour are hurricanes, it is possible to have winds twice that speed. So to differentiate between what we might call an ordinary hurricane and a real killer storm, the Weather Bureau divides them up into categories, depending on wind strength. Category One contains winds of 74 to 95 miles an hour. Okay, that'll knock down a few trees and signs. Category Two, up to 110 miles an hour, knocks over mobile homes and can get under poorly constructed roofs. Category Three has winds of up to 130 miles an hour. Now you'd have big trees coming down and some roofs coming right off. But Category Four can reach 155 miles per hour, and that's more than double the speed of an 'ordinary' hurricane. It's real nasty. You really want to be battened down tight in those circumstances, or your roof will almost certainly go."

"Sounds horrific. A 150-mile-an-hour wind. Hard to imagine."

"It's not the ultimate."

"You mean there are stronger winds?"

"There have been. Not very often, thank God. In fact only about four this century, at least in the Western Atlantic."

"And that's Category Five, right?"

"Right. When you get that, whole buildings, and I mean properly constructed buildings, can get blown down."

"But what would cause a Category Five to happen?"

"Well . . ." he signalled for fresh cappuccinos. "Nobody actually knows. Nobody actually knows enough about why hurricanes spawn at all. Sure we know they won't form unless the water temperature is high enough. But that's not to say they will appear the moment the temperature reaches 26½° Centigrade. Just as we don't know why they sometimes fizzle and why they sometimes keep on building. The jet streams have a lot to do with it. Those are the upper atmosphere winds, which are very strong but have nothing to do with barometric pressure or heat; they're caused by the earth's rotation. If they happen to be blowing over where a hurricane is forming, they can scatter the rising air before it becomes a system. Again, when a hurricane hits land it tends to dissipate, because land temperatures aren't as stable as those of the sea."

"Is that why, after they have tracked west across the ocean and reached America, they generally turn back?"

"Not really. That is part of the earth's rotation also."

Jo regarded her notes. She had enough for a small book. "That's all just great," she said. "But tell me one thing more, Richard: how dangerous are hurricanes? I mean, compared with earthquakes or volcanoes or things like that? I know they can push up tidal waves . . ."

"We call them storm surges," he murmured.

". . . in places like Bangladesh, and drown a lot of people, but those are exceptional circumstances, surely, with vast low-lying areas exposed to the sea? The porter in my apartment says his father told him about the '26 hurricane down in Florida, which killed a lot of people."

"Over four hundred," Richard said. "Florida was much more sparsely populated then than now. Jo, in terms of energy release, a hurricane is the most destructive of all natural phenomena, and that includes volcanoes and earthquakes. Just for example, even a small hurricane generates as much energy as several atomic explosions added together. There is no radiation, of course, and no searing heat. But it is still the mightiest force known to nature."

"I hadn't realised that."

"Very few people do."

"So it's the wind which causes the most damage."

"Oh, no. It's the water. Figure this: a Category One storm will push up a storm surge of maybe five feet above normal water level. Now, remember, it is not a wave, nor is it a rise of tide. It is a surge, which may arrive several hours before the wind and start flooding low-lying coastal areas, and then continue for as long as the wind is blowing. And this surge gets bigger with every increase of wind. A Category Three storm could have a storm surge of as much as twelve feet above normal."

"And Category Five?"

"The highest storm surge we have recorded is about 20 feet above normal. But it could go higher than that. And this, of course, is on top of the tidal range, which could be a big one if it was a spring tide, so that on top of the surge there will be waves of as much as 50 feet high, breaking."

"My God! Thank heaven we don't have things like that in New York."

"You could. Don't forget Gloria."

"Back in 1985," she recalled. "Oh, yes. We were all panicking like mad. But she didn't turn out to be half as bad as people expected, or as you weather forecasters said she would be."

"That was because the Big Apple is one hell of a lucky city," Richard told her. "Consider these points. Gloria was a Category Three storm, big enough in all conscience, but a long way short of the biggest possible. Then she passed east of New York, the centre, that is. That's very important, because of that anti-clockwise movement I was telling you about. In the northern hemisphere a hurricane pushes out its strongest winds and biggest seas to the right of it as it moves, and thus in a west moving storm the extreme conditions are always found in the northern half – what sailors call the dangerous semi-circle. The front quarter of this semi-circle is the most dangerous of all. With Gloria, as she was moving north by the time she came up here, that quadrant was on the north-east, that is, always out at sea. If she had come ashore, if, say, the centre had crossed the coast over Atlantic City, it would have been a different matter: you'd have had the strongest winds blowing up Broadway. And then again, when Gloria did come ashore, on Long Island, she did so at low water. If she'd gotten there at the top of a high tide there could have been incalculable damage, and even loss of life. So you see, it could happen."

"But will it ever?"

He grinned. "You'll have to ask God that. But it most certainly could, given the right atmospheric conditions, or I guess I should say, the wrong conditions."

"Is there anything that could be done to avert it, or mitigate the damage, if it were to happen?"

"There's not a thing anyone can do to avert a hurricane. The only practical step which can be taken to mitigate the worst effects, provided warning is received in time, would be to evacuate the whole threatened area."

Jo stared at him in amazement. "You mean, if a major hurricane were likely to hit New York, you'd evacuate the city?"

He shrugged. "If a really major storm were taking a bead on us, I'd certainly recommend it." Another grin. "And then shoot myself when it veered off."

"I guess someone else would beat you to it," she smiled. "This is all great stuff, Richard. Now let me ask you that last $64,000 question: is there going to be a major storm this year?"

"That's another one for the deity, I'm afraid."

"But aren't there some signs you can use?"

"Sure. And as it happens, we have them. The ocean temperatures are somewhat higher than normal for the time of year. And this warmth is pretty widespread."

"So you think there could be a big one?"

"I think there is going to be a lot more hurricane activity than usual, this year. I won't go further than that."

"Well, as I said, that was just great. Now I have to put it all into readable English." And then forget all about you as soon as I am given another subject to interview, she thought. But today she didn't want to do that. Perhaps because her quarrel with Michael had left her feeling isolated; however long she had lived in America, this was his country, not hers. Even the Donnellys, who had so willingly and enthusiastically taken her to their hearts, were his family, not hers.

Perhaps Richard felt the same way. "Do I see you again?" he asked.

"I'll send you a copy of the article," she promised. "But you know, what you've told me today has given me an idea. I'm sure an awful lot of people would like to know something more about hurricanes than the old wives' tales which is all they normally get. Have you thought of giving a series of talks, say at the end of a forecast? Especially now we're into June, and if there are going to be a lot of storms this year."

"Have you thought of the scheduling? Kiley would throw a fit."

"I've an idea he might go for it," Jo said, remembering that it was Kiley who had set up this interview to publicise his new boy. "And what I would like to do is conduct some interviews with the man in the street, get his opinion on what you had to say, find out just how much he knows about hurricanes, whether he believes one could ever hit New York, and so on. It could make interesting reading, and the two would tie in together. What about it? I'll have Ed Kowicz – he's my editor – give Kiley a call. And then, at the end of the season, I could interview you again."

"Sounds brilliant." His crooked smile played over his face. "But I'd hate to think you're not going to interview me again until October."

Park Avenue – Afternoon

"Where are we going, Mom?" Owen Michael looked down at the East River in puzzlement as they left school and drove over Manhattan Bridge.

"To the beach," she announced.

"Oh, jees, that's great!"

"But Mommy, we don't have any swim things," Tamsin complained.

"No problem. We'll buy new ones."

"I'm hungry," Owen Michael said, waiting breathlessly for her reaction.

"How does the thought of a double, double, king-size take you?"

"Neat! Fantastic!"

"Oh, Mommy! Smashing. But why? You usually call burgers non-food." The little girl bounced up and down in the back seat.

"They are non-food. But today's a special treat." She felt like a schoolgirl playing truant; it was that sort of a day.

She bought bright yellow swimsuits and towels for them all at a beachfront store. They swam first, then sat under a beach umbrella to eat their hamburgers, washing them down with Seven-Ups, and walking away licking ices. After another swim Jo's offer of a speedboat ride round the Jamaica Bay islands was promptly accepted. They started back at six and Owen Michael complained of hunger pains – so they found a restaurant and she handed the kids a menu. While they ate she went over her notes and added various comments or ideas – and found herself thinking of that crooked smile.

Owen Michael pushed back his chair. "Jees, if I eat any more my eyeballs will be pushed out on to my plate."

"Ugh! Don't be disgusting," Tamsin scolded. She, too, was full.

Michael was waiting for them in the apartment. "Jo! Thank God! I thought . . ." He looked miserable.

"Hi!' she breezed. "Like to fix me a drink while I bath these two?"

"Okay." He nodded. "I'll bring it to you."

While the bathing progressed, Michael paced between bathroom, bedroom, and lounge, hovering anxiously, searching her face every time she looked at him for indications of her feelings. He watched as the kids hugged her goodnight.

"Thanks, Mom, for a super treat." Owen Michael's arm squeezed her neck until it hurt.

"Yeah, thanks, Mommy. What'll we do next?"

"Well, on Saturday, how about the zoo up at Prospect Park?"

"Ooh, yes. Terrific. Dad . . ." Owen Michael looked up at his father. "Couldn't you come too?"

Jo bent over Tamsin's bed, deliberately not looking at Michael.

"I . . . er . . . well," Michael hesitated. "What do you reckon, honey? Would you like me to come?"

Jo stood up and faced him. "Yes, Michael, I would."

He strode across the room to take her in his arms. "Oh, my sweetheart," he whispered. "I love you. I'm so sorry. Forgive me."

She hugged him back, and the kids stood on their beds to join in.

"What about the race?" she whispered.

"Well . . . maybe they can manage without me for one weekend."

"Oh, Dad! Then you can teach me to water-ski," Owen Michael begged.

"And me?" Tamsin squealed.

Jo looked on, beaming. Had it really worked? Certainly it was time to forget that crooked smile.

NATIONAL AMERICAN BROADCASTING SERVICE OFFICES, FIFTH AVENUE

Evening

"God, but it's hot out there." Jayme, Richard Connors' secretary, delicately patted perspiration from her neck as she came into the office; she had nipped out for a sandwich between newscasts. "Even without the sun I bet you could fry an egg on the sidewalk. And it's only June. What do you reckon it's going to be like come August?"

"Worse than Florida," Richard commented. He was trying to concentrate on the various weather reports, which were certainly interesting, but was finding himself instead thinking about Jo Donnelly. He wondered if anything might come of her suggestion that he do a series on hurricanes. It was something he'd love to tackle, supposing Kiley would go for it. Although, he supposed, the real decision would come from that snapping turtle on the top floor.

But he wondered even more if she had suggested the idea – with its implication that they would work together – from a purely professional point of view, or if she might have had an ulterior motive? But how could she, happily married as she was and with kids. Maybe if he and Pam had had kids . . . but that had been yet another thing on which they had differed.

Jayme leaned over him. "Anything interesting on the way?"

"More of the same for us, I'm afraid. But the first storm of the season is down there. Just came in."

"Where? Let me see."

He prodded the map, as she rested one breast on his shoulder; she was already half in love with him. "There, in the middle of the Caribbean. They've just up-rated him into a Tropical Storm; winds around the centre are sustaining 45 knots. So he has a name: Anthony."

"And is Anthony going to become a hurricane?"

"Could be. The water temperature down there is certainly high enough. But he's not going to interest us; starting where he is, he'll almost certainly head off into the Gulf of Mexico."

"Now there's a shame," Jayme remarked. "If he'd come up here, maybe we'd get some rain to cool things off. You know what, Richard? I'll bet you ten bucks we're on water rationing before another month is out. Can't you conjure up a storm for us?"

Richard was studying the charts plotting the course of the jet stream. "I don't think I'm going to have to do that," he said. "I think one may come along of its own accord."

JUNE

The First Two Weeks

SUNDAY 4 JUNE

The Four Seasons Restaurant, New York

The Four Seasons restaurant hummed with muted conversation around the vast shrubbery where prospective diners sipped aperitifs and greeted friends and guests. It was a constant source of interest to Jo Donnelly, as an Englishwoman, to observe the variety and general informality of clothes American women wore to dinner in one of New York's leading establishments. In London it was not unusual to see long gowns and black ties – certainly most women would be in smart summer dresses, at least, but here no one seemed to bother; skirts and blouses, suits, slacks, even jeans, were apparently acceptable. A pity, she thought, so to downgrade a special evening.

Michael smiled at his wife, and was aware how lovely she looked tonight; the neck of her white dress was cut wide and low, revealing the deep tan on which a two-carat solitaire diamond pendant gleamed, matching the sparkle of her ear-studs as she moved her head. She wasn't beautiful in the modern film star style, yet she outshone any other woman in the room. The angle of her head, her sleekness and dignity, had always attracted him, always would . . . if only – what? If only she'd let him lead his own life? Stop nagging? Give up her damned journalism? Stick to the role of wife and mother? But if she did, could, would she still be the lively, dynamic personality with whom he had fallen in love?

"Penny for your thoughts." Jo squeezed his hand. He told her. After all, they had come here to round off their wonderful weekend together – and to discuss where they went from here.

It was the opening they needed.

"Can you understand that I am just not that sort of person?" Jo gazed into his face, pleading for his understanding.

"Can you understand that I need excitement and stimulation – like yacht racing? That's the sort of person I am."

"Yes, of course. And if it's not yacht racing it must be something else. I see that." She took his hand from the cocktail table and held it between both of hers, on her lap. "But as I see it, yachting as such is not the problem. Time is the point at issue. Time to be with your wife and family. Surely modern marriage isn't just a quick fuck and a wave of the hand in passing, as one flits from job to amusement and back? No," she shook

49

her head as he tried to speak. "Don't get me wrong. You and I have the same problems – I just think I schedule my life better than you, so as to do justice to each of my roles. And I've cut out of my life all other interests until Owen Michael and Tamsin are much older."

"What other interests?"

"Sport. When I left England I was in the top division of the squash league, remember? And I was also a county class tennis player."

"If you would only give up your . . ."

"Don't say it, please. I sacrificed sport for a career and that's that. Look at it this way; I spend an average of six hours a day, thirty hours a week, on journalism, and eight hours a day, plus all weekends, say sixty-five hours a week, on home and family. And I spend all vacations with Owen Michael and Tamsin."

Michael frowned. "Eight hours a day? How do you work that out?"

"Seven till nine in the mornings; half twelve till two lunch time; and six till half ten evenings."

"Well, I do almost that."

"True. But it's the weekends and holidays which are causing the problem." She held up her hand again as he opened his mouth. "I am going to make you an offer. I'll promise to cut down my journalism by an average of one hour a day, if you'll promise to spend alternate weekends with the kids and me, and take two weeks' vacation with us every summer, plus the winter skiing. And alternate public holidays."

The head waiter appeared at that moment to lead them to their table, so Michael had several minutes to consider his reply. "Well, put that way, I suppose it sounds fair," he admitted, as an under-waiter spread a napkin across his lap. "I hadn't analysed the situation down to hours, as you seem to have done, and I'd gotten the idea that I was spending that much time with you anyway. It's just a pity the Bermuda Race this year is sailed at roughly the same time Dad and Babs always go down to Eleuthera, and you know how disappointed they'd be if they didn't have the kids with them every summer. But what with the preparations and all that . . . you do realise the Bermuda Race is the big one?"

"I know. It will be an enormous sacrifice to miss it . . ." Jo started.

"Miss it? You mean . . ." He paused to study her expression. "Oh, God, yes, I see you do."

He was miserable, torn both ways, and she watched his torment with pity . . . but what was the alternative? "It won't be forever," she said gently. "In five years the thought of a holiday with us old folks will bore the kids silly. You'll be able to do what you like, then."

"Does this mean you want me to sell my share of *Esmeralda*?" Michael asked over his avocado and prawns.

"Good Lord, no! Can't you just cut down the amount of time you spend on her?" She didn't want to be unreasonable.

"I can do that, of course. But the Bermuda Race . . . we have a real chance this year, of winning our section. And we're a team, with me both skipper and navigator."

"Michael. You have said you have a chance of winning every year for the past seven, and you never have. Surely some of the others can navigate? Sam could replace you as skipper."

"Cheers." He raised his wine glass and drank.

"Cheers! Well?"

"I guess Sam could," he agreed reluctantly. "Larry could navigate . . ."

Jo noted the reluctance with a sinking feeling. Would this mean a ghastly summer holiday, with Michael sulking all the time because she had dragged him away from his sport? "You have no idea how much fun it is down there," she said. "All the family – Marcia is certain to bring Benny down to show off the house – and Lawson and Belle always come up from Nassau . . ." she paused. "It all boils down to a matter of loving, doesn't it?" she asked, without taking her eyes from her plate. "Which do you love more, your wife and kids, or your yacht?" He didn't answer, but she felt his eyes on her, and looked up. Her heart lurched as she whispered, "Michael? How important to you is our marriage? Do you want to save it, honestly, or do you want us to split up?"

His eyes closed momentarily, hiding his thoughts. He drained his glass and a waiter immediately stepped forward to take the bottle from the ice bucket, and dry it on a napkin before refilling both glasses.

When the man retreated, Michael held the tips of Jo's fingers and looked at her rings – the big emerald-cut diamond solitaire left to him by his grandmother and given to Jo on their engagement, the diamond eternity he had bought her when Owen Michael was born, and the plain platinum wedding band he had slid, nervously, on her finger in the splendid surroundings of St James's, Piccadilly, in front of a vast congregation of family and friends . . . what a let-down it would be to everyone, not least himself, to admit the marriage had failed.

His eyes held hers as he whispered back, "My dearest Jo, our marriage, our love, is far more important than anything else in the world. It's a deal. I promise to cut back on the time I spend on *Esmeralda*. And I will hand over to Sam for the Bermuda Race."

Tears of happiness stung her eyes as she said, "And I promise to cut back on my journalism."

Their lips met above their climbing wine glasses, while the head waiter and his team stood watching benevolently.

MONDAY 5 JUNE

Office of *Profiles* Magazine, Madison Avenue

The phone purred beside Jo, and she flicked the open switch, unwilling to spare a hand from the article she was composing on Richard Connors. "Josephine Donnelly, good morning."

"Jo? Marcia here. How're you doing?" Her happy voice trilled out of the box.

"Never better. How about you? What's new?"

"Something fantastic. I've got to tell you all about it. Are you busy right now?"

Jo looked down at her pad; there was a lot to be done, and Ed wanted this on the press by Friday. But Marcia sounded so excited and eager to relay her good news. "Not too busy. What's happened?"

"Can I come over for a coffee?"

"Sure, little sister. Any time."

"Like right now?"

"I'll meet you at the place on the corner."

"Ten minutes. 'Bye."

Jo sighed, and folded her pad away. Ten minutes later Marcia rushed into the coffee shop, panting. "I'm so excited I could die." The dishevelled young blonde squealed as she pranced in and planted herself in the chair across the table.

Jo giggled, and signalled the waitress to bring another coffee. "Okay, so what's it all about?"

"It's so fabulous I don't know where to start."

"Try the beginning, sweetie."

"Well . . . you remember I told you that Benny's mother owned an apartment building?"

"Yes." Jo wrinkled her nose. She hadn't seen the house, but knew it was in Greenwich Village and in rather a run-down state.

"Well, the two guys who were renting the basement have moved out, owing two months' rent, so Annamarie has repossessed it. Now she says we can have it."

"Oh, how super." Not quite as exciting as Jo had expected.

Marcia saw her expression and grinned. "But that's not all. The lease on the first floor ends in two months, and the old darling says she won't renew it, so we can have that, too."

Jo frowned. "What are you going to do with two apartments?"

"Steady, girl, steady; that's not all, either. The old chap on the second floor is in hospital. His wife says he has terminal cancer, and so she is leaving to keep house for her brother. Isn't it fantastic, all that happening at once? So Benny's mother says we can have the whole house."

"Gee, Marcia, that's fabulous. But the rent . . ."

"No, no, she's not renting it to us. She's giving it! We thought she meant selling it, and we didn't think we could raise that kind of money, but she says she has enough income from her other houses; seems Benny's father left her three. So she's making the deeds of the house over to us. And," she went on as Jo made to congratulate her, "there's more yet." She opened her purse and produced a sapphire and diamond engagement ring. "Benny says that if we want to be respectable home owners, we'll have to get married and have children. Look what he bought me with the money he got from the sale of that purple and red sea scene." She slipped the ring on to her finger and held it up to the light. "We are now officially engaged."

"Marcia! How absolutely marvellous." Jo leaned across the table to give her sister-in-law a kiss. "Congratulations, Babe, congratulations. Have you told your folks?"

"Not yet. I telephoned Babs and told her we'd like to come out tomorrow night. Can you and Michael come?"

"Sure we can."

"Because Belle and Lawson are flying up from Nassau, and Dale has promised to be there too. We'll surprise them."

"Big Mike will blow his mind."

"I guess he will. We're taking Benny's mother, too. We'll have a surprise family party."

"And I'll prepare the food," Jo said excitedly. "Over at the cottage where Babs won't see it."

To think that only a few days ago she had been the most miserable woman in New York.

TUESDAY 6 JUNE

Bognor, Connecticut

"Run, woman, run! Move your fat ass," Big Mike shouted, then threw his racket into the air. "Christ! She's missed it. Would you believe it?"

"Will you shut up, you big turkey? If you hadn't played the ball right on to Neal's racket when you had an open court . . ." Babs laughed as she went up to the net to shake Meg's hand. "Anyway, you'd have beaten us in the end. You were just too good for us today. Thanks for a lovely game.''

There was applause from the gallery. Jo and Michael, who had arrived with the children and sat watching the final set, rose to greet the players as they came off the court.

"Lovely of you to call round." Babs kissed her eldest son. "Let's all go inside for a drink." The court had been levelled out of the gentle slope behind Pinewoods, and the sun had begun to dip towards the surrounding trees. "Were you thinking of staying for supper?" Babs asked Jo as they walked down the gravel path together. "I haven't anything very interesting in the house, as Mike and I had thought of going out. Could you come with us?"

"Bit difficult with the children," Jo hedged. "But I've quite a nice lasagna ready at the cottage. I can pop back and fetch it, later. Won't take me more than five minutes," she lied, picturing the vast feast she and Marcia had prepared and which the latter was looking after, while she and Michael paved the way for the big surprise. They had to be sure Babs and Big Mike were at home when Marcia and Benny walked in.

When the Robsons had left, still anxious to talk about their new purchase – they were leaving for the Bahamas at the end of the month – Babs and Big Mike went up to change while Jo and Michael went home to fetch the 'lasagna'. The older couple suspected nothing, despite the children's conspiratorial glances – they had been sworn to secrecy.

Half an hour later, Babs squealed with delight as Marcia dashed into the house and hugged her parents. "Sweetie! Don't you look lovely. What a beautiful dress. And Benny! Wow!" She did a double-take. "Don't you look smart. I don't think I've ever seen you in a suit before. You guys going to a party?"

Benny was looking distinctly uncomfortable – but Marcia had insisted.

Jo, Michael, Owen Michael, Tamsin and Dale crowded the doorway behind Marcia and Benny, and Babs stared at them too. "You're all dressed up as well. What is this?" She looked from face to face in suspicion.

Jo prodded the shy and nervous Benny in the back, prompting him to speak. "Er . . . well . . ." he coughed and looked pleadingly at his beloved, who didn't attempt to help – but smiled encouragement. "Well, Marcia and I-have-decided-we-want-to-get-married, and we've brought my Mom too." Words spilled out in a rush, and an equally shy, short, plump, middle-aged woman in an obviously new, smart, two-piece, was dragged into the room from the hallway.

Big Mike leapt up to join the whirl of excited hugs, kisses and hand-shakes, beaming from ear to ear, while Babs' eyes filled and she kept repeating, "I'm so happy I could cry," while her husband made a grab for the car keys, saying, "I'm shooting down to the store for some champagne."

"Not necessary, Dad." Michael produced a huge cool-box from behind him. "Here we are, all chilled and ready."

No one noticed Jo slip upstairs to the phone, and five minutes later the excitement started all over again as Lawson and Belle walked in.

Benny was left in no doubt as to the popularity of his proposal. His natural reserve was swept away on the tide of Donnelly enthusiasm and soon, with the added help of champagne, he was chatting freely, arm round his mother, explaining her generosity and all they planned to do with the house.

Jo was kept busy organising food from the car to Babs' oven, but she had time to join in every few minutes. She loved watching people – speculating on what made them tick. Big Mike, Babs and Michael all relieved that Marcia was at last 'going legit', becoming respectable; Benny's mother, Annie as she liked to be called, swamped by the noisy and affectionate welcome, trying to keep her end up with Benny's encouragement; Belle, who couldn't give a damn about respectability, thrilled by her younger sister's happiness, and Lawson . . . but Lawson seemed to hang on the periphery of the fun, obviously preoccupied.

Babs followed Jo into the kitchen. "If only I'd known you were all coming I'd have gotten food in and ready, but I guess we'll have to send the boys out for some takeaway, to feed twelve of us. Your poor lasagna can't . . ." She realised Jo was grinning, and stopped. "What have you been up to?" she sniffed. "That's not lasagna . . . why, that's one of your lovely baked hams . . . and what's under there?" She pointed to a large tray concealed under a dish towel.

Jo whipped the cloth away to reveal twelve halves of grapefruit, cut and piled with brown sugar steeped in sherry. "Those just need to go under the grill for a few minutes, the vegetables are on, and the sauce made."

Babs hugged her. "Jo, you are a doll. You've got it all organised. Say, have I got time to go up and change? I feel awful in these old pants."

Her daughter-in-law laughed. "Babs, you make old pants look divine – but if you want to put on your mother-of-the-bride outfit, you go ahead. Nothing's going to spoil if you're quick."

Minutes later Big Mike came into the kitchen. "Where's Babs?"

"Changing. You've time, if you want to," Jo assured him.

It was not an assurance he wanted. "What's wrong with what I'm wearing?"

Jo looked at the ancient sweater and cords. "Not too much, I guess, providing you're not embarrassed."

"Embarrassed? Dammit, they're clean . . ." He noticed a greasy mark over his stomach. "Well, nearly."

"Where's that beautiful jumper Marcia gave you for Christmas?"

"Not that purple and yellow monstrosity?"

"Yeah, that's the one. She'd love to see you wearing it. She's been so worried that you didn't like it," Jo coaxed.

"She's damn right . . . oh, okay." He grumbled off towards the stairs.

The meal was a great success. The table wasn't built for twelve people, but they made it, Owen Michael and Tamsin, in smart suit and party dress, being allowed to stay up for the important occasion. After they had all held hands while Big Mike said grace, there were innumerable toasts and gradually the noise level rose as the wine took effect and everyone's voice grew louder in an effort to compete with the rest.

"I have an announcement to make too," Jo said, when she could make herself heard. "You'll never guess who's vacationing with us at Dolphin Point next month."

They looked at her, and Michael drank some more champagne.

"My husband," Jo said, smiling at him.

"Son of a gun," Big Mike said. "I never thought we'd get you down there again."

"Well . . ." Michael said.

"Won't that be during the Bermuda Race?" Dale asked his brother.

"Well . . ."

"I'm so glad you're coming down." Babs squeezed Michael's hand.

"Yeah. Well . . ." Michael looked at his father, and then at Lawson. Big Mike understood the glance, as did Lawson. Big Mike nodded, motioning him to wait.

By 10.30 the children were virtually asleep in their chairs, and Jo took them up to bed. The others voted to clear away before taking coffee in the lounge; Benny and Dale collected glasses while the women dealt with dishes and leftovers.

"Cigar?" Big Mike asked Lawson.

"Love one."

"Come and take your pick. They're in my study." Followed by Michael, he led Lawson across the hall into the small room lined with loaded bookshelves, to the comfortable armchairs arranged before his desk. "Sit down and help yourself." He pushed a big silver box across the table, dropped into the swivel chair behind the desk, sat waiting as they all sucked vigorously for a few seconds. Then he said, "Well?"

"The ball's in your court, Big Mike," Lawson said. "Dolphin Point is officially on the market as of now. So . . . we're going to have to make a decision."

"Big interest?"

"Some, already."

"Local?"

Lawson shook his head. "A million US is a bit steep for the average Bahamian." He grinned. "They'd hardly get foreign exchange for such a purchase, and if they don't apply questions might be asked as to where they got the money – like do they maintain an illegal American account?"

"I thought everyone down there was as corrupt as hell," Michael remarked.

"There's a lot of corruption, sure. But you still can't be too blatant about it. No, our main interest is coming from Florida. The realtors over there are looking for some alternatives to those millionaire ghettos they have up in Boca Raton and Palm Beach. Once they get in the act . . ."

"So what d'you want from me?" Big Mike asked. "I'm thinking about raising the money, but I need another few weeks. And I want to have another look at the property."

"And you're not coming down until mid-July? It'll be gone by then. Can't you make it sooner?"

"No way. We're up to our ears trying to float a stock issue."

"Look," Lawson said. "All it needs is a hundred thousand as a deposit. That'll tie it up, Big Mike."

"Which we lose if it doesn't work out," Michael commented.

"It has to work out," Lawson insisted. "Look, did Big Mike give you the figures?"

"He talked about maybe a couple of million profit."

"That was off the top of my head," Lawson told him. "Since then I've been getting down to facts and quotes. Listen! I can lay electricity to that whole property for a hundred grand. There's no water, but hell, no property in North Eleuthera has mains water. But I can build a cistern big enough to serve the whole area for another hundred, and a catchment area to serve the cistern for fifty – hell, it's just a big sheet of sloping concrete."

"So we're up to 250 grand on top of the million," Big Mike pointed out.

"Sure we are. But then we split those 42 acres into quarter-acre lots. 168 of them. And you know what I reckon we'll get for them, with water and electricity? Forty thousand dollars each. Work that one out."

Big Mike pulled his calculator towards him, jabbed the figures. And whistled. "Six million, seven hundred and twenty thousand dollars."

"That's right. Five million profit. Half for me, half for you."

Big Mike and his son exchanged glances. "We were thinking of a three-way split."

Lawson hesitated, then grinned, and shrugged. "Okay, if I get my normal two per cent for every lot I sell."

"Done," Big Mike said. "I'll have that $100,000 in your account tomorrow."

Michael poured them each a glass of port. "Seems a bit unnecessary for me to come down at all," he remarked.

*   *   *

They all drank coffee in the kitchen. "Now then," Babs said. "Let's talk about this summer. You going to honeymoon on Eleuthera, Marcia?"

"Well . . ." Marcia looked at Benny. "Would you be terribly upset if we didn't, Babs? Actually, we don't mean to marry until the winter. Right now we want to fix the house up first. Our house," she added proudly.

"Of course I'll be upset," Babs said. "But I reckon you're probably doing the right thing."

"You can count us in," Belle said, smiling at Lawson. She was dying to tell her mother and sister about the McKinley deal, but he had sworn her to secrecy until her father gave her the nod.

"I'll be there," Dale agreed.

"And Jo and Michael and the grandchildren," Babs said. "Oh, it's going to be such fun. How long is it since you were on Eleuthera, Michael?"

"Not since he started racing, seriously," Dale observed.

"Seven years," Michael said, thoughtfully.

"You'll find it's changed," Big Mike said. "Boy, have I got some things to show you."

"I'm looking forward to it," Michael agreed.

He wasn't entirely convincing, Jo thought. But he wouldn't go back on his word. And she knew he would enjoy it, when he got there. She'd been feeling rather guilty about him, ever since Sunday night. But she knew she had made him do the right thing.

She smiled at them all. She hadn't been so happy since her wedding day. And she felt the happiness was shared.

"Here's to the summer," she toasted. "It's going to be just great."

FRIDAY 9 JUNE

Park Avenue

Two days later, Ed told her that Kiley had agreed to give Richard an extra five minutes on Friday evenings following the early newscast, to chat about the weather, and about hurricanes in particular; he had been encouraged by Anthony down in the Caribbean, even if Anthony, after briefly reaching Category One in the Gulf of Yucatan, was now fading fast. "So," Ed said. "If you're serious about doing those interviews with the 'man in the street', you'd better get with it." He had raised no objection when she told him she wanted to cut down her office hours, and do more work at home, but a project was a project.

58

Jo was momentarily taken aback. She had not actually planned out how she would go about it; interviewing the man in the street was not her forte. Normally her meetings were with people used and eager to be interviewed, set up by the magazine. So how did one buttonhole some perfect stranger and get his opinion on something as remote as a hurricane? Then she realised that she had at least one natural starter, Washington, the giant black man who had worked as porter in the apartment block ever since she had first lived there, and who had once told her how he had been frightened as a child in Florida by tales of the 1926 storm.

"Couldn't hardly happen, nowadays," he said, when she asked him about it again. "They have all that sophisticated gear to tell everybody days in advance what's going to happen."

"So living in South Florida wouldn't bother you, now," Jo persisted. "Even if you know that by the law of averages Miami has to get hit again by a big one some day?"

"Depends on whereabouts I'd be living, Mrs Donnelly. Think maybe I'd get worried if I was one of those rich folks out on Miami Beach. My son and his wife took his mother and me down to Miami on a holiday two years ago . . ."

"Yes, I remember you telling me about it."

"Didn't think too much about hurricanes at the time, but now you mention it, I don't see how they're going to get all those people off that sandbank, over the causeways, in time – even with plenty warning. And that's if everyone moves kind of quick. You know what folks are, Mrs Donnelly. They won't make up their minds to go until the last minute, and then there'll be one big traffic jam and panic and everything you can think of."

"Washington, have you ever thought that a hurricane might hit New York, one day?" Jo watched his face as he considered the question.

"Nope," he said at last. "Never came into my head. Hurricanes don't get this far north."

"Only because the water's too cool. But suppose one year warm water spread up here, as it must have done the year Gloria came so close?"

"Heck, I remember her," Washington said. "Jees, that was something, eh? But she was a kind of freak, wasn't she? I guess anything in the world can happen."

"And if it happened once, it could happen again, couldn't it?"

"I guess it could, ma'am. But you don't get freaks very often. I wouldn't expect to see another Gloria in my lifetime. And she didn't even hit us, Mrs Donnelly."

"She only just missed us," Jo reminded him. "Well, I hope you're right that it can't happen again for a while, because I've been told it's quite possible. If a hurricane were heading this way, what would you do?"

The automatic glass doors swung open and a man crossed the foyer. Washington got up to speak with him, returned to call one of the apartments, and directed him to an elevator. When he sat down again, he shrugged. "Hard to say."

"Suppose warnings were out on TV, that one was coming straight for the Battery, would you leave town?"

He nodded, slowly. "Yes, ma'am, I reckon I would. If there was going to be a big one coming straight at us, I reckon I'd do just that. Get the wife and my daughter and little one, and call my son to do the same. Yes, reckon we'd all drive off to stay with my brother until it was over."

Again the automatic doors opened to admit several people, and Washington stood up.

Jo got up too. "Looks like you're going to be busy for a while, so I'll leave you now. NABS will be doing a short feature on hurricanes after the Friday forecast at six o'clock. I'd be interested to hear what you think of them, some time. And thanks very much for the interview, Washington. I'll let you have a copy of the magazine when this article is printed."

Washington beamed at her as they left the office. "That'll be great, Mrs Donnelly, just great. And I'll be sure to watch for that feature. Thank you, ma'am."

Monday 12 June

Grand Central Station

Jo gazed around the cafeteria, looking for a likely subject, and saw one sitting alone at a green-painted, glass-topped table. "This seat taken?" she asked.

The elderly woman smiled. "No. Sit down, honey. Feel free. Busy up here today."

"Railroad cafés usually are at this time of day, and especially this one." Jo surreptitiously inspected the woman while she examined the menu: neatly permed white hair, framing a carefully made-up face, turquoise polyester pants and loose, flower-printed shirt. She tried to sum her up: lonely, probably widowed, not too much money . . . yes, this would be a likely subject. She closed the menu and asked the waitress for a chicken salad and coffee.

"Salads are real good here," the woman told her. "My name's Lila Vail."

She was making it easy by being so friendly. "I'm Jo Donnelly."

"You eat here often?" Lila asked.

"Not really. I live in New York."

"Well, so do I, right now. With my sister." Lila giggled. "Her name's Talma. But we call her Tootsie. Wouldn't you?"

"Yes, I would," Jo agreed. "What location?"

"One block south of East Houston. Where are you?"

"Park Avenue, just off 48th."

Lila drank her coffee; their respective locations, Jo thought, socially as wide apart as Mayfair would be from Brixton in London, were threatening to end the interview before it began.

"Can you remember a summer so hot so early?" she asked.

"Oh, sure," Lila said. "Only moved up here from Florida less than a year ago. When my Hughie died. Well, heck, Tootsie's a widow too. It seemed right for us to get together, and she wouldn't come down there. She can't take the heat, right? So I thought I'd give the Big Apple a try for a couple of years. Right?"

"Right," Jo agreed again. She wanted to sound interested, but she was disappointed; she had been looking for the opinions of genuine New Yorkers. Still, having started . . . "Just like that weatherman on NABS. Do you ever watch him?"

"You mean Richard Connors? When we're at home, sure. I used to watch him on Miami TV, too."

"Of course you would have. He's an expert on hurricanes, so they say."

"Isn't everyone?"

"Did the thought of experiencing a hurricane ever bother you, in Florida?"

"No way, my dear. As far as Hughie and I were concerned they were just so much hot air." She threw back her head and laughed at her own joke.

Jo tittered politely. "But if you had heard a hurricane warning and been told to evacuate, would you have left your home for a safer area?"

"Oh, no! Safest place is your own home with shutters over the windows." The older woman's tone was condescending. "Might have a few trees down in the yard. Need to pick your washing in, too." She laughed again.

Jo ignored that one. "The most serious problem would be the surge of water . . ."

"Our house was two miles from the sea. That never bothered us."

"But could you be sure it never would? In a really big hurricane the surge would penetrate much farther than that. There is no high ground in South Florida to stop it."

"Don't you worry, my dear. I've lived in Florida for years. I know about hurricanes. And I can tell you there's more crap – if you'll pardon the expression – more crap talked about them down there than you'd believe possible. In all the years we were there we never had a problem."

"But did you have a hurricane?"

"Of course we did. They have them all the time, in Florida."

Jo frowned. "I thought no major hurricane has hit Florida since 1949?"

"That's nonsense. Every year we had the warnings, and we put the shutters up and the wind blew and we had thunder and lightning and rain . . . if that's not a hurricane, what is? But they never troubled us. But you know what gets people worked up and scared of them? Self-styled experts like that pretty-boy, Connors. Every June, there he was on Miami TV, telling us to prepare, and that at any time there could be this big storm, the storm of the century, he would say, and how it was going to do unimaginable damage . . . absolute crap. And now they tell me he's gonna give a series of talks on hurricanes up here? What a waste of time."

There must be thousands of people down south who think like this, Jo thought. What a terrible problem for the authorities, if there was a severe storm, like a Category Five, or even a Three or Four, heading straight for all those high-rise condominiums, as Washington had pictured. But it was no use arguing with the old dear, or even getting annoyed because of her criticisms of Richard. She tried another tack. "Do you believe a hurricane could ever hit New York?"

"New York? You're putting me on." Lila drained her coffee cup. Lonely she might be – Tootsie only really came alive when playing bridge – but the sort of chat this girl had to offer was a dead bore. She signalled the waitress for her check.

"Yes, I must be getting along as well," Jo agreed. "I found your comments very interesting, Lila. You know, I'm a journalist, and I'd like to write a feature on this subject – what people really think about hurricanes. Would you mind very much if I quote you?"

Lila beamed, flushing with pleasure. "Mind? I'd be delighted. You let all those people know that Lila Vail thinks all this sensationalism over hurricanes is a load of crap. What paper do you work for?"

"A magazine called *Profiles*."

"Never heard of it. But I'll look out for it in the future. Nice meeting you, dear. Now, I must hurry; my train's due in a few minutes. I'm going down to Philadelphia for a few days to stay with my daughter. 'Bye, dear."

"'Bye, Lila." Poor, deluded old duck. Jo watched her making for the platform, small suitcase clutched firmly in her hand. But could she be right? Then her mind returned to all Richard had told her, and once more the possibility became frighteningly real.

Park Avenue

Florence was waiting at the elevator as Jo stepped out. "Just going to get Bert's vacation jacket from the dry-cleaners and I'll pick up the children from school on the way back. Be about half an hour."

"Are you going to Coney Island again this year?" It amazed Jo that so many New Yorkers spent their vacations on that unattractive strip to the south of the Narrows, so close to home.

"Same as ever. Sometimes we talk about a change, but we always end up there. We like to get ourselves a good tan on the beach, once a year." Stepping into the car she held the door open as she added, "A gentleman called. I said I thought you'd be home by four, and he said he'd call back. Didn't leave a name."

"Thanks, Florence," Jo said. "Can't think who that could be." Which was a lie. As it couldn't be Ed – who would certainly have left his name and instructions for her to call him – it could just be Richard. She didn't know if she wanted that or not. She knew she should congratulate him on being given the extra screen time, but she hadn't as yet, because she felt guilty every time she thought of him, and remembered her mood after that silly row with Michael. How long ago that seemed . . . and it was only a couple of weeks.

Her remote keyboard chattered away in her office as she knocked the interview with Lila Vail into shape, but her eyes drifted repeatedly to the phone, willing it to buzz – it was 4.15.

When it did, she nearly jumped out of her skin. She flicked the switch and Richard's voice filled the room. "Hi there. Have you heard the good news?"

"Yes," she said. "Terrific. And I've started on my interviews with the 'man in the street'. Got some useful reactions, too."

"Great. I'd love to hear them."

"I'm bashing them out now. I'll send you copies."

"I rather thought we might have a meeting," he said. "My first chat is on Friday, and maybe I could work in some of the comments you've accumulated."

Jo waited.

"We could get together for lunch," Richard suggested.

Jo stared at the phone. It was a totally sensible idea. They were sharing a project, and pooling ideas was obvious. So why did she again feel guilty? That was absurd in an adult career woman. "Why not?" she asked.

"Well, what about tomorrow?"

"No. I can't make tomorrow. I could manage Thursday."

"Okay. Thursday would be great. Will you come along here, or shall we meet at that pizza place?"

"I think the pizza place. About 12.30?"

"I'll be there." There was a moment's silence, as if he had considered saying something more, then he said, "See you."

"Yes," she agreed, discovering herself to be slightly breathless.

"Mommy, Mommy, I have a stomach ache." Owen Michael stood in the doorway, his face a mask of misery.

"Darling! I didn't hear you come in. Just a moment. Yes," she said, "Thursday at 12.30, Mr Connors. Goodbye."

There was a moment's pause before Richard said, "Goodbye."

The phone went dead, and Jo turned to face a worried Florence.

"It's a fact Owen Michael ain't too good," she said. "Says he has a bellyache. That's the third time this month. I guess he don't like my cooking."

Jo put her arm round her son's shoulders. "Where is the pain, sweetheart? Tell me."

"All over, in no particular place."

Jo could see this was no imaginary tummy ache; the boy's eyes swam with tears which his ten-year-old pride was fighting to hold back. "Is it the same pain as the other day?"

His chin bobbed up and down as he nodded.

"Then I'm going to take you along to see Dr Knapps right now. Maybe he can tell us the problem and give you something to fix it."

MONDAY 12 JUNE

The Mercy Clinic, Avenue of the Americas

"Dr Knapps is on vacation, Mrs Donnelly, but Dr Glenville can see your son."

"That'll be fine," Jo responded. "Just as long as he can tell me what's wrong."

They sat in the waiting-room thumbing through dated journals for over half an hour, and inevitably, by the time they were called into the consulting room, Owen Michael's pain was gone.

Dr Glenville was one of the several partners who owned and operated the clinic, and with Dr Knapps he shared the pediatric section. He was a charming, elderly man, who smiled benevolently, though failing completely to conceal his tolerant scepticism. Owen Michael lay on the examination couch while the doctor pressed his abdomen and asked questions, then when he was satisfied, Dr Glenville said, "Hm. Let's see. Your school year finishes in a couple of weeks, I believe."

"Yes, sir." Owen Michael nodded politely.

"So you're about to begin your exams."

"On Monday, sir."

"Hoping for good grades, I guess?"

Owen Michael grinned. "I hope so, sir."

"He's starting High School in September," Jo explained.

"So you've been working extra hard. Exams can be tough, can't they?" Owen Michael nodded vigorously.

"Find any subject very difficult? How's your math?"

"Math is no problem. English grammar and literature are the worst."

Dr Glenville smiled, and nodded. "Not too difficult to diagnose a nervy young stomach at this time of year, is it?"

"Well . . ." Jo hesitated. "He really was in pain, doctor. I know he was."

"Of course he was, Mrs Donnelly. Psychosomatic pain can be just as unbearable as the real thing. What we have to do is relax those stomach muscles. I'll give you a prescription . . ." He sat at his desk and scrawled something indecipherable on a pad. "This'll settle him down."

WEDNESDAY 14 JUNE

52nd Street

The two filing clerks Jo spoke to in the main *Profiles* office had never heard of Richard Connors, neither were they the slightest bit interested in hurricanes. Nor was the man on the newsstand from whom she usually bought a paper on the way to work. But when next morning Jo asked Nancy Duval, who was shaping her hair with expert snips of her scissors, the hairdresser gave a tremendous response.

"I was in the Bahamas once," Nancy said, "when there was a warning. God, I was scared." The blonde curls bobbed up and down as the girl gesticulated at Jo in the mirror. "Took Bill hours, and three vodka Martinis, to calm me down. Gee, if one of those things ever hit New York . . ."

"It's highly improbable, of course," Jo said, beginning to worry about the proximity of the scissors to her ears. "It would have to be the result of freak weather conditions. You know, an exceptionally hot, dry spring, raising the water temperatures way above normal, and . . ." She paused, to stare into the mirror, and watch the sweat beads gathering at Nancy's mouth and temples, despite the air-conditioning in the salon.

"Like this one now," Nancy suggested.

"There have been hot springs before," Jo pointed out. "The chances must be a thousand to one against anything like that happening."

"I was always a sucker for long odds. My father gambled away a fortune on horses, always going for short odds, but you'd be amazed by the number of times I raked in the cash from outsiders. Thousand to one against it may be, but it still gives me the creeps to think about it."

The conversation was certainly slowing down the trimming job, but it was good for business, and Jo asked, "Do I guess right that, if there was a hurricane warning for New York, you'd leave?"

"Leave? You can bet your goddamn ass I'd leave. I'd be leading them all the way out of town, 'cept I reckon no one would see my heels for dust."

"Bill might not want to go," Jo suggested.

"Correct. Bill will not want to move – but he will, even if I have to drag him away by the hair."

"And your three children . . ."

"Yep. I'd throw them all in the car, lock the doors, and drive like crazy. There." She stepped back. "That looks better."

Jo looked at the results in the mirror. She could have sworn the left side was shorter than the right, but she had been here long enough as it was. "Yes, that looks great. Thanks a million."

"Say, you vacation in the Bahamas, don't you?" Nancy inquired. "You ever seen a hurricane?"

"I don't think so," Jo replied, deciding against supporting Big Mike's upgrading of their storm of three years earlier.

WEDNESDAY 14 JUNE

New York City Library

Jo's Mercedes was in for a service, so she left the salon and walked down to the library; she needed some more youthful reactions. There was the usual assortment of people sitting or lounging on the steps. Most were in groups, but there was one young man, wearing a dirty sweatshirt and shorts, gym shoes and a broad-brimmed western style hat – through the band of which was stuck a hash pipe. He was sitting on the steps and reading a newspaper, and did not look up as she stood behind him. "You're wasting your time, sister," he said. "I don't have 'em."

"Have what?" Jo inquired.

"You ain't taking a survey on Aids?"

"As a matter of fact, no," she said.

At last he raised his head. He was quite a good-looking boy, early twenties, she estimated, spoiled only by the looseness of his mouth, the laziness in his eyes. "Well, what d'you know," he said. "What *do* you know," he repeated, as he inspected her from her ankles, slowly up the length of her summer skirt, which was inclined to sheerness in the afternoon sun, to her breasts. "Well, if you're looking for a fuck, I guess we'll have to use your place." He grinned. "I ain't got one."

Jo opened her mouth and then closed it again. She wished she had chosen someone else. But his reaction might be interesting. "My name is Josephine Donnelly," she said. "I work for *Profiles* Magazine, and I am doing some research on hurricanes."

The young man leaned back and tilted his hat over his eyes. "Siddown," he suggested.

Jo hesitated, then chose a relatively clean piece of step. It was the middle of the afternoon and they were surrounded by at least a thousand people: but she was careful to keep out of arm's reach.

"You are something," he remarked. "I like your feet."

"Thank you," she said. "You ever been in a hurricane?"

"But I like your ass better. You know what I'd like to do to your ass?"

"No," she said. "What about the hurricane?"

"Bit of breeze," he said.

"You've seen one?"

He shrugged. "Can't say I have. You gonna let me feel your tits?"

"No," she told him. "What would you do if you were told a hurricane was coming straight for New York?"

"Nuts," he declared.

"It could happen."

He sat up again. "You gotta be dumb."

"Imagine it," Jo recommended.

He gazed at her for several seconds. "I'd stand out there in the rain and say, hallelujah."

"You'd be blown away by the wind."

"That I'd have to see. Like your tits." He suddenly reached for her, and she had to leap to her feet. "You scared of men?"

"I'd like to see that too," Jo remarked. "You being blown away." She hurried down the steps.

She caught a cab; she was too angry to walk, and the heat was intense – the air-conditioning inside the automobile had little effect and she mopped her face with a Kleenex. Her skirt and blouse were damp and crumpled, and the waistband was saturated. Her contentment of the morning – how much had that had to do with the thought of lunching with Richard? – had quite dissipated beneath the insults of that vulgar lout.

A haze lay over the city, and the avenues were like brick ovens, the highrise buildings reflecting the heat on to the traffic and pedestrians, the stench of melting tar filling the air. Every few minutes dust and paper swirled up in a flurry of hot air and then subsided on people and cars as suddenly as it had started. A cacophony of motor horns screamed before their drivers' frustrations and wheels rolled only a few feet before jerking against their brakes.

"It's these fucking trucks stopping in the middle of the street while they unload that causes this fucking foul-up," the driver fumed. He rolled down his window and shouted, "What the fucking hell's the matter with you, you anaemic asshole? Can't you carry those pissy little boxes a few extra yards instead of bringing the whole fucking city to a standstill?"

"You mind your fucking . . ." the culprit yelled back, but his comments were silenced as the cabbie rolled up his window again.

"Heat's bad enough without goddamned assholes like him snarling us up. Jesus, lady, did you ever know heat like this in June before?" He mopped his bald pate with a very dirty red and white spotted handkerchief. "Now, if I was a metio . . . a metori . . . a weather forecaster, I'd say there was a fucking big storm coming."

Jo's head jerked up to look at him, her annoyance dissipating. Here was the perfect man in the street. She flicked her notepad open. "I've been told there could well be even a hurricane up here. What do you think?"

"A hurricane? Fucking hell, lady, this is New York, not goddamned Miami." He revved the engine, moving the cab a few yards before braking again.

"Everyone thinks it'll never happen to them; even people in Florida and on the Gulf Coast," Jo said. "But it could. What about Gloria? New York was pretty lucky to escape her."

"Bullshit! New York was damned unlucky she came so close. Won't be another that near in a thousand years."

Jo smiled to herself at his total conviction. "Just supposing there was a hurricane warning broadcast on radio and TV for the New York area, would you get yourself and your family out of the city?"

"Out of the city?" He strained his neck to give her an incredulous look in the rear-view mirror. "What the hell for? You taking me for a dumb bunny, or something?"

She had to laugh, he was so like the dropout, although, for all his bad language, so much the pleasanter personality. "No. I'm a journalist," she confessed. "And I'm trying to get people's reactions to the possibility of a hurricane hitting the city, for an article."

"You want my opinion?" He still sounded incredulous.

"Yes."

"You can have it in one word: fucking bullshit. Sorry, that's two words. Both unprintable," he added, straight-faced.

"Thanks. May I quote you?"

"Sure. If you change the wording a bit. Look . . ." he took a piece of cardboard from the glove compartment and held it over his shoulder. "Here's my card. You can use my name, too. Al Muldoon."

WEDNESDAY 14 JUNE

Park Avenue

Michael stood at the cocktail bar with his back to the door, fixing a drink, when she came in. "Hi there," he said over his shoulder.

Jo frowned. He was home at least an hour early, and suddenly she had bad vibes.

He smiled very sweetly as he handed her a sherry on ice. "Let's sit down, darling. Boy, has it been hot today!" He set his bourbon and soda beside the chair, sat and stretched out his legs.

"Michael? What is it?"

"What's what?"

"Don't play games with me. You have something on your mind. Oh, my God!" She started to her feet. "Where's Owen Michael?"

"In the den."

"But he's all right?"

It was Michael's turn to frown. "Shouldn't he be?"

Jo sat down again with a sigh of relief. "Just that he had a tummy ache on Monday. He's been getting them kind of regularly. So I took him along to the clinic. Knapps was away, but Glenville saw him. Said he had a nervous stomach."

"You never told me any of this," Michael accused.

"Well, I didn't want to bother you, unless it was serious. But if it isn't Owen Michael . . ."

Michael gave as close to a sheepish grin as he was capable of. "It isn't Owen Michael. Fact is, my love . . . I won't be able to come to Eleuthera with you next month, after all."

"Why not?"

"Well . . . I had to call the guys, of course, and tell them I wouldn't be available for the Bermuda Race, and they were pretty upset."

"They were, were they?" Jo said.

"I did tell you that we reckon we have a good chance of a trophy this year," Michael explained. "But only if we have our best team. Sam and Larry flipped at the idea of me not skippering. Quite apart from being short of a crew member . . ."

"Are you going to tell me they can't find a volunteer to race in *Esmeralda*? To Bermuda? Any of those guys up in Newport would jump at the chance."

"Sweetheart . . ." He was still speaking very reasonably. "You can't just take along any beachbum on a race like the Bermuda. Every crew member on that has to be part of a team, used to working together. And . . ."

"No way! Absolutely no way, Michael. You made a solemn promise . . ."

"And on top of that, Sam says he'd rather not skipper in so important an event. It's one thing round the cans on Long Island Sound, but out there on the ocean . . ."

Jo sat back in her chair and crossed her legs. "Well, if they can't manage without you, they'll just have to scratch."

"Jo! It can't be done. I've given them my word . . ."

"You've what?" She jumped up and stood glaring at him. "You're not serious! So tell me, Michael Donnelly Junior, who do you intend breaking your promise to, your pals, or your wife and children?"

Suddenly he was on his feet too, standing over her, grinding his teeth in fury. "Goddamn it, you silly bitch," he hissed through his teeth. "I've been trying to break it to you gently, trying to explain the predicament I'm in so you'd understand . . ."

"Understand? Of course I understand! That you're a lying cheat."

"Don't you call me a liar," he threatened.

"Then you tell me what you are. Did you really and truly intend to drop out of the race this year? Ever? In which case you are an extraordinarily weak-minded character. Or did you just play the yes-man to me to stop me filing for a divorce? Which unquestionably does make you a liar."

She knew he wanted to hit her, but stood her ground, while the knuckles of his balled fists turned white – as white as the anger in his face.

Then he turned away, picked up his glass, drained it, and returned to the cocktail bar. "You really are the most selfish, self-centred, demanding bitch of a wife any poor sod could ever get landed with," he remarked, quietly, affecting a calm belied by the rattle of the decanter on the rim of his glass.

"Really?" She sat down again. "Do you base that opinion on the fact that I am asking you to keep your promise to spend some of your non-working hours with your family? And to take a vacation with them, for the first time in eight years? Do you realise Owen Michael and Tamsin cannot remember ever having vacationed with their father? Or do you sincerely believe that a husband and father should be permitted to break any promises to his family without recriminations of any kind? Perhaps I'm still somewhat naïve about marriage relationships in the States. Back in England, that sort of male chauvinism died with Queen Victoria."

"I guess it's your training as a journalist which enables you to twist what people say to suit your purpose," he retorted. "Well, I warn you, it won't wash with me. I agreed to holiday with you this year, all things being equal. But I can't let the guys down, and I don't mean to." He drained his second drink and slammed the glass down on the counter. "If you can't understand that, then that's it. I see no point in trying any more. I'm obviously wasting my time. In future, I'll just please myself – and the children. This atmosphere you repeatedly create is certainly having a bad effect on them. Nervous tummy? You're goddamned right Owen Michael has a nervous tummy. Who wouldn't in his circumstances?" He opened the door. "I'll be in the study if the children want me; I've some phone calls to make."

Jo realised her mouth was open, and closed it. She was too stunned to think for a moment. Vaguely she wondered if Michael really believed what he'd said . . . or if perhaps it was true, and it was all her fault. Either way, it was hard to see how the situation could continue. But the alternative was just as hard to imagine. It had been easy a fortnight ago, in a fit of fury, to say that she was going to Tom Wilson when her head was spinning with physical as well as mental grievances; there had been little time to think of the stark realities of divorce. Now, sitting alone in silence, she tried to visualise the possible outcome. The children having to grow up in two separate homes, each parent at least subconsciously trying to best the other with extravagant presents to them, while the kids themselves, like so many others she knew in such circumstances, learned to play one against the other, becoming rude and aggressive in their demands, knowing that the parent at issue dared not scold or chastise them lest they run to the other for 'protection'. And what of the Donnellys? Babs and Big Mike, Belle, Marcia and Dale? She had come, over the past eleven years, to regard them as her family, because she liked them all so much. But in a matter of 'sides' – as she had reminded herself before – they would have to be loyal to Michael, even if they knew he might be in the wrong! So where did that leave her? Ostracised? By both family and mutual friends, struggling, on a dramatically reduced income, to retain popularity with the children.

Her earlier anger and resentment was replaced by self-recrimination. How the hell had she been stupid enough to marry Michael in the first place? She had known of his drive for kicks from the day she met him. In her innocence she had imagined that would slacken off after marriage, that he would become a real family man like his father. Now she knew better, should she consider giving up her career to do as he asked, and devote her time to being wife and mother? But if she did that, and the relationship continued to deteriorate, she would be left with absolutely nothing. Homeless, friendless, and jobless – that would be ridiculous.

The door burst open and Tamsin ran in with a wail. "Mommy, I can't understand my math problem, and Owen Michael won't help me."

"Let's see if I can, Baby." Jo drained her glass and followed the child from the room, grateful for the distraction.

That night Michael reeled into the bedroom as high as a kite, waking Jo from a deep sleep. Having thrown his clothes all over the room, he clambered into bed and immediately fumbled for her breasts. She pushed him away but he came on, grabbing her arm and twisting it painfully.

"What's the matter, then?" he demanded, his voice thick and slurred. "Have you let that silly quarrel upset you? Come on, girl, forget it."

"No way. Get out of here and leave me alone. You stink." The water bed sloshed alarmingly as she struggled away from his reach until finally she was on the floor, and he was lying diagonally across the bed looking down at her, laughing.

There was no way she could get back into bed without virtually being raped – so she took the only alternative, rushed naked through the door and down the corridor to the spare bedroom, locking it behind her before climbing into one of the single beds. Michael didn't try to follow her – he was probably already asleep.

Next morning Jo woke late and hurried back to their bedroom to dress. Michael was out cold, snoring, mouth wide open, dishevelled hair over his face. She looked down at him and shuddered.

WEDNESDAY 14 JUNE

Key West, Florida

Mark Hammond leaned against the wall of the telephone booth. "Well," he said. "That was Barbara. She's fizzling so fast someone could have pulled a plug. I don't figure it, old buddy. What kind of sea temperature do you have up there?"

"25°C,' Richard told him. "It's climbing."

"Well, there isn't a water temperature under 26½°C anywhere south of Bermuda. So both Anthony and Barbara spawned, became hurricanes pretty quickly, and now have fizzled again."

"There's some jet stream activity," Richard told him.

"Yeah. But not enough. I just don't get it. Anyway, I'll be with you tomorrow, we can talk about it then."

"Tomorrow?"

"Sure. I told you I was coming up for a day or two this month."

"Oh, Jesus," Richard said.

"Come again?"

"Looking forward to seeing you," Richard said. "It's just that I have a rather important lunch date then."

"So, I won't get there until afternoon. See you then. Maybe you'll have worked out what's happening. By my book, both those storms should have been biggies."

"So maybe there'll be a real biggie this summer," Richard said. "Give you something to spot. See you." He was on too much of a high to care about hurricanes right that minute, even if he knew he should. He had encountered JC in the elevator only yesterday afternoon, and the great man had remarked, "Where's all this hurricane activity you promised us, Richard? Seems the goddamned things can't get off the ground. Or do I mean the sea? Haw, haw, haw. But it'd make people more interested in these chats of yours if we were to have something to hang them on to. Right?"

The old fool appeared to think he could conjure them out of thin air, Richard thought. But JC's excesses didn't really matter; tomorrow he was lunching with Jo Donnelly. So she was a married woman. But then, once upon a time he had been a married man.

JUNE

The Last Two Weeks

Thursday 15 June

East 57th Street

Richard Connors replaced the telephone and switched on his television screen: he had the morning off, and Julian was doing the ten o'clock forecast. Julian was coming along well – even if there was nothing to report. There was another tropical storm, just off Martinique, and this one was being named Christopher, but Richard didn't expect it to do much – it was already small and tight, and yet without hurricane force winds. It was being the damnedest spring, the hottest in New York for some time, and with summer only a few days away – and yet muted hurricane activity. A summer, he realised, which could leave him with egg all over his face, as he had confidently predicted, on the air as well as to his superiors, that there would be several major storms this year.

A summer which could end with him on his way back to Florida!

His ebullience of half an hour ago had faded, as it had a habit of doing when he found himself trapped in the minute apartment which was all he had been able to find. The fact was, he wasn't a home maker, at least on his own. He had moved in here a fortnight ago, and boxes of books remained stacked in a corner waiting for him to put up shelves. The place would look less bare when he had hung his pictures, but he didn't want to do that until he had redecorated the room – he couldn't live with that hideous shade of orange, and he hadn't even decided what colour would be an improvement. He leaned over and took a can of Budweiser from the box beside him, pulled the ring, and gulped a couple of mouthfuls. The bedroom had been easy to fix; he'd spent most of his time on it, working at odd hours, and felt quite pleased with himself. It had been his first attempt at Do-It-Yourself. He had also got his music centre working; it had been difficult to get the speakers in just the right positions in such a small area and he had had to be satisfied with a compromise – but he'd hardly listened to them: good music needed to be shared.

Bedrooms also needed to be shared. When Pam had finally walked off with that overmuscled piece of charred flesh, and they'd agreed to split, he'd been quite keen to sample independence again, have only himself to please, and get away from the constant emotional strain and bickering of a dead marriage. He had visualised himself as the happy bachelor, dating pretty girls when the mood took him, or staying late at the studio if he chose without feeling he was giving Pam an excuse for spending the night out with some pick-up. He had conjured up pictures of cosy evenings alone with his sort of music, his kind of TV programme, hamburger in one hand and beer in the other – comfortable and contented. Well, just about every evening since moving in he had had his music, his TV, his beer and his hamburger available – but what the hell had happened to the contentment? He'd pondered over the question long enough to know the answer: he was lonely for a woman. What about the pretty girls? The NABS building was stuffed with them, everyone eyeing him over their typewriters or round their coffee machines, offering him a lay any time. Closer at hand, there was Jayme, just dying to get him between the sheets.

The trouble was that he was too damned choosy, and he was not really into one-night stands. He wanted the same woman there, every night, to talk with, discuss the day. Someone with common sense and intelligence. Companionship was what he was after, even more than sex. A companion to eat with, walk with, go to the theatre or art exhibition with, and still be a pleasure to sleep with. He had met only one woman since coming to New York who could fill that bill. A married woman with children. To get her, he would have to play his image to the hilt. And he wasn't sure he wanted to do that, with Josephine Donnelly. But at least they were lunching together. He could feel his way.

They ordered pizzas, salad and Frascati again, as if they were both consciously trying to recreate the rapport of their first meal here. It was too hot for the English two-piece she had been wearing on the previous occasion, but Richard loved her in the crisp pale turquoise cotton dress, with its full skirt. Loved her? That was ridiculous; he hardly knew her.

". . . interviews. When school finishes for the summer . . ." He let her chat on, hardly listening, just watching her. She seemed more brittle than the last time they'd met – tired, perhaps.

A word sank in. "Vacationing in Eleuthera? That'll be fun."

"It is," she agreed. "All the family will be there . . . well, nearly all."

A shadow had passed over her face. "But your kids will be there with you," he prompted. "You never did tell me their names."

"Owen Michael and Tamsin."

"Cute. How old are they?"

"Ten and eight. Have you any? Oh, no, I remember . . ."

"Wish I had, in a way, but it's probably just as well I don't, with the divorce and all that."

"That's true. Was it . . ." She hesitated before asking the question which had immediately leapt to her tongue. "Very traumatic?"

He shrugged. "I was told it could've been a lot worse. We both wanted out at the same time, and having no kids was a great help."

"Yes," she said, thoughtfully. She had not come here today to think about her own problems – rather to escape them. But of course they were inescapable now. And hideous. Just for starters, there was no chance, even if Michael would admit they no longer even liked each other, much less loved, that he would want out from his children any more than she could contemplate abandoning them. Richard was clearly waiting for her to say something, so she asked, "What's it like being single again, after years of marriage?"

He was about to tell her it was great to have freedom again, all those trite quips one usually trotted out when asked that question. Instead he said, "Awful. I hate it. I never dreamed how lonely it could be."

Jo shook her head in amazement. "That's incredible. I'd have thought you'd have any number of girl friends."

"Don't you believe it. Oh, there are lots of girls, yes. But . . ."

"What have casual girl friends and bright lights to do with sharing TV suppers with your favourite person?" Jo suggested wistfully.

Richard's eyes narrowed. "You know?"

All at once she was nervous. The conversation had crossed that invisible dividing line between professional colleagues casually discussing personal matters, and two people striving for at least mental intimacy. He had begun to bare his soul to her, and he was inviting her to do the same in return. Well, she thought, with some men it wouldn't matter, and she was in the mood to do just that – but this one was far too attractive, and right at this moment she was far too vulnerable. She laughed. "What married woman doesn't, occasionally? My husband spends most of his time yacht racing. Now tell me what you're going to say in your first hurricane chat."

He felt a stab of disappointment as she backed off, and tried to get his mind back to business. "Well, I guess I'll have to begin with outlining just what a hurricane is, and hope to God I have something real to talk about before JC cancels the show."

"JC? Oh, you mean Calthrop White."

Richard grinned. "That's the network ogre, all right."

"Surely he won't cancel the show after one programme?"

"He might. He reckoned that there'd be hurricane activity down south this summer which would give the chats a boost, and it just isn't happening. Oh, there have been three named storms, but they've all fizzled."

"Don't tell me: the jet stream has been knocking them off before they could properly form."

"You have a good memory. Trouble is, the jet stream hasn't been all that strong over the central Atlantic this summer."

"So what's the reason?"

He shrugged. "I told you, meteorology is still an inexact science. I simply don't know. It's as if something out there was straining to bust loose, and hasn't been able to, yet."

"Isn't that an angle for you to use?"

He shook his head. "I'd be torn to ribbons by my fellow forecasters, and if it didn't happen JC would have my guts for garters."

She was terribly aware of those black, mobile eyebrows, and that sleek black hair and the way he could smile with just half his mouth. She could see he was quite different from her first impressions of him – so much more real and sincere, and, she realised, *he* was vulnerable, too. She drained her glass and averted her eyes, watched other people come in to the restaurant and the feet of passers-by above them on the sidewalk.

There was a brief silence, then he asked, "Do you go racing with your husband?"

"No. Michael made it quite clear, a long time ago, that his sort of sailing is for men only."

He raised his eyebrows. "How does he relate that theory to women like Clare Francis or Naomi James?"

"I'm afraid Michael does not relate his theories to anyone, or anything," she said. "He just behaves and thinks as he sees fit." And now he would even more, she thought.

"Then what are your hobbies?"

Her turn to shrug. "Being Mum, I suppose. There just isn't enough time to do anything else, if I'm going to hold down my job as well."

"But . . ." He checked what he had been going to say.

"Oh, sure, we don't need my income. That's not the point, though, is it? I have a life to live just as much as Michael, and I love journalism. But spare time does go on being a wife and mother. You won't believe it, looking at me now, but I used to play a lot of squash in the winter, and tennis in the summer, but one needs to play three or four times a week to maintain any sort of standard, and I hate playing games badly, so I guess picking up the threads will have to wait until the children are older." She realised that she was, after all, baring her soul to him, and discovered that she didn't mind. In fact, she wanted to, because he was listening to her in perfect seriousness. She smiled. "I get what kicks I can out of music. Sometimes, after the kids are in bed – and when I can find a baby sitter – I go to a concert or a play . . . or just stay at home and listen to records. I have a super disc collection."

"Really? I think I do too. What sort of music? Classical?" He leaned eagerly across the table.

"Yes, mostly."

"CDs?"

"Oh, yes. Yours?"

"Naturally. I'd love to show you my set-up; it's the only part of the apartment that's properly finished. Do you have half an hour?" Then he almost visibly gasped at the thought that she might accept.

They stared at each other, both knowing the implications of his invitation. Richard held his breath, while Jo's mind raced through the list of fors and againsts. But she knew what she wanted to do. It was years since a man had looked at her like this; come to think of it, it was hard to recall if Michael ever had. So she might regret it . . . but her entire life right now seemed composed of regrets.

She smiled, shyly. "Yes, I have half an hour to spare," she said, quietly but decisively.

In the elevator, Richard apologised for the mess she would find in his lounge. "Guess I just haven't gotten around to deciding what to do with it. I'm not too hot on interior design."

"That's because you haven't got a woman prodding you all the time," she said without thinking, and wanted to bite her tongue. But she immediately saw what he meant, shuddering at the hideous orange walls.

He showed her the music centre and the neat cases of compact discs. "Take your pick. Anything there you like?"

Scanning the titles, she tried to think, tried to decide what to do if . . . wondered if coming here hadn't been the stupidest thing she'd done since . . . since marrying Michael. Aware that he was patiently waiting, she stammered, "I'm spoilt for choice. I love them all. How about some Chopin?"

The reproduction was exquisite. Standing beside the window, double-glazed against the Manhattan traffic, she closed her eyes, listening, absorbing. And when she re-opened them, he was beside her, filling her with an overwhelming desire to touch him – be in his arms. And he wanted it too; she could read it in his eyes.

Silently they moved together, eyes locked. Jo felt herself drawn against him and stood trembling, wanting – yet frightened, overawed by the magnitude of her reaction to him. Richard was not the first man to have touched her since she'd married Michael; there had been plenty of sly hugs and kisses at parties and smoochy dancing with some very attractive men. This was different. She was very aware of how great the gulf was between those fun flirtations and what she felt now.

"Jo?" His voice was scarcely above a whisper.

"Richard?" She felt his breath on her forehead and tilted her head to meet his mouth with hers. Suddenly she was vibrant, alive; a great surging joy welled up to fill her chest, her throat, her head, leaving her gasping under his soft kisses. His encircling arms moved up, and with fingers threaded in her hair he held her face in both hands and gazed at her, smiling – the famous Connors smile. But this was genuine.

"Darling Jo. I have dreamed of you for the past fortnight, praying, hoping, and fearing it might all never happen." He crushed her against him as Chopin's Revolutionary Study filled the room.

The feeling of utter contentment blotted out all reality. The fact that she was married, irrevocably, that this love could only be an illicit, secret thing, that she could never stand on the proverbial hilltop and shout it to the world, or even admit it to her closest confidante, was irrelevant. All that mattered was the steady beat of his heart against her ear, his arms, his love.

Love? Oh, yes, it was love. Love like she could never remember feeling until now. A joyous, two-way thing, transmitted between them through kisses, caresses, and the way they looked. And, pressed against him, she knew he wanted more. As did she. When he turned her towards the bedroom she made no resistance, but then stared at him in consternation as the doorbell rang.

"Oh, goddamn," he said. "Just give me a moment."

She stood in the centre of the room, watching him as he went to the door. Now was the moment to regain sanity and leave. But she wasn't going to do that. She wanted only to have him back in her arms.

The door was open. "Hi, old buddy," Mark Hammond said. "Got in a shade earlier than I'd hoped."

"Remind me to put a bomb in your plane next time you go on patrol," Richard said.

SATURDAY 17 JUNE

Bognor, Connecticut

"Come on in, Mom, it's lovely," Owen Michael called from the swimming pool.

"It's a bit early in the year for me," Jo replied from her lounger.

"Don't know why I bust a gut putting in solar heating," Big Mike groused. "No one seems to use the pool any more often."

"We do," Tamsin shouted.

"Huh? You two used to break the ice to get in. Hasn't made a cent of difference to you," their grandfather retorted.

Reluctantly, Jo heaved herself up and went to the edge of the pool to dip a toe in. "Hey, that's quite warm."

"Fooled you," Big Mike grinned. "The heating isn't even on today."

Jo dived, her slim body slicing through the water under the children to tickle their feet and bring shrieks and squeaks as they splashed to get away.

"Shame Michael isn't here," Babs murmured. "I thought he was only going to race every other weekend?"

"Yep. Something wrong there. You can see it in Jo's face," Big Mike replied in a low voice. "It's my bet he means to do the Bermuda Race again this year."

"Oh, no! Do you really think so, after his promise to come to Eleuthera?"

Jo swam back to where they were sitting, kicked her legs and bounced up to perch on the pool edge beside them. "That's just super. Have you really turned off the solar panel?"

"Not off," Mike explained. "I've switched it to heating the house water alone. The weather's been so warm recently the pool hasn't needed it."

"We've had a record spring," Babs remarked. "Temperature-wise, anyway."

"Jo! Why's Michael up in Newport this weekend? Is he preparing *Esmeralda* for the Bermuda race after all?" Big Mike was not renowned for his tact: if he had a question he usually asked it.

Babs flushed and waited.

"Yes," Jo replied, not looking at them. She had not meant to discuss Michael with them – no doubt he would tell them his plans when he was ready. Besides, she had not wanted to think about Michael since Thursday afternoon. She still couldn't make up her mind whether she was glad or sorry that navy flier had walked in on them. He had been as embarrassed as they, but the ice had soon been broken, and they had sat around chatting and drinking coffee and beer until four. That he had been an old friend of Richard's had been sufficient to make him a friend of hers. That he was Richard's secret source of information about the weather made him an absorbing personality, especially when he had talked about the long, weary hours flying over the Atlantic, investigating every piece of cloud cover for signs of that circulation which would mean warm air rising too fast for safety.

And while he had talked, she and Richard had glanced at each other, the physical desire slowly subsiding, to be replaced by what? She wasn't sure. When she had realised the time and hurriedly left, he had come with her to the door. "I'm real sorry about that," he had said. "Can we meet again? Mark will only be here a couple of days."

"I'll call you," she had promised. But she hadn't yet. Mark might still be there, and besides . . . it had never occurred to her in her wildest daydreams that she would ever cheat on her marriage. Even if that marriage was over? That was something she had to be certain of.

"Oh, dear." Babs' tone was indicative of her concern; she was well aware of the implications of Michael's absence.

Jo felt their eyes on her, knew they were itching to learn if the old wounds had been reopened – if they only guessed at the truth they would have a fit. But they would have to be told something. The children were at the far end of the pool, racing from one side to the other, splashing and shouting. "Yes," she admitted. "We did have another quarrel, a big one, Wednesday night. When he told me he'd decided to race after all. I'm sorry I didn't tell you sooner – I thought he'd have done it himself. Maybe I was hoping he'd change his mind back again."

"Perhaps he will," Babs ventured.

Jo shrugged her wet shoulders and said nothing.

"Well . . ." Mike shook his head. "You knew he was a keen sportsman before you married, and if this is the way he wants it to be . . ." He paused, lamely.

"Quite. And he knew I was a keen journalist. Only I've kept my side of the bargain and cut back my work. So where do we go from here?" She wondered if they could help her solve her dilemma, even if inadvertently.

Alarm bells were sounding in Babs' brain. "Oh, my dear, I'm quite sure something can be worked out."

"What?" Mike asked.

Jo looked from one to the other. "If you can come up with some good suggestions, I'm all ears."

"Can't you discuss it together . . ." Babs started.

"We have. And it always ends in a slanging match." When your son doesn't actually hit me, she thought, but she wasn't going to tell them that.

They sat silently watching the children. The sky was an uninterrupted blue, but for the birds which occasionally swooped from the branches of one pine to the next. Gazanias and mesembrianthemums spread their colourful petals to embrace the warmth while bees hummed a ballet over the borders.

Mike rolled his feet off the lounger and stood up. "When's he coming home? I'm going to talk to him."

"I've no idea," Jo said. "We're not exactly communicating at the moment. But anyway, it's a waste of time. He'll know I've told you, and he'll accuse me of running up here whining to you." She tipped her weight forward, flopped into the pool, and swam to the far end and back, long, lazy strokes with the minimum of splash. She leaned her arms on the coronation and looked up at Mike and Babs, seeing the anxiety in their eyes. "I'm sorry. So sorry. He says it's all my fault, and naturally, I think it's his. I suppose we just have to accept that we're not compatible."

"Compatible, shit," Mike growled. "Don't give me that. Folks are as compatible or incompatible as they make up their minds to be. Look . . ." He sat on the edge of the lounger again, leaning towards her. "Don't get me wrong. I think he's behaving like a lousy son of a . . ." He threw Babs an apologetic grin. "Louse, breaking his promise, but dammit, it is his life, and if he wants to spend all his leisure time sailing . . ."

"He should never have got married in the first place," Jo interrupted bitterly. "He's like someone who buys a puppy to fuss over and pamper, and then abandons it when he gets bored or it proves too much trouble. Michael is bored with marriage, with me, and with his children."

"Oh, Jo! That's not fair!" Babs protested.

"Okay, maybe I'm wrong. But you tell me why he wants to spend so little time with us?" She could feel tears starting to sting her eyes.

"Well, you know how much he loves *Esmeralda* . . ." Babs' voice was gentle and coaxing.

"You're damned right I do. More than home, family, children . . . more than anything. Maybe I should just let him get on with it, and offer up grateful thanks to God for the few times he does spare us a little of his company. Well, I'm sorry, folks, but that's not my idea of a marriage. I didn't marry Michael just to be his maid, valet, bear him children, and be available for his sexual satisfaction whenever he requires it. I want a companion, too, to share things . . . like our children, holidays, the fun there is in life doing things that families do together." She scrambled out of the pool, grabbed her towel, and rushed up to the house to shower . . . and weep.

When she reappeared, made up and smiling in a pretty sunsuit, Babs jumped up and ran to put her arms round her. "Dearest Jo, we all do love you so much. Please don't give up, please. Anyway, don't let it get you down. We'll all have a talk with Michael, and maybe . . . if you'll just be patient."

Jo hugged her back. "I love you all too, remember?"

"Then you're not thinking of . . . well . . . separating? Or anything like that?"

She was actually considering the dread word, divorce. But she couldn't tell them that. Certainly she didn't intend a separation, which could only make matters worse while solving nothing. "No. No, I'm not," she promised. But Babs and Mike both noticed she wasn't smiling.

Monday 19 June

Park Avenue

The phone on Jo's desk buzzed, and she picked it up, heart pounding. She still hadn't called Richard, although she had almost made up her mind to, knowing full well that it meant she would go to bed with him. But Michael had returned from Newport as aggressively contemptuous of her as ever.

So perhaps Richard had grown tired of waiting; Mark would have gone back to Florida by now.

"Josephine Donnelly."

"Washington here, Mrs Donnelly. There's a . . ." Washington hesitated. "Gentleman down here to see you."

"Gentleman?"

"Says his name is Stuart Alloan. Says you and he are old friends."

"Stuart Alloan? I've never heard of him. Oh, well, you'd better send him up." She was preoccupied, at once with thoughts of Richard and with researching her next assignment, Nino Fabretti, the famous guitarist, who was going to be in New York the following week. Stuart Alloan? She looked at her watch; it was half past three, and Florence and the children had not yet got home from school.

The doorbell rang, and she looked through the peephole, while releasing the locks. All she saw was a face, which was certainly familiar . . . then the door was pushed in with a violence that all but knocked her over. "What on earth . . ." She gazed at the young man in the dirty sweatshirt and jeans, and the cowboy hat.

"Hope I didn't hurt you, ma'am," he said. "You remember me? Name's Stuart Alloan."

Jo drew a sharp breath. "Yes. I remember you, Mr Alloan. How did you know where I lived?"

"You told me your name and the magazine you worked for, ma'am. They gave me your address."

That stupid girl, Jo thought; am I going to have a word with her. But first, this lout had to be removed. "What do you want?"

He looked her up and down. Working at home, she wore only a housecoat, as he could certainly tell, however tightly she had retied the cord before answering the door. "Well," he said. "I thought you might have a copy of that article you were gonna do on me."

"Not on you, Mr Alloan. On hurricanes. But the magazine only comes out once a month, and the article is in July's issue. Sorry. So if you'd like to leave . . ."

He had closed the door behind him, and now looked around the lounge. "Say, some place you got here, doll. Must be money in writing for magazines, eh?"

Jo discovered her heart was pounding quite painfully, and she was feeling a little sick. The nearest telephone was in the study – on the far side of the intruder. And Nana was in the kitchen, asleep; she would be awakened by a call, but the kitchen door was shut, again behind the intruder. How on earth had she been so careless? Simply because her brain had been entirely filled with thoughts of Richard. But there was no use in losing her head. "The apartment belongs to my husband," she said. "Who will be home any minute."

"Is that a fact?" he asked. "You know that's what they all say?"

"They all?" She licked her lips, slowly backing across the room towards the brass-edged glass table. It was used to display ornaments, one of which was a tall, slim statuette, cast in bronze, on a marble pedestal. It could be a serviceable weapon. "You mean you make a habit of calling on women in the middle of the afternoon?"

He pointed at her. "Don't gimme any sauce, lady. I kinda like you. All of you. I really came up to see if you was ready to show me those tits."

Jo reached the statue, and wrapped her fingers round it, breathing a sigh of relief as she lifted it from the table. "If you don't leave right now," she said, "I am going to brain you, and then hand you over to the police."

His finger was still extended. "Now that's fighting talk, doll. You know what I'm gonna do? I'm gonna take that thing and stuff it right up your ass. You'll like that, eh?"

He came round the sofa, and Jo inhaled. She hadn't expected to be challenged. But then she hadn't expected anything like this to happen at all. Not in her own apartment, guarded by Washington . . . but she had told Washington to send Alloan up without checking further – Washington had all but told her, without actually being rude to a possible friend of hers, that he didn't like the look of the fellow. "I mean it," she warned. "I . . ."

Alloan moved far more quickly than she had anticipated. She swung the statue, but he easily evaded it, and then caught her arm with a strength that surprised her, twisting it so that she yelped with pain and dropped the ornament to the floor with a thud. Then his other arm went round her, clutching her against him, and his fingers were tugging at her housecoat, tearing it open to fumble inside, digging into the flesh of her breasts and buttocks. She gasped and twisted and used her elbows and kicked at him, and managed to get away, although leaving the gown in his hands as she stumbled forward and fell across the back of the sofa.

Before she could recover he had seized her shoulder to hold her there, head down, legs flaying. While he also picked up the statuette. "Now," he said. "Just let's part these pretty little cheeks . . ."

"No!" she screamed, hating herself for being so terrified. "No, please . . ."

The front door opened and Florence and the children stared at the scene in front of them.

"Florence?" Jo shrieked. "Call Washington. Call the police. Call . . ." She realised the hand had left her shoulder as Alloan straightened, and did so herself, turning and kicking as hard as she could for his crotch. Momentarily distracted by the intruders, Alloan did not defend himself and gasped with pain.

"Nice work, Mom," Owen Michael shouted, running into the room, seizing a large Chinese vase, and smashing it over the man's head.

Alloan was still bent double, clutching his genitals . . . and he had dropped the statue. Jo grabbed it again in both hands, swung and hit him on the head with all her strength.

"May I ask just what the shitting hell has been going on?" Michael Donnelly stood in the centre of his lounge and looked around him.

"Oh it was terrible, Mr Donnelly," Florence said.

"A man was here," Tamsin shouted.

"Assaulting Mommy," Owen Michael declared.

"Mommy was all bare," Tamsin informed him.

"But Mommy bopped him one with the statue," Owen Michael assured him, proudly.

"And Owen Michael hit him with the big vase," Tamsin added.

"Blood everywhere," Florence managed to get a word in.

"You were all bare?" Michael echoed, looking at Jo who was now fully dressed.

"Washington came, and the police, and took the man away," Tamsin said.

"The sergeant said Mommy had been awful brave," Owen Michael went on.

"And he said Owen Michael had been brave too," Tamsin added loyally.

Nana barked and attempted to frisk; even if she had missed the actual combat, she hadn't had such an exciting afternoon in years.

Michael continued to glare at Jo. "I think you kids had better go do your homework," he said. "Your mother and I would like to have a little chat."

"Yes," Jo agreed, understanding that her ordeal was not yet over. "Run along, children. Thank you so much, Florence. I think you saved my life, literally."

Michael waited until they had all left the room, taking Nana with them. Then he said, "Perhaps you'd like to explain." His voice was deceptively quiet.

"Well . . . there's not a lot to explain, Michael." She sat down. "This druggie broke in here and tried to assault me . . ."

"In the altogether?"

"He pulled off my housecoat," Jo said, refusing to lose her temper.

"Is that a fact. Druggie? Broke in here? How the hell did he do that? This is supposed to be a burglar-proof building. What the hell do we pay round-the-clock porters for?"

"Well, I suppose the fault was mine. Washington called to say there was this man to see me, who said he was an old friend, and without thinking I said to send him up. I was working, and just never thought, I guess."

Michael went to the bar and poured himself a drink. "You expect me to believe that? Jesus Christ, entertaining hashed up dropouts in my apartment in the middle of the afternoon . . ."

"I ought to kill you for saying that," Jo said.

He half turned, and flushed. "You going to pretend you didn't know the guy? How did he know to come to this apartment and, no other?"

"Sure I knew him," Jo snapped. "He was one of the people I interviewed for my hurricane article. Nothing more than that."

"How'd he know your name?"

"I told him my name," she shouted.

"A streetside layabout?"

"An interviewee. I always tell them my name, and who I work for."

"Who you work for." His momentary embarrassment had disappeared now he had discovered another handle to twist. "That goddamned stupid job. Do you realise it could've got you raped? The kids hurt. And Jesus . . ." He looked at the empty pedestal. "Do you have any idea how much that shitting vase cost? I demand you give it up. Now."

She stared at him. But she had been frightened; she could almost be tempted. If he would co-operate. "And if I do, will you come to Eleuthera next month?"

"You have got to be joking." He pointed. "You have nothing with which to hit me, sweetheart. You're the one out of line on this one. And I'm the poor bastard whose wife's name is going to be splashed all over the newspapers. I suppose you have to give evidence at the trial?"

"Of course I do. Don't worry, they tell me it won't be until after the yacht racing season."

"Bitch," he commented. "But you are giving up that job. Now."

"Go to hell," Jo told him, and went into the bedroom. She had had just about all she could stand.

THURSDAY 22 JUNE

East 57th Street

The concept of what had happened had set Michael going, in an almost obscene way, Jo thought. That the idea his wife had been wrestling naked with a strange man should start the vibes was horrible . . . but that night he wanted to return to her – she had slept in the spare room since their quarrel – and when she refused to let him they had another flaming row.

Yet what had happened had set her going too. It had been the unacceptable face of sex, but so were her relations with her husband. She wanted to lie naked in a man's arms, feel them about her and him against her – but the arms had to be loving rather than angry or hating or claiming a right.

And in any event, having read the morning paper, she knew she had to contact Richard. But in fact he contacted her, at the office, just after she had finished enduring the comments and sympathies of Ed and the staff, and the apologies of Jeannie Ryan for having divulged her address to a total stranger.

"Jo?" Richard's voice was fraught. "I've just seen the paper. My God . . ."

"Nothing happened," she assured him. "The guy was just hashed up."

"But . . . the papers say he broke in and assaulted you. That he's being charged with . . ."

"Attempted rape. He didn't get very far."

"It says you knocked him out."

"With a little help from my friends."

"Oh, Jo . . ."

"I'll tell you all about it when we meet."

"When?"

"I could make Thursday."

There was a moment's pause, and she could hear him riffling the pages of his diary. "You got it. Ah . . . I could arrange some time off."

"Yes," she said. "I would like that."

So here she was, Jo thought; Josephine Donnelly, would-be adulteress. It was the oddest feeling of her life, to be sitting across this now so familiar table, gazing into those now so familiar eyes, knowing that they were both doing nothing more than going through the formalities. But she had been doing this all week, existing on a cloud much higher than seven, hardly aware of what she was doing as she had been waiting for this moment. Fortunately, Ed had put her preoccupation down to her 'ordeal', as he called it. So did most other people. Neal and Meg had called to say goodbye, as they were off to Eleuthera. They had looked forward to seeing her there in a couple of weeks. "A good lie in the sun will put that horrible experience behind you," Meg had trilled, every word redolent with outrage. Eleuthera? Eleuthera was a million miles away right this minute.

There were no banalities, about 'how're you doing?' or 'I wondered if you were going to call'. They were two people who were thinking with a single mind.

He paid the check and they walked along the sidewalk together. Their hands brushed, and once or twice they exchanged a quick squeeze of the fingers. Nobody appeared to notice, although they both had the feeling that anyone could look at them and tell they were on their way to bed.

In the elevator, he said, "I'm afraid I've started stripping the wallpaper."

"Good for you. What colour have you chosen?"

"It's an off-white, really."

"Sensible."

She waited while he unlocked the door, trying to control the pounding of her heart. She had not felt like this since the first night of her honeymoon. But then, she hadn't felt like this then, either.

"Voilà! It really is a mess."

She gazed at the half bare walls, the piles of loose paper, the layer of dust . . .

He closed the door, slipped the chain into place. "I'll get it straight, eventually. And the bedroom's clean as a whistle."

She turned, and was in his arms, pressing herself against him as they kissed. "My darling girl," he said. "I'm going to say something stupid."

"Then don't say it. Don't say anything at all." She released him, opened the bedroom door, and went in, terribly conscious that she was leading here where she should perhaps have waited to be led. But it was her nature, and she couldn't risk any weakening of her resolve.

The door closed again, and he was in the room with her. Facing away from him, and carefully avoiding looking in the mirror, she reached behind her and unzipped her dress. She wore no slip in the summer, but for that reason always a bra. She shrugged her shoulders and the dress slid down to her thighs. She stepped out of it, reached behind her again, and touched his hands. "May I?" he asked.

"Yes," she told him, and waited, as the clip was released, and he carried the brassiere forward with his hands as they moved round, under her armpits, to hold and caress her breasts. She gave a little shiver, but it was pure ecstasy at the gentle loving of his touch – the last two pairs of hands to touch her there had been vicious.

She let him hold her for several seconds, then reached down to slide her pants past her hips. He let her go, and she stepped out of them, drew a long breath, and turned to face him. If the family habitually skinny-dipped when in Eleuthera, it was a very long time since any man other than her husband had looked at her naked – in a bedroom. Suddenly she was afraid he would be disappointed in this slightly overweight wife and mother. But his eyes told her she had nothing to worry about.

He was undressing himself, and he was perfection, the hard muscles gleaned from years on the grid only slightly softened by age, the glowing desire at once beautiful and reassuring. Then it was natural to be taken in his arms and held close, to feel his fingers sliding over her buttocks, to reach down herself to hold and caress, and then to lie beneath him, feeling him from her mouth to her toes. She had no thought of orgasm, just an immense contentment as she felt him questing.

Second later he was filling her, and her senses were soaring. She loved, and was loved. And she was in love, she realised . . . for the second time in her life.

THURSDAY 29 JUNE

The Cape Verde Islands

"There." Eisener had assumed his favourite position, on the flightdeck between the two pilots, and now he pointed.

Mark followed the direction of his finger and gave a low whistle. The big bird was flying through empty skies, as usual, and over a calm ocean, but she was a very long way away from home; Mark had already called Pedra Luma in the Cape Verdes, the group of islands that lie six hundred miles off the westernmost bulge of Africa and which were now less than a hundred miles east of the aircraft, and asked for permission to land for the night and refuel, before returning to Key West.

The reason for the extended flight had been an unusual phenomenon which had manifested itself over the past week; the pressure over the Cape Verde Islands had dropped much lower than usual for the time of year, and the result had been a much greater accumulation of cloud than usual. This had first shown up on satellite, and Eisener had determined to take a closer look. Now they gazed at an apparently unbroken carpet of white, lying right over the horizon even at 20,000 feet.

"That thing must stretch clear back to Africa," remarked Bob Landry, the co-pilot.

"Yeah," Eisener said. "Where are we, Mark?"

"Eighty miles due west of Praia, capital of the Cape Verdes. They're expecting us, but all the islands are under that lot."

"It's big," Eisener agreed. "What do you make of it?"

Mark didn't know what to reply. He had never seen anything like it in his life. He had called New York just before leaving Key West, to discuss the satellite picture with Richard . . . but Richard had been in no mood to talk about hurricanes. Even Richard. Because the clown had gone and fallen in love, with that married chick he'd been trying to seduce in his apartment when he'd been interrupted. Fooling around with married women caused nothing but trouble, in Mark's opinion.

While here could be what they had all been waiting for, all of their lives.

"There's no trace of any circulation," Landry remarked.

"No," Eisener said. "But by golly, if that mass should start to circulate . . ."

"Yeah," Mark muttered. "Jesus Christ, if . . ."

"Let's take a closer look," Eisener decided.

JULY

The Second Week

TUESDAY 11 JULY

National American Broadcasting Service Offices, Fifth Avenue

"That is it," J. Calthrop White declared. "Kill it, Kiley."

Kiley twisted his fingers together. "It's getting quite good audience support, JC . . ."

"You mean half a dozen telephone calls."

"Well, people don't usually telephone after the weather report . . ."

"Yes, they do. And the people who are telephoning are the same who were watching the weather programme anyway. That programme has had not the slightest effect on our ratings."

"That's true, JC, but there could be something any day. According to Connors . . ."

"That asshole? Bringing him up here is the biggest mistake you ever made, Kiley. And at seventy-five grand a year . . . Jesus Christ! He's made us the laughing stock of the networks with his warnings that this could be the year of the big storm, or at least of exceptional activity. All because it's hot? For Chrissake, it's too damned hot for hurricanes, that's what it is. How many have we had so far?"

"Well," Kiley said, "the last was named Eric . . ."

"So that makes five. Just five, in six weeks since the start of the season. And every one has gone flatter than one of my wife's pancakes in less than a week."

"Yeah. Connors says he can't understand it."

"He couldn't understand a tornado in his back yard."

"Well . . . there's this big system out in the Cape Verde Islands . . ."

"The Cape Verdes? Holy shit! That's four thousand goddamned miles away. And it's been there for damn near a month, just sitting. That isn't going anywhere, Kiley. It's pure convection. We want programmes which are going to boost our ratings. That's damned important right now. Having the capital isn't enough to convince those goddamned Limeys we can run a network. They want proven results. And bids for that franchise need to be in the first of next month."

Kiley nodded. "How's the financing going, JC?"

"Goddamned Irish shit," JC said. "Still saying it can't be done at such short notice . . . and in the summer. What the hell has the time of year to do with it? You know something, Kiley, it's because that asshole of a son of his wants to spend the whole goddamned summer racing. And now Mike tells me he's packing it in as well and going to the Bahamas for at least a fortnight. Says he does it every year and can't change his plans now. Nothing to worry about, he says; my partner, Cal Palmer, is handling everything. For Chrissake, Cal Palmer. That bid has to be in August One." White brooded for several seconds, then raised his head. "Now you listen to me, Kiley . . ." He wagged his gold pencil. "You kill those goddamned chats. And I want you to get this straight: Connors' contract will not be renewed next spring. You got that?"

"I've got it, JC," Kiley said, unhappily.

WEDNESDAY 12 JULY

Bognor, Connecticut

"Saturday," Babs said happily. "Oh, Saturday. It's just incredible that another whole year should have rolled by. But you know what, Jo, honey, every fifteenth of July I feel kind of reborn. How I love that place."

Jo watched the children playing in the pool. School had broken up a week before, to her great relief. Owen Michael's stomach ache had developed into an almost nightly feature during the exams, and she had worried herself sick – when she had been in the mood to be worried. But, as Dr Glenville had prophesied, with the ending of the pressure it had just disappeared.

"When Big Mike retires . . . heck, it's only in a couple of years," Babs reflected. "I reckon we're going to move down there, permanently."

Jo turned her head in surprise. "Not sell Pinewoods?"

"Well, I don't think we will. I mean, Michael will take over as head of the firm. So why shouldn't you take this place? You don't want to spend the rest of your life in a New York apartment."

"Um," Jo said. She had realised that Babs, and no doubt Big Mike as well, had interpreted her almost euphoric happiness of the past month as meaning she and Michael had at last patched up their differences; fortunately Michael, absorbed with getting *Esmeralda* ready for the big race, which started this weekend as well, had not noticed any difference in her demeanour at all. He had hardly been home long enough to do so, anyway.

She still had no idea what to do about it. She had now been to Richard's apartment five times, had met him for lunch on nine occasions, had called him at least three times a week or been called by him. Most of the calls had been made from the privacy of her study at home, but sufficient had been from the office to cause a certain amount of gossip. She was dipping her hand into the fire without caring if it was burnt.

Simply because she was in love. But even through the euphoria she understood that she could not live the rest of her life as a lie – any more than she could give up the children. Because that was what would happen if Michael found out. So maybe nowadays there was no guilty party, in the eyes of the law; there was still the discretion of the judge as to who was the more fitted to bring up the children – a husband who, if his true love was a boat, could yet provide them with the loving family background of grandparents and aunts and uncles, or an adulterous mother who would have to bring them up in a tiny Manhattan apartment . . . all she would be able to afford on her salary from *Profiles*.

It was a sodding world, she thought. She had always dreamed of one day inheriting Pinewoods. The thought that it could happen in a couple of years . . . but did she want it, now?

"All packed?" Babs asked, determined to keep the conversation going.

"Not really. I'll pack Friday."

"You sure leave things late."

"Well, there's not all that much to pack, for just the three of us," Jo pointed out. "Shorts, shirts, that's it. Anyway, I have Michael's dinner party tomorrow night."

"Oh, yes, I'd forgotten that. Will it be the usual crowd?"

"The crew and their wives, yes."

"What are you giving them?"

"Veal," Jo told her. "After onion soup. And baked Alaskas to follow."

"For twelve? Isn't that a bit ambitious."

"Florence is a whizz with baked Alaskas. Anyway, it won't be twelve. Only Sam and Larry are married."

"Well, you ought to have fun." Babs hesitated, choosing her words. She and Jo hadn't really had a chance to talk about much for the past three weeks or so, but with the girl so obviously happy . . . and yet there remained an undercurrent of tension. "I can't tell you how happy it makes Mike and me to see you . . . well, to feel things are okay between Michael and you again."

"Um," Jo said.

"Sure I know it's one hell of a disappointment, him not coming down to Eleuthera with us . . . I feel the same way about Marcia. But she has her Benny . . . what a sweet couple they are."

"And they're doing something together," Jo said before she could stop herself.

"Jo! You're not still angry about that?"

"No," Jo said, with complete honesty. "Michael is welcome to spend all the time he wants in his plastic bathtub."

"Just let him do this race," Babs recommended. "And win his class. That's all he's ever wanted to do, win his class in the Bermuda. Then we'll talk him into letting go a little."

WEDNESDAY 12 JULY

Park Avenue

"Hi," Richard's voice drifted over the phone. "Tomorrow?"

"I can't," Jo said.

"You're kidding."

"I have to prepare a dinner party for Michael's crew."

"Hell . . . and you're off on Saturday?"

"So I'm free . . . Friday evening. I'll get a sitter. Michael will have left for Newport by then." She waited; they had never had the opportunity to spend even part of a night together. She had become utterly wanton. But she wanted this to happen, and then . . . she knew that three weeks on Eleuthera would give her the time to think, to know what she had to do.

"Oh, Jo," he said. "That'll be just marvellous. I have to do the ten o'clock forecast."

"So I'll watch it, from your lounge."

"Sweetheart. Say, I have some news."

"Good news?"

"Well, some of it's good, some of it's bad, and some of it's just interesting. What'll you have first?"

"The bad."

"Ah. JC has killed the chat show."

"No! But why?"

"Seems his ratings people have told him it hasn't had any impact. No storms, you see."

"But there could be one."

"Sure. As a matter of fact, I'll give you the interesting piece next."

"Shoot."

"You know that huge cloud mass over the Cape Verdes I've been telling you about, and showing on the box."

"Yes." Suddenly she was breathless.

"It's started to shift."

"Where?"

"Slightly to the west. Only slightly. But Jo" – now his own voice was excited – "Mark says there are signs of circulation."

"Oh, boy," she said.

"Pleased about that?"

"Shouldn't I be? It'll vindicate everything you've been saying."

"Maybe. The circulation is still very weak. Highest sustained winds aren't much over 20 knots; that's just a good sailing breeze."

"But it'll grow from that."

"It could. And if it does, well . . . it has to come ashore somewhere. Not a nice thought for those people in the way."

"Where would you expect that to happen?"

"From where it is now, anywhere. But most probably the northern West Indies. Say Haiti or Puerto Rico."

"So I'll worry about them. But Richard, can't you plonk that information on White's desk and convince him the show should go on at least another week?"

"Nope. For two reasons. One, it would be begging, and begging JC is one thing not on my agenda. And secondly, there is every possibility this one will turn out to be a damp squib, just like the other five we've had so far. It's still pretty early in the year, and while I'm prepared to bet there's going to be a big storm this year, I'd rather go for the end of August, early September. Anyway, if it does prove something, it'll be mud in JC's eye. And it'll give your article a boost. When is it out?"

"Next week. I won't be here, but I've arranged for Ed to let you have a copy."

"Something to keep me warm while you're away. Three weeks. I am going to go stark, raving mad."

"Are you?" she murmured.

"Yeah. You never asked me what the good news was."

"No, I didn't," she said. "Tell me?"

"Only that I love you."

"I love you too," she said.

Thursday 13 July

Park Avenue

Florence was in despair – the cooker wouldn't work and she couldn't get anyone to come and repair it.

Owen Michael had a tummy ache all over again.

Ed phoned; would she like to do a series on André Previn?

Tamsin had a fight with the girl on the floor below.

And to cap it all, Nana was sick on the lounge carpet – the third time in two days.

Jo handled it all, but even the children noticed how she repeatedly grinned, for no apparent reason. Florence was most impressed by the calm way she coped with the disastrous afternoon, though she did wonder if her young employer realised that the dinner she and her husband were giving that night would be wrecked if someone didn't get the cooker working in time.

Jo got on the phone and threatened the maintenance people with publicity on their inefficiency – which brought a Mr Fix-It to tackle Florence's problem within twenty minutes. She sat Owen Michael in front of the TV and told him to relax – presumably he was getting worked up over his father's imminent departure for Newport and his own flight to Miami and thence Eleuthera . . . but if he was going to have to go through life with a bellyache every time he got excited he was going to have a hard time.

She sang as she scooped up the mess on the carpet and washed the stain, and gave Tamsin a brief lesson on basic judo – while Ed sat at his desk impressed, not to say overwhelmed, by Jo Donnelly's enthusiastic reception of her latest assignment, which she promised to research during her vacation and undertake the moment she returned. Maybe, he thought, she has something going for Previn.

Jo's mood lasted all evening. Wearing a stunning little cocktail number, she welcomed Sam and Sally Davenport – Sam was Michael's best friend as well as his second-in-command on the yacht – Larry and Beth Simmons, Jon Tremayne, Pete Albicete, and Mark Godwin. Mark was as shy as ever – he was by some distance the youngest and newest of the crew – but the others she had known for years. Actually, she liked them all, and could understand the good fellowship Michael enjoyed with them; she would have enjoyed it too had she been allowed to share. But Sally and Beth did not seem the least resentful of their husbands' preoccupation, and joined in the enthusiastic counting up of reasons why they should win their class this year.

Michael was at his beaming best. He was always a superb host, and he was obviously pleased that Jo was making such a magnificent effort to play the beautiful and loving wife. Certainly she was convinced, unless he had been doing some locker-room confiding, that none of the others had the slightest idea that they had not shared a bed for a month, or that their marriage might be on the edge of disintegration. But then, she supposed Michael was not aware of the latter either.

The party was a great success. Thanks to Florence, the meal was first-class and the baked Alaskas superb, and due possibly to the power of Jo's cocktails and the wine that followed, everyone became hilariously jolly. Anecdotes and laughter rocked the apartment – and the elevator as the guests departed – and when Jo and Michael returned to the lounge after saying their goodbyes, and he put his arm round her, kissed and thanked her for a marvellous evening, she was in far too happy a mood to push him away.

So that later she found it impossible to ban him from his marital rights, as she had done ever since their last quarrel. But she froze. Suddenly he was alien and unwanted. She switched her mind away, tried to blot out his touch, his weight, his presence in her, and instead distract her brain with thoughts of Richard. Richard's face above hers, his breath, his arms, his body pressing down, filling hers . . . as he would be doing tomorrow night. Momentarily her back arched ecstatically, and a moan of pleasure reached Michael as he climaxed.

He smiled with satisfaction as he left her, congratulating himself on standing his ground until she'd learned to control her stupid selfishness and become human again.

FRIDAY 14 JULY

Park Avenue

Jo didn't sleep. She hadn't climaxed, had deliberately switched off. She felt guilty, soiled, disloyal – to Richard. She was angry that force of habit had led her into allowing Michael to make love to her. She hated herself for it; she no longer belonged to him. Jo and Richard – Richard and Jo.

Then, as the sleepless night passed, reality took over, and a black cloud of gloom shadowed her mind. The future seemed absolutely insoluble. Of course a lot of women ran a perfectly happy marriage and kept an afternoon lover on the side, but she couldn't imagine how they did it. She couldn't make love to two men concurrently. Either she loved – or she didn't. And now she loved Richard – not Michael. But her whole life revolved around being Mrs Michael Donnelly junior, with everything that that implied, socially, domestically, and sexually. To refuse Michael might be to alert him to the fact that she no longer wanted or needed him, and then . . . when she thought of the children she felt sick. Therefore the sensible thing to do would be to put Richard out of her mind – never see him again.

With stinging eyes and a painful weight of dread in her stomach, Jo fought for sleep until, sticky with perspiration, she left the bed to turn up the air conditioning and hunt in the bathroom for the Panadol.

"I can't find my red sports shirt or my yacht club sweater," Michael complained, stuffing clothes into a duffel bag. "Where have you put them?"

"Haven't touched them," Jo called from the bathroom, where she was desperately trying to wake up.

"Well, will you look, please? I'm in a hurry. I want to be in Newport for lunch."

"For God's sake, the race doesn't start until Sunday."

"True. But there's a lot of preparing to be done. Or hadn't you thought of that?"

"Judging by the amount of time you've spent in Newport these last six weeks one would have thought *Esmeralda* could have been re-fitted and ready a dozen times." She scrubbed her face with her towel and lurched into the bedroom.

"Do you know," he remarked. "Just for a moment, last night, I thought you had finally come to your senses – but I can see it was just alcohol. Now for God's sake be reasonable and try to help."

Jo strode silently into the dressing-room, looked through the neat stack of shirts and sweaters, and carefully drew out the 'missing' items. "There, under your nose," she said quietly, and strode out again.

"You stupid bitch," he growled. "Are you going to keep up this farcical performance every time I go yachting, for the rest of our lives?"

"As long as you continue to break promises, hurt your children's feelings, and disappoint Owen Michael in particular by your selfishness – yes, I probably will." She was too hungover to care what she said at that moment.

"You don't give a damn about the kids, you're only thinking about yourself! Anyway, they couldn't care less what I do with my spare time; they're perfectly happy. But I'm damned if I am. You'd better start pulling yourself together or there is going to be one big parting of the ways. I'm not going to put up with much more."

"You're not?" Jo exploded. "You . . ."

"That's correct. Now come on, for Christ's sake. I've got to go. Let's part friends, okay?" He was standing in the bathroom door, waiting.

Jo sighed. She had all but said something irrevocable, and was still tempted. But that made no sense . . . at least until she had had the time to think. "Okay," she said. "Let's find the kids and we'll all say goodbye together."

Tamsin and Owen Michael appeared from the family room and watched as the gear was dumped by the door.

"You going to kiss your Daddy and wish him luck in the race?" Michael asked his daughter.

She ran into the room and hugged him. "I do hope *Esmeralda* wins, Daddy. But I will miss you. I wish the race was some other time so's you could come to Dolphin Point with us."

"Perhaps Granpa will be able to go down there at a different time next year," her father suggested.

No question of his not racing next year, Jo noted. She also noted that Owen Michael was looking rather pale, and was unusually quiet, hanging back in the doorway.

"You'll look after Mommy and Tamsin while I'm away, won't you?" Michael held out his hand to the boy.

Owen Michael managed a smile. "Sure, Dad." He shook hands. "I hope you have good winds for the race."

"I'll settle for Force Six there and back, nothing more than 30 knots. But however strong the wind is, your Daddy will cope," Michael told him.

"Are you going to come down to Eleuthera and join us when the race is over?" the boy asked.

Michael glanced at Jo and then away again. "No. I won't be able to do that. The fellows want to spend a week or so cruising around Bermuda before we come home. But you be sure to have lots of fun down there. Come back real brown, and bring me a tooth from the biggest shark you spear," he quipped.

"Wow! Don't know about that," Owen Michael responded.

Michael turned to Jo. "Look after yourselves." He waited.

"And you come home with that cup." She reached up and kissed his cheek. "Goodbye. Keep in touch with Sally, so that if we can't raise you on the radio we can get an update from her."

"That's my girl." Michael hugged her and the children, and headed for the elevator. He turned to wave one last time, and was gone.

Jo had a great deal to do herself. She decided to leave the packing until after lunch, but went out straightaway to take Nana to the kennels. Nana actually enjoyed her own yearly 'vacation', with people who had cared for her since she had been a pup, and other dogs in compounds all around her with whom she could engage in barking matches. But it was necessary to tell Mrs Hellman that she had an upset stomach, and discuss her general health, and have a cup of coffee, and it was past 1 pm before Jo regained the apartment, her heart slowly beginning to sing again as she realised that within six hours she would be in Richard's arms. She was greeted by Dale.

"Hi!" she said in surprise, presenting her cheek for a kiss. "What brings you here?"

"I dropped by to see if I could give you a lift to Kennedy tomorrow," he said. "And found Florence worried stiff."

"Florence? Worried about what?" Florence would be departing for her own summer vacation tomorrow, as soon as the family had left and she had locked the apartment up.

"It's Owen Michael. He's got stomach cramps so bad he's been yelling with pain."

"Oh, my God! Where is he?" She ran towards the family room.

"In bed."

She changed direction and rushed in to kneel beside the boy. "Darling, what's happened?"

Owen Michael was curled up on his side, hot, flushed and shivering. An arm reached out for his mother, and fresh tears streamed down his face. "Mom. It's so bad I can scarcely breathe," he sobbed.

Jo put a hand on his forehead and gasped. It was burning hot. "Okay sweetheart, we'll do something right away." She spoke quietly and calmly, but she was seething with angry fear. That idiot Glenville . . . she turned to Dale. "Will you carry your nephew down to the garage? We'll take him straight along to the clinic." And she intended to see Dr Knapp, no matter where he might be – she had no intention of wasting her time with that doddering old fool any more. She had no doubt at all that far from having a nervous tummy, Owen Michael was genuinely ill.

Florence quickly put a clean pair of pyjamas and a bathrobe into a bag, and Dale drove the Mercedes while Jo sat beside Owen Michael in the back, holding him across her lap. The traffic was still heavy, and she felt very like using some of Mr Muldoon's language as they crawled from one traffic light to the next, while Owen Michael whimpered with pain.

But at last Dale parked outside the Emergency Admittance at the Mercy Clinic and ran inside to call up a stretcher, which quickly appeared. Jo walked beside the boy as he was wheeled into an examination room. The black doctor who had answered his bleeper hurried in and with a polite nod turned Owen Michael on his back and gently pressed the bared abdomen.

The boy screamed, and Jo jumped in alarm. "I want to se Dr Knapp," she said.

"He's not here right now," the doctor said, and gave instructions. A nurse was sent hurrying away, and reappeared seconds later with another doctor, and the two men conferred in undertones as they examined the boy together, then the black doctor led Jo out of the door to where Dale was waiting.

"What is it?" Jo asked anxiously.

"We both think he's probably got a perforated appendix. He will need immediate surgery."

"Perforated?"

"Yes. The indications are that it may have abscessed and burst, spreading septicaemia throughout the abdomen. If that is so, he is very seriously ill, and should be operated on immediately."

Jo and Dale both saw the concern in the kind black face, and were frightened.

"Is he in danger?" Dale asked.

"His situation is critical," the doctor said carefully. "But if we get him on the table right now, we should be able to pull him through." He looked at Jo, awaiting the necessary permission. "It has to be immediately, Mrs Donnelly."

Jo took a long breath, and nodded.

FRIDAY 14 JULY

The Mercy Clinic, Avenue of the Americas

Big Mike Donnelly ran along the hospital corridor, gasping for breath. Babs followed more slowly, only because her legs were shorter. "Jo!" Mike gasped, catching sight of his daughter-in-law in the waiting room. "Where is he?"

"In theatre," Jo said miserably.

"Is he . . .?"

"They're operating now."

Babs arrived, panting. "Where's Tamsin?"

"I called Florence," Jo told her. "She's stayed at the apartment with her."

"Michael . . ." Big Mike began.

Jo's shoulders heaved. "The hospital are still trying to reach him. We contacted the yacht, but he wasn't there, gone off to lunch with some friends or something. I . . ." She turned as a white-uniformed nurse appeared in the doorway. "Mrs Donnelly? We have your husband on the line. You can take it in the office."

"Thank God for that," Big Mike said, and he and Babs crowded into the small room behind Jo.

"Michael?" she asked. "Michael, is that you? . . . Yes, I know the race starts at dawn tomorrow . . . yes, I know you have a lot to do, but Michael . . . oh, for God's sake will you listen to me? Owen Michael is ill . . . yes, very ill. He has acute appendicitis . . . yes, I'm talking from the hospital. Michael . . . yes, they think he's going to be all right . . ." She listened for a few moments, then exploded. "For God's sake, he's your son! He needs you . . . The hell with the goddamned race . . . I told you, they think he's going to be all right. They think. But he needs you here. Your son needs you, Michael. We need you, here . . ." Another long pause as a deep flush crept up from her neck to suffuse her angry face. "You are a shit!" she screamed into the phone. "Do you hear me? A lousy shit. Go play with your plastic toy."

She slammed the phone down, and gazed at the nurse, who gazed back, silently.

"Oh, Christ!" Big Mike muttered.

"He wouldn't come?" Babs asked, disbelievingly.

"He asked me twice if the doctors thought Owen Michael was going to be all right. Then said there would be no need for him to come." Jo's voice was toneless. "He couldn't let the guys down, he said. The guys . . ." She looked at her father-in-law.

Who sighed. "Yeah . . . well . . ."

Another of the phones on the desk buzzed. Jo spun round, but the nurse had already picked it up. "Yes," she said. "Oh, right away." She smiled at Jo. "Dr Matthey is waiting to see you, Mrs Donnelly."

"Oh," Jo said, suddenly as breathless as her in-laws. "Is he . . . I mean . . ."

"I think you'll find Dr Matthey has some good news for you, Mrs Donnelly," the sister said.

Big Mike and Babs waited for her to return. "I just don't know what's gotten into Michael," Babs said. "I mean, refusing to come back . . ."

"Well," Big Mike argued. "He was right. I mean, if Owen Michael really is out of danger, and with the race starting tomorrow . . . I mean, do you have any idea how much time and money those guys spend on that boat? Christ, they devote their entire spare time to it . . ."

"Then Jo is right, and none of them should be married," Babs said.

"Now really, sweetheart, because a guy has an all-consuming hobby doesn't mean . . ."

"You were a sailing nut when we got together," Babs reminded him. "And you gave most of it up, because I got seasick."

"Yeah. Well, maybe I wasn't quite as keen as Michael."

"You were just as keen," Babs pointed out. "What you mean is, maybe you weren't as big a shit as Michael."

"He's your son too, dammit."

She nodded. "Maybe the truth is that I wouldn't let you be like that. Here she is."

Jo almost looked happy, but for the lines of exhaustion and despair that streaked away from her eyes. "He's going to be okay."

"Did they . . .?"

She nodded. "The appendix was perforated, as they thought. His whole stomach was in a terrible mess, but Dr Matthey says they cleaned him up just in time. Now, it's only a matter of recuperation."

"Have you seen him?"

"Through the screen. He's still out, of course. But he looked so peaceful . . . and his temperature and pulse are under control, Dr Matthey says. He also says I can see him again tomorrow morning. God, I feel like a drink."

"And you shall have one," Big Mike promised. And grinned. "I feel like one myself."

They found a bar just round the corner from the hospital. "Jees, what a foul-up," Big Mike muttered, and gazed at his wife.

She knew exactly what he was thinking; it was now nearly five in the afternoon and they were due to leave for Eleuthera in not much over twelve hours time. "We'll cancel our holiday, of course," she said.

"Of course you won't," Jo protested. "You can't. What about Belle and Lawson? And Dale?"

"Yes, but we can't leave you . . ."

"I'll be all right. The doc says that if all goes well, Owen Michael may be able to leave the hospital by next Friday, and then, if he just rests up for a few days, he should be as right as rain. Look, you're planning on spending at least three weeks down there, aren't you?"

"Well, that was the idea," Big Mike said. "What with the letters and telegrams I've been getting from Neal Robson complaining that this doesn't work and that doesn't work and how can he get hold of a plumber and an electrician . . . Christ, doesn't he realise he's living on a Bahamian out island? That's the whole point of the thing. If he wants plumbers and electricians on call he should've stayed in Connecticut."

"What Mike is trying to say is that we have to try to sort things out for the Robsons," Babs explained. "From what I hear Meg has been in a permanent state of hysterics since the first night, when she found a ground spider on her bed. If only they'd had the sense to wait for us . . . I guess you're right, and we should go . . . but you can't cope on your own with the hospital to visit every day and Florence due for her vacation as well. Listen, we'll take Tamsin, and then you and Owen Michael can follow on down just as soon as he's well enough to travel. You'll have a week, anyway. How about that?"

"I think that would be splendid," Jo agreed; she didn't even want Tamsin around right this minute. She just wanted to sit and think . . . about the end of her marriage.

"Heck, it'll work out just fine," Big Mike said. "You stay up here another ten days or so, and Michael will be back from Bermuda. You can all come down together. Why didn't we think of that before?"

"We did," Jo told him, and remembered that she had another phone call to make.

JULY

The Third Week

Saturday 15 July

Park Avenue

The buzzing phone finally reached down into Jo's deep subconscious, startling her into a violent leap out of bed, to stand naked and disoriented, momentarily unable to identify the disturbance, not knowing what time of what day . . . Richard had been horrified to hear about Owen Michael, and readily accepted that she would not be able to make it that evening. She had sent Florence home, packed a bag for Tamsin, and then the little girl had been driven out to Bognor by Big Mike and Babs; she would spend the night with them before leaving. Alone, emotionally and physically exhausted, Jo had taken two Panadol and collapsed into bed, falling asleep immediately.

And now . . . she registerd the phone summons at the same time as remembering Owen Michael's operation. Panic stricken, she grabbed the bedside handset . . . and gasped with relief at the sound of Belle's voice. "Where are you? . . . Still in Nassau? . . . Oh, you're going up today. Yes, the folks should be down some time this afternoon. They have Tamsin with them. How did . . . oh, of course, yes, Babs. Yes. It was bad . . . a burst appendix . . . No, he hadn't come round when I left, but the doctors seemed to think he was going to be okay . . . I'm going in this morning, and I'll call you when I get back . . . oh, hell, of course I can't. Listen, I'll call the post office in Whaletown; they have a phone, and they can get a message to you via Joss . . . No idea. He complained of stomach pains and I took him along to the clinic, but Knapp wasn't there . . . some idiot named Glenville. I think he's the senior partner . . . I agree, nothing but preconceived ideas, and too damned lazy to make a proper examination . . . You're damn right, I am going to have plenty to say to them in the next few days . . . no, that depends on how long they need to keep an eye on him before letting him out of hospital . . . Oh, we'll get there, don't worry about that . . . and give mine to Lawson, too. Thanks for calling. 'Bye.''

The bedside clock said 10.30; she had slept for more than twelve hours – and she had to be at the hospital in half an hour. A quick shower and a glass of juice revived her, and in cotton dress and toe thongs she dashed out to the elevator.

Owen Michael was awake. He managed a feeble smile which made Jo want to cry; he looked so ill, lying propped against his pillows, black circles round his eyes, while the intravenous dripped monotonously. She kissed and stroked his forehead, and whispered softly to him.

"Why did Dr Glenville say it was exam nerves, Mom?" he asked in a low voice.

"Because he's lazy and incompetent. Some boys and girls do get exam nerves, so he thinks that's the cause of all tummy aches."

"Where's Tamsin?"

"She's gone down to Dolphin Point with Granpa and Granma. Don't worry, we'll be joining them in a few days."

"When will Dad get here?" he asked, hopefully.

Jo hesitated; this was the question she had been dreading. The temptation to lash out at Michael as she had done at Dr Glenville was enormous. But it would be very wrong of her to upset Owen Michael at this moment. "I don't think he will be able to make it, darling," she said. "The . . . the start of the race was brought forward, and he was already at sea when I tried to reach him. I'm still trying to raise him by radio, but I don't know if I'll make it . . . and anyway, now that you're on the mend, you wouldn't really want him to abandon the race, would you?" She hated Michael even more for forcing her to lie to their son. But the boy knew how ill he had been and would have been heartbroken to learn that his father had still not rated him important enough to 'let the guys down'.

"I guess not," Owen Michael agreed, not entirely convinced. "Will we really be able to get to Dolphin Point after all, Mom?"

"Of course we will. Just as soon as the doctors say so."

"I'm glad you stayed behind with me, Mom." Owen Michael smiled, and dozed off.

MONDAY 17 JULY

Park Avenue

Two days later Dr Matthey pronounced that Owen Michael was definitely on the mend, and quicker than he had anticipated. "I think you can take him home Friday, Mrs Donnelly," he said.

"That would be great. How about travelling after that?"

"Where do you want to go?"

"I want to fly to Miami, and then fly across to Eleuthera."

"You have a reason for doing this?"

"Sure. The rest of my family is down there vacationing."

"Is that a fact. Well . . . I would say a couple of weeks lying in the Bahamian sun, or rather, the Bahamian shade, Mrs Donnelly, is just about the best way of recuperating I could think of. Sure, go ahead and take him down. But . . ." he held up his finger. "Lying in the shade is the operative word, right? No diving or snorkelling. And no fishing either. Nothing which can put any kind of strain on that belly of his."

Jo nodded. "He'll lie in the shade, Dr Matthey, believe me. And thank you."

She was so relieved that once she was back in the apartment she gave in to the long suppressed need to have a good cry. Then she wanted to do things. For two days she had seen no one, spent all her time at the hospital. Now she telephoned her travel agent and got seats on the following Monday's plane to Miami and thence on to Eleuthera by the local airline. Next she called the post office in Whaletown, a long and tedious business as she had to go through international and then wait hours while, as she knew from past experience, the one operator in the little Eleutheran village either chatted up her boyfriend or painted her toenails.

"Dolphin Point," she shouted. "Mr and Mrs Donnelly. You know Mr and Mrs Donnelly."

"Ah guess ah do," the girl said. "They was in here yesserday, lookin' for messages."

"Well, I have a message for them," Jo said.

"But they ain' heah today," the girl pointed out, patiently. "They don' come in every day."

"I know that," Jo said, with equal patience. "But Josh Albain lives just round the corner from the post office. Will you give him the message, and he can take it out to the house."

"Well, ah will, if ah sees him."

"You'll see him," Jo said with determined optimism. "Will you ask him to tell Mr Donnelly that all is well, and that we will be down next Monday."

"Next Monday," the girl said. "Who's callin'?"

"Just say Jo."

"Jo? You a boy?"

"No," Jo said. "I'm a woman."

"I di'n' think you sounded like a boy," the girl agreed.

"I'm Josephine Donnelly. You must remember me. For God's sake I've been in your office often enough."

"Well, hi, Mis' Donnelly. Why you di'n say so right off? Sure I goin' give Josh the message. Sure."

"Thank you," Jo said, and hung up. She felt exhausted.

But she called Marcia. Marcia had been in touch throughout the weekend, asking if there was anything she could do to help; Jo hadn't taken her up because she just wanted to be alone. But she had to tell her the good news.

"Oh, sweetie, that is just marvellous," Marcia trilled. "I am so happy. Can I go visit the boy?"

"He'd love it."

"I'll do that. And listen, you going to have a meal with Benny and me?"

"That's very nice of you."

"How about tonight? We can have it here. We're winning, slowly. We actually have one room finished."

"Ah . . . May I give it a day or two more, Marcia? I'm very tired."

"Sure, sweetie, sure. You just give me a call when you're in the mood."

Jo replaced the phone, and stood by the lounge window looking down at the Manhattan traffic. The brief spurt of almost manic happiness and energy had departed as suddenly as it had come. Now she felt somehow disoriented from all the busy life down there; her whole body felt limp. She knew she was still exhausted by fear and emotional trauma and by her anger and bitter resentment at Michael's attitude. He had telephoned on Saturday to ask how the surgery had gone, and had pointed out that, as all was well, she had been behaving hysterically. Then he had presumably gone to sea with his boat; according to the newspapers the race had started on time on Sunday. He was having the time of his life while his only son was fighting the biggest battle of his life, so far.

What a swine! How could she have married him? More important, how could she stay married to him? She slumped into the soft white cushions of the settee and lay back – numbed. Jumbled thoughts flashed to mind, then vanished. She could hear herself assuring Babs and Big Mike that she wouldn't consider divorce – but it didn't seem possible not to.

To divorce, apart from the children, would mean Richard. What about Richard? They were lovers, but he had never mentioned marriage. For her to mention the word divorce might send him running a mile. So that would prove him to be a cad. She didn't want to have to take the risk of finding that out. In her present situation he was the only rock to which she could cling. If he wasn't already off her – she had promised to call him as soon as she felt up to it . . . and that had been Friday night. But she still didn't feel up to it.

She had hardly eaten for three days. Now she opened a can of soup and had an apple, which made her feel slightly better. Then it was time to return to the hospital where Owen Michael was sitting up watching TV, and, apart from his pallor, looking almost normal again. She almost wanted to cry again with relief.

That evening she curled on the beanbag, half watching whatever appeared on the screen, dozing off periodically, relieved by Owen Michael's progress but increasingly disturbed by thoughts of the horren-

dous complications involved in the breakdown of her marriage. It would
be bad enough going through a divorce if one didn't have children, but
what the split would do to Owen Michael and Tamsin she dreaded to
think. And for all that Babs and Big Mike had seemed very upset by
Michael going on with the race regardless of Owen Michael's illness, she
still doubted if they'd ever forgive her if she broke her word.

The phone buzzed insistently, above the noise of a big shoot-out on
TV.

It was Richard. "Mrs Donnelly?" he asked, formally.

"Oh, hi." Immediately her spirits lifted.

"Are you alone?"

"Yes."

"Sweetheart! How have you been? I've been half out of my mind with
worry. I know I'm chancing my arm, but I just had to call. How's the
boy?"

She told him about Owen Michael's recovery, and how she really
had not felt up to doing anything over the weekend but visiting him.
Deliberately she never mentioned a word about Michael, but when she
had finished he said, "Hold on a minute. Where does your husband figure
in all this? Don't tell me he's gone out and left you alone?"

"Gone out!" she exclaimed. "Oh, he's gone out, all right. Right out
into the Atlantic. I told you he was leaving on Friday."

Richard paused, before slowly responding. "Out into the Atlantic? You
mean on his yacht? But couldn't you get a message to him through one
of the port radio stations?"

"I got a message to him before he ever left Newport."

"And he went anyhow?"

The incredulous note in his voice made tears sting her eyes. "Of
course," she said huskily. "He's racing, you see. Nothing else matters."

"Not even his son's life? Didn't he know how serious the situation
was?" he persisted.

"I told him. Before he left Newport."

Richard heard the sob in her voice. "Would you like me to come over?"

To her apartment. Washington was off duty, but the other porter,
Edwardes, would be there, and would record the visit, as he was required
to do. But what did it matter?

"Yes. Yes, please."

At another time, in a different mood, she would have been aware that
a decision had been taken, that from here on this was her man and she
would belong to him, body and soul. Now she only knew she urgently
needed all the love, sympathy and understanding he had to offer. She
needed his strength and gentleness, and his love.

The bedroom mirror reflected a drab, defeated creature – a refugee
from a terrible disaster. And wasn't she just that? Hadn't the life she had

been building, striving to achieve, for the past twelve years – ever since agreeing to marry Michael – just been swept out from under her feet? It was all gone – finished. And now?

Jo stripped off her T-shirt and headed for the bathroom. A cold wash would help her to pull herself together. Then she could start picking up the pieces . . . and begin all over again. Water dripped from her chin over the vanity basin as she reached for a towel – and the lobby phone buzzed. She just had time to slip into a clean shirt and brush her hair before opening the door.

It was almost like welcoming a true husband home from the office. She nestled gratefully into Richard's arms and allowed a glorious peace and comfort to envelop her. It was like arriving at safety after a tortuous and dangerous journey – finding the place where one belonged. In the lounge Richard sat on the settee and asked what she would drink. He explored the cocktail bar, filled two glasses, and returned to sit beside her, watched her sip her drink, saw the worry and pain which had lined her face in the few days since he had last seen her – and it hurt him. He longed to take her away from this magnificent apartment, full of hellish protection, blot out all her unhappy past – and his own. Then a thought occurred to him. "What have you eaten today?"

"I had some soup, and an apple," she said guiltily, waiting for his reproach.

It didn't come. Instead he got up and said, "Put on a lively tape while I fix some food," and she heard him opening and shutting doors as he searched through the kitchen.

From the icebox and fridge he produced melon and prawn cocktail, and a huge Spanish omelette filled with chopped ham, sweet peppers, onions and herbs, together with a salad.

An open bottle of Californian white filled two glasses each, enough to lift Jo's spirits, when Richard said, "Let's drink to Owen Michael, who has, I think, unwittingly provided the key to some big decisions. Thank God he's mending quickly. And now, a toast to us, and our future – together!"

Jo gulped and choked. "Together? Aren't you jumping the gun a bit?"

"Well, I hope not. It's what we both want, isn't it?"

She gazed at him, and nodded, the background scherzo gradually absorbing the pace of her response.

"Great. Then that's settled. It's Jo and Richard – Richard and Jo from here on in. That's the important decision. The how, where and when are comparatively minor details, to be sorted out later, when your husband comes back from his race."

"Yes, Richard," she agreed meekly, but a sparkle had crept back into her eyes, and her breathing had quickened as the joy and confidence of this man swept away the last lingering clouds of uncertainty. Because he would solve all the problems; she had to believe that.

"That was delicious. You're a marvellous cook." Jo sat back, smiling across the empty plates.

"Only with simple things. Nothing exotic. Now . . ." He stood and collected the dishes. "Yogurt, followed by coffee."

"Great. Here, let me . . ."

"Sit down, woman. Your turn will come, but not today." But she did get up later to pour brandies to sip with their coffees.

They changed tapes while clearing the kitchen together, stood watching rows of head and tail lights lining the streets below, in opposite directions, and when the current tape finished Jo looked at her watch and said, "Time for bed," gazing at him for a moment before adding, "Coming?"

She instinctively led him to the spare bedroom, neither of them would be happy in Michael's bed. But this was the night for which she had been waiting, and longing, for more than a month.

"Do you know," Richard said, "how many times I have dreamed of just this moment?"

"*This* moment?" Jo asked, resting her head on his shoulder. They had climaxed virtually together, for the first time, and she was aware only of contentment.

"Yes. I'll tell you a secret: there have been dozens of women I have thought about, that I'd like to have in bed with me. But only one or two I've really wanted to spend the night with."

"One or two," she remarked, jokingly.

"Only one, now." He looked down at her. "Will you marry me?"

"Oh, God, if I can, Richard. If I can. If . . ."

"I know." He held her close, and then suddenly the tenderness was replaced by tension.

"What's the matter?" She raised her head.

"It's just past midnight. There's a system I should get an update on."

Oh, God, she thought; not a workaholic. "I thought you were off for the evening."

"I am. But I told Julian, that's my assistant, that I'd keep in touch before going to bed. I mean, to sleep," he grinned. "It's that big thing just west of the Cape Verdes. You remember."

"I remember," she said. "What's it doing now?"

"Moving west. Slowly. But it was showing signs of tightening. I know Mark was worried about it when last he called. He was out there today again, and promised to let me have an update."

"So you want to go off and look at a map."

"I don't particularly want to, but Julian is expecting me, and won't stop tracking until I get there. I could come back," he suggested tentatively.

"I'm expecting you'll do that," she said. "But just to make sure you do, I'll come with you and take a look at this map too."

TUESDAY 18 JULY

National American Broadcasting Service Offices, Fifth Avenue

The studio was quiet. The late-night news programmes were finished, and now there was only a midnight chat show going out, to be followed by two old movies. Richard took Jo into the weather room, where Julian was sifting through various charts. "Well, hey, Richard," he remarked. "What kept you?"

"I was dining out," Richard told him. "You remember Josephine Donnelly, from *Profiles*?"

"Hi, Jo," Julian said. "Don't tell me, you want to look at that system." He laid an enlarged photograph on the desk. "I'll tell you, it *is* a system."

Richard studied the print, and Jo looked round his arm. She could make out the coast of Africa, and the offshore islands; they had been inked in. Stretching from immediately west of the Cape Verdes – which were now clear of cloud – a considerable distance out into the Atlantic was a white mass, very like the whipped cream on the photograph of hurricane Anita in Richard's office, with just the traces of a circulatory movement.

"Your friend Mark Hammond called," Julian said. "He just got back from having a closer look. Flew right into it, and couldn't find any clearly defined eye as yet, but he says it's tightening all the time."

"Course?" Richard asked.

"Oh, just north of west, and moving real slow. Not more than ten knots. Mark says it still hasn't got winds of more than forty knots round the centre. But as I said, he reckons it's going to improve on that."

"It's enormous," Jo whispered. She was realising that if Anita had seemed to cover the entire Gulf of Mexico, this system lay across a good half of the Atlantic Ocean.

"It's the biggest I have ever seen," Richard agreed. "Where's the jet stream?"

Julian pulled out the latest weather chart, and pointed. "Moving north all the time."

"Christ almighty!" Richard commented.

"Is that really so important?" Jo asked.

"Yes," he told her. "The jet stream is one of those rivers of air I was talking about. It's the only one we can really identify, as a matter of fact. It's very big, very high, and very fast; you really are talking about phenomenal speeds up there, two hundred miles an hour plus. Usually it has only a marginal effect on surface weather; obviously, when it's blowing from the Arctic towards the south you get cold upper altitude winds and a general drop in temperature, and vice versa. It's also very important to high altitude flying, either for or against – it can make quite a difference in time between here and London, for instance, depending on whether a pilot can use it or has to buck it. But it is also useful for dispersing hurricanes.

"You remember I told you, when hot air rises very fast and very high you have a hurricane. Now obviously, the higher that wind can get into the atmosphere, without dissipating, the stronger the circulation around the centre of the depression is going to be. The jet stream plays an important part in this. In fact, I am pretty sure it's been responsible for the fact that not one of those five storms we've had so far this year have developed. It's been unusually far south, you see, and coming out of the central Pacific, too. So those storms each started their upward spiral, and when they got above 10,000 feet, the jet stream blew them apart, and they collapsed. But if it's now moving north, this system could be left to develop as much as it wants. And it has the time." He looked at the map again, and then at the satellite photograph. "Ten knots, you say, Julian? Working on where the centre should be now, that means five days to Puerto Rico, on that course. Five days over some of the warmest water we've had for yonks."

"So you reckon this could be the big one," Jo said.

He shrugged. "After what's happened so far this year, your guess is as good as mine. But it is one hell of a big system. If that circulation does increase . . . we could have a problem."

"Your ultimate storm?"

He grinned. "Any system could become my ultimate storm, if all the conditions were right."

"And you've just said they could be right, now."

"Well . . . yes. But they've seemed to be right before, and we haven't had that big one. The odds are against it happening this time."

"If it does become a storm," she asked, "what might it be called?"

"All the names are selected before the hurricane season even begins." Julian looked at the list pinned up over his desk. "As it will be number six for this year, it'll be a she, and her name will be Faith. Now, how can a system with a name like Faith cause any damage?"

"Let's all have faith that you're right," Richard quipped, and held Jo's hand as he escorted her out of the office.

FRIDAY 21 JULY

Over the Atlantic

The aircraft bucked and dropped, soared again and dropped again. The cloud seemed to be clinging to the windows, resting on the wings, threatening to force them down. Sweat stood out on Mark's face as his hands gripped tight on the wheel, and Landry was equally tense. Only Eisener, his mind totally caught up in his job, was relaxed, staring ahead of them.

"There it is," he said.

The clouds parted as if a magician had waved his wand, and they were under blue skies. However often Mark had flown into the eye of a tropical storm, he never failed to marvel at this moment, when he could look up and up and up at the heavens, and then, on either side, at the solid wall of cloud surrounding him.

Eisener was looking down. "Big stuff," he commented.

Mark looked down too, and caught his breath. They were only a thousand feet up, and down there the seas were nothing but white, leaping and churning. The thought of coming down into that . . . but it would at least be quick; the plane would break up in about five seconds.

"Take her up," Eisener commanded.

The aircraft soared, and back into the cloud. Up and up she went in a spiralling ascent, to break out again into brilliant sunshine a few minutes later. But now she was above the clouds, and they could look back down to the huge, swirling area of white. "Fifty-three knots of wind at the centre," Eisener said, having checked his instruments. "We have ourselves a storm, gentlemen. What's her name?"

Mark looked at the list which hung by his earphones. "I guess she's a girl named Faith," he said. "You reckon there's any charity down there, Doc?"

"Nope. And even less hope, for those who can't get out of the way."

JULY

The Fourth Week

Saturday 22 July

Park Avenue

The telephone jangled. Jo put it on open speech; she had an idea who it might be. She had in fact expected this call yesterday.

"Hi," Michael said.

"Hi."

"Just got in. Well, last night."

From his voice, she had an idea he had spent most of the night drinking.

"Aren't you going to ask me how we did?"

"How did you do?" Jo asked.

"Well . . ." His voice was triumphant. "There are a couple of protests to be heard today, but it's as near a certainty as you can have that we've won our class." He waited for a moment, then asked, "Aren't you going to congratulate me?"

Presumably the fact of having won the race made everything that had gone before irrelevant, at least in his eyes. "Congratulations," she said.

"It was some race," he told her. "Flat calm to begin with. Would you believe on Monday morning we could still see the hills around Newport? Then light airs. Now that's where real skill comes in, taking advantage of every puff of wind, entering the Gulf Stream at just the right place . . . the guys all agree it couldn't have been done without me."

"I'm sure they're right," Jo agreed.

"Then the winds picked up and we had a good breeze for the last couple of days. The ship behaved like a dream. Now tell me, how's the boy?"

"Doing well."

"Still in hospital?"

"No, I collected him yesterday. But he still has to rest. He's in bed."

"Great. Then everything has gone all right."

"Yes," she said. "Everything has gone all right."

"Well, that's great. What are your plans?"

"Owen Michael and I are flying down to Eleuthera on Monday."

"The doctor given you the okay on that?"

"Yes."

"Well, great. He'll like that. And it's bound to do him good."

"What are *your* plans?"

"Well, like I told you before we left, the guys and I thought we'd take a week cruising around Bermuda. There's some great snorkelling and fishing to be had here. And there's nothing for me to hurry back for, is there? Not with Owen Michael on the mend and all of you down in the Bahamas."

"Nothing at all," Jo said, and hung up. She gazed at Richard, who had arrived just as the phone had rung, and was mixing them Bloody Marys. Now he looked back at her. She had wanted him to hear the conversation, but she felt she had to offer some explanation. "He has this marvellous facility of remembering only what he wants to remember, and forgetting everything else," she said. "We had the most vicious quarrel over the phone when he wouldn't abandon the race because of Owen Michael's illness. I called him some terrible names, virtually in public. But now all is sweetness and light, because he's won his damned race. Not that he is going to change any of his plans, of course."

Richard handed her a glass. "You sound kind of bitter."

"Don't you think I have cause to be?"

He gave one of his half smiles. "I'm a prejudiced witness. But I would say you have every reason to be bitter."

She drank, sat on the settee, brooded out of the undraped picture window at the skyline of New York, gleaming in the morning sunlight; Richard had come here so regularly during the past week she had ceased worrying about the porters. Now, presumably she should be worrying about Owen Michael's reaction. On Dr Matthey's recommendation she had given him a sedative last night to make sure he had no ill effects after the excitement of coming home. But he was going to wake up any minute. "So what would be your solution?"

"You know it. Divorce Donnelly and marry me."

"I wish it were as simple as that."

"Everything in life is simple, if you just make up your mind to do it. And divorce is no more difficult than anything else. The guy's a heel. Or he sure comes across that way. And there's no real question of guilt, nowadays, either. Just a matter of will."

"You have got to be joking. Don't you think I've gone over this time and again in my mind? Guilt? There may not be any in the eyes of the law, but I wouldn't have much chance with friends and family, now would I? I commit adultery with you, while Michael is committing adultery with a yacht?" She sighed. "Believe me, Richard, I'd move in with you tomorrow, if it weren't for the children."

"That is a legal matter, my love, and I don't think it will be a problem either. I told you, courts don't consider guilt or innocence in divorce cases these days. The decision will be based entirely on which parent is the better one to have custody of the children – for their good. Well, when Donnelly's behaviour, not only about Owen Michael's illness but over the whole vacation scene, the way he's always away from home, is brought out, I don't think any right-minded judge would hesitate for a moment as to who should have them."

"Court," she said, and hugged herself. "Judge. The whole thing sounds too terrible for words."

"It isn't, really."

"Because you've been through it. I guess maybe it's different for a man. Anyway, from what you've told me, it was a mutual decision – and there were no children involved. Michael wouldn't go along with that, especially if it meant losing Owen Michael and Tamsin. Anyway, he's a Catholic, so he'd thump that tub. He'd fight tooth and nail, and he'd fight dirty, too. Every last bit of dirty linen in our lives would be hung out to dry. And even if I did get custody of the children, think of the effect the whole thing would have on them. Not only the split. They'd have to be allowed to spend time with Michael every so often, and boy, would he attempt to turn them against me."

"Like I said, the guy's a heel. But Jo . . . are you going to spend the rest of your life in misery for fear of him and what he might do? That's emotional blackmail, even if he hasn't started to apply it yet."

She smiled. "Then what about you? Do you really want to take on two hooligans?"

"As long as they're your hooligans, I'd like nothing better."

Her smile became genuinely warm. "Yes, I think you would. I know you'd make a good father. Oh, Richard, how I want to . . . look, give me a little time to think, will you? When I come back from Eleuthera I'll have it all sorted out in my mind, I promise."

He frowned. "I wanted to talk to you about that. I don't think you should go down there right now."

"But I have to. I told Michael I was going. It'll be quite all right; Dr Matthey says that as long as I make sure Owen Michael just lazes about, does no diving or anything like that, a couple of weeks in the Bahamas would be the best possible thing for him." She touched his hand. "And for me. It's pretty difficult to make decisions about us, knowing I'm going to see you in half an hour. You're just too close. My mind is full of you, rather than what's best for us. Can you understand that?"

"Sure I can. But I wasn't thinking about Owen Michael, Jo. Or about us. I was thinking about Faith."

Her turn to frown. "What do you mean?"

"Haven't you been watching my forecasts?"

"I haven't really felt like watching anything this past week."

"Well . . . I didn't mention it before, because I didn't want you worrying about Tamsin."

Jo sat up straight. "You mean Faith's a biggie?"

"Not yet. But she's doing everything she isn't supposed to do. Or maybe it's everything she *is* supposed to do, if she means to cause the maximum trouble. You remember she was moving fairly slowly, but even so she should have reached the Caribbean by now. But she's slowed down even more, almost stalled in fact. Yet with no deviation in course; she still has a bead drawn on Puerto Rico. And her winds are increasing all the time. We expect her to be upgraded to Hurricane by tonight."

"You mean she could pose a threat to the Bahamas?"

"We have no means of knowing. She could go straight across Puerto Rico into the Caribbean, she could turn up north before reaching the islands – neither would pose any threat to Eleuthera – or she could hit Puerto Rico and then turn north, which would carry her in a straight line up the eastern Bahamas. I'm afraid that's the most likely course for her to follow."

"Oh, my God. When will this happen?"

"Well, there are storm warnings in Puerto Rico right this minute. If she were to do what I suggest, and travelling at her present speed, she could be in the Bahamas by next Wednesday."

"Oh, Christ," Jo gasped. "I must get hold of them."

"Don't you think they know? They'll have been watching the Miami forecasts."

"Perhaps. But I really must try."

SUNDAY 23 JULY

Park Avenue

She was too worried to be good company that night. She found it difficult to accept that North Eleuthera would ever be hit by a major storm, and even if it was, she reminded herself that Lawson and Belle knew all about hurricanes, having lived in the Bahamas for years, and Big Mike and Babs and Dale were also perfectly able to take care of themselves. Yet when she remembered three years ago those seas getting higher and higher, until they had almost threatened to lap over the rocks below the house . . . and Tamsin was there.

In the morning she telephoned the Whaletown post office. Inevitably it took her over an hour to get through, and then the line was bad. "Hi, there, Mis' Donnelly," the girl said. "I give Josh that message for Mr Donnelly, and he got it, 'cause he tol' me so when he was in las' week."

"Thanks a million," Jo said. "I have another one for him."

"He don' come into town on Sundays, ma'am."

"I know. But if Josh could take the message again . . ."

"Josh don' go out to Dolphin Point on Sundays."

"I know that too. But if he could perhaps make a special journey . . . it's very important. I want Mr Donnelly to call me here in New York. Can you ask him to do that?"

"Ah guess ah can give Josh the message, Mis' Donnelly, when he comes outa church."

"I'd be most terribly grateful. And do remember to tell him it is most urgent."

"No problem, ma'am. You have a nice day, heah?"

Obviously, if anyone around Whaletown had heard there was a potential hurricane a few hundred miles south of them they weren't worrying about it – but then, she remembered that in those sunkissed islands nobody ever really worried about anything . . . until it happened. And obviously she couldn't hope to hear from Big Mike before tomorrow. And what was she going to say to him when he did call? Even if she told him she had changed her mind about coming down – as she had, not so much for herself but for Owen Michael: Dr Matthey would hardly approve of exposing the boy to the tensions and possible risks of a hurricane – he was very unlikely to pack up and come home just because there was a storm in the vicinity; he would remind her of how they had survived the last Tropical Storm to hit Eleuthera – just a doddle. Nor was there any way he could send Tamsin back alone. She was almost tempted to farm Owen Michael out and rush down and pick the little girl up . . . but she couldn't leave him at this stage, not even with Marcia. Her anger with Michael grew. If ever a family needed two parents it was now.

Marcia! There was an idea. She could drive down to Greenwich Village for a cup of coffee and hear what they thought about it. She just had to talk to someone, and Richard was at the studio. Besides, Richard was too close to the subject, took it all perhaps a shade too seriously. Marcia's approach to life was essentially practical.

She told Owen Michael she was going out for half an hour, installed him in front of the television set, and discovered both Marcia and Benny in overalls, surrounded by paint and wallpaper, hanging on to step ladders as they painted the ceiling in the first-floor lounge. "Hey, Jo," Marcia called as she entered the room. "Have you heard there's a storm could be gonna hit the Bahamas?"

"Yes," Jo said.

"I'll bet you wish you were there to see the fun," Benny said.

"Fun?" Jo asked. "I'm worried sick. Tamsin is there."

Marcia slid down her ladder to give her a hug, managing to transfer some wet paint from the back of her hand to Jo's blouse as she did so. "Now, Jo, you know she'll be all right. Dad and Lawson and Dale are there, and Babs and Belle . . ."

"That's what I keep telling myself," Jo agreed.

"So there is absolutely nothing for you to worry about, believe me."

"I know you're right," Jo said miserably.

Marcia felt a surge of sympathy. "Come on, old girl, let's put on some coffee. When's Michael coming home?"

"I have no idea," Jo said. She didn't want to get involved in chatting about Michael with any member of his family, at least, not until her own decision was irrevocable – as if it wasn't already.

Marcia, who had been kept informed of the situation by her mother, decided against pressing the subject. "Well, *I've* got some news for you, anyway." She glanced at Benny and winked, before leading Jo down the creaky old stairs to their new kitchen.

Jo tried to put her worries and resentments out of mind and look interested. "Tell, then. What is it?"

"Well . . ." Marcia grinned as she filled the machine. "It looks like we'll need to advance the date of our wedding."

"You're not . . .?"

"We are. At least I am – pregnant."

"Oh, terrific! Accidental, or deliberate?" Jo was truly excited for them both.

"Bit of both, I guess. We'd decided to start a family just as soon as we were married, and just stopped bothering . . . never imagined it could happen so quickly."

"Have you told Babs?"

"No. It's such a hassle, trying to get in touch with them down there. And it's not something you can say over the phone. I'll tell her when she comes home; it's only another fortnight."

"How do you think she'll take it?" Jo herself had no idea. Illegitimate babies might not be the catastrophe they had once been considered, but Babs and Mike were practising Catholics, even if Marcia wasn't, most of the time. How did one confess something like an illegitimate pregnancy?

"Well," Marcia said, practically, "Benny and I are getting married. We'll just have to bring it forward, I guess."

"Um." Jo felt her sister-in-law was refusing to consider that her parents might be upset. She gulped her coffee. "Well, I have to get back to Owen Michael."

"How is he, anyway?"

"Thriving. Except that I haven't told him yet we're not going down to Eleuthera tomorrow."

"You're not? You don't mean you're staying here because of that storm?" Marcia gave a shriek of laughter. "Oh, Jo, you really are a worry wart."

"Well, I don't think Owen Michael should be exposed to any excitement right now," Jo said stiffly, and then relented. "Look, why don't you and

Benny come over for supper tomorrow night. Save you cooking." She knew Richard was working that evening.

"Hey, Mom," Owen Michael shouted as she entered the apartment. "There's a hurricane making for Puerto Rico. It's just come through on the news. Did you know that?"

"I heard something about it," Jo lied. "But it's not a hurricane, darling, just a tropical storm. They've called it Faith."

"It's a hurricane," Owen Michael insisted. "They just said so. It has winds of eighty miles an hour at the centre."

"Oh, my God!" Jo muttered.

"Say, Mom, do you think it could hit the Bahamas?"

"Of course it won't hit the Bahamas. Puerto Rico is hundreds of miles away."

"Ah, shit! I was hoping we could get down there in time."

"I do wish you wouldn't use that word," Jo remarked. "And Owen Michael . . . we are not going to Dolphin Point tomorrow."

"Not going?" He turned away from the screen in dismay.

"Dr Matthey has changed his mind." Jo was becoming a most efficient liar; on the other hand, she had no doubt at all Dr Matthey would agree with her. "He thinks you should stay here for at least another week."

"Aw, Mom . . ."

Jo went into the study and closed the door. Eighty miles an hour was at the very bottom end of the hurricane scale, but the storm hadn't even reached Puerto Rico yet. She dialled Richard's office number.

"Hi," he said. "Did you get through to your folks?"

"It's an Out Island, remember?" she told him. "I left a message for them to call me, but I don't expect to hear before tomorrow morning. Richard, is it really true that Faith is now a hurricane?"

"It's true," he said. "And quite honestly, I don't like the look of her one little bit."

"You mean she could build?"

"I mean she is doing just that."

"But you still don't know if she'll hit Eleuthera."

"I can't have any idea about that until she hits Puerto Rico, which is expected in another twelve hours. Normally we can form some idea of what will happen then by reading the water temperatures, she'll look for the warmest. Trouble is, this year the waters in the Bahamas are just as warm as in the Caribbean. In fact there are temperatures of over 26° Centigrade all the way up to Canada; big sharks have been reported north of Cape Cod, and they only go up there when their food fish move north, and those smaller fish move with the plankton which drifts up there with the warm water. Added to that the way the jet stream has gone right up north . . . Faith has the whole north-west Atlantic to play in."

"Jesus," she said. "Richard, I really am worried."

"Well, take it easy," he recommended. "When I said she's building, there's still no indication of her getting above a Category Two Storm."

"How big is that?"

"Well, say something over 100 mph winds."

"100 mph? Oh, my God! Richard, wouldn't I be justified in asking them to come home?"

"Sure, you would. No one sits out a hurricane who doesn't have to. As to whether they'll still get a flight . . . you'll have to make them hurry. How's Owen Michael?"

"He's fine," she said absently.

"Would you rather I didn't come round tonight?"

She hesitated. She wanted him so badly. But she didn't want Owen Michael involved – not yet; he was still unaware of Richard's visit on Saturday morning. "No," she said. "I want you to come. But make it later, after Owen Michael's in bed. He's still pretty weak and easily tired; I'll have him tucked up by half past eight. Is nine okay?"

"Sure. I understand. But I may not be able to stay very long. I'll have to get back here by midnight for a late update; the big white chief likes his number one weatherman on duty when the weather happens to be making news."

"How's the old bastard taking it?"

"With a pinch of salt. Expects it to fizzle, like all the others so far this year."

"I wish he was in Puerto Rico," Jo said. "Maybe you should send him there to see for himself. Anyway, I don't mind if you can only come for an hour. As long as you don't feel I'm wasting your time." It would be disappointing to see him for so short a time, but it would be better than nothing.

"Oh, we men are called upon to make these sacrifices from time to time," he teased.

Jo giggled. "The sacrificial altar will be ready at nine."

"I'll be there," he promised, laughing.

Owen Michael was sound asleep when Richard turned up.

"Have you eaten?" Jo asked, after they'd kissed.

"No, but don't go to any trouble."

"I haven't had anything, either. Go park yourself in the family room. I've got something ready on a tray."

They drank soup from mugs and tore meat off grilled chicken pieces with their teeth, saying little and obviously with much on their minds.

"Do you want to know what I think you should do when Donnelly gets

back, and you return from Eleuthera, supposing you ever get there?"
Richard broke the silence, eventually, wiping grease off his fingers with
a paper napkin.

"Tell me."

"You move out of here, into your place in Connecticut, with the
children, and have him served with a petition immediately. You have a
pretty good case for mental cruelty and your best chance of getting
custody of the kids is to leave me right out of the picture, so he can't
counter-claim on adultery."

"Yes, I guess you're right," she agreed, and reloaded the tray. "There's
no point in delaying, if I'm not going to get down to Dolphin Point." She
noticed his eyes kept straying to the clock. "You don't have to go for an
hour yet, do you?"

"No. But I have to be there *in* an hour. May I come back afterwards?"

"Please," she smiled, and then frowned. "You're uptight. Is it Faith?"

"I guess so." He sighed.

"I didn't ask if there was any more news of her. I imagine you'd have
told me if there was."

"Sweetheart, I don't want to worry you with unnecessary details, when
we don't yet have any idea where she's heading or how big she's going
to be. You've seen enough hurricane tracks charted by now to know that
from her present position she could go anywhere."

"Yes, yes, I know that, but there's something on your mind. Come on,
let's have it. What are you holding back?" She wanted to know the worst.

"Well . . . the first reports are starting to come in from Puerto Rico.
The hurricane winds were beginning to hit San Juan just before I left the
studio, and the torrential rain was already said to be causing landslips
and widespread damage. The system is still moving very slowly, too, just
on ten knots, which gives it so much more potential."

"That isn't what you're not telling me," Jo insisted.

He gave another sigh. "Mark called in just before I left. He'd just
returned from the area. He says there has been a significant change in
the track, from just north of west, to north-west. That's good for Puerto
Rico, of course; they'll remain in the less dangerous semi-circle, down
there."

"But it's not good for the Bahamas."

"No. However, it's still early days. The system is still huge, covering
such an enormous area, that it's difficult to see how the eastern Bahamas
at any rate can avoid getting at least some of it, now. If you can get your
people out of there, I most certainly would."

Monday 24 July

Monday 24 July

Park Avenue, 11.00 am

The phone buzzed at eleven in the morning. Jo had deliberately stayed in, waiting for the call, pretending to do some more research on André Previn – she had not told Ed she was still in New York, just to be left in peace – but she couldn't concentrate. The weather update had revealed no deepening of the storm, and, as was always the case, lying in Richard's arms had totally reassured her, but all through the night she had been aware of the feeling of imminent disaster hanging over her; the system was still drifting north – and it was still expected to deepen. "Hello," she gasped, as she picked up the study phone, carefully closing the door to make sure Owen Michael couldn't overhear.

"That Mrs Michael Donnelly, junior?"

"Yes. Yes, it is."

"Hold the line, please. I have an overseas call for you." The American operator did not close her key, and Jo could hear the well-known Bahamian voice saying, "You can use the firs' boot', Mr Donnelly."

"Dad?" she shouted. "Is that you?"

"Jo? Hi, sweetheart. I got your message and came right in. Nothing wrong, I hope? Owen Michael still okay?"

"Yes. But Dad . . ."

"So how come you're not coming in today? You're sure he's okay?"

"Yes, Owen Michael's okay. We're not coming in because of this . . ."

"And Michael? Say, how did the race go?"

"He called Saturday. He's won his class, I think."

"Attaboy!" Big Mike shouted. "I knew he could do it. He must be over the moon. And he's okay?"

"Yes, he's okay," Jo said wearily.

"Then what's all the fuss about? We thought you had an emergency, that's why I came hustling into Whaletown to call."

"There *is* an emergency," she shouted. "Haven't you heard about Hurricane Faith?"

"Sure," Big Mike said equably. "Seems she gave Puerto Rico quite a clout. Mostly rain, though."

"Yes," Jo said. "Well, she's giving Haiti quite a clout this minute. And with a lot more than just rain. Have you heard about that?"

"The goddamned electrics have been on the blink out at the Point," Big Mike explained. "And I'm having some trouble with the generator. So we didn't get last night's forecast, except from the radio, which didn't say much. Didn't sound too bad, though."

"Dad," Jo said, trying to speak calmly. "Faith is expected to carry winds of more than a hundred miles an hour by tonight: that is going to be twice as strong as we had three years ago. She's a Category Two storm and she could deepen further. And she's coming straight at you."

"Is that a fact. Well, I guess I'll have Josh dig out those shutters again. Actually, we could do with some rain; the cistern is kind of low."

"Dad," Jo said desperately. "We're not talking about a little bit of rain. I think you should all get out of there while you can."

"What, run away from a bit of wind, bang in the middle of our vacation? Heck, sweetheart, you're starting to sound like Meg Robson. Boy, am I gonna have fun telling her about this."

"But Dad . . ." Jo felt like screaming. "A hundred miles an hour . . ."

"The house can take it. So can we."

"I'm thinking about Tamsin," Jo said, bluntly.

"You don't have to worry about her. Do you think I'd let anything happen to that little girl?"

"I want my daughter brought home!" Jo shouted.

There was a moment's silence; she had never spoken to her father-in-law like that before. At last he said, "You really are worried."

"Yes," she said. "Yes. I really am worried. Please, Dad, please."

"Well, if you feel that way . . . tell you what I'll do, sweetheart. I'll hustle back out to the Point and chat it over with Lawson and Belle and Babs. Then I'll call you back tomorrow morning."

"And tell me what flight you'll be on," Jo begged.

"Ah . . . yeah, I'll call you back."

The phone went dead, and Jo rested her head on her arms in despair.

DOLPHIN POINT, NORTH ELEUTHERA, BAHAMAS

11.30 am

A piercing scream electrified everyone in the house.

"Holy shit! What was that?" Dale dropped the saw on the garage floor and ran outside.

"Tamsin! Where is she?" Babs also emerged, from the kitchen.

"Oh, my God!" the voice shouted. "Neal! Oh, my God!"

"That's our Meg," Dale commented.

"Tamsin was with her," Babs snapped.

And at that moment the little girl called, "Granma! Granma! Come quickly."

Barefooted, Babs ran across the heavy flagstones that composed the central patio of the house, paused to accustom her eyes to the brilliant glare of the Bahamian sun, then hurried down the path through the hibiscus hedges towards the sea, closely followed by her son.

Tamsin and Meg were standing beside an old boat engine, eyes gaping, rigid with horror . . . and staring back, tongue flicking viciously as he slid out from a rusty aperture, was a large snake.

"Dat no problem, ma'am. He jus' a fowl snake," Melba the cook announced coolly, having followed to investigate the excitement. "He don't hurt. I call Josh. He fix he."

"Meggie. Oh, my darling Meggie!" Neal arrived to take his wife in his arms.

"It's horrible," Meg sobbed. "To think it was there, all the time, when I was looking at the engine . . ."

"You probably woke him up," Dale pointed out.

"Are you quite sure he's harmless, Melba?" Babs asked. "He looks enormous." She pulled Tamsin away as foot after foot of the reptile oozed out of the engine casing on to the path.

"He ain' poisonous, ma'am, but he might squeeze'm all of us. Yeah, he sure am a big one, all o' ten foot." Looking as nonchalant as she could, the large black woman backed off as well before turning to call, "Oh, Josh! Where you? Bring 'um yo' cutlass."

Josh, half the size of his wife, came running down the path behind them.

"Mornin', borse." He nodded to Babs, who was the senior of his employers present. "What seem to be de trouble?"

"Come fix dis fowl snake, man," Melba commanded.

Josh approached, and checking behind him that the onlookers were well clear, swung his machete, decapitating the snake with a single blow. "Dere. No problem, borse."

"Ugh, what a stink." Tamsin screwed up her face.

"Is de blood. It powerful. Josh, take um away, quick," his wife ordered.

The Americans watched in fascination as the gardener balanced the long, dripping body at the end of his knife, holding it at arm's length, and carried it down to the shore to fling it into the sea.

"It's horrible. Horrible," Meg said. "Oh, Neal, this place just gets worse and worse. We shouldn't ever have come here. I want to go home."

"Now, Meggie . . ." Neal held her close, and looked above her head at Babs; they had gone through this almost every day of the vacation, as some other incident which bore no relationship to the cloistered existence of Bognor, Connecticut had occurred.

"Let's all go have a rum punch," Babs decided. "Mike'll be home from Whaletown in a minute. You can tell him all about it."

"I want to go home," Meg wailed, as they escorted her back up to the house.

Lawson Garr heard the scream, and rolled on his back. "Sounds like Meg," he remarked.

"Blow Meg," his wife replied, remaining on her stomach, pale bottom turned up to the sky. Dolphin Point curved away from the mainland of North Eleuthera to form the southern arm of a huge, shallow bay; the northern arm was composed of a series of small islands which had grown out of the reef, of which Palm Island, on which there was a settlement, was the largest. There was a supermarket and a post office on Palm Island, and at a distance of only three miles, it was the nearest civilisation to the Point – but the Donnellys preferred as a rule to drive the ten miles into Whaletown as opposed to getting out the small dory Big Mike kept moored to the wooden dock, and braving the spray as they crossed the entrance to the sound, where the Atlantic rollers creamed into the narrows and could make the passage treacherous for small boats.

Those rollers were breaking on the rocks only a few feet below where Belle and Lawson were lying, for if the bay side of the Point was a stretch of magnificent yellow sand beach, shallow for perhaps fifty feet from the shore to make a perfect aquatic playground, it was also overlooked by both the houses, and inclined to attract snorkellers from Palm Island. The Atlantic side was all rock, but there were patches of sand, and these were the Garrs' favourites. Here they could sunbathe nude, and make love as the mood took them. Seven years into their marriage, Lawson and Belle still adored each other.

"You don't think I should go find out what's troubling her?" Lawson asked.

"No, I don't. She is a pain in the ass." Belle put out her hand to find him, and giggled. "You have a sand-coated willy."

"Yeah, well, I'll give him a wash just now."

He remained sitting up, and after a moment she rolled over as well, her golden brown splendour also coated with sand. "What do you see?"

"Not a damn thing. Except forty-two acres of rolling green money."

Belle sat up too, rested her head on his shoulder. "I still can't believe it." But she did, now. They had told Babs and Dale when they had all got down, and that had seemed to make it official. Babs had been a little doubtful at first; the thought of spending a million bucks speculating in land was against her New England instincts, but as they had all walked over the property, and seen Neal Robson slowly turning green, she had warmed to the idea. "When do the diggers come in?"

"Next month," Lawson said. "I thought we might stay on up here and keep an eye on things."

"Mmm. I'd like that. Just you and me. We could go nuddy all the time."

He turned his head to kiss her. "Well . . . after Josh and Melba go home, why not? You reckon on wearing me out?"

She kissed him back, and removed some sand from where it mattered most. "I reckon on having a damned good try."

They listened to the toot-toot of a horn. "There's Dad!" Belle scrambled to her feet, scooping up her towel as she did so but not bothering to do more than drape it across her shoulder, as, like some reincarnation of Aphrodite, she strode towards the dirt road. Lawson hurried behind her, his own towel round his waist; there was always the chance that it might be someone other than Big Mike – not that the thought of his wife sending some poor sod into a mind-boggling spin did anything more than delight him.

Big Mike braked as he saw them emerge from the bushes that fringed the road. "Holy shit!" he commented. "You could cause an accident."

"That would be incest." Belle sat beside him, and Lawson also got into the front seat. "What's up with Jo? The kid all right?" Lawson was fond of his niece and nephew, even if he was glad he and Belle had no children of their own; there was not only the risk of that magnificent sun-browned body being damaged, but a child would have interfered with their essential intimacy.

"The kid is fine," Big Mike said as he turned into the drive beside the generator shed. "Jo's scared about this hurricane."

"What hurricane?" Belle asked as the car stopped.

"The one that's been knocking around Puerto Rico. Faith."

"That's hundreds of miles away."

"Puerto Rico may be, but not Faith, apparently. Seems she's moving this way, and is beating the shit out of Haiti right this minute. Jo says she could have 100 mile an hour winds."

"That," said Lawson, "is a lot of wind."

"Yeah." Big Mike brooded on his holiday home. Built on a low ridge some thirty feet above the water, the setting was idyllic. Casuarinas lined the shoreline beneath it, and before them a garden of hibiscus, oleanders and yellow elders grew out of ground-filled rockholes in the coral limestone which made the Point. The house itself was single storeyed and U-shaped, bedrooms to the right, living rooms and kitchen to the left as he faced it, linked by a wide roof which half covered the flagstoned patio from which they looked across the shallow waters of the sound at Palm Island. The only other house on the Point, the Robsons', was a quarter of a mile away, where the ridge dwindled to a mere ten feet above the beach. Mike thought Dolphin Point was the loveliest place in the world – and the most secure. So he'd been a little scared three years ago when there'd been that storm, but there'd been no damage. Fifty mile an hour winds! But Jo had been talking about double that. "She wants us to go home," he said.

"Go home? Half way through our vacation? She has got to be kidding," Belle said.

"Well . . . I guess she's worried about Tamsin? What do you reckon, Lawson?"

"Hundred mile an hour winds," Lawson said thoughtfully. Born and bred in Nassau, where his parents had lived since the early 1950s, and having holidayed in Eleuthera even before he'd met Belle Donnelly, he could remember storms like Betsy and David. "Maybe it'd make sense."

"Lawson!" his wife said.

"We'll talk to Babs about it." Big Mike grinned. "I just gotta hear what Meg has to say."

12.00 noon

"A hurricane!" Meg Robson screamed. "Oh, my God! This is it. Absolutely it. Why we ever bought this place I can't imagine. I told you it was a stupid thing to do, Neal. I told you."

"Now, Meg . . ." Neal said unhappily.

"I want to go home. I want to go home, now!"

"Well, you can't, now," Lawson pointed out. "There won't be any planes out of North Eleuthera until tomorrow, now."

"And anyway, we have to shutter the place up," Neal told her. "We can't just walk away from it. Mike, I don't suppose you guys would give us a hand?"

"Sure we will," Mike said. "We have to shutter this place up too. In fact, I'll get Josh on to it now, before he goes home." The servants generally left right after lunch. "Josh!" he bawled. "Josh!"

"Heah I is, borse." Josh appeared from the garden.

"You heard about this storm down in Haiti?"

"I did heah somet'ing, borse."

"You reckon it's gonna come up here?"

Josh looked at the sky; it was a perfect blue, marred only by fine weather clouds . . . but there were cirrus streaks high up, indicating wind not too far off. "Could be, borse. Is the time of yeah."

"Yeah? Well, I tell you what, you go on down to the generator shed and bring those storm shutters up."

"Now, borse?"

"Right now," Mike said.

Josh ambled off, somewhat disconsolately.

"Now I tell you what we're gonna do," Mike announced, signalling Dale to mix up another batch of rum punch. "We are going to have another drink . . . you too, Meggie, and then we are going to have lunch, and then we are going to put up the shutters, and then we are going to listen to the six o'clock forecast, and then we are going to make a decision on what we are doing next. We'd look a right load of billygoats if we went chasing back up home to get away from a storm which wasn't even gonna come near us, right? Tonight is time. I told Jo I'd call her back tomorrow and tell her what we were doing."

They gazed at him, and Babs squeezed his hand; she loved it when Big Mike was being masterful. "I think that's absolutely right, sweetheart."

Josh was back on the edge of the patio. "Borse, them shutters ain' no good."

"What? Holy shit, what do you mean?"

"Well, borse, they been sittin' down in that shed t'ree year' now, and they all warp up. There ain' no way them bolts goin' fit in them holes."

"Oh, Jesus Christ," Big Mike groaned. And looked at Lawson. "What the hell do we do?"

"We get some good nails and we board them up."

"Nails? In my window frames?" Babs demanded.

"It's better than having them blown out," Lawson told her. "You got a good supply of nails, Dad?"

"Of course I don't have a good supply of nails," Big Mike groused.

"Okay, there's time. Josh, when you go home this afternoon, you buy all the nails we will need at the store, and bring them out with you tomorrow morning. Right?"

"Okay, borse. I goin' do that. I goin' bring my nephew to help an' all. He is good with nails." He ambled off again.

"Fucking country," Big Mike growled, revealing his first trace of nerves. "Can't even leave some wood lying around without it warping. You'd better check yours out, Neal."

"Mine are all brand new. Had them made the moment I got down here." Neal smiled triumphantly. "We have nothing to worry about."

6.00 pm

"Okay, folks," Big Mike shouted to the world in general. "News time."

They straggled into the lounge, having spent an exhausting afternoon helping Neal to put his shutters into place. Dale mixed up rum cocktails while they took their places in front of the TV set in various stages of undress, not very interested in the news, although Mike had tuned in to a Miami station rather than the local Bahamian telecast, whose weather coverage was sketchy to say the least. Before the news was finished the Robsons had joined them.

"Now, sssh," Big Mike told everyone. "This is important."

"And now for the weather, and that hurricane, folks," said the anchorman. "Faith is her name, and she could be heading our way. How about an update, Gordon?"

The camera switched to a smiling young man standing in front of a huge map.

"Remember when this station had that gorgeous Richard Connors?" Belle asked her mother.

"Oh, yes. He's in New York, now, you know, with NABS. I think Jo knows him."

"Does she? You must ask her to get me his signed photo."

"Oh, yeah?" Lawson inquired, giving her an affectionate squeeze.

"Will you guys shut up," Big Mike shouted. "We want to listen to this."

"Well, hello, there," the young man named Gordon was saying. "I guess I'll begin with Hurricane Faith, because she is a full hurricane now. As to whether she poses any threat to South Florida . . . We have Dr John Eisener standing by at the Coral Gables Hurricane Tracking Centre to give us the latest update on that. Good evening, Dr Eisener."

The meteorologist came up on the huge monitor. "Good evening to you, Gordon."

"What's Faith doing right this minute, Doctor?"

"Well, Gordon, as you know, the storm passed over Haiti last night. Then it was blowing a good ninety miles an hour around the centre, and there was some pretty heavy rainfall as well. We've reports of seventeen inches of rain in three hours."

Gordon gave an obliging whistle of amazement, as if he did not have all the figures on the desk before him.

"We had some hopes the storm might begin to dissipate over the land,"

Eisener continued. "But it regained strength the moment it hit open water again, and if anything the circulation increased; winds at the centre are now just short of a hundred miles an hour, with gales extending some hundred miles from the eye. It's position is here . . ." He turned to another huge wall map and touched it with his wand. "That is about a hundred miles south-east of Mayaguana, in the south-eastern Bahamas, and it is moving north at about 15 knots – it has quickened its progress considerably over the past few hours. Mayaguana is already experiencing gale force winds and heavy rain, and a hurricane warning has been issued by the Bahamian Government to cover as far north as Cat Island." The wand flickered out again to touch the large island just south of the southernmost tip of Eleuthera. "We would expect that warning to be extended to include Eleuthera and even the Abacos by this evening."

Meg Robson moaned, and Big Mike remarked, "Holy shit!"

"Faith is moving just west of north, you said, Doctor?" Gordon asked. Eisener nodded. "That's right."

"Do you expect that track to be maintained?"

"Well, Gordon, as you know, one can never be certain with tropical storms. There are so many factors involved. But given what information we have, the absence of any jet stream activity in this vicinity, the water temperatures, and so on, yes, I would expect her to continue on her present track for at least twenty-four hours. That would take her just east of Eleuthera and the Abacos and thence north to Bermuda."

Gordon was giving his viewers a reassuring smile. "In other words, in your opinion this storm poses no real threat to South Florida."

"Unless there is a substantial alteration of course during the next few hours, that is, unless Faith swings sharp westerly and begins to make for New Providence, then I would say there is no real threat to the Miami area. There'll be some big seas on the coast, mind . . ."

"Ideal for surfers," Gordon suggested.

"Oh, indeed. But we'll continue to monitor it, hour by hour. One of our pilots will be out there first thing tomorrow morning, checking it out."

"Thank you, Dr Eisener. I'm sure that's what our listeners wanted to hear. Now let me ask you one final question. Is this a dangerous storm?"

Eisener moved away from his map, and the camera brought him into close focus. "Gordon, you know as well as I that any hurricane is potentially dangerous. Faith is not a major hurricane; sustained winds of 100 mph put her into what we call Category Two. But that is still a lot of wind. The folks in the Bahamas should prepare themselves for very high seas topped by storm surges of maybe six feet, which will mean considerable flooding in low-lying areas. The probability of flooding will be increased by torrential rain, and there will be considerable lightning activity. Certainly they should take every precaution, and people in isolated areas should prepare to be cut off for a day or two, maybe longer. Finally, Gordon, we must always bear in mind that this storm has the potential to deepen, and become a Category Three. That would put her in the same class as Gloria of a few years back – and I don't have to remind you that Gloria was a very dangerous storm indeed."

"Thank you, Dr Eisener." Gordon beamed at them. "So there you have it, folks. A spot of bother for the Bahamas, maybe, but nothing to worry about here in South Florida. So sleep easy in your beds tonight. Now for Gordon's forecast for the next twenty-four hours. It will be partly cloudy tonight, and . . ."

Big Mike was on his feet to switch off the set. "Holy shit! Nothing to worry about here in South Florida," he mimicked. "We're not *in* South Florida. That asshole wouldn't be so Goddamned complacent if he were here. Well, that's it, folks. The holiday is over. Tomorrow morning first thing we are gonna put those shutters up, and then we are going to catch the first plane out of North Eleuthera travelling west." He looked around their faces. "Right?"

"Right," Meg agreed.

"Right," Babs and Neal said together.

Lawson looked at Belle, who shrugged. "If we are all going to fly out of here tomorrow, hadn't someone better go to the airport and book our seats?" she asked.

"At nearly seven o'clock?" Lawson asked. "You have to be joking. There won't be anyone there."

"Surely they don't close the airport before dark?"

"Of course they do! How the hell else would the drug planes get in?"

"Lawson, now is no time to be funny," his wife snapped.

Lawson handed her a full glass and kissed her nose. "Lover, I'm not funning, I'm serious. But if it'll please you I'll try to raise someone on the CB." He picked up the handset. "Palm Bay Airport. Palm Bay Airport, will you come in, please." He waited a moment, while they all watched him, and Dale mixed some more drinks. "Any taxi, Palm Bay area, any taxi, come in please. This is Dolphin Point calling." Another wait. "Hell, this is a waste of time." He switched off the set. "I'll try again in the morning."

"That won't be necessary, boy," his father-in-law assured him. "We are all going to the airport in the morning. We won't need a reservation."

"Suppose there are no seats?" Dale inquired.

"Look, the people who get out of here are going to be the ones at the airport, ready to board, not the ones sitting at home relying on a reservation. Right?"

Belle looked at Tamsin, sitting by herself, eyes big as saucers as she watched the adults. "Come on, honey," she said. "Supper for you, and bed."

She fed the little girl and then walked her across the patio; she was thoroughly enjoying playing Mom for the first time in her life.

"Aunt Belle, why can't we stay and see the hurricane?"

"Because, honey, it won't be very nice."

"Why? I'd love to stay and watch it."

"You wouldn't be able to see anything. The windows will be shuttered and the house all dark inside, even in the daytime. It'll be very boring."

"We could go outside and watch," Tamsin suggested.

"Honey, you'd be blown away! You can't imagine how strong the wind will be." She drew a floral-printed sheet loosely over the child. "Now you get some sleep."

"I don't want to sleep. I want to stay here."

"So do I, honey. But we can't." She kissed her, and felt a thrill of pleasure as the girl's arm slid round her neck.

"I love you, Aunt Belle."

"I love you too," Belle said, and switched off the light.

After supper was cleared and the dishes washed up, Dale suggested they should all play Trivial Pursuit, but Big Mike wouldn't hear of it. "For God's sake, don't you realise we have a hurricane coming straight at us? Come on, get with it. Help your mother pack up all the food; we can't just leave it in the freezer: the electricity will be the first to go. Belle, why don't you make some sandwiches for tomorrow: it'll probably be lunch time before we take off."

"Michael Donnelly!" Babs remonstrated. "You are going to give yourself a heart attack. That storm can't be here until the day after tomorrow. It could veer off in any direction by then."

"It could," Big Mike agreed. "But if we wait to see if it does, lover, and it doesn't, we're in the shit."

Babs sighed; she could see that he was really worried. "Okay, okay. Let's get cracking, you guys."

Everyone started doing something, half-heartedly. Mike's fear was communicating itself. This was obviously something far more serious than the storm of three years before. But a full hurricane? Those were things you only read about in the overseas news. Belle finished making the sandwiches, then went outside to put the crusts in the trash can, found her husband standing behind her. "It's such a brilliant moonlight night," she said, watching the light streaming across the water. "And there's not a breath of wind."

"That's a bad sign," Lawson told her. "It means Faith is coming closer, and even if she only sideswipes us, we're going to know all about it, even home in Nassau."

She turned, into his arms. "Can it harm us, Lawson? The property? The deal?"

"A 100 mile an hour breeze? No chance." He grinned. "Not permanently. It may blow one or two things down, but we can always put them back up again."

"Lawson," she said, nestling against him. "How about starting a family."

"You kidding?"

"I'm only thirty-three."

"Yeah, but . . ."

"Wouldn't you like to be a daddy?"

Lawson realised she was serious, kissed the top of her head. "If you're going to be the mummy, sure. Come to think of it, there's not a hell of a lot else to do, during a hurricane."

TUESDAY 25 JULY

DOLPHIN POINT, NORTH ELEUTHERA, BAHAMAS

Dawn

Just before dawn Belle was awakened by a rain squall which blew in the mosquito screen. She reached for a light, but the power was off. Lawson was still snoring contentedly, so she got up herself to close the window, grazed her foot on the sharp corner of the screen, and swore. But she soon fell asleep again when she regained the bed.

When she awoke again, to broad daylight, rain was thrumming on the roof.

Melba and Josh arrived at seven with their nephew, Goodson. Josh touched his sharp-peaked cap which proclaimed: 'It's better in the Bahamas'. "I brung me nephew like I said, borse, to help wit' de shutters. We soon get um fix. Den, if it's okay wit' you, borse, we likum get home again, quick. Got some tyin' down and t'ings to do before de storm hit.''

Big Mike, towering over him, clapped him on the shoulder. "Josh! Am I glad to see you. And Goodson. Sure we'll all work on the shutters together and then of course you must get home. Perhaps you could lift some of us to the airport on your way; we can't all fit into my car, together with the bags.''

Josh frowned. "You leavin', borse? You t'ink dere goin' be planes?''

Goodson said nothing, just shook his head.

"There have to be planes," Mike insisted. "What about the two which stay overnight and fly out about 10.30 in the morning? If we hurry we can catch those, can't we?'' His tone was suddenly anxious.

"Not today, borse. Dey done gorn. Flew out las' night. De wife's niece, she de agent. She tol' us dey done gorn.''

"Holy . . . !'' Mike bit off the word; Babs didn't like him to swear in front of the servants.

But Babs, having appeared in a dressing gown, was just as alarmed. "But surely you're expecting them back?'' Her eyes were wide.

"Couldn't say about dat, mam. You could ask de wife to see if she can raise dat girl on the CB.''

"The electrics are still out,'' Mike growled. "Josh, run down to the shed and start the generator. Christ, if we had gone down to the airport yesterday afternoon instead of trying to call them, we could've caught those damned planes."

"Beggin' yo' pardon, borse," Josh put in. "But them planes was all full. People was lef' standin'. Frien' o' mine is one of de taxi drivers. He tell me las' night dere was quite a fight out dere, people pushin' and shovin'. Seems agents in de States done sold two tickets for each seat."

Blood drained from Big Mike's face. He stood, shoulders hunched, in the shelter of the porch as wind and rain scattered casuarina needles and bits of palm frond across the patio, opening and shutting his mouth as he fought to control both his anger and his fear. "Get those electrics going," he told Josh again. "Babs, as soon as we've power you go see if you can get any sense out of that girl at the airport. The rest of us had better get started on these shutters."

"What about Neal and Meg? We told them we were leaving at 8.30. Meg'll have hysterics if we don't go."

The thought of Meg having hysterics could always bring a grin to Mike's face. "So we won't tell her, until 8.30. Lawson! Dale! Come on, you guys, let's go."

Heads down against the weather, they hurried behind Josh to the generator shed, while Belle, followed around the house by Tamsin, began making breakfast.

Babs knew Melba was more likely to get some sense out of a Bahamian than she, so she got the cook to use the CB. "It early, min'," Melba pointed out.

"But she should be there, shouldn't she?"

"I don' t'ink so," Melba said. "Not today. But she got CB at home. I goin' try she dere." She called, over and over again, until at last a sleepy voice answered. "Ooh!" Melba shouted. "Is dat you, Chris'abel?" Her voice shrieked above the crackling and opposing traffic on the air, and the banging of the hammers nearer at hand as the shutters went up.

"Yeah," a young female voice replied.

"You got any flights today?"

"Ah dunno."

"Di'n' dey tell you?"

"What?"

"Ah said, di'n' dey tell you if dey was comin' back?" Melba shouted even louder.

"Dey di'n' say not'ing."

Babs flushed with exasperation. "How soon can she find out if they are coming, and when?" she asked. "Can't she telephone Miami?"

"She ain't got no phone," Melba explained.

"But she can call from the post office, surely," Babs said. "It can't be far."

"Is a fac' is jus' across de street," Melba agreed. "Hey, Chris'abel," she bawled into the microphone. "You still dere?"

"Yeah."

"How you goin' know if dey comin'? De borse heah askin' why you don't phone?"

"Dey don' like me phonin', lessen I got seats."

"Tell her she has seats," Babs hissed. "Seven seats. For God's sake, we'll charter the whole plane."

"Hey, Chris'abel, I got a charter for you heah. You can call and tell 'em so?"

"I could try," Christabel volunteered. "But I ain' know iffen dey goin' come back today. You all ain' heah dey got storm comin'?"

"Oh, God," Babs moaned. "That's why we want to leave."

Melba looked at her sympathetically, then turned back to the radio. "Chris'abel, you listen to me good. You call Miami and tell dem dese folks goin' charter. You do that."

"Okay. I goin' do dat."

"Will she let us know?" Babs asked. "How soon?"

"When you goin' know about dis t'ing, Chris'abel?"

"Ah dunno. Maybe one hour."

"Okay," Babs said. "One hour. And she'll call us right away."

"You do dat right away now, Chris'abel," Melba commanded her niece.

"Suah t'ing. But I ain' t'ink dey comin' back. Not today."

"Just try," Babs begged.

"An' you call us heah and tell us what dey say," Melba said.

"Yeah," Christabel said.

Babs sighed, her face long and drawn, and returned to the lounge. Mike saw her through an as yet unshuttered window. "Well?" he demanded.

Babs related what she could recall of the conversation.

"Jesus Christ!" Mike exploded. "Not coming back? Not even for a charter? What the hell is going on? They can't just maroon us."

"Well, maybe we should go out to the airport anyway, just in case a plane does come in."

"Beggin' yo' pardon, mam, but if it was me ah woul'n't go wastin' my time out dere. Better spend de time preparin'." And seeing their horrified expressions, Melba put a comforting hand on Babs' arm. "Is all righty, all righty. We all sat out dem Betsy and David. Few trees down an' a bit o' floodin', but dem hurricane's no big deal. No cause'n for gettin' a stroke worryin'. You all got good shutters. Jus' be sure you got plenny food, water and candles, and oil for de hurricane lamps. Dat all yo' want. Better someone go drive down de shore to Whaletown and get supplied. Tin stuff, 'cause de fridge'll go wid de electrics."

"I don't believe this," Big Mike fumed. "We are just going to be abandoned on this fucking sandbank . . ."

"But can't we keep the generator on?" Babs' mind was on the food in the freezer.

"Sure t'ing, mam, but ev'ry once in a while it got to have oil and water, and yo' tank don' hold too much fuel. Den yo' cable from de shed to de house does be overhead; wind or limb off a tree can bring it down. Anyway, dat generator ain' too big. Yo got de fresh water pump for de toilets, de water heater, lights, freezer, fridge . . . it goin' burn up before it take care o' dem all one time."

Lawson and Belle joined the discussion. "She's right," Lawson said. "It'd be better not to turn the thing on except for emergency lighting."

"Maybe we should see if the power is back on and give it a rest right away," Belle suggested.

"Thank God we cook with gas," Babs said. "It's to be hoped there's plenty in the cylinder."

"Dolphin Poin', Dolphin Poin'," said the CB.

Melba hurried back into the kitchen and grabbed the mike. "Dat you, Chris'abel?"

"Yeah."

"You got t'rough already?"

"Naw."

"Den what happenin'?"

"Is Nassau callin' heah," Christabel said. "Dey tellin' me de airport is close'. All de airports in de eastern region is close'. You hear me?"

"Yeah," Melba said slowly. "I heah you. Dese folks gonna be too disappointed."

"Ah can' help dat," Christabel said. "I goin' now."

Melba replaced the microphone, and turned to face the white people. "You heah dat?"

"We did. Thank you, Melba, for trying." Big Mike sighed and shook his head in exasperation. "Well, that's that, folks. The decision's been made for us. We sit it out." He straightened his aching back. "Come on, you guys, let's finish getting these shutters up so these people can go home."

"What about the food supplies and the candles?" Babs asked. "Someone'll have to go down to Whaletown."

"Will it be safe going over Big Leap?" Dale peered at the rain lashing across the patio, and thought of the place where the island narrowed to such an extent that the sea came right up to the road.

"Give me a list and I'll drive down and see," Lawson volunteered. "I shouldn't think the seas are over the road yet; there isn't all that much wind."

"I'll come with you," Belle declared. "If that's okay with you, Babs."

"Sure. And listen, you'd better call Jo and explain the situation. Tell

152

her there's nothing to worry about." She looked at Lawson, seeking reassurance for herself.

Lawson grinned. "We'll be snug as bugs in rugs behind these shutters."

"Can I come too?" Tamsin asked.

Belle hesitated. There was no question how exciting the child would find the narrow roadway. It was always a fascinating place, with the clear, calm, aquamarine waters of the sound on the west while just yards away to the east the great dark blue swell of the Atlantic surged up to the rocks only feet below. But today the swell would be building to horrendous size, thrilling, exciting, but possibly, by the time they returned anyway, quite dangerous, even to Big Mike's heavy old Buick. No place for youngsters.

"No, honey," she said. "It'll be quite nasty and certainly too wet to get out of the car and see anything."

"Wouldn't it be quicker to take the boat across to Palm Island?" Dale suggested.

"No way," Big Mike replied. "Cross the entrance in that swell? Anyway, as soon as we've put the last of these shutters up, we're taking the boat out and tying her down."

"You can't take her out until Lawson gets back with the automobile," Dale objected.

"I'll borrow Josh's before he leaves. Now, have you got that list ready, Babs?"

Babs had been scribbling away. "I don't know if I've thought of everything."

"Candles?"

"Yes."

"Batteries?"

"Yes."

"Tinned soup and beans?"

"And some more Log Cabin Syrup for our breakfast pancakes," Tamsin reminded her grandmother.

"Oh, lover, I nearly forgot. We'll need some more eggs, too." Babs scribbled some more, gave Belle the list. "You hurry, and take care."

"We'll hurry." Belle kissed her mother. "Who's going down to tell the Robsons?"

Babs sighed. "I guess it'll have to be me. I tell you what: add a really strong sedative to that list, if you can find one. We may need it for Meg."

8.30 am

The drive down the coast wasn't easy with the windscreen smeared by the worn-out wipers as they were constantly deluged by the muddy water filling the holes in the road – Big Mike had bought the Buick third hand from the garage in Whaletown in preference to facing the expense of bringing a car across from the mainland. They bounced and weaved until a good stretch of tarmac carried them down to the neck, where they paused awhile, waiting to see if an occasional rogue wave might crash into the wide, deep gully below and swamp the road.

"The sea hasn't worked itself into a fuss yet," Belle said, urgency boiling inside her; if her first reaction had been a desire to stay and sit it out, she had got caught up in the general fear of the rest of the family, and now felt as apprehensive as them of what was coming. "Come on, Lawson, let's go."

In fact the seas were not yet high, although there was a considerable swell building from the south-east, but with the heavy rain clouds beginning to break up to allow patches of blue and even occasional glimpses of the sun, it was rather a beautiful day. Only right down on the sea horizon, hardly visible, there was a ridge of cloud so dark as to be almost blue black. They passed the neck without incident and arrived at Whaletown fifteen minutes later. A very strange Whaletown. Instead of the doors and windows of the brightly painted houses standing open, spilling children and animals on to the street, and women in gay dresses and bandannas sitting in the shade gossiping while they plaited straw for the baskets and hats they sold to tourists, everything was closed tight, windows boarded, chairs, tables and plant pots stowed away, and men working in the mud with ropes to tie down suspect roofs.

The little wooden supermarket was filled with chattering women in dripping dresses, fast emptying the shelves. Belle grabbed the last packet of candles while Lawson selected batteries, then they filled two store baskets with canned food and joined the long, slow, check-out line. In the end, Belle left Lawson to cope and, head down against the still gusty wind, pants soaked by the intermittent rain, made a dash up the hill to the post office. "I want to make an international call," she said, pushing wet strands of yellow hair from her eyes.

"Dere ain' no lines," the girl said, continuing to paint her nails.

"None at all? Who's using them?"

"Nobody heah," the girl said. "Dere ain' no lines out of Nassau. Everybody speakin' at once."

"Oh, for God's sake. How soon will there be a line?"

"Ah dunno. Maybe dis afternoon. But I got a list heah of twelve people wantin' to call out. You wan' me put you down at the end?"

Belle hesitated. But there was no way she was hanging about until this afternoon – or coming back into the village. Jo would just have to wait. "No," she said, and went back to Lawson.

The rain had virtually stopped as the car headed north again. Belle and Lawson watched anxiously as they came down the steep hill to the Big Leap neck, but the Atlantic was hidden from view by a high wall of rock.

"Nothing but spray seems to be coming over," Lawson commented, bending over the wheel. "So let's go."

Belle braced herself, feet on imaginary pedals, hands on the dashboard, eyes staring to the right, waiting for the ending of the rock wall to reveal the ocean.

The road was quite clear as the blue automobile careered down the hill through the potholes and levelled off on to the concrete surface. Then Belle saw it – a massive wall of surging green water rushing straight at them. "Foot down!" she shrieked. "Go, go, go!"

A quick glance through the window, and Lawson responded. "Jesus!" he yelled.

The giant wave crawled up the cliff face at the far end of the neck, higher and higher, then burst against the concrete structure of the bridge. An umbrella of water opened high over the road, hung there as though waiting for the car to reach it. They were committed; it was impossible to brake in time – they could only urge the Buick on, and pray.

The water descended on the roof like a mountain of rock. They were engulfed, swept across the road and crushed against the concrete parapet. Belle saw and felt it all happen as though in slow motion; felt herself being thrown into Lawson's lap, felt the car tip over, teetering on its left-hand wheels, held her breath waiting to crash, upside down, on to the rocks beneath, but miraculously the parapet held and she was flung back against the passenger door, Lawson with her, as the car righted itself. And amazingly, the engine was still running, Lawson having managed to keep his foot on the gas pedal. Now he regained the wheel and gunned her, pressed her on, sliding, swinging through the water – and then they were clear. The floor of the car was awash, the wipers were lying distorted on the hood, and the engine spluttered as they rolled up the hill on the other side, where Lawson let it coast to a halt.

Several minutes passed before either of them spoke, or moved. They had both faced an horrific death, and death is a very private thing. Then Lawson took Belle's face between his hands and kissed her, hard, on the mouth.

"Oh, lover," she said. "I thought we'd had it."

He grinned at her. "We are indestructible, you gorgeous critter. But I tell you what . . . I'm not crossing that bridge again until Faith is only a memory."

Dolphin Point, North Eleuthera, Bahamas

11.00 am

Belle jumped out into the mud to open the garage door for Lawson to drive the Buick in, but found the Mako had been stored in there, so he parked hard against the back of the house. They had passed Josh, Melba and Goodson on their way home to Whaletown just after leaving Big Leap, and stopped to warn them of the possibility of a big sea crossing the road; but they decided not to alarm the family any further by telling them of their experience; they were just thankful to have survived – and if the roof of the automobile had been dented by the water crashing on to it, Big Mike would hardly notice until after the storm.

The living room was quite a shock.

"Beds?" Belle and Lawson exclaimed together.

Babs laughed. "After you'd gone, Melba took charge. She said we'd not be able to get across to the bedrooms when the storm hit, so I'm afraid it's going to be dormitory style for the next couple of nights."

"Surely mattresses on the floor would have been enough?" Belle remarked, gazing at the furniture, all pushed back against the walls to make room for the beds.

"That's what we thought, but Melba decided otherwise. Thank heavens this is a big room."

"Isn't it gloomy." Dale peered at a wedge of daylight showing through a gap in the plywood boarding. "What the hell are we going to do with ourselves all day?"

"Play games and read stories," Tamsin informed her uncle gleefully.

"Oh, no, I don't believe it." His horror was only pretence.

"There's a hell of a lot of work to be done before we can play any games," Big Mike announced. "The stuff Lawson and Belle bought has to be unloaded and put away. And if for the next forty-eight hours we are all six of us going to be living in one room, then it's got to be kept tidy. Tamsin, you can help by putting the games on that shelf and picking up those shoes. Now, the rest of us have to stow all the patio furniture and get all the darned potted plants into the garage. The men will bring them up, and the women can put them away." He frowned at Belle. "You okay, sweetie? You look all shook up."

"Just wet."

"Well, change. The last thing we want is someone sneezing all over the place. Say, did you get hold of Jo?"

"No chance. There will be no lines before this afternoon at the earliest."

"Oh, heck," Babs said. "She'll be worried out of her mind."

"So, she'll just have to worry," Big Mike said. "Now remember, you two," he told the women, "I want the pots placed against the far wall of the garage, beyond the boat."

"That's extra work," Babs objected. "Why not leave them this side?"

"For everyone to climb over when they go to the john? That's the only one this side of the house. Or do you intend to trek outside through the storm to the bedroom every time you need a leak? Don't argue, woman, just do it."

For a moment Babs looked ready to retort angrily, then she grinned, and feigned a punch to his stomach. "You big bully," she said. "Okay, we'll do it your way. But you have a job to do too: go on down that hill and see if you can talk some sense into Meggie. She's having hysterics."

"Christalmighty! That's all we need," Mike growled, but he went off, while the others got to work, pretending it was enormous fun, laughing and teasing each other as trailing vines got caught around their feet and they tripped over the patio furniture or bumped into each other as they carted it inside – but Belle knew they were all frightened. Hurricanes were something beyond their ken; huge storms so violent that they hit the headlines, with reports of death and destruction left behind them. She and Lawson had seen the film *Hurricane*, on video, in which an entire island community had been reduced to an empty sandbank, and had wondered if a major hurricane could really be that bad, or if the film had just been an horrendous dramatisation – like *Jaws*.

Belle recalled newsreel pictures from Galveston and Houston when Alicia had struck there a few years before. There had been shots of vast seas, even bigger than she and Lawson had just seen, and flying debris which had shattered plate glass windows. Yet Melba and Josh, going home to their little wooden house which had apparently withstood all the hurricanes to hit Eleuthera for the past thirty years, had not seemed too perturbed.

Most frightening of all was the way the sky to the south-east was changing, filling with high, tumbled, hard-edged white clouds, behind which was solid black, and the way the wind would shriek into a squall every couple of hours, hurling raindrops at the shutters, and then die away into a flat calm. It was like watching the slow, relentless approach of a vast, ruthless enemy army, and already having to fight off its skirmishers.

*　　*　　*

157

Neal Robson's house was some twenty feet lower down the ridge than the Donnellys', on the bay side, which meant that it was actually somewhat sheltered from any winds blowing out of the Atlantic. Babs and Melba had been down earlier to make sure it was adequately stocked with candles and batteries, and the bathtub filled with water in case they could not pump any up from the cistern. In fact, with Neal's new shutters on the windows, the house looked as well protected and prepared as it could possibly be, but Meg still sat huddled on the settee, starting up with a moan every time there was a gust of wind. "I wish we were home," she wailed. "Oh, God, why can't we be home?"

Big Mike looked at Neal, who looked back and shrugged. "She really is scared. I wish to God we could have gotten her off the island."

"Well, we tried, goddamn it," Mike said. "Look, if it's getting you down, you can always move up the hill with us. We have lots of room, and I guess it could get a little scary here on your own."

"Oh, Neal . . ." Meg began, and then checked herself as her husband shot her a glance.

"We'll stay with our house," Neal said with dignity.

"Okay," Mike said. "But remember we're just up the road. I reckon we can talk to each other on the CB even with our aerials down; we're only a few hundred yards apart, for Christ's sake. Now Babs is expecting you for lunch, remember? See you."

He walked back up the beaten earth path – marked on the map as a road – between the casuarinas on his left and the rocks and ocean on his right, looking up at the sky, picking out the little streaks of white alto cirrus, the forerunners of real wind. He'd done that at sea, as a young yachtsman, when expecting a gale. Sure, he had a few butterflies in his stomach, but that was to the good. It was like waiting to drive off from the first tee on the morning of the club tournament, if you weren't keyed up you'd shoot a hundred.

So come on, you bastard, he thought. Come on and do your damnedest.

PARK AVENUE, NEW YORK

3.00 pm

Jo waited in all morning for the phone call from Eleuthera. When at lunch it hadn't come she called herself, and waited for even more than the usual hour while her ears were deafened by clicks and thumps. "I'm sorry," the American operator said at last. "It is quite impossible to get through to either Nassau or Eleuthera. The lines are absolutely jammed."

She felt as if she had been kicked in the stomach. Perhaps they had got out already. But if they had got out, and reached Miami or Fort Lauderdale, surely they would have called from there. Desperate for reassurance, she called Richard.

"I'm afraid it doesn't look too good," he told her. "Faith has just about laid Haiti flat. She was then packing winds of 100 miles an hour, and let's face it, a lot of Haiti is shanty town: almost any strong winds knock those huts down. But first reports of the damage are horrifying. Now she's moving straight up the eastern Bahamas."

"Is she maintaining these wind strengths?" Jo asked.

There was a moment's silence. Then she heard him give a kind of gulp. "She could be strengthening."

"What do you mean?"

"Mark called me an hour ago; he'd just got back from flying into the eye, and he reports sustained winds of 110 miles an hour. That is moving into Category Three country. We're talking now about a major storm. And I mean, major."

Jo felt herself breaking out into a sweat all over. But she kept her voice even with an effort. "Tell me."

"Well, it'll be a strong enough wind to lift a car off the road, and that sort of thing. But Jo, from your father-in-law's point of view, I guess as long as he's securely shuttered and has a good roof, the house'll be in no danger. Especially as, if the storm maintains its present course, he'll be in the western semi-circle. That's far and away the least dangerous place to be."

"But what about tidal surge?"

"Sure there'll be a tidal surge. You could expect nine to twelve feet above normal. On top of the waves, of course."

"Which will be how high?"

"Well . . . is there deep water right up to the point?"

"On the Atlantic side, yes."

"Then you could be talking about thirty-, forty-feet waves. But you told me your father-in-law's house is on a ridge . . ."

"Yes," she said. "Maybe twenty-five feet above normal sea level."

"Oh. How close to the sea itself?"

"Maybe a hundred feet."

"And there's no reef offshore? You're certain?"

"Not on the Atlantic side. For God's sake, Dolphin Point is *part* of the reef. Oh, Richard, I'm so frightened . . ."

"Take it easy, darling. Take it easy. That's the worst prognostication. For the dangerous semi-circle. On the western side of the storm the seas will be much lower. The wind strength, too. Look, I have to go now, to prepare the next forecast. There's a mass of information coming in. But I could get round later. Would you like me to do that?"

"Oh, yes, please," she said. "I want you here."

Dolphin Point, North Eleuthera, Bahamas

6.00 pm

Having disconnected his aerial, and laid it flat beside the house, Big Mike was unable to use the television, but he invited the Robsons over again that evening to listen to the news on the portable radio. There was a great deal of static, but they were able to gather that Faith was now packing winds of over 110 mph round her centre, which made her by some way the biggest storm to threaten the Bahamas since the 1930s, but that the centre was still well over 100 miles away and some 70 miles out to sea. He switched off the radio, and looked around the tense faces. Already the house was trembling to occasional gale force gusts, and there was a good deal of distant thunder, while every so often rain squalls swept across the headland.

"Okay, you guys, relax," he announced. "We're in the safe semi-circle. Sailors call it the navigable semi-circle. So by God, if a ship can be navigated we can sure as hell sit it out. Now, I reckon we should break open that case of champagne. Just to put ourselves in the mood."

"Good idea," Lawson agreed. "I'll do it."

"I've been thinking," Meg said. She was obviously full of Panadol and had been quite calm during the broadcast. Now her eyes were bright. "Wouldn't it make sense for us all to go into Whaletown, and put up at the hotel there?"

"I think she has a point," Neal said, determined not to show his own fear, but clearly nearly as terrified as his wife. "We can't do anything more to protect the houses, and no one is going to come along and break in while there's a storm raging. And in Whaletown . . ."

"You'd be one hell of a lot worse off," Big Mike pointed out. "What makes you think any house down there is safer than ours here? Most of them are built of wood. And it's virtually at sea level, too, more likely to be flooded."

"But there'd be other people . . ." Meg groaned.

"You don't call us people? The more people you accumulate in one place the more likely it is that someone's gonna get hurt."

Meg looked at her husband with beseeching eyes, begging for guidance.

Lawson came back from the kitchen with a tray of full champagne glasses, and Neal drank his at a gulp. "I guess Mike is right," he pronounced. "Of course we're safer here."

"Anyway," Lawson put in. "You'd never get across Big Leap, now. Those seas'll come way over it."

Meg gave another moan of sheer terror.

"The word is safe," Mike pronounced. "Here you are safe. Take my word for it. Any place else . . ." he shrugged. "I wouldn't like to say."

"This is French champagne," Babs remarked.

"So I lashed out. Actually, I forgot to tell you with all this going on; Michael has won his class in the Bermuda Race."

"Hey," Belle cried. "Ain't that something? Oh, I'll drink to Michael. I bet he's so happy he raced instead of coming down here."

"Even if Jo isn't," Dale said quietly.

"Well . . ." Belle flushed. "Racing, or doing something dramatic, is Michael's life. It always has been."

"I hope he gets home before this storm reaches Bermuda," Babs said. She wanted to change the subject, to avoid splitting the family into taking sides – remembering the telephone conversation at the hospital she had a terrible feeling that such a situation was going to arise anyway, in the not too distant future.

"My God! What's that?" Meg Robson screamed as there was a heavier than usual squall, accompanied by a crash from outside.

"A branch from a tree," Mike told her. "If we didn't need them for shade, I'd cut the whole damned lot down. It's impossible to tell which branches are getting ready to fall and which are good and strong. Anyway, none of them are going to do us any damage. Now, you folks staying to supper?"

"I think we'll get on back while we can," Neal decided. "Thanks anyway."

"But you'll remember we're here if you need us," Babs reminded him.

"Tell you what," Mike said. "Your generator running?"

"I was going to put it on when I got back," Neal said.

"You do that. Then give me a shout on your CB, so we can make sure we hear each other."

Neal nodded, and as it was not actually raining at the moment, escorted Meg outside.

Mike closed and bolted the door. "They're scared as shit."

"So are we all," Babs pointed out. "115 miles an hour. That sounds one hell of a lot of wind."

"We'll ride it, Babs," Lawson said reassuringly, and rumpled Tamsin's hair; the little girl had been strangely silent all evening. "Won't we, Tammy?"

"I wish Mommy were here. And Daddy," she added as an afterthought.

"Think of all the exciting things you'll have to tell them," Belle said. "Now, let's get supper." She looked at the door. "What's that roaring noise?"

"That's the sea getting up," Lawson told her. "The surf pounding on the rocks. It's going to be a wild night, folks."

The CB was spluttering. "Can you hear me, Mike?" Neal was asking.

Mike thumbed the handset. "Sure. Loud and clear. Well, maybe not all that loud or clear, but I sure can hear you. Keep in touch."

PARK AVENUE

7.30 pm

"Well, hi," Jo said, opening the door. "I didn't expect you so early."

"I came as soon as I could get away," Richard explained.

"And I'm glad to see you." Jo stepped back, and shrugged. "Owen Michael," she said. "This is a friend of . . . of your father's and mine, Richard Connors. You must have seen him on TV."

"Say, are you really the guy on TV?" Owen Michael shook hands, impressed. "Will you write in my autograph book?"

"Any time," Richard agreed.

"I'll get it." He ran for his bedroom,

Richard stared at Jo.

"It's okay," she said. "It doesn't really matter now."

"I wasn't thinking of that."

She frowned, suddenly realising that he looked as if he'd seen a ghost. "Richard? What's the matter?"

"I came over to tell you . . ." he hesitated.

"What?" she almost screamed at him.

"Faith's done a dirty on us," he said.

"What do you mean?"

"Well, she maintained her course until she was past the southern tip of Eleuthera . . . Eleuthera is damn near a hundred miles long, you know."

"I know," she said. "I holiday there, remember? It's just a glorified sandbank, hardly a couple of miles wide anywhere. So where's the storm gone?"

He swallowed. "She's turned due west."

"Due west? But . . . oh, my God!"

"Yes," he said miserably. "Her new track will take her right over central Eleuthera. That means North Eleuthera will be in the dangerous semi-circle. The most dangerous quadrant, in fact. And Jo . . . she's increased in strength again; winds at the centre are blowing 120 miles an hour."

"Oh, God," Jo said. "Oh, God." Her knees gave way and she sat down. "Do you think they know?"

"Well, surely they'll be listening to the radio for an update every hour," he said. "And they'll be taking every precaution."

"But there's nothing any of us can do," she moaned.

He sat beside her, put his arm round her shoulders, ignoring the boy who stood in the doorway. "Not a thing. Except pray."

Dolphin Point, North Eleuthera, Bahamas

9.00 pm

"Why do hurricanes always come at night?" Tamsin asked.

"Well, honey . . ." Belle, engaged in tucking her in, looked at her husband for an explanation.

"They don't," Lawson said. "They just seem more scary at night. Anyway, we don't even know this one is going actually to reach here tonight. These are just the first squalls."

"But maybe it will, and by the time you wake up tomorrow, it'll be all over," Babs said reassuringly.

Tamsin buried her face in her pillow. "I wish the thunder would stop."

"Thunder can't harm you, sweetheart. Now try to get some sleep."

Big Mike stood looking out through one of the sliding glass doors; there was a board for this too, but they had left it off until they knew the storm was close, to give them some light and occasional air. "First squalls, huh?" he remarked, and Lawson joined him. "What do you reckon it's blowing out there?"

"I reckon it's gusting about 70 miles an hour. If the forecasts are right, and the storm is out to the east, we shouldn't get much more than this. Say, there's a forecast on radio in a few minutes; we'd better listen."

"Forget it. We're in the middle of it. I don't want to listen to some kid in a snug studio telling me what I'm experiencing."

The thunderstorm was fierce, the flashes of lightning so bright they gleamed through cracks between the shutters and lit up the glass in the door as if someone had switched on the outside lights; the wind whined and the rain squall slashed at the house, but it passed over quickly enough, and it was obvious that the storm had not yet in fact arrived, but Lawson preferred not to argue with his father-in-law who, he could tell, was distinctly nervous.

And it was coming closer, as even after the squall had passed over and the wind dropped somewhat, the thunder continued to growl in the distance. Around the supper table the atmosphere had been one of tense joviality, tempered with apprehension, as they had eaten various leftovers which would go off first. Although, by mutual consensus, the Donnellys had decided against taking Lawson's advice and had topped the generator up with oil and water to keep it going – Big Mike having calculated there was just enough fuel to last the night and claiming that it was absolutely necessary to keep in touch with the Robsons – they knew that from tomorrow they would be without electricity, and probably for some days.

Big Mike continued to stare through the door. "I guess we should put this final shutter up."

"Not necessary, yet." Lawson shook his head. "Faith is still a long way away. Relax."

Mike glared at him, suddenly irritated by the casual confidence in the younger man's voice. "How come you know so much about it, eh?"

"I was in Martinique when David struck, oh, must have been more than ten years ago."

"Was that a big one?"

"He carried 100 miles an hour plus winds just like this one is supposed to do. Come on, Dad, settle down and let's talk about what we're going to do with all of that money lying just up the road."

It was the sort of chaff the entire family indulged in all the time, but Big Mike felt like hitting him. Then he remembered Korea. He could picture all the boys sitting around a tiny fire in the native hut laughing and leg pulling in whispers, no one giving a hint of his inner terror that at any moment a bunch of Commies might burst in on them after silently despatching the pickets. Fear is exhausting, it saps your strength, and you can't live with it, only alongside it. To survive, you must constantly deny it, boost your morale and your determination to win – and boost those around you as well.

So he grinned, and said, "Well, let's see now . . ."

There was a particularly loud bang, which brought Tamsin upright in her bed, weeping with terror. Mike and Lawson jumped to their feet, ran to open the glass door and peer out. They were between rain squalls, although the air was damp with the spray thrown up by the sea on the outer side of the point, so they ran outside in opposite directions, buffeted by the wind, which was now a sustained 50 miles per hour. Dale followed them, and Belle and Babs stood on the patio, Tamsin between them, wind whipping their hair and clothes, to look over the garden down at the dock. Usually the water was only three feet deep down there, and mirror calm; now four foot waves crashed over the wooden platform. Built of heavy planking nailed on to stout tree trunks drilled into the seabed, normally it looked sturdy enough to withstand anything ... but Belle wondered how long it could take a battering like this – or worse.

The men came back, looking wet and windswept, and mystified. "Can't imagine what the hell that was." Dale shrugged. "It can't have been on the property."

"Must have been," Babs said. "The noise seemed to come from right out here."

"Well, we couldn't find anything wrong."

Tamsin had to be tucked in again, but before she could settle a palm frond fell with a crack and a thump. "See, Tammy," Lawson told her. "Those fronds are only falling now, but when Faith gets closer they'll fly horizontally. That's why the windows are boarded up, so they can't smash through the glass."

"What would happen if they did?" the little girl asked. "Would the rain get in?"

"Worse than that. The wind would get in, and if it did that, it ... would blow everything all over the place." It could also well lift the roof off, he thought – but he didn't tell the little girl that; she was scared enough. He looked at his watch. "I'll just go check the generator."

He opened the door and stepped outside. He was actually enjoying the weather, having experienced such a storm before and survived without injury – although that had been in an hotel, with lots of expert help around, and the responsibility of survival someone else's. But he liked to feel the wind and sea spray swirling through the trees even when it wasn't raining. It went with his mood, his sudden surges of euphoria; he had had to live with debts and financial threats for so long it was almost unbelieving that the end was finally in sight.

DOLPHIN POINT, NORTH ELEUTHERA, BAHAMAS

10.30 pm

Lawson returned, dripping water.

"What's it like out there?" Dale looked up from his book.

"Wild, man, real wild. But beautiful, too."

"Guess I'll go take a look. I could do with some fresh air."

"For Christ's sake be careful," Big Mike warned. "We don't want to be sending out a rescue party."

"Forget it, Dad; I'm not a kid," Dale protested.

"You don't think?" For a moment there was a smile on Big Mike's face as he watched his son go. He loved all of his children. He had enjoyed his business career, often at the cost of time that could have been spent with his family. Now he was easing back, letting Mike junior take over – at his own pace – leaving himself more time with Babs and the kids. Not that they were really kids any more. Not even Dale, the baby of the family, the crazy, leggy youngster who had just walked off his campus one day because he'd been bored, who didn't seem able to stick at any job, who sometimes came home with that vague, staring look caused by marijuana – at least, Mike hoped it was only marijuana – yet who had so much love and caring to offer. He would find his way, given time – and understanding.

Just as Marcia had found hers. Marcia had never been an easy girl to understand, especially during the period when she had dyed her hair purple and worn it in those hideous spikes, with zany clothes to match. God, he had felt so embarrassed when she had arrived home one evening during a dinner party he and Babs had given for the new candidate for Governor of Connecticut. They'd had the eight people they most wanted to impress round that table when Marcia strode into the dining room and said, "Hi, folks!" He could remember the expressions on the guests' faces, ranging from astonishment to horror. He had wanted to get up and paddle her backside, but before he could get his breath back Babs had reacted, wonderfully, he agreed, looking back. She had risen and put an arm round the girl, immediately. "Hi, sweetheart, how lovely of you to look in on us. Let me introduce you." And she had led the monstrosity round the table, proudly introducing the 'artist of the family'. The effect had been miraculous, both on the guests and on Marcia, when everyone had understood she was not a creature from outer space and could actually speak intelligently, they seemed to warm to her and made complimentary remarks about her after she'd left. While as for Marcia herself, mysteriously the hideous hairstyle had vanished soon after and her gorgeous natural blonde colour was restored. Yes, Babs had handled that quite brilliantly, and now Marcia had her Benny and even a house of her own. And maybe kids, some day. It hurt Big Mike that only his Protestant English daughter-in-law had so far given him grandchildren.

He did not suppose Belle and Lawson ever would now, with their expensive lifestyle and their precarious realty business down in Nassau. Belle and Lawson worked and played too hard ever to consider kids, although they had a big house and lots of space, and a beach front – ideal for bringing up a family. It was a really lovely house, yet Mike and Babs never felt quite comfortable staying there, despite the invariable warmth of their welcome. It was too clean, too perfectly arranged, no untidy piles of books thrown on a chair; no sewing, no dog or cat. And they never had ordinary meals, or warmovers. Belle would speed home from downtown Nassau in her Lotus at 6.30 with four vacuum-packed New York strips and a brown store bag filled with exotic fruits, vegetables, and salad-makings, and bottles of French wine and, wearing a pretty pinny to protect her silk dress, would set the table and prepare her purchases for dinner within fifteen minutes, in time to greet Lawson's return and join her guests for drinks on the patio.

Mike gazed at them now, saw the look of affection they exchanged as Lawson, having dried himself, settled on the arm of Belle's chair, and then he found himself thinking about Belle's older brother. One couldn't help wondering if Michael should ever have had a family – he spent so little time with them. The kids seemed bright and happy enough, but the thought of Jo at her job all week, and their father even more preoccupied, made him feel angry and hurt for them. Big Mike didn't approve of working mothers . . . yet he couldn't blame Jo. He remembered her saying all along that she would go back to journalism, and at least she spent every moment of her spare or vacation time with her children – but Michael had never warned anyone that he would devote virtually all of his leisure hours to sailing, before he was married. Sailing! He had finally won the race he wanted more than any other. God, where was he now? Once this storm had passed Eleuthera there was every possibility it would make straight for Bermuda. But Michael would know how to handle it, wherever it was.

Michael Donnelly junior. Big Mike smiled, recalling how excited he'd been when the boy came home from college to say he'd like to take up the offer of a place in the firm. Michael Donnelly and Son, Stockbrokers. That had been a thrill. And so was the speed with which he had learned; nobody could have cottoned on to a business faster. Made one feel quite confident about handing over more and more clients, giving the boy responsibility. He allowed his eyes to drift to a framed photograph of his son, the blond giant of the family, skimming up the beach on his wind-surfer, strong, bronzed, laughing . . . and totally confident. Christ, he thought, what would I give to have him here now. He dropped his lids over stinging eyeballs.

"Mike, what is it? What's getting at you, lover?" Babs' hand stroked through his thinning hair.

"Guess I'm feeling bushwhacked after putting up those shutters. Gotten myself a bit of a headache."

"Man, it is blowing out there," Dale announced as he returned, dripping wet. "Where are the towels, Babs?"

Dolphin Point, North Eleuthera, Bahamas

11.30 pm

They called Neal, and were told everything was all right down there. "But say, have you had a weather update?" he asked.

"Who wants a weather update?" Mike asked. "We can give those guys one ourselves."

"I tried to get one on my portable," Neal said. "Only heard the end. Something about crossing the coast around midnight. Crossing what coast?"

"Search me," Mike said. "Must've got their numbers wrong. I'll give you another shout later." He replaced the handset and gazed at Lawson. "What coast? There isn't any land out there before Africa."

"Yeah." Lawson was frowning. "You don't suppose . . . hi, Dale, when you were outside just now, where was the wind coming from?"

"Ah . . . just north of east, I'd say."

"Oh, Christ!"

"What?" Mike asked.

"When I went out just after supper, it was still south-east. That means the storm has turned – west! The coast they're talking about is Eleuthera. It could be coming straight at us."

"What do we do?" Babs asked, trying to keep the panic out of her voice.

"We board up that last door," Lawson said. "Come on, Dale."

They went outside, and Tamsin raised her head. "Granpa? How will they get back inside when they've nailed up the door?"

"Through the garage, my love." He looked at the women. "Well, there's damn all we can do now except wait. I suggest we go to bed."

"I'm all for that." Babs disappeared into the garage cloaks and reappeared in a very respectable long cotton nightdress.

"I'm staying in this," Belle said; she had worn a glamorous silk kaftan all evening. "Now, whose bed is which?"

The living area of the house was a large inverted L. At the top of the leg was the kitchen, divided from the dining area by an island of counters, and beyond the dining table the heel of the L normally contained a cocktail table and chairs, and a collection of shells arranged on shelf units, whilst the remaining 'foot' held the cane settee, chairs, tables and a whole wall of books, a stereo music centre and the television set. The rectangle formed by the two inner sides was the garage.

That morning, with Melba's help, the television set and settee and armchairs had been pushed together into the cocktail area to make room for the beds; first a small one for Tamsin, then a small double for Babs and Mike – pulling rank, Belle called it. She and Lawson shared a single, while Dale settled himself quite comfortably on the settee.

"Mike! You haven't put your pyjamas on," Babs protested as he made to crawl across her legs.

"You're damned right I haven't," Mike retorted. "Nobody is going to part me from my pants tonight. Lord knows what I might have to get up and do in the middle of the night."

That raised some laughter from the others, but the tension was back and increased now they realised that they were not going to escape the full force of the storm, after all. The noise was tremendous. Certainly the wind was maintaining a good 60 miles an hour, with a lot more in the squalls, while the thunder rumbled constantly and the sound of the waves hitting the rocks was like a pride of lions growling outside the door, and the rain slashed against the shutters like machine gun bullets; there was hardly any let up in the squalls now. And there remained the awful feeling that the worst was yet to come.

Then the entire house seemed to shake with a sudden increase in wind.

"Oh, my God!" Babs said, and sat up. But they were all sitting up, save for Tamsin, who had mercifully fallen asleep.

"I'm going to put the kettle on," Belle announced. "It's nonsense to pretend we're going to sleep. How about some coffee?"

"Brilliant idea," Babs agreed, also getting up.

"I'll settle for whisky," Mike said, heading for the drinks cupboard.

"Pour one for me too, Dad," Lawson said, watching his wife as she moved around the kitchen, his body responding as it always had, ever since the day he had first seen her. In the privacy of their own room he would stand behind her, running his hands over the thin silk of that kaftan, feeling the smooth contours of her breasts, arousing her nipples into hard points. He would help her shed the garment, shed his own, and stand hard against her, holding her and kissing her before . . . instinctively he crossed his legs and glanced around at the others, wondering if his reaction had been noticed. He sighed. No chance tonight, even if there was a hurricane.

Belle made coffee, Mike poured whisky. Everyone was trying to act as normally as possible, but now the house was shaking regularly, making them wonder just how strong it would prove, and every so often there came a crash from outside, as of something being torn loose.

"Whatever kind of whisky is this, Dad?" Dale asked. "I never tasted anything like it before."

"Neither have I." Mike forced a laugh. "But it's half the price of the Haig down on Palm Island."

"Well, I guess it's good enough to get drunk on," Lawson said. "But what the hell it's going to do to our guts I wouldn't like to say."

They tried to settle down again; this time Mike switched off all the lights save for the one in the kitchen; the CB continued to crackle, and the fan to whirr, but he was really very pleased with the way the generator was standing up to all its extra work. So maybe it would burn out by morning; he'd cheerfully buy a new one just to get through tonight.

The house seemed to jump into the air. At the same time the entire room filled with brilliant light despite the shutters, and the accompanying peal of thunder was so loud it left them all dazed. Babs inhaled the scent of scorching wood. "My God!" she shouted. "We're on fire!"

Tamsin screamed.

"We've been hit, that's all," Dale snapped.

Mike was switching on the lights. "Well, they're still working." He stared at the television set, which was cracked and blackened. "Jees! The bolt must have struck the aerial, even lying down."

"Big Mike, Big Mike," said the CB. "You guys all right?"

"Sure we are," Mike told him. "You get hit?"

"No, but it sounded awful close."

"Yeah. We had it come to call. How's Meggie taking it?"

"I've put her to bed, with Panadol and whisky."

"Best thing. Keep in touch."

Babs had her arms round Tamsin, crooning reassuringly, but she looked at her husband, eyes wide with terror.

Big Mike looked back, and then twisted his head. "What the shit is that?" he demanded.

They all turned to look at the door, listening to a different sound to any they had ever heard before – except for Lawson.

"Sounds like an express train," Dale muttered.

"Christ," Lawson said. For all his studied insouciance, and his previous experience, his face was pale. "That's the hurricane wind." He attempted a smile. "I guess Faith has arrived, folks."

WEDNESDAY 26 JULY

Half Past Midnight

"Christ!" Big Mike mopped his face with a towel. The noise was continuous, whip-like cracks of lightning striking the rocks, the pounding of the rain on the shutters and the roof, the roaring of the seas, and above all the banshee-like howl of the wind, all merging into a mind-numbing cacophony. "How long does this last?"

"Maybe a couple of hours, until the eye passes through," Lawson told him.

"Well, I think everything's working like a charm," Belle declared. "We have electricity, we don't have any water leaking in, and we've only been struck by lightning once. Who's complaining?"

"Talking about the genny, it's damn near twelve hours since it's had oil or water," Lawson remarked. "I guess we'd better do it now, before the full force of the storm arrives, then we're in the clear until well into tomorrow."

"You mean, go out in that?" Dale asked.

"He's right," Big Mike said. "I'll do it."

"No way," Babs declared. "You think I'm in a hurry to collect your insurance?"

"If we don't do it, and she runs out of lubricating oil, or overheats," Mike said patiently, "she'll just stop."

"So let it," Babs said, refusing to concede that the generator might be a she. "We have the candles and the lamps."

"Look, lover," Mike said. "I promised Neal we'd keep in touch, didn't I? How the hell am I to do that without power?"

"I'll come with you," Lawson volunteered.

"And me," Dale said. "The three of us can hang on to each other. Form a kind of chain."

Babs looked at Belle, who shrugged; she was used to her menfolk being macho.

"Well, hurry back," Babs said.

"You bet."

The wind was now blowing full from the north-east, against the garage doors. One of the glass doors on to the patio, facing west and thus sheltered, had however been left with just boards covering the glass itself so as to allow an exit away from the wind if necessary, and the three men cautiously went outside, Belle closing and bolting the wooden-shrouded door behind them.

"Jesus," Lawson commented, as they pressed themselves against the wall. The scene in front of them was dramatic in the extreme. It was utterly dark, but yet bright as day every few seconds from the continuous lightning flashes. They looked at the normally calm waters of the sound, in which there were now six foot waves, topped with foaming whitecaps, tumbling over each other as they raced at the curving beach and pounded the sand, surging onwards into the palmettos and casuarinas that lined the coast. The dock had already disappeared, although whether it had broken up or was just under water was impossible to say. But several trees were down already. And this was the lee.

Big Mike took a long breath – there was too much noise to say anything – and flicked his flashlight on and off to tell the others he was going round the house. Clinging to the wall, they edged round the lounge and kitchen into the patio area; here they were still protected by the wall that connected the two halves of the house, but from here they had to leave that shelter if they were to reach the generator shed.

There were two doors leading out of the patio, one at each end of the wall. Mike signalled them to make for the south-facing exit, as the wind was still north-east. This they pulled inwards, and sidled through. Once again it was necessary to take a long breath before turning the corner of the wall, into the wind. Mike was first round, to be seized by a giant hand, it seemed, and flattened against the wall. The surprise, as well as the force being exerted on his body, caused him to let go of the flashlight, which fell to the ground, fortunately without smashing, and was retrieved by Lawson, on his hands and knees, before it actually blew away. Spreadeagled against the wall while still on his feet, hardly able to breathe because of the wind tearing at him, the flailing rain and spray stinging his face and chest, Mike gazed in horror at the garden, the uprooted trees, at the generator shed, still a hundred feet away, and then beyond. Another hundred feet across the unmade road the rocks began, and out there was the Atlantic. He had thought the waves in the sound big. Now he looked at immense walls of water, twenty, even thirty feet high, topped by another six feet of curling crest, smashing themselves into the rocks with a force which seemed to make the entire Point tremble, hurling spray hundreds of feet into the air. And already there was water on the road, flowing towards the drive and the generator shed.

"Holy shit!" he shouted. But nobody heard him as the words were torn away by the wind. Although the other two were clearly having the same emotions.

Mike tried to think, but could only understand the imminence of catastrophe. He didn't know if they could reach the generator at all with such a wind battering at them, but even if they did, how long would the engine continue working once salt water got at it? It was a diesel, and theoretically should run for as long as it had fuel, oil, water and air, but he had never seen one put to the test. And as Lawson had said, the full force of the storm had still not arrived – although obviously the wind was increasing every minute . . . and the seas were rising every minute, too.

There was a banging sound from the wall alongside them. Grateful for the recall, Mike signalled the others back round the corner, and they tumbled through the door to arrive beside Belle, both her hair and her kaftan blowing in the wind, and wielding a frying pan with which she had banged the wall.

"What the hell are you doing outside?" Lawson shouted at her.

"Neal is on the CB," she bawled back. "They're being flooded. And Meg's having hysterics. He wants out."

"Oh, Jesus," Mike growled. He put his mouth to his daughter's ear. "Okay, tell him we're on our way."

"So rain's getting in. What the hell is a little water?" Dale demanded as they crouched in the shelter of the bedroom wing, looking down the hill.

"I told them we'd get them out of there if they called for help," his father reminded him. "And now they're calling for help, right?" In fact he was suddenly alarmed by something he had earlier considered a good thing – the Robsons' house was at least fifteen feet lower than his own, so it didn't have to be rain water that was causing the flood. "Let's go."

"Crawl," Lawson told them. "Don't attempt to stand."

By staying on the bay side of the road, where the land sloped off to the west, they could obtain some shelter from the wind, and by keeping as close to the ground as possible they obtained even more. Mike was reminded of trying to stay alive in Korea, and in every way this was hardly less dangerous. Lightning was striking all around them, every few minutes a branch would come crashing down, while those that didn't were whipping to and fro immediately above their heads. To cap it all was the thunder booming like a continuous artillery barrage from close at hand, and the rain which thudded into their bodies like so many bullets.

But they made progress, creeping along the grass verge of the road to the dip down to the Robsons, and there falling to their stomachs in consternation. Below them, the sea had already crossed the road. The full force of the waves was still being contained by the rocks, although the surge was so high that spray was being flung over the crowns of the tallest coconut trees. But the overspill of each wave, some two feet of water, was flowing across the road, round the Robsons' house, and thence down the west side of the Point to the sea. Mike realised that quite apart from whatever might be happening at the neck, Dolphin Point was in danger of being cut in two right here, exactly where the Robsons' house stood.

The others understood that too, and they didn't have to be told to hurry. Lawson led the way, in his anxiety standing up, and promptly being knocked down by the next gust, which sent him rolling into the bushes before he came to a stop against a tree. Mike gazed after him in alarm, but Dale continued on his way, crawling, up to the flowing water, and then attempting to cross it. It swept him sideways, but down the Robsons' drive, which was resembling a fast running river, and up against the house.

"Oh, Christ!" Big Mike muttered, wondering if he was about to lose two-thirds of his family. But Lawson was sitting up, rubbing his head, and grinning ruefully at his own stupidity. A moment later they had joined Dale against the house; they were so wet anyway that the fact they were crouching in the middle of a stream hardly mattered. Cautiously they made their way round the house, and had almost reached the lee, when they were arrested by a huge ripping sound, as if a giant was tearing an enormous telephone book in two. Lawson recognised it, and looked up; Dale and Mike followed his example and watched the roof begin to peel back, like the lid being removed from a sardine can, while shingles tore off and scattered in the wind.

"Holy shit!" Mike screamed, and reached the door to bang on it. A moment later it was opened. Inside was dark, as even the candles had blown out; Neal's generator must have failed only seconds after he had called for help – no doubt because the sea had reached the shed. Mike shone his flashlight into the interior, saw the floor covered in water, saw Meg lying on her face on the settee, a pillow over head, rocking back and forth in terror. Neal was by the door, white-faced and shaking.

"The roof . . ." he gasped.

Mike nodded. "Let's get the hell out of here," he shouted. The tearing noise was growing louder.

Lawson and Dale dashed inside and pulled Meg from the settee.

"God!" she screamed. "God! We're going to die. Oh, God, we're going to die," she sobbed.

"No way," Lawson told her. "But we're going to get wet."

"Look out," Dale shouted, and the roof finally went with a gigantic whoosh, shattering itself in the trees. Rain and wind and salt spray descended on the wrecked house, like playfully destructive giants. Furniture was picked up, whirled around, and then hurled against the walls. Glass shattered. The heavy dresser came crashing down. Even Meg's screams were lost in the noise, as the humans were also thrown about by the spiralling wind, but she was clearly both screaming and sobbing as Mike and Dale dragged her, and themselves, to the door and out into the open. For the moment they were again sheltered by the walls, but that wasn't going to last very long, Mike knew, as he heard a tremendous crash from the windward side. The house was being systematically demolished. He pointed up the slope towards his own house, and Dale nodded; the water around them was getting deeper by the moment.

It was slow going. Meg was too exhausted to fight any more, either her rescuers or the elements. She didn't want to do anything but lie down with her hands over her head – and drown. Neal was hardly in better shape. And once they left the shelter of the wall they had to contend with both the wind and the water, nearly a foot deep and rising, increasing in force all the time. Slowly and painfully they half pushed and half dragged the Robsons up the slope, gaining some protection from the trees, yet knowing that at any moment one might come down on top of them; the noise of uprooting trunks almost competed with the howl of the wind. Mike gave a gasp of relief when a lightning flash revealed that his house was still intact. But the same flash showed him that water was swirling around the generator shed. His heart seemed to skip a beat. Here he was, rescuing his best friends – but what was he taking them to? If the water continued to rise . . . he panted in fear, and self-reproach, that he had exposed his family to this, gave a moan of temporary relief as the door opened to his bang, and Babs and Belle were there to help them inside.

Here too it was utterly dark, save for an oil lamp Belle had lit, which guttered and threw weird shadows on the wall. And there was water on the floor, but this was fresh, rain water driven under the shuttered doors by the force of the wind. Mike and Dale carried Meg to the nearest bed and laid her on it. "Oh, God," she moaned, while water drained from her hair and clothes into the mattress. "Oh, God! We're going to die. I know we're going to die."

Tamsin started to cry, and Babs sat beside her to comfort her.

Dale and Mike had forced the door shut and shot the bolts, and Mike could catch his breath. "Give Meg a shot of brandy, Belle," he said. "Come to think of it, we'll all have one."

Belle poured.

"The house is gone," Neal said, sitting down with his hands dangling between his knees. "Just like that."

As if they hadn't seen it go, Mike thought.

"Here, drink this," Belle said. "It'll make you feel better. Dad. Dale. Law . . ." Her voice suddenly stopped, as she peered into the gloom. "Where's Lawson?"

"Eh?" Mike jerked his head. "He was just behind us." He looked at his son. "Wasn't he?"

"I don't know," Dale said. "I never saw him after that wind got into the house."

"Lawson!" Belle gasped. "Lawson!" she screamed.

"For Christ's sake, he's just outside." Big Mike wrestled with the door, and got it open, peered into the raging darkness. He felt sick. He knew Lawson wasn't there.

"You left him behind!" Belle shrieked. "You left my husband behind!"

"He must have fallen," Babs said reassuringly. "He'll be all right. Lawson is indestructible."

Mike looked at Dale, who looked back. Anyone who had fallen and been unable to move in the vicinity of the Robsons' house would have drowned by now.

"Indestructible," Belle muttered. "He said so, by the bridge. But he's out there, maybe hurt." Her voice started to rise again. "I must go to him."

She ran for the door, and her father caught her round the waist. "Don't be a fool. You'll be killed."

"Lawson is out there!" she screamed at him.

"I'll go see. I'll get him," Dale volunteered.

"No," Babs snapped. "No way!"

"He's my husband!" Belle snarled at her.

"And Dale is my son," Babs snapped back.

"We have to try," Big Mike said. "Come on, Dale." He shuddered as he opened the door. The thought of facing the horror out there was nearly more than he could stand.

But even worse was the horror looming in the comparative safety of the building. His family was beginning to disintegrate. And the house too. Perhaps they were all going to die – not only Lawson.

PARK AVENUE, NEW YORK

12.00 noon

"Reports from the Bahamas," said the NABS newsreader, "are uncertain at this time as to the full extent of the damage caused so far by Hurricane Faith. The capital, Nassau, seems to have escaped the worst of the storm, which passed more than 50 miles to the east of New Providence Island, although there has been considerable damage from the very heavy rainfall, and also the storm surge. It seems certain that Cat Island, Long Island, and the Exuma Cays have all suffered extensive damage as well. However, it is feared that the worst effects of the storm may have been felt on the large island of Eleuthera, as owing to the late alteration in Faith's course the eye passed over the very centre of the island, at about two o'clock this morning."

"Oh, my God," Jo whispered, sitting and staring at the screen. Owen Michael reached out and clutched her hand. Neither had done more than doze in their chairs all night, waiting desperately for news, which had never come.

"All contact has been lost with the northern half of Eleuthera," the newsreader continued, "but it is estimated that in the vicinity of the eye the wind force touched 130 miles an hour, and the results could have been catastrophic. I have with me here our weatherman, Richard Connors. Good morning, Richard."

"Good morning, Dave." Richard, Jo knew, had been on duty all night, but he looked fresh and clean shaven, if unusually serious.

"Now, Richard, first of all, can you tell the folks what sort of weather those people on North Eleuthera might have experienced, at the height of the storm?"

"As you've just heard, Dave, there would have been exceptionally heavy rain." Richard spoke into the camera, looking directly at Jo. "Accompanied by almost continuous thunder and lightning."

"How about the wind?"

"130 miles an hour," Richard said. "That is enough wind, Dave, to blow a man off his feet, and then some. Enough to overturn any mobile home. Enough to blow or suck out any unshuttered window."

"TV aerials?"

"Certainly lost."

"What about the buildings themselves?"

"Solidly built and well-shuttered stone structures should have been all right," Richard said. "I say shuttered, because once the wind with that kind of force gets inside any house, it can act like a tornado, and lift everything in there right out. The building really wants to have every single window and door on the windward side shuttered tight, and those to leeward ready to close the moment the eye passes through and the wind changes direction."

"So you reckon that if the folks on Eleuthera knew what was coming at them, and took the proper precautions, they'd have been all right."

Richard sighed. "I'm afraid there's no guarantee of that, Dave. You see, wind doesn't actually do the greatest damage in a hurricane, so long as it's kept out. It's the storm surge that takes lives and destroys property. For the folks on Eleuthera, everything will have depended on their height above sea level, and their distance from the sea. Unfortunately, as I understand it, it's not possible to get very far from the sea on that island. With a storm which has been building for as long as Faith, and packing winds of 130 miles an hour, one can expect a storm surge of maybe 15 feet above normal, and that's the surge I'm talking about. Close to the shore you'd have to add waves of maybe 30 or 40 feet on to that. Now, according to my map, there are considerable areas of Eleuthera which are only a few feet above sea level, much less 20 feet."

"So what kind of conditions could people in those areas expect?"

"Those on the eastern, windward side of the island, or on exposed headlands, could expect to have seas like that breaking around their houses. Those on the leeward side would be better off, but could still expect to be flooded."

"And would solidly built stone houses stand up to 20 foot waves?"

"I'm not an architect, Dave, but I don't think any house, in Eleuthera or anywhere else, is built to withstand that kind of force. Even breakwaters, designed to keep out the sea, are sometimes breached by seas that big."

"So you think the Nassau authorities are right to expect that there has been a major disaster up there."

"I hope and pray not, Dave. But I think we have to brace ourselves for the worst."

Owen Michael's fingers were biting into Jo's arm, and she freed herself and put her arm round his shoulders. Even though Richard had earlier warned her what he would have to say, each word had still thudded into her brain like a bullet.

"Now, Richard, latest reports indicate that the storm has turned north again after passing over Eleuthera. I don't want to pre-empt your forecast, but can you tell us where she is now?"

"Sure." Richard got up and walked to the wall map, which was already marked with an X. "She's right there at this moment. The co-ordinates are 27°18'N. latitude, and 77°3'W. longitude. That puts her approximately 250 miles east of Melbourne, Florida, so you see she suddenly gathered speed after striking Eleuthera, and is in fact now travelling at more than 20 knots."

"Is that good, or bad?"

"On the whole, good; it gives her less time to build any more."

"So does she pose a threat to the mainland United States?"

"At this moment, no. There's a gale warning up along the entire Florida and Georgia coasts, and the folks down there are getting some pretty strong winds. But they're on the weaker side of the system. As long as Faith stays offshore to the east, they're not going to suffer anything more than some beach erosion. The big winds and seas are out to the north-east of the centre."

"Well, that's good news, anyway. So . . . any ideas where this lady is going next?" Dave asked.

"Well, she's travelling just east of north at this minute, so I reckon the folks in Bermuda need to look out . . ."

"Oh, shit!" Owen Michael muttered. Jo did not admonish him.

". . . but she was doing that before, and then suddenly made west. That could happen again."

"You mean she could still come back and hit the States?"

"Dave, even if she maintains her present course, she will brush Cape Hatteras. I reckon we need to keep a close eye on her for the next couple of days."

"And will she maintain her present force, do you think, or will she weaken as she hits the cooler waters of the North Atlantic?"

The camera suddenly zoomed in to Richard's face as he stared into the lens; the director had obviously been briefed as to what the answer would be. "There are no cooler waters up here right this minute," Richard said. "This is the hottest summer we've had in years, and the water temperatures are way above normal. As long as Faith is moving fast she should remain as she is, but she certainly won't weaken – and if she slows down again, she could well build."

"Build to what?"

"Right now she's blowing around 140 miles an hour at the centre. If she works up winds of more than 150 mph, Dave, the sky's the limit. Faith is already a big, dangerous storm. She could become one of the biggest storms we've ever seen. There's no way of telling yet. We just have to watch what she does, very carefully, over the next few days."

"And we know that you're going to do just that, on our behalf, Richard. Thank you. That was Richard Connors, our weather expert, warning us all to keep an eye on a certain lady named Faith. Now, finally . . ."

Jo flicked the switch.

"Heck, Mom," Owen Michael said. "Do you think Tamsin is all right? And Granpa and Granma?"

"I wish I knew. We must just . . ."

The phone buzzed. Jo leapt out of her chair and ran to it.

"What's the news from Eleuthera?" Michael asked.

Her heart slowed with disappointment; she had really hoped, quite unreasonably, that it might be his father. "There is none. All communication has been cut."

"That's what they're saying here too," Michael agreed. "We'll just have to assume they're all right."

"You know Tamsin is down there?"

"Of course I know Tamsin is down there. You sent her, remember?"

"With your parents."

"That doesn't alter the fact that the poor kid has had at the very least a traumatic experience, while you've been sitting on your ass in Manhattan."

"If you just rang up to abuse me," Jo said, "I suggest you get off the line. But perhaps, before you go, you might like a word with your son."

"Hi, Dad," Owen Michael said. He had been bewildered by what he had heard of the exchange, but there could be no doubt that he wanted to hear his father's voice.

"Hi, son," Michael said. "How was the operation?"

"Not so bad, Dad."

"And is all going well, now?"

"Pretty good. Mom says we may be able to go down . . . oh, I guess we won't, after all." He looked at his mother.

"We'll have to see," Jo told him.

"Yeah. Where are you now, Dad?"

"In the Royal Bermuda Yacht Club. We're going to stock the boat this afternoon and leave at dusk."

"Leaving? Where are you going?"

"We're coming home," Michael told him. "We don't want to be here when Faith arrives."

"Heck . . . are you sure you can make it?"

"Sure I'm sure. If necessary we'll motor; we're taking on extra fuel. Oh, sure, we'll be home in about three days. We'll beat that storm. Tell your mother I'll call her from sea tomorrow, and that she'd better have an update on the Eleuthera situation for me by then. Got it?"

"I'll tell her, Dad. Have a good trip."

"Looking forward to it," Michael said.

"Give me that." Jo took the phone away from her son. "Listen, you should stay in Bermuda until the storm is past."

"Stay here? You have got to be crazy. This island is totally exposed. I told the boy, we'll be home long before that hurricane gets here; it's travelling north-east, we'll be heading north-west, and we'll have a 48-hour start. What I want is the earliest possible news from Eleuthera. I'll call you tomorrow."

The phone went dead.

Jo replaced the receiver and looked at her son.

"Mom," Owen Michael asked. "Why did he sound mad at you?"

"Because he is mad at me, I guess."

"But why?"

Jo rumpled his hair. "Grown-ups are always getting mad at each other, Owen Michael. You enjoy being young while you can."

The phone rang again, and again she grabbed it.

"Hi," Richard said.

"Oh, thank God," Jo gasped.

"I've been trying to reach you for the past five minutes."

"I had Michael on the phone. Richard . . . is there any news?"

"Nothing as yet. But listen . . . I spoke to Mark just before the news programme. It was one of his buddies reported the northern turn and the present position, but he's out again this afternoon to make another check. I asked him to take a close look at Dolphin Point when he's done. He'll tell us what's happened."

"Oh, thank God, Richard. Thank God!" But, she wondered, did she really want to find out?

THE BAHAMAS

4.00 pm

"That system just seems to get bigger and bigger every time we look at it," Landry remarked.

"It *does* get bigger every time we look at it," Mark agreed.

They had emerged from the clouds and climbed to twenty thousand feet, yet virtually as far as the eye could see beneath them to the north was white and black, swirling, looking just as menacing as it was possible for a weather system to be. Even at their height there was the occasional buffet of wind spiralling out of the eye.

"Take those co-ordinates, Mac," Mark told his navigator, "and send them back to Coral Gables." He was without Eisener on this trip; the doctor was in constant demand to appear on television screens throughout the eastern states. "I think we can confirm that she's still on track."

The co-ordinates were pushed in front of him. "She seems to be slowing up again, though," Mackenzie said.

"Yeah. That'll make everybody real happy. Okay, gang, let's take a look at Eleuthera."

He put the aircraft into a steep turn, and they raced to the south. Below them the clouds started to break up, and as they sank into them they could see patches of white-streaked blue water. Now the buffeting increased, but it was mild compared with what they had experienced earlier that afternoon when they had flown into the eye.

"Land," Landry commented.

"The Abacos." Mackenzie had returned to the flight deck after sending off the message. "They don't look too bad."

The amphibian had sunk lower yet, and was now flying at 5000 feet. Below them the seas were still tumbling, but the settlements they passed over looked reasonably intact, although they saw several boats washed ashore, and one or two lying sunk in the clear water.

South of Abaco was the twenty-mile wide north-east Providence

Channel, deep water, in which the white-topped waves could be seen as the aircraft dropped to 3000 feet. And by now North Eleuthera was in sight. Mark turned to the left, to pass down the eastern, Atlantic side of the island, heard a low whistle from Landry as they looked down on Palm Island, the roofs torn off, the collapsed buildings, the fallen post office aerial, the wrecked boats and overturned vehicles . . . but there were people down there too, working at clearing the damage; one or two waved at the plane. Palm Island was some forty feet or so above normal water level, and the town was on the bay side – it had obviously escaped the worst of the surge.

Mark waggled his wings and went on. His chart told him he was over Dolphin Point, thrusting out into the Atlantic, the waves surging at the narrow entrance into the sound, and smashing on the rocks. The Point was quite heavily wooded with pines, and coconuts by the shore, and he looked at what might have been a gigantic lawn cut by an equally gigantic motor mower; there were scattered trees everywhere. He also looked at an island, for it had been entirely cut off from the mainland by a torrent of water which was still pouring across from the sea into the sound. There was no sign of habitation at all.

"Lucky nobody lived there," Landry commented.

"Somebody did," Mark said quietly, his heart lurching. His glide down had carried him ten miles south of the Point, and now he banked again, over the airstrip – which had turned into a lake.

"Holy shitting Moses!" Mackenzie commented.

They looked down on Whaletown, or what was left of it. The settlement seemed to have divided into two parts; a wall of raging sea had burst through from the Atlantic side, just as at the Point, carrying everything in its path into the calm waters of the bight enclosed by the curve of Eleuthera. The shattered remains of houses and cars could be seen in the shallows, and as the plane dipped lower yet, floating bodies could also be discerned. But there were also people on the land, waving to attract their attention.

"Tell Sparky to call Nassau," Mark snapped. "Tell them there is a major emergency at Whaletown and that Palm Island will also need assistance. Relay that message to Key West as well. They'd better send some medical supplies just as fast as they can. But they have to use seaplanes or amphibians – the airstrip is out of action." He flew lower yet, waggled his wings again to reassure the people that help was on its way, and then turned back to the north and west.

Now they were only a thousand feet up, following the remains of the road. Dolphin Point was cut off twice, for the bridge connecting it to the mainland had also collapsed. Lower and lower Mark dropped the plane, peering down into the wrecked foliage beneath him.

"Hey," Landry snapped. "There's someone there."

"Eh?" They were out over the bay. Mark put the plane into another steep turn, dropping now to 200 feet and throttling back.

"There!" Landry pointed.

Something white was being waved, a few hundred yards north of where the water had broken through. Mark turned again, studying the bay now; since the eye had passed through, the wind had begun blowing from the opposite direction, west, which meant that the bulk of Eleuthera had been between it and the sound, and the seas in there had gone right down, although it was by no means calm. "Check the chart," he told Mackenzie. "What kind of depths can we expect?"

"Eight to ten feet on average. But . . . Christ, you're not thinking of putting her down? There are sandbanks all over the place."

"And you've no clearance," Landry pointed out, deciding against reminding his skipper that he would also be breaking every rule in the book.

"Fuck that," Mark said. "How long do you think one or two people stranded there are going to survive? The help is gonna go to places like Whaletown first. And I have an idea those folks are Americans. You guys with me?"

Landry and Mackenzie looked at each other. "You're the skipper," they said together – even though all their careers were at risk should he pile up.

"Okay," Mark said. "Let's dummy it first time."

He took the amphibian down almost to water level while they studied the changing colours beneath them. "That looks best," Landry decided. "Nearly unbroken green for a good half mile."

"Kind of narrow," Mackenzie objected.

"It's the best we have," Mark said. "Get your belt on."

He turned the plane yet again, and now definitely set her down. Into the wind, she almost skimmed the few remaining trees on Dolphin Point, then the floats touched the water, sending huge spumes of spray away to either side, and the hull bumped again and again on the shallow waves. But he held her on the narrow ribbon of green water – there were patches of white to either side – and she came to rest, rising and falling on the gentle swell. Mark turned her, and motored back as close to the Point as he dared, then closed the throttles. "Get that anchor down," he told Landry, "and let's prepare the boat."

The inflatable was thrust through the door, and the cord pulled; it burst into rubber. Landry had already unclipped the outboard, and passed it down to Mark, who was first in. "Okay, Bob," he said. "Mac and I will go see. You and Sparky stay here."

The outboard chattered, he took the tiller, and they moved towards the shore.

"What the hell is that?" Mackenzie asked as they entered the shallows.

"Looks like an automobile," Mark said, steering to avoid the upturned vehicle, which had been carried some thirty feet from the shore.

"You're damned right. A blue Buick. How the hell did it get there?"

"The sea, I guess. And I'll tell you something, Mac: I have an idea it's gonna stay there."

"There's someone!" Mackenzie pointed as they neared the beach, going dead slow now, for here there was all manner of debris, from house timbers to pieces of furniture, some with sharp enough edges to puncture even the thick rubber.

Mark stared at the tree line, and the man who stood there, waving his shirt. He was a very young man, although haggard and drawn.

"Thank God!" the man said. "Oh, thank God," staggering down to meet them.

The dinghy grounded, and Mark stepped into the shallow water with the painter to drag it clear. "You alone?"

"No," Dale said. "No, there are others."

"Where?"

Dale gestured at the trees, and Mark followed him, Mackenzie at their heels. They looked to their right, at where the sea still flowed into the bay; there had been a house there once – they could still see part of the walls.

They climbed a shallow slope, picking their way through tangled fallen trees and branches, gazed at the wreckage of another house. This one had stood up to the wind and sea better than the first, but was still virtually collapsed, two walls and the roof down, furniture scattered in every direction; a 24-foot Maki, its hull stove in, rested in the centre of what had been the kitchen. Farther off, towards the head of what had once been a drive, a large generator rested on its side; there was no evidence that it had ever been enclosed in a shed.

"Over here," Dale said.

Mark parted the bushes, and looked at the people, who were huddled in the shelter of the two remaining walls. He guessed they must have been there for more than twelve hours, and the rain had probably only cleared about four hours before. There was a middle-aged man, heavily built, but somehow shrunken by his experiences; another middle-aged man, much smaller, whose face was streaked with tragedy; a middle-aged woman, eyes red with weeping, clutching a little girl to her breast – the girl stared at Mark with enormous eyes; another middle-aged woman, who did not seem aware of his presence at all, just rocked back and forth, while tears streamed from her eyes; and there was a quite beautiful younger woman, wearing the remnants of a torn kaftan and nothing else, who also seemed oblivious of his presence – she wasn't weeping, and her face was composed, but it was also utterly closed, as if the world outside her tortured mind had no meaning.

"Can they move?" Mark asked Dale in a low voice.

"I think so."

"Well, let's get them down to the beach. We can be in Miami in half an hour. Say, I sure am glad that you all survived."

Dale's shoulders sagged. "We didn't all survive," he said.

PARK AVENUE

6.30 pm

Jo's hands trembled as she picked up the phone; if the night had been bad, the long afternoon's wait had been worse.

"Jo?"

For a moment she didn't recognise his voice. "Dale?"

"Yeah."

"Oh, Dale! Where are you?"

"Miami."

"Oh, thank God for that. Tamsin . . ."

"She's okay. A bit shocked, I guess. I guess we all are."

Waves of relief made Jo quite dizzy; she felt sick with joy, had to force herself to speak rationally. "But you got out. Are the planes flying?"

"No. We were brought out by a navy amphibian on weather patrol."

"Mark Hammond!" she shouted. "Oh, thank God for Mark. Dale, was there much damage?"

He gave what might have been a bark of laughter. "Yeah. You could say that."

"Tell me!"

"There's nothing left, Jo."

Jo frowned at the phone. "What do you mean, nothing left?"

"I mean, nothing." Dale's voice rose an octave, and she realised he was quite close to hysteria. "Every goddamned, fucking thing has been blown flat."

"The house?" She was still incredulous.

"Yeah. The sea just came over the point."

"Oh, my God. The Robsons . . .?"

"Even worse."

"But they're all right?"

"If you can call it that. Meg's in hospital, under sedation. I reckon Neal should be there too."

"What about Babs and Dad?"

"They're not too good, either."

"But Tamsin's okay. Can I speak with her?"

"She's been put straight to bed. I guess we're all suffering from exposure. And shock. Listen, we're coming up tomorrow morning. Can you meet us?"

"Sure. I'll let Marcia know, too. Oh, I can hardly wait."

"Yeah. Listen, bring two cars. We'll have Belle with us."

"Oh, great. Yes, I'll have Marcia bring her car as well. Lawson's gone straight back to Nassau, is that it?"

There was a short silence. Then Dale said, "Lawson didn't make it."

"He . . ." Jo swallowed. "You mean . . ."

"I mean he's dead. Drowned."

"But how? I mean . . ."

"He's dead!" Dale shouted. "I don't know how it happened. Nobody knows. One minute he was there, and the next he wasn't. He must have fallen and been washed away by the sea. We just don't know."

"Oh, God," Jo said. "Oh, God. Then Belle . . ."

"Yeah," Dale said. "We'll see you tomorrow."

The phone went dead, but it was several seconds before Jo replaced it.

NATIONAL AMERICAN BROADCASTING SERVICE OFFICES, FIFTH AVENUE

7.00 pm

J. Calthrop White beamed at his telephone. "But that is great news, Mr Palmer. Great news! Monday, you say, that's fine. Yes, sir, just fine. Say, any words from the boss? . . . Yeah, I guess he'll be in touch as soon as communications are restored. I guess he had a little rain down there, eh? Haw, haw, haw. Anyway, you did it without him. My congratulations, Mr Palmer." He replaced the phone, grinned at Kiley. "Palmer has Kohler's picking up seventy-five per cent of that issue. Now that is a stockbroker. I'll tell you, Kiley, I have been shitting blood this past fortnight with that oaf Donnelly and his shitty son away, but by Christ their business runs better without them. Now you listen to me: I want our bid on the desk of the Licensing Authority in the UK first thing Monday morning. Get on to the bank and tell them we need a guarantee of $100 million, and that it'll be supported by Kohler's. Got me?"

"Yes, sir, JC." Kiley hesitated. "I have Connors outside."

"Well, send him in. Send him in." White leaned back expansively, grinned at Richard as he came in. "Richard!" he said. "I saw your forecast. You really socked it to them. Yes, sir. Now everyone's talking about this hurricane thing. What's the latest word on it? Is it really as big as you said?"

"She's a big system, JC."

"Bigger than Gloria?"

"She's about the same strength as Gloria right now, but she covers a bigger area. And she could deepen further. In fact, I think she will; she's still over warm water."

"And heading at us?"

"No, sir. Thank God! She's moving slowly north by east, which is presently taking her parallel with the coast, at a distance of about two hundred miles."

"Ah." White looked somewhat disappointed that imminent and newsworthy catastrophe could not be expected. "But in your forecast you said she could still come ashore on the mainland."

"It's a possibility."

"But you wouldn't rate it more than that. You reckon there's no real danger to the mainland."

"I didn't say that, JC. We won't be out of danger until that storm is past Newfoundland. She turned west once, she can do so again."

"It could present us with a tricky situation," White mused. "As I say, this storm is causing a lot of comment, so much so I have half a mind to slot you in for another of your chats, slightly expanded, maybe, to talk about this storm in particular, and what it could do."

"What she already has done, JC, in the Bahamas."

"Yeah. But nobody cares what happens down there. It's what could happen up here that people want to know about. But we have to be careful. If we start hollering wolf, and nothing happens, well . . . we lose viewers. There were adverse comments on your talks for that very reason, remember, about how you were trying to be sensational."

"I remember," Richard said, grimly. "Everything I said was proven fact."

"Maybe. But these ginks up here have never seen a hurricane, and just don't believe anything can be that fierce. What I am getting at is, if we go to town on this one, she has to be a threat, at some time in the next few days, or we are going to have egg all over our faces. How do you reckon the chances of that?"

"I think she's a potential threat now, JC. I would like to see the mayor take some precautionary steps, tomorrow."

"You would? What kind of precautionary steps could he take? How do you stop a hurricane?" White smiled at the concept of Mayor Bill Naseby holding up his hand like some kind of latter day Canute and commanding the winds to cease blowing.

"Well, at least he could hold a comprehensive review of his evacuation plan, and publicise it, so people would know when to leave and what route to take."

"What do you mean, evacuation plan?"

"Just that, JC. A plan to evacuate all low-lying areas of New York in the event Faith were to prove a serious threat."

"What kind of area are we talking about?"

"Well the whole coast and Jamaica Bay area. And half of Manhattan is less than 50 feet above water level; that could all be flooded."

"You mean he has a plan to evacuate Manhattan?" Kiley spoke for the first time.

"I have no idea. But he should have."

J Calthrop White stroked his chin, the light of battle in his eye; he loved a political wrangle, and he was no friend of the Mayor's party. "That could be interesting," he said. "And give us an angle. I tell you what you do, Richard. First thing tomorrow you round up some data. Get one of the regular news team . . ." He looked at Kiley.

"What about Kimmelman? He's as sharp as a razor, and he's been an investigative reporter for some time. In fact, he could handle the whole thing while Richard got on with . . ."

"No," White said. "This is Richard's baby. But I agree, send in Kimmelman as a back-up. Take him off whatever he's doing now, and send him with Richard to do a little sleuthing." He pointed his gold pencil at Richard. "Find out what plans there are, if any. Try the police and the fire department, and anywhere else you can think of. And try the Mayor's Office, too. Then report back here, and we'll make one or two plans of our own."

"Yes, sir," Richard said enthusiastically.

The pencil continued to point. "But just bear in mind that if we take on City Hall and make this into an issue, such as pointing up the inadequacy of their plans, we have to win. That means we have to be sure of our facts. Don't let me down on this. And we need that hurricane to come at least as close as Gloria did."

Or I'll be on the next plane down to Miami, looking for my old job back, Richard thought. "I won't let you down, JC," he promised. Although how the hell he was supposed to tell Faith what to do he had no idea. He frowned as he gained the elevator: did JC really want Faith actually to strike the city, in order to make a political killing?

9.00 pm

"Hi," Richard said on the phone.

"I thought you were coming over," Jo said.

"Sorry, I can't tonight. I have a lot on. JC is again looking on me with a smile."

"Oh," Jo said. "Because of Faith?"

"Yes. Jo . . . I spoke with Mark. Jo, I'm most terribly sorry about your brother-in-law."

"Yes," she said.

"But at least Tamsin is safe."

"Yes," Jo said. "I'm eternally grateful to Mark for what he did. I want you to tell him that, Richard. But right now, I don't know whether to laugh or weep. I guess I've been doing a bit of both. So has Owen Michael – I had to give him a sedative and put him to bed."

"It's that kind of situation. I could drop by tomorrow."

"No," she said. "I'll be tied up tomorrow. They're coming up."

"Oh," he said. "It's going to be a rough day."

"Yes," she agreed. "Look, I'll call you when I can."

"Okay. Say, where's that husband of yours? Still in Bermuda?"

"No. I guess he's left by now."

"Left to go where?"

"Return to Newport."

"Can you get in touch with him?"

"I suppose so . . ." Jo snapped her fingers; she should have done so before, to let him know his folks were all right.

"Well, I would if I were you, and tell him to stay put. At sea is no place to be with Faith about."

"I've already told him that. But as I told you before, he makes up his own rules."

"Then he's a fool as well as a rat. But if you don't want to be a widow, I'd call him again." He blew a kiss down the line, and was gone.

Jo sat gazing at the phone for some seconds, then picked it up again to call Central Exchange for a shore to ship radio link.

THURSDAY 27 JULY

New York Police Department Headquarters, Park Row

10.00 am

"Evacuation plan? What do you mean, evacuation plan?" asked the New York Police department spokesman, an Assistant Commissioner, to whom the two television reporters had been referred by the Mayor's Office.

"We would like to know," Richard repeated patiently, "if there is a file plan for the evacuation of Manhattan in the event of a serious emergency."

The Assistant Commissioner stared at him from under arched eyebrows. "The evacuation of Manhattan?" He looked at Rod Kimmelman, whom he obviously knew. "Who *is* this guy?"

"Richard Connors," Kimmelman explained. "He's into weather."

"That's right," the Assistant Commissioner agreed. "I knew your face was familiar. Thought at first I must've seen you in a mug shot. Now I remember, you're the guy who's been scaring people half to death with your talk about an ultimate storm. Well, welcome back to the real world, Buster. How the hell do you expect us to evacuate Manhattan? Have you any idea how many people live in this city?"

"Maybe ten million," Richard ventured.

"And a hell of a lot of them are right here on this island. So where do you want us to evacuate them to? And why?"

"Suppose there was a six-second warning, or whatever," Kimmelman put in. "That the Russians were sending ICBMs over. What would happen then?"

"The sirens would go, and people would take to the fall-out shelters."

"And everyone knows where they are?"

"They should do. We don't keep their locality a secret, and it is the duty of every citizen to know where his nearest fall-out shelter is. Christ, we've been begging the public for years to be aware that something like that could happen."

"Would you say they have done that?"

"I wouldn't like to offer an opinion on that. But it wouldn't matter. We have a highly trained Civil Service organisation in this city . . . in this state. There'd be wardens telling the people where to go."

"Ten million people flooding the streets, and wardens telling them where to go, with maybe only a few minutes in hand? How many wardens do you have? One million?"

The Assistant Commissioner pointed. "You guys trying to be funny? Sure not everyone will make it. We all know that in the event of an atomic war there's going to be casualties, maybe as high as sixty per cent. The Pentagon talks about megadeaths. Who am I to argue with the Pentagon? And what the hell has an atomic attack to do with the weather?"

"Nothing," Richard agreed. "Save that I'd like to ask, these fall-out shelters, where are they?"

"Why don't you go look them up on the map? They're everywhere, and they're adequate. No goddamned Commie is going to catch us napping."

"Well, would I be correct in assuming that they're all in subways, cellars, and that kind of thing? In fact, underground."

"Well, Jesus," the Assistant Commissioner remarked. "I've never heard of putting fall-out shelters in penthouses."

"Would I be right in assuming that the entire area between 34th Street and the Battery is less than 50 feet above sea level?" Richard persisted, refusing to abandon his smile.

"Don't ask me, Mr Connors. I'm not the City Engineer."

"Well, I can tell you that according to the ordnance map, it is. So if a lot of people were to start going down into subways and cellars, you are talking about them going down to sea level or even beneath it. What would happen if you had a tidal surge of 25 or 30 feet coming through the Narrows, and your population had all taken refuge in the fall-out shelters?"

The Assistant Commissioner looked at Kimmelman again. "Say, what the hell is this guy talking about? Atomic bombs or weather?"

"In his book, they're the same thing," Kimmelman explained.

"Thirty feet of water coming through the Narrows?" The Assistant Commissioner scratched his head in bewilderment.

"Look," Richard said. "All I want to know is this: does the NYPD have an emergency plan for the evacuation of the city of Manhattan in the event of a situation which might require such an evacuation, but not necessarily an enemy atomic attack? It could be an outbreak of plague, an incipient earthquake, or a major storm. Anything which might make the use of fall-out shelters irrelevant or even dangerous."

"Think maybe of a 24-hour warning of a Commie attack, rather than six minutes," Kimmelman suggested brightly. "A whole Commie task force somehow spirited across the Atlantic and ready to invade."

That was a tactical error. The Assistant Commissioner gave him a withering look. "And you want me to tell you guys that, to blare over the networks? Next thing the Commies would be blowing all the bridges, and where would we be then?"

12.00 noon

J. Calthrop White glanced down the page of notes. "We could have a whole barrel of dynamite here, Richard," he remarked. "So you're pretty sure there is no evacuation plan?"

"Pretty sure, JC. Partly because the only real emergency the authorities seem able to consider is an atomic attack, when there wouldn't be time to evacuate the population anyway. There is no way anyone down at City Hall seems able to envisage the damage a major hurricane might do."

"But you can. And you're sure of your facts."

Richard drew a long breath. "Yes, JC, I think I can envisage the probabilities."

"Don't let me hear that word 'think' again." He glanced at Kiley. "How much time can you give him without screwing the schedule up?"

Kiley studied the chart he had brought into the office. "Three minutes at the end of the early evening forecast, by cutting two news items."

"Okay, Richard, use that time, and blast them this evening." White pointed his pencil. "This storm isn't going to fizzle, I hope."

"I don't . . ." Hurriedly Richard changed what he was going to say. "No, JC, it isn't going to fizzle," he said, and fled down to the weather office. "When the hell," he complained to Julian and Jayme, "will the average layman understand that pinpoint weather forecasting, with a system like Faith, is just not a practical proposition? And this set up, where I have virtually to guarantee that she's a real threat to New York, is just ridiculous. We should all be praying for her to turn due east and lose herself out at sea. Where the hell is she now, anyway?"

Julian showed him the latest chart.

Richard frowned. "But for Christ's sake, she hasn't moved more than a couple of miles in six hours."

"That's right," Julian agreed. "She's stalled."

"Two hundred miles south-east of Cape Hatteras," Jayme added. "They're reporting 70-mile-an-hour winds down there, and high seas. And that's the navigable semi-circle."

"Stalled," Richard said, and sat at his desk. Stalled, he thought. That would at least maintain interest in Faith for another couple of days, which would give JC time to launch his attack on the incompetency of City Hall. But stalled! The most dangerous storms in history were always those which had stalled, because then they could go anywhere. Sometimes they even turned back on themselves, like Betsy in 1965, which had stalled, then reversed itself after passing the Bahamas and gone back to hit the islands with renewed force just when everyone supposed the worst was over. And Faith's present position was just over 500 miles from New York. He looked out of the window – it was raining, from a total overcast sky, but the wind was light; as Jayme had said, they were still to the west of the storm, the area of least danger, and they were beyond the gale limit. "What wind strengths?" he asked.

"Oh, they're big," Julian said. "The last navy plane into the eye recorded 150 miles an hour."

"Just short of a Category Five. Shit!"

"And the Hurricane Centre reckons she could still build," Julian added. "They're sending another plane out in a couple of hours."

"So . . . you going ahead with blasting City Hall?" Jayme asked.

"If you do, and Faith does fizzle," Julian said, "what do you reckon JC's reaction would be to that?"

Richard brooded for a few seconds longer. Then he said, "I don't see that it matters if Faith fizzles or not. If she does, it may take the heat off the administration, and have everybody calling me a scaremonger – which they're doing anyway – but that doesn't alter the fact that she *could* hit here, and that even if she doesn't, one day a major storm most certainly will, and therefore that the city should have a plan to deal with it."

"So you're going ahead," Julian said.

"Yes."

"Attaboy," Jayme shouted, and kissed him.

Kennedy International Airport, Jamaica Bay

2.30 pm

"I can't believe it." Marcia twisted her fingers together. "The whole place, destroyed! Lawson . . . my God! I just can't believe it."

"Well, pull yourself together," Jo told her. "They're on the ground." She squeezed Owen Michael's hand. "You okay?"

"Sure, Mom," he said. But he wasn't; there were dark shadows under his eyes. Partly from lack of sleep, she knew. But also partly from shock. The family had been so secure in their ebullient togetherness. The biggest threat that had ever hung over them had been the possible separation of Michael and herself, and few of them had even been aware that it was there. How criminally irrelevant it seemed now. But Tamsin was only moments away.

Passengers started streaming through the gate from the Miami flight, greeting friends and relatives, or hurrying straight through for the taxis. The reporters moved closer; Jo had no idea who had told them to be here – probably Cal Palmer; she had felt obliged to call him and let him know Big Mike was all right.

"There they are!" Marcia ran forward, checked.

Meg Robson was first off, helped by Neal. They wore obviously freshly bought clothes, and had no luggage. They glanced at Marcia as if she had been a stranger, ignored Jo and Owen Michael altogether, and hurried for the exit.

"Say, were you on Eleuthera?" one of the reporters called, running behind them.

"Go away," Neal snapped. "Leave us alone."

The reporter hesitated, then rejoined his rivals, who were moving forward to block the corridor as the Donnellys came out. Jo and Owen Michael and Marcia were in front of them as the television cameras started to whirr.

"Oh, Babs," Marcia cried, taking her mother into her arms. "Oh, Babs." Like the Robsons, the Donnellys were in new bought clothes.

"Tamsin!" Jo swept the little girl from the floor, hugged her and kissed her, then held her away. "Are you okay, darling?"

"Yes," Tamsin said, in a small voice. "The whole house fell down. Oh, Mommy . . ." She burst into tears.

Jo held her close again. "You're okay now, honey. You're home. Nothing can hurt you here. Dad!" Still holding Tamsin, Jo kissed Big Mike, looked into his eyes. "Oh, Dad!" She couldn't think what to say.

He hugged her tightly, then turned his attention to Owen Michael. Jo looked past him at Dale, who held Belle's arm. How incredible, she thought, that Dale, the family layabout, had come through the ordeal better than anyone, while Belle . . . beautiful, statuesque, strong, indomitable, erotic, laughing, totally indestructible Belle . . . she might have been looking at Babs' older sister.

"Hi, Jo." Dale kissed her.

"Belle . . ." she put her arms around her sister-in-law.

"They haven't found him," Belle said. "He could still be alive, you know. People survive." Tears spilled from those gorgeous eyes and dribbled down her cheeks.

"How bad was it, Mr Donnelly?" the reporters were asking.

"Was the island really knocked flat?"

"Do you have any idea of the loss of life?"

"How strong would you estimate the winds were, Mr Donnelly?"

"They've been talking about giant waves, Mr Donnelly? How high would you say the seas were?"

"How'd your property make out, Mr Donnelly?"

All the while the little group, the last off the aircraft, had been straggling towards the exit. Now Big Mike stopped, and turned, and faced the pack at their heels. The TV cameras zoomed in on his face. "Yes," he said. "It was hell. The island was knocked flat. My property is destroyed. The waves were bigger than anything I have ever seen. And yes, there was loss of life. Now get off my fucking back."

They reached the automobiles. Marcia took Dale and Belle. Babs and Tamsin and Owen Michael got into the back of the Mercedes, Big Mike sat in front with Jo. "We've food at the apartment," she said. "And Cal Palmer wants you to get in touch. He says it's urgent."

"Just drive us out to Bognor," Big Mike said. "We want to go home. Cal can wait until tomorrow."

"At the earliest," Babs agreed.

Jo hesitated, then hooted to attract Marcia's attention, and made for the Whitestone Bridge and the New England Thruway. "Is there any chance . . ." she hesitated, unwilling to say his name for fear of setting Tamsin off again.

"None at all," Big Mike said, understanding. "I guess part of the roof or some of the furniture must've hit him on the head. We just didn't know. We were so busy wrestling with Meggie . . ."

"Belle blames us," Babs said. "She doesn't actually say it, but she does."

"But . . . it could've happened to any of you," Jo said.

"Sure," Big Mike said. "But it happened to Lawson. And then . . ." he sighed.

"She wanted the men to go back and look for him, right away," Babs explained. "But they couldn't, really. They'd have been killed too."

Jo gained a small insight into the traumas these people must have experienced during that dreadful night.

"Neal and Meggie blame us too," Babs said. "For persuading them to go down there in the first place."

"For heaven's sake," Jo protested. "They're adult human beings. They vacationed with you and loved it there . . ."

"I know. But all that money, just washed away . . . Neal hadn't yet taken out insurance."

"And Lawson got drowned saving their goddamned lives," Big Mike growled.

Another fall-out from Faith, Jo thought: the end of a forty-year friendship. "How bad is the house?" she asked. "Your house."

"There are a couple of walls standing," Big Mike said.

"Oh, then you can rebuild it," Owen Michael suggested.

"Rebuild that? Shit! I am never setting foot on that goddamned island again if I live to be two hundred."

"What about McKinley?" Babs asked.

"He can keep the hundred grand," Big Mike said. "So I made a mistake."

Jo had no idea what they were talking about.

"Where's Michael?" Big Mike asked.

"As far as I know, he left Bermuda last night, for Newport."

"You been in touch?"

"Yes," she said. "I've been in touch."

"But isn't that storm now heading for Bermuda?" Babs asked.

"Oh, I've told him that, twice. And got a 'silly little woman' reply." She didn't tell them about the abuse she had also received when she finally got through to the yacht and apparently dragged Michael out of his bunk to speak with her: the lack of interest he had shown even in Lawson's death, once she had told him Tamsin was safe. "He reckons he'll be home long before Faith can catch up with him. Anyway, they're travelling in different directions: he's making north-west, and the storm north-east."

"Michael will be all right," Big Mike said. "That boy knows what he's doing. No goddamned hurricane is gonna bother him."

PARK AVENUE

10.00 pm

Jo refused an invitation for supper, although Marcia decided to stay; presumably to tell them of her pregnancy. Jo opted to drive the children back to town. She wanted Tamsin all to herself, and she wanted the little girl to sleep in her own bed that night. And every other night for a long time to come.

Besides, staying out at Bognor would have meant re-living the storm, over and over again, entering into Belle's angry anguish, Big Mike's sense of failure, Babs' bewilderment that such a thing could have happened to them. Only Dale had accepted what had happened, and was prepared to look forward rather than back. Jo wanted Tamsin to forget about the whole ghastly episode just as quickly as possible.

It was drizzling, although there was no wind, and it was past eight when she regained the apartment; she fed the children and put them straight to bed. She had been tempted, as soon as she realised that she and Owen Michael were definitely not going to Eleuthera this year, to reclaim Nana. But the dog was booked in for another week, and with Florence also away she felt she had enough on her plate with just the two children. For that reason too she had not yet informed Ed that she was still in New York, although obviously he must now suspect that she had returned: according to her Ansaphone he had called twice that afternoon, and wanted her to get in touch. Well, she thought, like Cal Palmer, he could wait at least until tomorrow. Richard had also called, but she knew by now he would be in the studio and working up his ten o'clock forecast; she'd call him back after that.

She poured herself a glass of milk, fixed a plate of salad and cottage cheese, and sat herself in front of the TV. She didn't really care what she was watching, knew she was merely waiting for ten o'clock; and there he was, outlining Faith's position, which had moved only a little north of her midday fixing. She was taken aback when the forecast ended and the anchorman said, "In view of the importance we attach to the matter, and the amount of interest the broadcast has aroused, we are now going to repeat Richard's comments of earlier this evening." Richard promptly reappeared on screen, but wearing a different tie; this was a recording.

"There is no doubt," he was saying, "that from her present position Faith can do anything and go anywhere. There is no human habitation within five hundred miles of her centre at this moment where the utmost precautions should not be being taken . . . now! That includes this city of New York. With winds of approximately 150 miles an hour round the centre, she could do unimaginable damage were she to move west and come ashore here. Try to envisage that force. A man finds difficulty in walking against a 25-mile-an-hour breeze; Faith represents six times that power.

"Now, we all hope and pray that such a catastrophe never occurs, but it would be a serious dereliction of duty on the part of the authorities, all the way up to the Mayor, not to have a comprehensive plan for dealing with such an emergency, should it ever happen, and not to make that plan known to the public. Our experiences of the past years, particularly along the Gulf Coast and in Florida and the south-eastern states, have proved beyond a shadow of a doubt that human lives, at the very least, can be saved by systematic evacuation of low-lying areas, if those evacuations are undertaken early enough. We all understand what an immense task it would be to evacuate Manhattan, Staten Island, Long Island, and Atlantic City, just for examples, but it must be understood too that any land below 30 feet above sea level could be at risk in the event of a major hurricane making a landfall in this vicinity, and even areas as high as 50 feet could be seriously affected in the event of a Category Five storm. And there is no use waiting for the hurricane to arrive before ordering such an evacuation. The greater the number of people to be warned and moved, the earlier it should happen. The plans for such an evacuation, street by street, with each street knowing the exact route to take, should not only be ready and known, but should be up-dated annually."

He leaned forward. "Now I must tell you that at the time of taking to the air this evening, we at NABS have been unable to discover the existence of any such plan, either from the police or from the Mayor's Office." He paused significantly. "We now invite the city authorities to accept our offer of free air time, either tomorrow morning or evening, so that you folks sitting out there may be given the vital details of their plan for your safety, should the need arise – always supposing such a plan exists. This is Richard Connors, for the National American Broadcasting Service."

Jo switched off the set, and mixed herself a drink. Coming on top of everything else that had happened today, she felt numbed. Richard hadn't given her a hint that he was planning to go outside the realm of weather forecasting and get involved in city politics. Presumably he had been ordered to do so by J. Calthrop White. She wondered what the official reaction was going to be.

Ten minutes later the phone buzzed, and she knew it would be him, so she took it in the study. "Hi! Who's a big bad bear, then?"

"What did you think of it?"

"Richard Connors, ace reporter, straight from the shoulder. It was great, but you'd better not apply to City Hall for a building licence in the near future. Or any kind of licence, come to think of it – even a marriage one. And haven't you missed the boat? Faith seems to be spending her energy on empty ocean."

"You could be right, although she actually seems to be re-stocking her energy from that ocean. But it's a fact: right this minute she isn't posing a threat to anyone. When I made that statement at six o'clock, she was still stalled and could've gone anywhere. Now she's on the move again, still very slowly, only ten knots, but more north than east. She's now definitely missed Bermuda, and is going straight up the Gulf Stream into the North Atlantic. Actually, she could pose less of a threat than Gloria did. All we're likely to get is some more of this rain, which everybody is enjoying."

"Oh, gosh. Did you know that when you repeated your attack on City Hall?"

"Yeah. I suggested it might be a good idea to hold the repeat until tomorrow, but JC has the bit between his teeth, I guess. Anyway, you know, whatever Faith does, the city does need an evacuation plan, because if it doesn't happen this time, it's going to happen some time. And she could still turn nasty. We know she's a maverick, and she's still one of the biggest storms in history. Certainly the biggest we've seen this far north this century. She's on the verge of becoming a Category Five. We don't have anything bigger than that. When you have something that big sitting out there only 400 miles away, virtually on our doorstep, you have to regard it as a threat."

"Makes sense to me. Let's hope the Mayor agrees with you."

"Who's sounding all cheerful, then?"

"Of course I'm cheerful. Oh, sure, I should be in mourning for poor Lawson, and Big Mike seems to have lost just about his shirt, financially as well as literally . . . but I have my little girl back, safe and sound and tucked up in bed just behind this wall. Richard, do let me know next time Mark is coming up. I want to thank him personally."

"I'll do that. What news of your husband?"

"Oh, he's somewhere . . . oh, my God!" What Richard had told her was only just registering. "Between Hamilton and Newport."

"Holy Christ! How far out?"

"Well, he left last night, say at seven, and he was going to motor if he couldn't sail. Supposing he could maintain seven knots, I suppose he'd be just about two hundred miles from Hamilton."

"Then he has time to turn back. He's about three hundred miles east by north from the storm . . . but if he keeps on he's going to enter the dangerous semi-circle."

"He left because he thought the boat would be in more danger in Hamilton than out at sea."

"Christ, what does he think will happen to his precious boat if Faith catches up with him? Jo, we're talking about lives, not boats. The point is that Faith is already just about past Bermuda. Unless she makes a sharp right turn they're not going to get anything but a swell. It's up to you, but . . ."

Jo looked at her watch. It was nearly 11.00 pm. "I'll raise him, just as quickly as I can. But when do I see you?"

"Just as quickly as I can get away from here," he promised.

Friday 28 July

Midnight 30

Sam Davenport climbed through the hatch of the racing yawl *Esmeralda*, sniffed the air. It was utterly dark with the moon and stars obliterated by the cloud cover, from which intermittent drizzle had turned everything on deck clammily wet. But the wind remained light, and the sea calm, although with a big swell out of the south-west; *Esmeralda* had all sail set, but she was also motoring.

"That forecast wasn't so good," Sam remarked.

Michael Donnelly sat aft, just visible in the glare of the binnacle lamp, one hand resting on the wheel. He wore orange oilskins over bathing trunks, but the hood was thrown back to make room for his cap – at the moment he was only seeking protection against the rain. "She's close, eh?"

"350 miles."

"That figures. We must just about be crossing the top edge."

"Not according to the forecast," Sam said.

"Eh?"

"She's altered course, heading more north than we are. She's still south-west of us."

"How fast's she moving?"

"About ten knots."

"And we're making a steady seven. She won't catch us. Nothing more than a gale, anyway."

"Yeah. Well I hope you're right. I got the news before the forecast. Some of what happened in Eleuthera was horrendous. They're talking of several hundred dead, and damage running into millions."

"Yeah," Michael agreed. "Including my brother-in-law and one hell of a big property deal." He shrugged. "That's the way the cookie crumbles, I guess. You ready to take over?"

"Sure." Sam swung his leg out of the companionway, then checked. "Hello, somebody's calling."

"Don't tell me," Michael groaned. "It'll be Jo again. She's a pain in the ass, sometimes."

Sam gave his skipper a curious glance; he had never heard Michael speak to Jo as he had done last night, or refer to her in such terms, before.

He ducked back into the cabin, thumbed the handset. "You're right," he called. "It is Jo."

"Well, take the helm," Michael said, and went below. "*Esmeralda*," he said. "What's the trouble now? Over."

"There could be a lot of trouble," Jo said. "What's your position? Over."

"Will it mean anything to you? We're chugging along, mostly under power. We're . . ." He switched on the chart table light and squinted at the chart. "I won't give you the co-ordinates, because you wouldn't understand them. Let's say we're approximately 220 miles north-west of Bermuda, right on track. And that there are four guys trying to get some sleep. Over."

"Have you enough fuel to get back to Hamilton? Over."

"Sure, we have enough fuel to get back to Hamilton. We have enough fuel to motor into Newport. Why should we want to go back to Hamilton? Over."

"Faith is coming your way again, Michael. Didn't you get the midnight weather forecast? Over."

"Sure we did. She's over 300 miles away from us, and only making a couple of knots more speed. So she's altered course. We still have time to beat her in. Over."

"Not if she increases speed, and the experts here think she may do that. Listen to me, Michael. This could be the biggest storm this century. I have spoken with a weather forecaster here and he says your only safe course is to go back to Hamilton. The storm is already past Bermuda and is very unlikely to turn back now. But she's going to cross directly over your route to Newport. Over."

"I know what Faith is doing," Michael said. "And I know we can beat her in. Going back to Bermuda is out. I'm coming home. If Faith gives us anything, it'll be a little wind so we can quicken up. Now tell me, did the folks get in? Over."

"Yes," Jo said. "Yes, they got in. Over."

"And Tamsin's okay? Over."

"Yes. She's fine. Michael, for God's sake, will you listen to me and go back. Over."

"Look, you go back to bed and let me run this ship, eh? We'll be in Newport Sunday night. You be there to meet us, right? *Esmeralda* over and out." He replaced the handset, looked at the four anxious faces peering at him from their bunks. "So what's eating you guys?"

"Maybe she's right," Larry remarked. "And we should turn back."

"And if Faith alters course easterly again, as she's most likely to do, we run slap into the middle of her," Michael told him. "This baby has been altering course more times than a ship with a broken rudder. We know we're ahead of her now. We are going to stay ahead of her."

"But if she does quicken up . . ." Pete said.

Michael shot him a glance. "That's supposing Jo and her tame weather forecaster have it right, which I doubt. Say, what's gotten into you guys, anyway? You scared of a little wind? Listen, this ship is damned near hurricane proof, because I made her that way. And we're gonna make even more sure. If you don't want to sleep, there's plenty for us to do. So, all hands turn out."

They grumbled, but grinned as well; they had the utmost confidence in Michael as a skipper – and he knew the best possible way to stop them from worrying was to keep them busy.

"Okay," he said. "Switch on the deck lights, Sam. Now, let's get organised. Larry, I want lifelines strung, from pulpit to pushpit; make sure they're secured to strongpoints, both masts, and the winches – if they're needed, they'll have to take the weight of a man. Jon, break out the deadeyes and prepare to screw them over the ports the moment I tell you. Pete, I want every possible vent plugged, ventilators taken out and their caps screwed down tight. Stow the anchor below and remember the hawsepipe. If water gets in anywhere it'll be there and we could wind up with half the ocean in our chain locker; use rolled up towels and dirty clothes. All deck lockers are to be padlocked as if we were leaving the ship in Nassau. Mark, I want you to cook just about everything we have, in one vast stew, then break it up into say six meals, and store each one in a separate container – if we're caught in the storm for any length of time we're going to need regular food and there's going to be no time to cook. And I want every man to check his personal safety harness. So let's get to it."

"I'd like to call Newport and tell Sally what we're doing," Sam said. "Especially as I reckon we'll be out of radio range in another couple of hours. Can you take her again for half an hour?"

"Sure, if you reckon she'll want to hear from you in the middle of the night." Michael returned on deck. "And when you've done that, carry extra lashings over the battery boxes and the radio gear – if we should get knocked down they could just come loose."

He took the helm, settled himself, thought of Jo working herself up into a fuss, and grinned. Silly bitch. Then he frowned. Jo had been behaving badly the last couple of months. Something was happening, or had happened, to change her personality. His frown deepened. Or someone. Just where the hell was she getting all this weather information from, anyway?

His fingers tightened on the wheel. There was going to have to be some very straight talking between them, when he got home.

Park Avenue

7.00 am

By the time Jo had managed to contact the yacht, Richard had arrived and he listened to the conversation.

"You have to hand it to the guy," he remarked when Jo finally hung up. "He has the confidence of a champion. And if he makes it home *I'll* have to hand it to him." He grinned. "Don't get me wrong. I hope he does make it."

"So do I," Jo said. No matter how irreconcilable their differences, Michael was her husband, and the father of her children – and they had experienced a lot together. "Do you think he can, Richard?"

"If he can get himself to west of the path, sure he can."

In the circumstances she didn't feel like making love, and Richard could understand that. They had a cup of coffee each, then he kissed her goodnight. "I reckon you want all the sleep you've been missing the last couple of nights," he said. "And I have a forecast at seven."

"So when do *you* sleep?" she asked.

"About ten minutes in every hour, on the settee in the office. I haven't been home for four days. Jayme keeps me supplied with coffee and doughnuts."

"You're going to make yourself ill," she protested.

He winked. "By this time next week the world will be back to normal, and we'll be wondering what all the fuss was about. I'll call you."

To her surprise, Jo did sleep, very soundly, but she set her alarm, and awoke at a quarter to seven, in time to switch on the TV while her coffee percolated.

Richard smiled at her, but his eyes were grave. ". . . latest co-ordinates are 35°15′N. latitude. 70°20′W. longitude." He moved to the huge wall map. "That puts Faith 300 miles due east of Cape Hatteras, and you'll see . . ." his wand touched the last position, "that she is now moving north-east again, but still slowly, only about ten knots. She is just over 400 miles south-east of New York, and you'll see from this picture that the cloud mass extends outwards for all of that and more. In fact, the rain we've been having the last couple of days is definitely what we might call an outlier from Faith. Well, we needed the rain; if that's all she gives us, we're going to be very lucky people. And in fact, if she maintains her present track, she is going to move straight out into the Atlantic and trouble no one any more . . . except any shipping that happens to be in her way. They should all by now have moved out of her path in any event, if they have any sense."

Jo opened her atlas, and began measuring off distances. By her reckoning the storm was within 200 miles of where she reckoned *Esmeralda* should now be. 200 miles and the gap was closing. Her hand hovered over the telephone . . . but almost certainly the yacht was now out of radio range from Hamilton, and not yet within range of any mainland station. And even if she could raise them and Michael were to listen to her, she didn't know what he could do about it now.

THE GULF STREAM

7.00 am

Dawn is usually the best part of the day, at sea. At dusk it is possible to witness the most magnificent sunsets, with the huge red globe inching its way beneath the horizon, and seeming to spread as it does so, so that when it is a third gone it appears to be sitting on a crimson plinth. But once the sun is gone there is nothing but the lonely hours of darkness ahead, so that, even in summer, around two o'clock in the morning it is sure to get pretty chilly.

Dawn is the promise of a whole new day. The appearance of the sun, rising out of the ocean with all the majesty of a sunset, but invariably in softer colours, brings an immediate suggestion of warmth. For those on watch there is the certainty of warming coffee, filling breakfast, and then a snug berth for four hours. For those getting up to take over, it is no hardship to sit in the cockpit of a yacht, sipping coffee, and enjoying the burgeoning day.

But some dawns can be angry. This morning the wind was still light and fitful, but the sun rose, blood-red, out of a mountain of high piling clouds, and the swell was bigger than before, so large that when *Esmeralda* sank into a trough the horizon disappeared. And now there came the first of the squalls, driving rain in front of the wind, stinging the skin and causing drops to leap out of the sea. "You'd better wake the skipper," Larry told Mark.

Michael was already awake. He had been fast asleep, but he had felt the yacht heel to the sudden wind gust even while unconscious. He rolled out of his berth, pulled on his oilskin trousers and top – he had slept in his clothes – and looked over Sam's shoulder at the chart table, and the forecast Sam had just scribbled down.

"There we are." Sam made a neat little pencil 'x' on the chart to indicate the yacht's position – he had just taken a Loran fix.

"And?" Michael asked.

"Faith is there." He pointed to another 'x' on the chart. "I make that 180 miles."

Michael frowned. "The bitch has altered course."

"Yes. And that's confirmed by the forecast. She's making north-east, and coming straight at us. Michael, you don't think . . ."

"No I don't," Michael told him. "She's doing exactly what I figured she would. Okay, right now we're in the dangerous quadrant, but 180 miles . . . how fast is she travelling?"

"Still about ten knots,"

"Eighteen hours to the eye. After midnight tonight. By then we'll be another 100 miles to the north-west, more if she gives us a breeze. We'll be in the safe quadrant then."

"The *safer* quadrant," Sam corrected. "I don't reckon there's any safe quadrant where this baby is concerned. And you do know that we're gonna have 100-mile-an-hour winds long before the eye actually gets to us."

"Listen, friend," Michael said. "I taught you navigation, remember. Any increase in strength?"

"Not really. Highest winds are still reported as 150 miles an hour around the centre. That's more than 130 knots. You ever been out in 130 knots of wind, Michael?"

"I guess not," Michael admitted. "We had 60 knots once, a couple of years ago. Remember?"

"I wasn't on that one," Sam said thoughtfully. "I've always been glad of that." Now he wished he had at least had that experience. "And the ship rode it all right?"

Michael grinned. "She rolled a bit. Everything depends on where we are when it hits us, and the direction it's coming from. Sea room is very important. And right now we have all the sea room in the world. There's only the Gulf Stream to worry about. The wind should back round to the north-east when Faith gets close. Put that over the Stream and we could have some steep seas. Shit, we could be climbing mountains. So what I want you to do is lay a course north for a while."

"North? But that'll take us up to Boston."

"So we'll go to Boston. Listen, Sammy, we can't head a hurricane wind. We have to go with it, right? Therefore, when it blows, it's gonna take us west no matter what we do. The further north we get now the slacker the Gulf Stream will be running, and the weaker the wind. Faith is making north-east. We'll get into the navigable quadrant yet. So we won't be heading straight for home. But if we can't make it in time, you know what the golden rule is."

"If you can't make port in plenty of time, keep the sea," Sam said unhappily.

"And that includes keeping well away from known hot spots," Michael reminded him. "We'll turn for home and the Gulf Stream when Faith has gone through."

"You're the skipper," Sam agreed. "I just wish I could call either Sally or Jo, tell them what we're doing? They'll be worrying."

"Do them good," Michael said. "We'll call them when we're through."

National American Broadcasting Service Offices, Fifth Avenue

Noon

"That was good work last night, Richard," remarked J. Calthrop White. "We'll have to think about giving you some more political broadcasting to do, eh?" He glanced at Kiley, who gave an anxious smile. "Now, all we need is for Faith to act up, and give people a good enough scare to ask the same questions we have; my information is that they are already doing that. So what the hell is all this talk that she's now heading out to sea?"

Richard couldn't figure out what the old buzzard was doing in the office on a Friday morning at all; he usually went out to Long Island on Thursday night, to prepare himself for one of his wife's lavish luncheon parties. But maybe he wasn't going home at all this weekend. "Well, JC, I'm afraid that's what she's doing."

"Hm. That's not so good. It'll give the administration a breathing space," JC pointed out. "Yes, indeed. That is a serious disappointment. They'll go back to the old theme of how a hurricane never will hit New York, and now they'll have Faith to add to Gloria to prove to the public that they're right. And we'll be accused of scaremongering all over again."

"Well, sir, in many ways their point of view is a correct one," Richard attempted to explain. "Hurricanes, until they come ashore, do tend to move in a parabola, as indeed do ordinary wind currents. They travel west in the lower latitudes, and they curve back to the north-east as they move higher."

"Then why did you say yesterday that Faith was still a possible threat to New York?"

"Because she was. She still is. She's a massive storm, she's still deepening, and she's moving very slowly . . ."

"But away from New York." JC believed in hammering the important point in any discussion. "All she's done is put down one hell of a lot of rain to spoil tomorrow's golf, and left us with egg smeared all over our faces." He pressed a switch on his intercom. "Alice, call the garage and tell Murray I won't be staying in town this weekend after all. Tell him to have the car ready in ten minutes."

"Right away, JC," the secretary replied.

JC stood up. "I'm not blaming you, Richard. I repeat, you did a good job. And you have the face to put these things across. You look honest, and even more important, you look sincere. Indeed you do. Sincerity is what grabs people. No doubt about that. But there's no doubt either that we'll have lost a lot of oomph when people tune in to your next forecast and discover this storm is heading out into the Atlantic. I mean to say, Gloria at least blew down a few trees in Connecticut, caused one or two deaths. This one isn't even going to do that. A real pity. Have a good weekend." He left the office.

Richard and Kiley looked at each other.

"Would you say I had better start looking for another job?" Richard asked.

"Well . . . I reckon he was pretty forbearing. But that's not necessarily a good thing," Kiley pointed out. "Trouble is, Richard, JC is the kind of man who just has to have someone to blame for anything that goes wrong. It's bad luck that you were elected in this case, but there it is. Wasn't it Napoleon Bonaparte who said he'd rather have a lucky general than a good one? JC identifies with Bonaparte on a good many things. Now, if Faith was to turn round and come back . . ."

"You'd say I was lucky," Richard observed in disgust. "And JC would be happy. You guys have got to be crazy. You actually want that storm to hit us. Do you have any idea what it would be like?"

"I saw the movie," Kiley said. "But New York isn't some Pacific sandbank. Or a Bahamian sandbank, either."

"The movie," Richard said contemptuously. "Did you notice how every time the director wanted his characters to say something the wind dropped, how there was no thunder or lightning, and how they climbed trees to survive? That was hocum. If Faith were to strike Manhattan there wouldn't be a tree left in Central Park. And a few other things are going to be blown about as well. Come over here." He went to stand at the plate-glass window looking down on Manhattan; it faced east. "Do we have any shutters for this window?"

"Are you crazy? We're forty floors up."

"Well, let me tell you something, Mr Kiley; if Faith hits here with winds of 150 miles an hour or more, that window is going to disappear. You remember that storm which hit Houston a few years back? It was losing force by then, and it had never at any time possessed anything near the strength of Faith, yet the wind sucked out glass like it was paper. This window . . ." he tapped it, "is going to go, and most of it will fall into the street in pieces as lethal as shrapnel. And if either you or JC happen to be in this office at the time, the odds are you will go with it. Now you tell me something: how many plate-glass windows of roughly this size are there in New York?"

Kiley stared at him.

"Okay," Richard went on. "Let me make it easier for you. How many windows are there in this building?"

"You're being hysterical," Kiley commented. "I have a luncheon date."

"Enjoy it, and pray that Faith keeps out to sea." And destroy Michael Donnelly? A man he loathed although he had never even seen him. But there were five other men out there with him, and he had no cause to loathe any of them.

He took the elevator down to the weather room in a thoroughly bad temper. Jayme was out shopping; he had told her he would need her over the weekend. Julian was on the phone, making notes. And his own phone was buzzing. He sat down. "Connors."

"Hi."

"Oh, my darling," he said.

"Any news?"

"Could be something coming in now," he said, as he saw Julian's eyebrows bobbing at him. "Listen, I'll call you right back."

"I'll be here."

He replaced the phone. "Give."

"That was your friend Mark Hammond. He got back to base fifteen minutes ago. He says Faith has sustained winds at the centre of 160 miles an hour, and that she's still building."

"160? Give me that." Richard took the pad and stared at the figures. "You ever seen wind speeds like that before, at ground level?"

"The ultimate storm, eh? But that ain't all." Julian took back the pad and flipped the page. "Mark says she's starting to wobble."

Richard found himself on his feet. "Where?"

"To the west. There is a definite movement west of north, Mark says. Look at the co-ordinates."

Richard stared at the paper, then reached for his phone. "Find out if Mr White has left the building yet," he snapped at the girl on the switchboard. "If you can, stop him. Tell him I have to speak with him again, most urgently." He replaced the phone, gazed at Julian. "That old bastard could be going to get what he most wants – a major hurricane right on his goddamned doorstep." Then he thought of Michael Donnelly, trying to get to the west of a storm which was now beginning to move west, and faster than he could sail his yacht. He sighed; Jo had to be told. But Michael Donnelly, and even Jo, were suddenly being upstaged, by Faith herself.

* * *

215

"I'm sorry, Mr Connors," the switchboard said. "Mr White has already left for Long Island."

"He has a phone in his car, hasn't he?"

"Of course, Mr Connors, but we are under strict orders only to call him once he has left the office for the weekend in an extreme emergency."

"This *is* an extreme emergency," Richard snapped. "Get him. And get me the Mayor's Office as well."

"The Mayor's Office?" The woman's tone conveyed a suspicion that he must have gone mad.

"And the police department."

"And the police department," she said sadly.

Richard replaced the phone, then picked it up again and dialled Jo.

"You really feel this is it?" Julian asked.

"This could be it. Those co-ordinates place the storm just 370 miles away from us, and she could be turning this way. If something isn't done about it, and quick, we could be looking at the disaster of the century. Hi, Jo."

"What's happening?"

"Nothing good. Listen. I want you to pack a bag, for yourself and the kids, and leave town."

"Do what?"

"You heard me, Jo. Leave New York. Go away for the weekend."

"Now? You're pulling my leg."

"I was never more serious in my life."

"But . . . will you be coming with us?"

"No, I have to stay here. Listen, Jo, I'm very serious. Didn't you tell me your in-laws have a house in Bognor, Connecticut?"

"Why, yes. But . . ."

"Go visit with them, just for the weekend. Bognor should be safe enough."

"I can't just descend on them, Richard. They're still suffering from shock."

"Well, they could be going to get a lot more shock in the next couple of days. Faith is moving west."

"West? Oh, my God! But Michael . . ."

"Yeah. I know. Maybe he'll be able to outrun her. That's all I can offer. But you, Jo . . ."

"I can't go running off when he's out there, maybe fighting for his life, Richard. I have to be here, in case he wants to get in touch. And anyway, I'm in the centre of New York. What danger could there be here?"

"For God's sake," he shouted. "Will nobody listen to me? Jo . . ."

"I have Mr White on the phone, Mr Connors," the switchboard said.

"Hell . . . I'll call you back, Jo," Richard said, and pressed the transfer button. "JC?"

"Something on your mind, Richard?" JC's tone was deceptively quiet. "Something important, I hope."

"I thought you'd like to know that hurricane Faith has stopped moving north-east."

"Yes?"

"And she's starting to wobble to the west."

"Does that mean she may be coming our way after all?"

"It certainly creates that possibility."

"Well, that is splendid news, Richard. Splendid news. Maybe she'll come close enough to wipe some of that egg off of our faces. Keep me posted. Call me this evening at home. Well done, Richard."

"JC," Richard begged. "If she does come west, she could pose a serious threat to New York."

"Well, that's what we've been saying all along, isn't it?"

"Yes, but now we have to stop warning and start doing. JC, I'd like to put out a hurricane alert, right now. I'd like to interrupt the scheduled programming to tell people that Faith could be making straight for us."

"Richard," JC said. "Listen to me, boy. I know how interested you are in this hurricane thing. But obviously you've let it get on top of you. Now here's what you do, and this is an order. You hand over the one o'clock forecast to Julian, with strict instructions to give the co-ordinates and the present wind strengths and nothing more, and you go home, and have a drink and a good lunch and a nap, and then you return to the studio this evening, and you call me and give me an update then."

"Mr White, we don't have those six hours to waste. This storm is carrying winds at the centre of more than 160 miles an hour, and she is still building. She is going to be the biggest storm this century. Maybe of any century."

"Great stuff. And we predicted it. *You* predicted it, Richard. Congratulations. It'll sure boost the ratings. And we'll get those chats of yours going again."

"Mr White. Faith is going to kill people. Maybe a whole lot of people. We have to do something about that, now. You have to do something. You have to call the Mayor, and the police, and get them to endorse our warning and move the people out of all low-lying areas."

"Richard, you are starting to sound hysterical. How far away is this system?"

"The centre is approximately 370 miles south-east of us. You could say, due east of Norfolk, Virginia."

"And how fast is she moving?"

"Approximately 10 knots. That is real slow, and that is additionally dangerous, because every minute she spends over the sea she builds some more."

"But she is still at least 36 hours away."

"36 hours isn't very long to evacuate Manhattan. And storm conditions, especially the rise of tide, will happen some time before the centre arrives."

"36 hours gives her one hell of a lot of time to change her course again, though." As usual, JC was concentrating on what he considered the essentials. "If we started sounding off the way you want to, and she went off again, as she could well do, Jesus would we be in shit alley. We'll issue our warning when we're absolutely sure she's gonna hit."

"Mr White, that will be too late."

"We have done our bit, Richard. We forecasted this storm, and we were laughed to scorn. Okay. Now it's up to the Mayor and the police, as you say, to do something about it. Hell, they must watch the forecasts too. Nobody can now hold us responsible for what may happen. If Faith does come close, you, me, the whole station, will have had one mighty lucky escape from an acutely embarrassing situation. We'd be crazy to go sticking our necks out again without proof positive. You can't have that before tonight. If Faith is still coming at us then, we'll reconsider the situation. But we do nothing further until then. Got me? Now either get off the phone and go home and take a rest, or let me have your resignation Monday morning. Have a good day." The phone went dead.

Richard looked at Julian, and Julian looked at Richard.

"I have City Hall, Mr Connors," the switchboard said.

Richard picked up the phone again. "May I speak with the Mayor, please?" he asked. "This is Richard Connors on behalf of Station NABS." He wondered why he was wasting his time.

"The Mayor has gone to lunch."

"I thought he might have. What time do you expect him back?"

"We don't, today. It's an official function which will last late into the afternoon and afterwards he's going straight home."

"Well, look, it is vitally important that I contact him, or at least get a message to him."

"Yes?" the man said.

"Is that possible?"

"No," the man said.

"But *you* can contact him, presumably. If it's important enough."

"If it's important enough, yes."

"Then will you do so?"

"Why should I do that, Mr Connors? If you wish to make an apology for the scurrilous attack you launched on this administration last night, I suggest you put it in writing."

"Okay, I'll apologise. But right now I want to talk to Mayor Naseby about the hurricane itself." Richard kept himself from shouting with an effort.

"The hurricane? Our information is that she no longer poses a threat to New York."

"Well, I have news for you. She does pose a threat, more than ever before. She is changing direction and could well be coming straight at us. You tell the Mayor that there is a distinct possibility that Hurricane Faith may hit this city within 36 hours."

"36 hours," the man said, thoughtfully.

"And that I consider it absolutely essential that he order the evacuation of all low-lying areas of the city, immediately."

"Evacuation immediately," the man repeated; obviously he was now making notes. "Immediately? You mean, like right now?"

"I mean, like right now."

"Mr Connors, the Mayor isn't going to be happy to be told this. And you're not his favourite person, right this minute."

"You ask him if he's going to be happy when he has a 20-foot wall of water rushing up Wall Street."

"20-foot . . . well, I'll call him, Mr Connors. But I must warn you that he doesn't like being interrupted when on an official function except in an emergency."

"I think this could just be described as an emergency," Richard said. "Tell him NABS is ready to broadcast such an evacuation order, with details of routes to be used, and call me back here. Right?"

He replaced the phone. Julian scratched his head. "Think he'll call back? Because if JC gets to hear of this, after telling you to cool it, he's gonna have your guts for garters."

Before Richard could reply, the phone buzzed again. "I have Assistant Commissioner McGrath on the line, Mr Connors."

"Oh, Christ," Richard muttered. McGrath was the man he and Kimmelman had interviewed yesterday morning. "He won't do anything on my say so."

"He won't do anything at all without directions from the Mayor," Julian pointed out.

"So you talk to him. Tell him we anticipate receiving such authority within the hour." He got up. "I'm going to obey JC's orders, at least for a while. Call me at Josephine Donnelly's apartment the moment you hear from the Mayor."

1.00 pm

"My God, you're sopping wet!" Jo exclaimed as she opened the door.

"Well, it's pouring with rain out there." Richard made to kiss her, then saw the children. "Hi."

"Hi, Mr Connors," Owen Michael said. "This is Mr Connors, the weatherman," he told Tamsin. "I have his autograph," he added proudly.

"Hello, Mr Connors," Tamsin said. "May I have your autograph too?"

"Sure. Just bring your book."

"Maybe you'd like to stay to lunch," Jo suggested, handing him a towel to dry his head; she had already spread his jacket over the back of a chair.

"That would be very nice, Mrs Donnelly."

"Have you any news on what's happening with Dad?" Owen Michael asked.

"Well . . ." Richard wrote in Tamsin's autograph book. "I guess he's having some rough weather out there."

"Dad doesn't worry about rough weather," Owen Michael declared.

"Well, that's great," Richard said.

"Fix yourself a drink," Jo said. "I'll have one too. And you two run along and watch TV until lunch time. They haven't been able to go outside all day," she said.

Richard watched the door close. "Jo . . ." he took her in his arms.

"Is it bad?"

"Bad, and getting worse. This is hurricane rain."

"And Michael?"

"I don't know, Jo. I just don't know. I simply can't imagine what it might be like out there. And it's going to get worse."

She sighed, and rested her head on his shoulder. "And you want me to go up to Connecticut."

"Don't you think you should? You have your children to think about."

"And not my husband?"

"Jo, you can't help your . . ." They both spun round as the phone buzzed.

Jo ripped it from its stand. "Jo Donnelly? Oh. It's for you."

Richard took it. "Anything good, Julian?"

"Not a damn thing."

"What did McGrath say?"

"You want his exact words? Get off my back, you punk."

"That sounds in character. What about the Mayor?"

"Ah . . . the guy at City Hall came back and said he'd been in touch

220

with the Mayor and had been instructed to tell us that when the Mayor wishes the assistance of the National American Broadcasting Service in running New York City, he will most certainly ask for it. What do we do now?"

"What *can* we do, save wait for six o'clock? I'll be along in a couple of hours." He replaced the phone, took the glass Jo was holding for him. She watched him pace the room, drink in one hand, while the fingers of the other clenched and unclenched. Anger, frustration, and worry were boiling in his mind, obviously, and she waited for the inevitable overspill.

Aware of her eyes on him, he stopped, and, shoulders hunched, spread his arms wide in a gesture of despair. "They just don't believe it can happen."

"Surely New York has been hit by a hurricane before," Jo said.

"Sure it has. And there's the trouble. Because the city was virtually undamaged on those previous occasions, they all reckon it can ride anything."

"I don't understand," she said. "If it was undamaged . . ."

"Let me give you a few facts. The last hurricane seriously to affect New York was Gloria. She passed over Long Island, right? A big storm, Category Three. Faith is already blowing 40 knots more than that. Then there was Belle, in 1976. She tracked over Long Island, too. But she was already collapsing, was only Category One when she came ashore. In 1960 there was Donna. Donna was a Category Three when she got up here, a big storm. But like the others, she was already turning north-east and went over Long Island. Same with Carol in 1954, and according to the records she shook people up and then some. But how many people remember back more than thirty years? They didn't give names before 1950, but New York had hurricanes in 1944, in 1938 and in 1916, all following the same route, a sweep to the mainland, then a sharp turn away to the north-east. So what's the operative phrase in all that?"

"The north-east?"

"Correct. And Long Island. The centres of all those storms passed over Long Island. That means that in each of those hurricanes New York was on the left, the western side of the track. The side where the winds are not only weaker but start to blow from the west earlier as the centre passes through. The side where the storm surge is minimal. New York has never been in the north-east sector, the dangerous sector. Do you know what mariners used to do in the days before forecasts, when the sky or the barometer indicated a big storm was about? They faced the wind, and knew the centre of the storm would be just over 90° to their right hand, in the northern hemisphere. It's a natural law, named after the Dutchman, Buys Ballot, who discovered it. So the ship would alter course to the left, to make sure it stayed on the weaker side, the navigable side. That's all New York has ever experienced, the navigable semi-circle."

"And you think Faith is going to behave differently from all the others?"

"Ultimately, no. I think she will turn north-east after hitting land. But it's where she hits land that matters, and right now, if this turning movement continues – and don't forget that she did just this over Eleuthera on Wednesday – she could come ashore south of Manhattan, and if she does that, with the kind of winds she is generating, it's going to be like nobody can even imagine."

"Surely those people, the Mayor and the police, can see that on the weather map?"

"No they can't, because it's not on the weather map, as yet. All they can see is a big storm behaving exactly the same as every other big storm. Up to two hours ago they were right. The fact that she has begun to turn west won't be clearly apparent for several hours." He drank some whisky. "The administration is at least basing its ideas on history. I feel they are dreadfully wrong, but I can't prove it until Faith's new track is clearly defined, and that may be too late. But you know, at the other end of the scale there are people like JC. He is mad. Quite insane. He actually wants Faith to hit New York so he can take the credit for his station having predicted it would happen, and thus score a big win over the Mayor. Can you believe that? He doesn't give a damn about the possible loss of hundreds, thousands of lives, doesn't seem able to assimilate the fact that he'll probably be amongst the victims."

"But doesn't he accept the fact that she is coming this way? And that if you put out a definitive warning now you'll still be scoring off the Mayor?"

"He won't take the risk that we might be proved wrong. He was pretty upset during the eastward movement, after our attack yesterday: quote 'we'll be left with egg on our faces' unquote. So now I'm banned from issuing any warning just in case she moves off again. The most important thing in life is JC's public image." He drained his glass, and Jo got up to refill it. "My darling . . ." He caught her wrist. "Will you listen to me? Believe me? Please?"

"I do believe you."

"Well, then, get out of town."

She took the glass to the bar, poured. "I can't, right now. God knows my marriage is over, Richard. But Michael is the father of my children. I have got to be where he can get in touch with me, tell me he's safe . . . or where I can be told of his . . . well, whatever happens. He's out of radio range right this minute; he only has an MF set, with a maximum range of 250 miles. But I know he'll call; as soon as he nears the coast."

He sighed. "Which will be when?"

"Well . . . he should be back within range by this evening."

"By this evening, if I have my way, this entire city will be under evacuation, and there are going to be some real traffic jams. Listen, you can call him from his folks' place, surely."

Jo hesitated. The last thing she wanted right this minute was for Big Mike and Babs, not to mention Belle and Dale, to hear the sort of slanging Michael had taken to dishing out to her. But she could see Richard was deadly serious. "Okay," she said. "Listen. I'll hang on here until seven tonight, and see if I can raise him then. And if Faith is still coming straight for us this evening, I promise I'll go as soon as I've spoken to the yacht."

"You don't really believe me, do you," he said sadly.

"Well . . ." She bit her lip. It was really impossible to imagine anything serious happening to New York. "Of course I do, Richard, but I really don't want to descend on the Donnellys in their present state unless I have to. Besides . . ."

He knew what she was thinking. "Listen, Jo, I have no doubt at all that this is one hell of a fine building, and can stand up even to 160 mile an hour winds. But what about that window?"

Jo looked at the picture window and frowned.

"That is going to explode like a bomb," Richard told her. "Do you really want your kids in here when that happens?"

"My God," she said. "I hadn't thought of that."

"So get out while you can. If you don't want to trouble the Donnellys, go to that cottage of yours."

"Sure. I'll do that."

"But not until tonight?"

"We'll have time. Won't we?"

He sighed, and nodded. "Okay. Tonight." He took her in his arms. "Promise?"

"Guide's honour."

"I'll be counting on that. I have an idea things are going to start to hum tonight, and I probably won't have the opportunity to call you. But if you're going to be out of town, I won't have anything to worry about."

"And what are you going to be doing? Aren't you at risk from flying glass as much as anyone?"

"Sure. But I at least know what to expect. And I have a job to do. I'll call you at Bognor, the moment I can. Now . . ." He kissed her to stop her protests. "Let's drink to Michael. I reckon he's doing it the hardest possible way, right this minute."

Afternoon

The squalls continued all morning, the wind speed gradually rising in each one, and the wind gradually backing as well, from south-west to south-east and then through east to north-east. Michael shut down the engine as even under reefed main and storm jib *Esmeralda* was making nine knots; but as the wind began to head him it was not possible to maintain a course as much north as he would have liked.

It was a peculiar day in that during a squall visibility would close down to under a mile, and they seemed alone in an empty grey world. Then the rain would pass, the clouds would break as they chased across the sky, and, at least on the top of the swells, they could see forever, the horizon at once sharp and serrated by the surging waves. On these occasions they became comfortingly aware of how busy a stretch of ocean this was. Steamers appeared and disappeared again, all heading north as fast as they could, and Sam chatted with one huge container ship, whose operator remarked, "Say, you guys know what's behind you?"

"We're keeping an eye on it," Sam said, blood tingling at the non-chalance in his voice.

"Well, good luck," the operator said. "Keep your whisky clean."

The swell was now mountainous, at least 20 feet from trough to crest, but still long, perhaps 300 feet between each crest. With each squall the crests rose another six or eight feet in curling waves, a foretaste of what was to come. Yet *Esmeralda* coasted along very comfortably under her reduced canvas, and she was as ready for the storm as human ingenuity could manage. Michael had sailed in the infamous Fastnet Race of 1979 when a freak storm had caused a large number of yachts to be abandoned and some fifteen men had been lost, and he remembered that the casualties had been caused by two main factors: premature abandonment of a ship for a liferaft, and failure of safety gear. He also knew that the greatest danger any yachting crew can face in bad weather is that of man overboard. And already occasional waves were overtaking the yacht; he was now steering with the wind on the starboard quarter to avoid the dangers inherent in running dead in such conditions, but even so water would often splatter over the stern, not solid enough to be considered pooping as yet, but again a portent of what was on the way, with the consequent danger of being washed out of the cockpit. Thus he had given instructions that no man was to leave the cabin without two safety harnesses, so that he could be clipped on to two strong points at the same time – he knew the force that could be exerted were the ship to be knocked down. He had also commanded that two men were to be on the helm at all times, one steering, the other ready to take over should anything happen. And still he tried to envisage all possibilities, but as the afternoon wore on he felt he could relax for a while. He had done everything he could. After they had eaten the first of Mark's stews, he told the watch below to turn in and try to sleep, but they all preferred to remain on deck, watching the horrendous cloud formations looming up from the south.

At two o'clock they were hit by their first thunderstorm. Sam disconnected all his radio equipment in case of a strike; the yacht itself was perfectly safe as the mast would act as a lightning conductor, allowing the electrical discharge to run down the steel shrouds and thence into the chainplates, from where it would plunge harmlessly over the side. But of course a strike in the vicinity of the aerials could blow all their electronic gear.

The first storm passed over quickly enough, but now the wind had freshened, the anemometer mounted at the masthead, some forty feet above deck level, showing a steady 35 knots with gusts of up to 60 knots, which was as high as the gauge would read. Even under shortened sail the yacht was racing along, soaring up the back of each swell and careering down the other side in a welter of foam streaking away from the bows. "Heck, if this keeps up, we could be in Boston for dinner," Larry quipped.

"She's going too fast," Michael decided, as the bows nearly buried themselves in a shorter than usual swell. "Let's have that mainsail down."

They handed the mainsail, stuffing the wet canvas on to the boom and strapping it down with twice the normal number of sailties. "Okay," Michael said. "Mark and I will take over now."

Larry frowned at him. "Pete and I have only been on two hours."

"Two-hour watches from here on. It's going to be pretty damned exhausting. Now all of you get below and lie down. I don't care if you sleep or not. Just get your heads down for a couple of hours."

He connected both his harnesses, made Mark do the same, settled himself on the bench seat behind the wheel. With only her storm jib and mizen up the yacht was travelling much more slowly, but still handling perfectly well off the wind; the mizen staysail was acting as a secondary, airborne rudder. And while the wind was now blowing a steady 45 knots with gusts clearly far more than that, and the seas were building all the time, it was a slow process; Michael knew it took several hours for the sea state to approximate actual wind conditions. On the other hand he was now definitely steering more west than north which meant that he was closing the Gulf Stream. That had to be crossed at some stage, but he had no doubt it was going to be hard going; running at an average of four knots the Stream reacted to wind blowing across it almost like a race, and could be the roughest water anywhere in the world.

He had been on the helm an hour, and was thoroughly enjoying himself, steering the boat up and down the ever-increasing swell, when Mark looked astern. "Oh, Christ!" he said.

Michael cast a hasty glance over his shoulder, although he had already heard the roaring from behind him. This was a big wave, all of 25 feet high, he estimated, and topped by another six feet of curling crest. "Brace yourself," he snapped, tensing his muscles. "Close the hatch," he shouted. For the hatch cover had been left open a few inches to allow some fresh air into the cabin, as the ventilators had all been sealed. Now it slammed shut, and Michael concentrated. His job was to keep the yacht before the sea; if he let her yaw away to either side she might broach – turn broadside to the waves – and be rolled over and over like a car falling down a steep slope.

The roaring became louder, and he hunched his shoulders. He glanced at Mark, white-faced as he looked astern, then he was in the middle of a foaming maelstrom of water, and the wheel was threatening to tear from his hands. The force threw him against the steel circlet and he gasped at a sharp pain, even as he realised that Mark had been hurled forward from his place beside him. But the harnesses held, and the boy came to rest just short of the hastily closed companion hatch, gasping and spluttering. The entire yacht was for a moment submerged as the water poured over the decks, only the masts sticking up out of the flailing sea. Then the bows came up again, and she surged back to the surface, wallowing for a few seconds. This was actually the moment of greatest danger, as she had completely lost way and could not be steered, and was thus entirely at the mercy of the sea. But the wave crests were sufficiently far apart, and the wind sufficiently strong, for the jib to fill and the ship to start moving through the water before the next wave came up to them.

"Holy smoke!" Mark pulled himself back to the helm. "Have you ever seen one as big as that before, skipper?"

"Yes," Michael replied, truthfully enough. He did not add that the only previous occasion had been in that Force Ten storm of a few years before, and that had been at the very height of the gale – not with possibly double as much wind still to be expected.

Yet he was pleased with the way things were going, so far at least. The ship was handling perfectly, and the gear was standing the strain. Soon there were other waves as big as the first, but in time they became almost commonplace, as the yacht reacted to every one with perfect balance. The wind was now howling like every banshee in the world cutting loose at the same moment and the needle on the anemometer read out was pressed hard on the 60-knot mark. The sea was entirely covered in flying foam, and entering the troughs was like diving down to the centre of the earth; there was no way they could have any idea what was happening within even a hundred yards of them down there. Not that there was much to be seen from the tops of the crests either. The rain teemed down like solid grey walls, and felt as solid, too, battering on the oilskins and pounding the decks. Yet it was totally exhilarating. They were fighting the elements, taking them on at their own game, and holding their own.

Just. A mammoth wave hit them and for a dreadful moment, as the stern was picked up high above the bow and Michael fought to maintain control, he thought they were going to pitchpole, go stern over bow, an incredible thought for a 48-foot yacht, but still a possibility in such seas.

"That's it," he bawled. "We have to get all sail off her. Get up the watch below."

Mark banged on the hatch cover and the others came out. They gasped at the conditions, but immediately understood what was required. Larry and Pete went forward, crawling, unclipping one harness and clipping it on again before releasing the next. Then they were on the foredeck and clawing down the sail. Again the yacht was pooped and awash, and Michael held his breath as he saw them being thrown about the deck like tin soldiers. Part of the grab rail snapped and Peter for a moment was over the side, but his harness held, and he scrambled back on board, and eventually the sail was handed and strapped to the deck. Meanwhile, Mark and Jon took down the mizen.

"Good work," Michael said. "Get changed."

"My turn on the helm, skipper," Jon said. "Sam will keep me company."

Michael handed over the wheel and considered the situation. Without sail at all the dangers of broaching were increased, although with all canvas gone the yacht was riding easier, and the wind was so strong that she retained ample steerage way. He had two other possible courses of action, apart from just abandoning any attempt at command and letting her lie ahull. Then she might well be rolled over – but he knew yachts had survived extreme conditions by merely behaving like pieces of jetsam. To retain command he could either put out a sea anchor or trail warps astern, both to slow her down to the extent where she would be overtaken by each wave rather than carried on with them, and to keep her stern on to the seas. Neither appealed, as putting an immense extra strain on both gear and crew. He decided to let her stand on for as long as humanly possible. "Just keep a look out behind you," he suggested, and thankfully crawled through the hatch into the warmth and dryness of the cabin. Only as he stripped off his dripping oilskins and the sodden clothes beneath did he realise how his muscles were burning with exhaustion – or how much his ribs were hurting where they had been crushed against the wheel. He rolled into his bunk, flopped from the bulkhead against the canvas leeboard in perfect relaxed comfort, listened to the immense roaring from all about him, and fell asleep. To awake as the world turned upside down.

6.00 pm

"Help!" Mark was screaming. "We're sinking! Help!"

Michael found himself lying on the cabin roof, while there seemed water everywhere, together with books and pots and pans and clothes and sailbags. Despite the utter darkness, he knew immediately that they had been capsized, and that it was probably a pitchpoling, ass over tit as he would say in the bar of the yacht club at home. If he was ever going to stand in that bar again. But before he could even gather his thoughts *Esmeralda* was coming upright again, throwing him on to the cabin sole. He groped for the companion hatch, which had flown open, splashing through several inches of water, hearing the shouts and groans from behind him, standing on Sam's priceless MF set, which for all its extra lashing had become dislodged and smashed on to the deck; from being a place of warm refuge, indeed, the cabin had turned in an instant into a trap threatening to drown them all.

Michael was more concerned with what had happened on deck, gave a gasp of horror as he saw the wheel spinning free. Before he could reach it, the next wave had reached them, and hurled the yacht on to her beam ends, that is, on her side so that the mast would have lain in the water, had there still been a mast, while tons of ocean poured over her. It seemed impossible that she would not fill and go to the bottom, but the yawl came up again, bobbing like a cork, the enormous amount of air in her hull giving her a total buoyancy.

Michael dived aft and grabbed the helm, twisting it to bring the ship straight as she rose to the wind. He tried the engine starter, but this was dead, and he guessed that the batteries must also have come loose. But the yacht did respond, if sluggishly, and just in time to ride the next wave, which, although huge and breaking, he knew could be only a fraction of the size of the rogue that had sent them over. Once he had her under reasonable control, he could start thinking and looking for his crew. He spotted Jon, lying on the deck several feet forward of the cockpit. One of the steel harness hooks had opened straight as if made of plasticine, but the second had held, and the young man was at least still with the ship, although he appeared to be unconscious. But to Michael's horror there was no sign of Sam Davenport.

"Deck!" he screamed at the hatch. "All hands on deck!"

Larry came up the companion ladder, fell into the cockpit with a splash; the well was self draining, but there were still several inches of water in it. Mark followed a moment later. "We're sinking," he gasped again. "The water's up to the bunks. Oh my God, we're sinking!"

"Pete's broken something," Larry gasped, more coherently. "Maybe his shoulder. He's groaning terribly."

"He's alive," Michael snapped. "Get forward and find Sam."

He himself looked aft. In addition to their safety harnesses, the men on watch each wore a lifejacket, and Sam would still be floating, although as *Esmeralda* was picked up by another huge wave and rushed forward he knew there was no hope of turning back for anyone. But he saw nothing astern save for the roaring seas, and now there came a reassuring shout from the foredeck. "Give me a hand," Sam was calling.

Mark and Larry formed a human chain to drag him back into the cockpit. Both his harnesses had failed, but the second one had taken the force out of the enormous power which had hurled him forward, enabling him to wrap both arms around what remained of the mainmast; that had snapped off just below the lower crosstrees, or spreaders, some fifteen feet from the deck; at least it had gone cleanly and disappeared, taking most of its shrouds with it, ripping them out of the chainplates; had it remained linked to the yacht they would have been dead in the water. And amazingly, the mizen still stood.

"We're sinking," Mark gasped a third time. "She'll be gone in a moment." He reached past them in an attempt to free the six-man liferaft, the canister containing which was still strapped to the deck on the transom.

Michael released the helm with one hand long enough to slap the boy hard across the face. Mark gave a shriek and tumbled to the cockpit sole.

"Get him below," Michael snapped. "Take Jon down as well. Give me a report on him and Pete. And on damage. And start the pumps. All the pumps. Get with it."

They hurried below, and he fought with the helm. It was still daylight, although the clouds were so low and the rain so continuous it was difficult to see more than the ship's length – which was no bad thing, he reckoned: every few minutes the evening would be cut open by a jagged lightning flash, and then the immensity of the seas all around them was horrifying.

It seemed an eternity, but could only have been a few minutes later that Sam reappeared. "Pete has broken his shoulder," he said. "We've strapped him up and I've given him a sedative, and we've tied him to his bunk. Jon is still out. I don't like the look of him at all."

"Is he breathing?"

"Yes. But skipper . . ." His voice trembled.

"Pumps?"

"No good. All the batteries have broken loose. They're all over the place. It must've been one of them falling that hit Pete. The radios are both out, and the instruments. Michael, maybe Mark is right, and we should abandon ship."

"For the liferaft? For Christ's sake, do you suppose a liferaft could survive those seas? *Esmeralda* is not sinking," Michael said, his voice harsh. "Yachts don't sink unless they are holed or catch fire. You know that as well as I do. The water in the cabin came in through the hatch when we were rolled over and then knocked down. So we've no electrics. Man the hand pump and get Larry and Mark bailing. But first, bring me up my harnesses."

Sam blinked, for the first time appearing to notice that his skipper was wearing not even a lifejacket, indeed, nothing at all save a gold Rolex wristwatch. He dived below for the gear, and helped Michael strap himself to the boat and the helm.

"Skipper . . ."

"Get to work," Michael told him. "Get bailing. All of you."

Sam disappeared, and a moment later a thin stream of water began to empty over the side. Another wave roared up with such force that Michael lost control, and the following one knocked them down again; he sat on the transom with water round his neck. But the hatch had been bolted tight shut again, and the ship came upright. Michael laughed aloud. He remembered Byron's 'Manfred' where the hero shouted his defiance of God and the elements as he stood on his mountain top. Well, here on the edge of the Gulf Stream was the biggest mountain top he had ever experienced. "You won't beat me, you bastards," he shouted at the clouds and the lightning and the rain and the waves and the wind.

As if in reply he heard a noise. It was a noise with which he was thoroughly familiar, that of a rogue wave coming up astern. "Oh, Christ," he muttered and turned his head, and felt exactly as if a mule had kicked him in the belly. Behind him the entire ocean seemed to be rising in awesome fury. The white streaked green wall went up and up and up, perhaps to 50 feet, and was topped by 10 feet of curling white foam. It reared above the yacht, a wall of water as high as a house, and now it was toppling over and falling.

Park Avenue

11.00 pm

After Richard had returned to the studio, Jo began making her preparations. There was a lot to do. First of all she telephoned Bognor. "Have you seen the forecasts?" she asked Big Mike.

"Yeah. Would you believe that fucking storm seems to be following us about? Thank God we're here."

"I thank God, too. Listen, Dad, I thought the kids and I might come up to you for the weekend. If everyone is right it's going to be a little unpleasant in town."

"Sure, do that, honey. What time tomorrow were you thinking of coming?"

"Well . . ." She hesitated. She had given Richard her word to leave that evening. But it would be most inconvenient – quite apart from Big Mike's pointed suggestion – and somewhat of an unpleasant drive in the darkness and the rain: she certainly didn't want to upset Mike and Babs all over again by suggesting there was any danger. Besides, even if Richard did manage to talk the Mayor and the police into ordering an evacuation of the city, they were extremely unlikely to get anything moving before dawn tomorrow. "How about first thing in the morning. We'll be there for breakfast?"

"Breakfast? Holy shit! That'll mean leaving the city before dawn."

"We're early risers," Jo assured him.

"Okay. We'll expect you. Any word from Michael?"

"Not as yet. He's out of radio contact right now. I'm going to try him again this evening. Do you reckon he's all right?"

"Sure I do. Especially if the storm is turning west and he's making north. He'll run out of it."

"I worry about the Gulf Stream. From what he's told me those waves can be horrendous."

"They can," Big Mike agreed. "I've seen them. But Michael can handle that."

He seemed to have entirely recovered his ebullience. "How are Babs and Belle?" she asked.

"Well . . . Belle is taking things easy right now." Which Jo guessed meant she was under sedation, probably the reason Big Mike didn't want noisy kids around before tomorrow. "Babs is doing well. She'll be the better for seeing you and the young 'uns. Breakfast, eh? See you then."

"The weekend in Bognor? Neat," Owen Michael said.

"Well, that means an early night, because I want to get started at the crack of dawn. Now, give me a hand with the packing."

She packed for a weekend, and then pinched her lip. Suppose that window did shatter and let a whole lot of rain in? Richard seemed to think it could. All of her treasured possessions . . . but wasn't she thinking of giving most of them up, anyway? Certainly she couldn't take them with her.

She fed the children and put them to bed. The six o'clock forecast had revealed Faith's westward turn, but not dramatically, and Richard had been studiously calm and relaxed about what he had had to say; she guessed he was waiting to be given his instructions by JC and decided against calling him to give him her change of plan. She'd do it later.

Instead she tried getting a shore to ship call through to *Esmeralda*, but after an hour the operator told her it was impossible to raise the yacht and that she must still be out of range. That was a lot preferable to wondering if she could have been dismasted and lost her aerials, so Jo agreed to try again tomorrow morning, immediately before leaving for Bognor.

By now she decided it might be a good time to tell Richard what she was doing, or rather, what she was not doing before tomorrow, and called the studio, but the switchboard said he'd gone out for a bite to eat. "Ask him to call Mrs Donnelly when he comes in, will you," Jo said. By now everyone in the world, she supposed, knew that she and Richard had something going – and she didn't mind.

To keep herself awake, she kept the TV on and watched some irrelevant mini-series, and promptly fell fast asleep, to awake with a start. There had been a succession of rain squalls slashing the windows on and off during the evening, and distant rumblings, but she was totally surprised by the sudden flash of lightning and the almost immediate crack of thunder right overhead. The whole apartment block shuddered again and again, a vicious reminder of what it might be like were the hurricane really to hit the city.

She got up and went into the bedrooms, but amazingly, both Owen Michael and Tamsin were still fast asleep. But that thunderclap had ended her last doubt about leaving.

Then she thought of Marcia and Benny. They should leave too, and also seek the safety of Pinewoods. She reached for the phone and punched out the numbers, tapped her foot impatiently as she waited for them to answer, but there was no response. Her watch showed eleven o'clock, so there was no possibility they would have gone to bed. Thus they had to be out, at a party. She'd have to try them again later. She replaced the phone, and heard Julian Summers' voice, hastily turned back to the set.

"We are interrupting this programme to bring you the latest update on Hurricane Faith. Here is Richard Connors."

Richard had changed his wet clothes and was again well dressed and immaculate, but his face was grave. "Good evening," he said. "This is Richard Connors, bringing you the latest information we have on Hurricane Faith. Faith is now a very big storm indeed, the biggest, in terms of wind speeds, ever recorded. She has sustained winds around the centre of approximately 170 miles an hour, and her present position is here . . ." He stood in front of the wall map and pointed with his wand. "The co-ordinates are 37°20'N. latitude, 71°46'W. longitude. That places her, as you can see, 280 miles east by north of Norfolk, Virginia, and exactly the same distance south-east of New York. You can also see from her track, that she is now definitely heading north-west. There was some doubt about that earlier this evening, but now it is almost certain that we are going to feel the full effects of the storm here. There is also some evidence that Faith is beginning to quicken. For the past two days she has been moving very slowly, at an average of 10 knots. Now the speed appears to be increasing, which means that she could be no more than 24 hours away from us, if that. In any event, she will be here not later than Sunday morning.

"Now this is a highly dangerous storm. I repeat, she is the most dangerous storm we have ever seen in this area. Because of her size and intensity, we have little previous experience to work on, but with winds this high we can expect extensive damage. This means most roofs are going to be at risk, and all windows and doors will be extremely vulnerable. There is no glass in the world will stand up to such a force. There may also even be a risk to complete buildings, unless they have been constructed to an exceptionally high standard. That is what the wind will do. But an even greater problem will be presented by the storm surge. It could be as high as 30 feet, depending on the state of the tide when the hurricane actually touches land, but the effects will be felt some five hours before the full force of the storm is encountered. Such a storm surge would mean the flooding of vast areas of land along the coast, and indeed of considerable portions of Manhattan itself. We at NABS feel that in these circumstances it is our duty to warn you that everyone living within five miles of the coast in the area stretching from Atlantic City to Newport, Rhode Island, must consider themselves and their property in grave danger. In the interests of human safety we urge everyone who can to evacuate these areas before tomorrow afternoon and certainly all those whose dwellings are situated less than 50 feet above sea level. For those who cannot evacuate, for whatever reason, instant preparations must be made for a period of up to 48 hours after the storm has passed through. Especially is this important for anyone trapped . . . remaining in a high-rise office or apartment. This is because extensive and prolonged power outages can be expected as well as a complete failure of the telephone system. Additionally, a refuge should be prepared in each apartment away from external windows and doors, and a store of drinking water ensured. The best way to do this is fill the bathtub, now, while there is uncontaminated water available – but that water must be used only for drinking purposes."

He paused, and took a sip of water. "We have contacted the Police Department and asked for their immediate assistance in effecting this evacuation, and we are looking forward to their co-operation. Now let me stress that there is absolutely no need for any kind of panic. Hurricane Faith cannot reach New York before tomorrow afternoon at the very earliest. Therefore there is ample time for every man, woman and child who wishes to do so to leave the city. We hope and pray that this may only be a precautionary measure, that Faith may again change direction and retreat into the Atlantic, and that the danger may be past by this time tomorrow night. But until it is past, we must repeat, if your home is less than 50 feet above normal water level, and if it is within five miles of the sea, it may become subject to flooding and structural damage during the next 48 hours. This station will of course remain on the air for as long as there is power, bringing you up-dates and information as they are available. This is Richard Connors, for the National American Broadcasting Service. Thank you."

Saturday 29 July

Pre-Dawn

12.10 am

"Whew!" Julian Summers said, and wiped his brow.

"So here we go," Jayme agreed.

Richard lit a cigarette, something he very rarely did.

"I must say," Julian remarked. "I am really amazed that you finally persuaded JC to put that message out."

"Or that McGrath agreed to co-operate," Jayme said.

Richard stubbed out the cigarette again; he had taken only two puffs. "I didn't persuade anyone," he said.

"You mean they got the message," Julian suggested.

"No," Richard said. "I couldn't get hold of JC until half an hour ago; although he told me to contact him after the six-o'clock update, he'd gone out to cocktails and dinner. Then he flatly refused to allow a warning to go out until Faith is within 100 miles of the city. Kept repeating that we had done all we could by forecasting what was going to happen; it was up to the city authorities to take whatever steps they thought necessary, and if they didn't, well, to quote his favourite expression, the egg would be over their faces, not ours."

"Holy Jesus Christ," Julian commented. "Does he have any *idea*?"

"None whatsoever. He's prepared to risk maybe a million lives to score a political point."

"Well, thank God the police woke up in time," Jayme said.

"Let's hope they do," Richard agreed.

She stared at him. "You mean . . ."

"I didn't waste my time trying to get them to move. I didn't have the time. New York doesn't have the time."

They both stared at him. "Let me get this straight," Julian said at last. "You put out that warning without JC's permission, and without any reference to the NYPD?"

"It was the only way," Richard told them. "It had to be done."

"You have any idea what's going to be happening down there once that message percolates?"

"So there'll be an upheaval. And the police will just have to step in and sort it out. Just as they should've been doing since this morning. But people will start to leave the city, and that's all that matters. Sorry, gang, to have landed you in it . . .''

"Oh, we're with you," Jayme said. "But I guess we'd better barricade that door."

"And take the phones off," Julian suggested.

As he spoke, Richard's buzzed.

"I think I'll take all calls," Richard said, and picked it up. "Connors."

"Oh, Mr Connors," the switchboard said. "A Mrs Donnelly called a couple of hours ago, while you were out. She asked for you to call her back, but you told me you were taking no messages until your late forecast."

"Thank you, Maisie," Richard said. "She'll be out in Bognor, Connecticut. Just a moment." He checked his address book, gave her the number. "Call her there, will you." He replaced the phone, looked at his staff. "It'll take JC a little longer than that to react, I guess."

PARK AVENUE

12.15 am

Jo realised that she had completely misjudged the rapidity with which the authorities would get to work once they were convinced there really was trouble coming. And of course Richard would not have thought it necessary to let her know because he would assume she was already safely tucked away in Connecticut. "Oh, damn," she muttered.

But it would still surely take an hour or so for people to react and get on the streets. She was already packed, and the Mercedes was topped up with gas.

She ran into Owen Michael's bedroom, shook him awake. "Get dressed," she said. "Quickly now."

He sat up, looked at his window, against which the rain was pounding. "Is it dawn?" he asked incredulously.

"Not quite," Jo told him. "But we're leaving early. Hurry." She went into Tamsin's room, got her up as well.

"But Mommy," Tamsin complained. "It's all dark and rainy out there."

"It'll be light in Connecticut," Jo promised. "Now do hurry."

She returned to the lounge, once again looked around her. She must have left the apartment something like five hundred times to drive up to Bognor, never with the slightest doubt that in two days' time she would be back, or that everything would be exactly as she had left it. Now, wherever she glanced, her eye picked up something of enormous personal importance, presents from her parents, school trophies, photographs . . . a kitchen drawer disgorged plastic carriers and she rushed from room to room grabbing miscellaneous memorabilia, throwing them into a jumble until the carriers threatened to split. The carriage clock in the lounge said twenty-five minutes past twelve and she grabbed it, dropped it into her anorak pocket, and jostled Owen Michael and Tamsin out of the front door, dashed back for three cans of Coke and some cookies, and finally they crammed into the elevator with their belongings.

"Mom?" Owen Michael was at last waking up. "It's only just gone midnight."

"I know, darling."

"What an hour to leave town," Tamsin commented.

"What's the idea, Mom?"

Jo hesitated. She had to be careful not to frighten them, or get them worrying about their own treasured possessions such as Owen Michael's collection of model airplanes. "I thought we'd surprise Granpa and Granma."

"Surprise them?" Owen Michael said. "Holy shit!"

"Now please, Owen Michael," Jo remonstrated, and breathed a sigh of relief as the car came to rest in the lobby. Washington emerged from the office, much to her surprise. "Washington," she said. "What are you doing here?"

"I'm on night duty this week, Mrs Donnelly, in place of Luke Edwardes." He eyed the bags. "You folks going off somewhere, then? It sure is a poor night out there."

"Owen Michael, go on down to the garage and get yourself and Tamsin settled," Jo instructed. "Take those bags."

"I can do that, Mrs Donnelly," Washington protested.

"You can help me with this big one," Jo said. She watched the children disappear down the stairs. "Didn't you see the latest up-date on the hurricane, Washington?" she whispered. "It's coming straight at us. So I'm taking the children out of town."

"You are? Heck." His breath came through his teeth. "No, I didn't see it. What channel carried that?"

"NABS, not half an hour ago."

"No, I was watching a film about . . . say, ma'am, when are they expecting the storm to hit?" His eyes were wide with alarm.

"Maybe tonight, maybe tomorrow morning."

"Oh! Then there's plenty time." He smiled.

"There isn't," Jo scolded. "Do you know how many people live in Manhattan? Maybe seven million. Can you imagine the traffic jams when they all decide to leave together? There could well be a panic."

Washington stroked his chin and slowly nodded. "Guess you could be right, Mrs Donnelly. And that warning was put out by that Richard Connors, I guess. He'd know what's going on. And he's a friend of yours, too."

So you must know what's going on as well, Jo thought, having seen Richard coming here at odd hours of the day, and night. But that wasn't important, at this minute. "Yes," she said. "He does. Washington, I think you should wake everybody in the building, and tell them to leave. And then leave yourself."

"Oh, I couldn't do that, Mrs Donnelly," Washington protested. "I couldn't leave anyhow until I was sure the building was evacuated, and I couldn't leave even then. Suppose somebody was to break in?"

"Washington, no one can expect you to sit here throughout a hurricane, surely. Okay, so you have to see everybody off the premises, but then surely you can go. Ring the agents and find out."

"At one o'clock in the morning? There wouldn't be anyone there, Mrs Donnelly. But I'd better go wake those folks up. They ain't going to be too pleased, either."

"And be sure you leave yourself the moment you can," Jo said severely.

"Yeah. I guess I could wake the old lady now and tell her to pack a bag," Washington decided. "Yeah. You say that storm is coming straight for us?"

"Yes," Jo said. "Straight for us." She ran down the stairs to join the children in the Mercedes.

New York Police Department Headquarters, Park Row

12.30 am

Assistant Commissioner McGrath yawned, stretched, and looked at his watch. "Christ! It's gone midnight."

The waiting police captains seated around the table exchanged glances; they could have told him that half an hour ago. It was his innovation, to hold these Friday night sessions when every conceivable important case or public event coming up the following week was reviewed in detail, numbers of men required on the spot allocated, and responsibility determined, so that every man would arrive at the office on Monday morning knowing exactly what he had to do – but they did drag on.

"Any coffee left?" the AC asked, and then got up to walk to the window and look out at Park Row. "Brother, is it raining out there." He blinked at the lightning flash which cut across the sky. "And doing everything else as well." Someone placed a fresh cup of coffee in his hand, and he turned back to face his men. "Anything left before we wrap it up?"

"Just the Garcia case," said Captain Harmon.

"Hell, yes, I'd forgotten that. When do we get Garcia back from Cleveland?"

"He arrived this afternoon. He's downstairs in the cells now. We're going to charge him Monday."

"Any trouble with Cleveland?"

"A few grumbles. But I pointed out they only have a trafficking charge. We have extortion and murder in addition to narcotics, and our warrant was signed before theirs. So they agreed we should have first crack."

"Will the murder charge stick?"

"Probably not, given Garcia's reputation for getting rid of witnesses. But I think we have him on the narcotics."

McGrath pointed. "If we can't fry the rat, I want him put away for so long he'll have forgotten which way Manhattan faces when he comes out. Got me?"

"We'll put him away, Chief," Harmon said soothingly.

"Just so long as you do. Keep me posted, every inch of the way. Okay. Let's call it a day."

The men started to get up, and the telephone rang. Captain Wright picked it up, listened. "It's the eighth precinct. For you, Harry."

Captain Jonsson took the phone, listening, brows slowly gathering into a frown. "So the weekend is starting early," he remarked, then listened some more. "Okay," he said at last, "I'm coming over. Put some extra men out. I'll be right there." He replaced the phone. "There's something strange going on. My people say the streets are suddenly getting real busy, and there's been some trouble after an accident."

"What do you mean, busy?" McGrath demanded. "In the middle of the night?"

"People leaving town," Jonsson explained.

"In the middle of the night?" McGrath asked again, incredulously.

"Going away early for the weekend," Wright suggested.

"That's what I thought," Jonsson said. "But there could be more to it than that. Lieutenant Lancing says there's damn near a riot going on because some character has skidded and blocked a road. Seems people are shouting they have to get out of town before Faith gets here."

"Who the hell is Faith?" Wright demanded.

"Faith," McGrath muttered. "Ain't that that hurricane out in the Atlantic?"

"Hell, yes," Jonsson said. "Well, look, Chief, I'd better get down there."

The phone was ringing again, and another message arrived from another precinct, telling of crowds and agitation in the streets.

"Fucking shit!" McGrath took over the phone himself. "Get me the Hurricane Centre in Coral Gables. I want to speak to the man himself, Eisener. Sure I know what time it is, and I don't give a damn. Get him on the line." He replaced the phone. "All of you guys get back to your precincts and put extra men on the streets. We could have a major traffic snarl up. And somebody find out who started this alarm."

"It was a television broadcast," said Captain Luther, who had just returned from checking with the duty officer. "That forecaster from NABS, Connors, went on the air just before midnight and issued a warning that Hurricane Faith is coming straight at us, with winds of 170 miles an hour."

"Holy Jesus, why wasn't I told at once?" McGrath bawled. "That crazy character . . . he was down here asking damn silly questions a couple of days ago, and then telling the world we didn't have any plans to deal with a hurricane. A hurricane! In New York! Shit! He wanted us to plan an evacuation of the city. An evacuation. Christ!"

"Well, Connors apparently told everyone to do just that," Luther said. "He predicted all kinds of damage, suggested that the city might just about be blown flat."

"New York?" Wright asked in consternation.

"For Jesus' sake, where'd he get the authority to do something like that?" McGrath bawled. "After that broadcast Thursday night I called the Mayor and asked him if he wanted us to take any steps, and he said to forget it, those weather boys are just a bunch of alarmists."

"Maybe it's a hoax," someone suggested.

"But how the hell did he get it across to so many people?" asked someone else. "You mean to tell me there are actually people watching television at midnight?"

"Sure there are," Luther told him. "Enough to get scared and start waking their neighbours."

"For Christ's sake," McGrath bellowed into the phone. "Get the Commissioner. And the Mayor. Sure, wake them up, if you have to. We could have a problem." He grabbed his other phone as it buzzed. "Oh, Dr Eisener, John McGrath, NYPD, here . . . Pretty good. Say, I'm sorry to wake you up like this . . . oh, you were up anyway? Well, that's great. Say, about this Faith thing . . . great balls of fire. You mean that fellow Connors could be right? . . . Oh, you didn't see it? Well, it seems he's issued some kind of 24-hour warning that New York should be evacuated, on his own authority . . . 24 hours is right? . . . Maybe less? Christ Almighty . . . Ah . . . Yeah . . . Yeah, that's what's bugging us. I mean, they always have veered before . . . Yeah . . . Yeah, sure, we can handle it . . . Yeah . . . Thanks a million, Dr Eisener. Keep us posted." He replaced the phone. "Seems that thing *could* hit us."

"Could?" Harmon inquired. "Or will?"

"Well, Eisener says it could still do anything, and he agrees with me that it should start to veer off to the north-east any minute now; seems it's picking up speed. But he thinks there's a real risk it might not turn off until after making a landfall, somewhere like Atlantic City, which would put us in the dangerous quadrant. He thinks Connors did the right thing. Well, hell, I sure don't agree with him. I'm gonna lock that guy up for causing a public nuisance."

"J. Calthrop White," Luther said. "He owns NABS. He'll have put Connors up to it. He has a running war going with City Hall anyway."

"I wouldn't mind locking that bastard up as well," McGrath growled. He banged on the telephone. "Come on, come on, get me those numbers."

"Well, they're all asleep, Mr McGrath," the girl protested.

"So wake them up. And come to think of it, wake J. Calthrop White up as well. Tell him I want a word. And somebody go out and get Connors. Come on, get off your asses. Move. We could have a panic in the streets."

THE STREETS OF NEW YORK

1.00 am

Jo started the engine, lined the Mercedes up, punched the red button on the wall, and waited for the steel doors to go up – and remembered Marcia! She had been going to call again, and had completely forgotten about it. But she couldn't abandon her sister-in-law down in Greenwich Village, which was definitely less than fifty feet above sea level and liable to be flooded out if Richard was at all accurate in his prognostications. Anyway at this hour of the morning it would only take ten minutes to get down there and pick up her and Benny, or at least tell them what was happening.

Though she knew the weather had been deteriorating all evening, she was unprepared for the density of rain that hit the automobile as she topped the ramp on to the street. And there were far more vehicles about too, than she had expected, nearly all heading north – it took her several minutes to edge into a stream, and then across it.

"Mom, this is terrible. Can't we wait till it clears? I'm cold." Owen Michael shivered and curled down in his seat.

"I'm freezing," Tamsin put in.

"In July? Forget it," Jo told them. But now at last turned south, she flicked on both heater and demister, leaning forward to peer through the dazzle set up by the lights of the oncoming traffic: the condensation was clearing as the heat got to it, but the screen was empty of water for only a brief second at a time, with each rapid sweep of the wipers. "Nana's rug is on the back seat. Wrap it round your legs, Tamsin."

"How come she always gets the rug?" Owen Michael grumbled.

"Because you're bigger and stronger," Jo told him, wishing he'd shut up and let her concentrate. The combination of rain, traffic and repeated red lights stretched the journey to Greenwich Village into twenty minutes, and one glance at the empty square of concrete beside Benny and Marcia's house, where they always kept their car, told Jo that they still weren't in.

The clock behind the wheel showed 1.25 am. They could of course still be out at their party. Equally, they could have seen Richard's telecast and already left; it was unlikely that Marcia would have worried about *her*. But still . . . Jo braked the care and got out. "I'm going to try ringing for a minute, just in case they're in after all," she told the children. "Maybe their automobile is in the garage again," remembering the idiosyncrasies of their ancient and battered Ford. She was soaked by the time she had satisfied herself that the house was empty, and hurried back to the Mercedes, dripping water everywhere, chewing her lip in indecision. She was still anxious about the young couple, but she couldn't risk waiting for their return . . . the traffic was building all the time.

Progress north was gradually slowed as the lights constantly changed at intersections, and the traffic steadily built up, with much shouting and swearing and honking on horns to suggest that quite a few New Yorkers had heard Richard's warning and decided to act on it. It occurred to her that the avenues farther east might be less congested; she could always cross back again later. Seventh, Sixth and Fifth all showed a mass of lights gleaming through the rain, but Park looked better, so she swung the Mercedes north again and made steady progress up-hill, round the Pan American Building, but still the number of vehicles around her was increasing, the blare of horns becoming more insistent, and the mood of the drivers deteriorating.

She passed 47th Street, 48th, their own apartment block, from the garage of which a steady stream of automobiles was issuing to indicate that Washington had been doing his job – 49th Street . . . "How long will it take to get to Bognor, Mom?" Owen Michael asked. "I've never seen the streets so busy."

"Everyone's going away for the weekend," Jo agreed. "I thought we'd be half way there by now." The lights changed, and she braked, drawing up slowly behind a white Chevrolet which inched forward in anticipation of the change back, and then leapt into gear immediately on amber. Jo followed . . . and she and Owen Michael yelled in unison as a blue Cadillac, engine racing to beat the lights which had already turned against it, smashed into the Mercedes' front wing, sending it spinning into the car on their left.

Tamsin screamed as another automobile hit the Mercedes from behind, throwing it at right angles to the street. Then there were other vehicles all around it, braying horns, screaming drivers . . . Jo shook her head, realising that she was not actually hurt, and looked at Owen Michael. If that bump had opened his stitches . . .

He managed a smile. "I'm okay, Mom."

She twisted in her seat and Tamsin sniffed. "I was so scared."

"Well, you had every reason to be." Jo opened her door and got out, into the rain. "You stupid idiot," she bawled at the driver of the Cadillac.

He ignored her, and his crumpled bumper, wrenched his automobile round, tearing off some of her wing as he did so, and joined the stream of traffic hurrying away from the lights.

"Bastard," Jo muttered, so angry she forgot to take his number, and bent to look at the damage. The right wing was pushed hard in against the wheel, and she doubted it would turn, at least without immediately tearing the rubber to shreds. She went to the rear, and saw an equal amount of damage. She needed a garage. And now the cacophony around her was tremendous, as other automobiles tried to pass her, and bumped against the next lane of traffic.

"Get that fucking wreck off the road," someone shouted at her.

"Yeah, lady, you're blocking the road," shouted someone else.

"How can I move the goddamned thing?" she shouted back. "I need a tow."

"Then let us help you," someone else bawled. The lights had by now changed from green to red and then back again to green. Now, before she could stop them, four men leapt from behind the driving wheels of their packed vehicles and ran to the Mercedes. They put their shoulders to the body and began to heave, cheered on by their passengers and immediately joined by several more frustrated drivers.

"Stop that!" Jo screamed. "My children are in there!" She grabbed at their shoulders, but they shrugged her off, and she slipped and fell on the wet street, only just being missed by an automobile in the next lane, which swerved round her, cannoned off its neighbour, and slithered away down the avenue.

Jo scrambled to her feet and ran to the Mercedes, which had been pushed on to the centre space, half on its side. She pulled the doors open, and Owen Michael and Tamsin tumbled out, gasping and crying. "Oh, my darlings," she shrieked. "Are you all right?"

Tamsin threw both arms round her.

"Yeah," Owen Michael said. "Yeah. But what's got into these people?"

Jo hugged him too, and looked past him at the Mercedes, which had now been pushed right over on its side; the men ran away from it, shouting and laughing. Jo watched them drive off, then saw a police officer making his way through the rain towards her, water dripping from his cap and cape. "Did you see what happened?" she shouted. "Did you see those men wreck my car?"

"Yeah," he agreed. "These people sure are in a hurry."

"Well, aren't you going to do something about it?"

"Me, lady? I'd need the goddamned National Guard to stop this bunch. They're scared stiff."

"But . . . my auto . . . look, you have a radio. Can't you call a garage for a tow truck?"

He peered at the twisted metal. "It sure is a wreck. Calling a garage wouldn't do any good; they'd never get here. That vehicle ain't going anywhere tonight, lady. I reckon you have to get hold of something else if you mean to leave town."

Jo stared at him in disbelief, then at the Mercedes, then again at the traffic streaming by behind gleaming lights and blaring horns. At that moment she hated everyone in the world, wanted to shout and scream in her outrage. But she knew that losing her temper was going to accomplish nothing – and there was Michael's Cadillac waiting in the garage only a few blocks behind her; as he had been planning to stay away at least a fortnight, he had driven up with Sam, who actually lived in Newport, rather than leave his car in the park for that time.

"Thanks for your advice, officer," she said. She wrestled the boot open, selected the suitcase she regarded as containing the most important items – she knew she could only carry one, and there was no question of Owen Michael hefting any weight – locked the boot again, told the boy to hold his sister's hand, and walked on into the rain.

NATIONAL AMERICAN BROADCASTING SERVICE OFFICES, FIFTH AVENUE

1.30 am

"I'm sorry, Mr Connors," the switchboard said. "But there is no reply from that number."

"Well . . ." She must have gone to her parents-in-law after all; presumably the reason she had just left a message for him to call her instead of specifying where was pure excitement. "Can you obtain from exchange the number of Mr Michael Donnelly? He lives in Bognor, too. Get the number, and call there for me, will you?" He replaced the phone, got up, and looked down at the street far below him. It, all New York, was now a constant ribbon of light, and the traffic was steadily growing. It was going to be a grim dawn, and already it was murky, with a gusty wind driving a succession of rain squalls in front of it, with darting lightning flashes serrating the gloom, accompanied always by a continuous rumble of thunder. Faith was coming closer – but if she held off until tomorrow there was time for most of those people to get away. If she held off until tomorrow. "How're you doing with the Hurricane Centre?" he asked Julian. They were alone now; he had told Jayme to get out while she could.

"I just can't get through," Julian confessed. "I guess every forecaster in the country is trying to ring Eisener."

"Hey," Richard said. "Wasn't Waring planning to keep a camera crew in Coral Gables over the weekend?"

Hal Waring was the producer of the weather programme on NABS. "Sure."

"Well, then, can't we raise them on the link?"

"At two o'clock in the morning that crowd will be in bed," Julian pointed out. "They were planning to start filming again at 5.30, in time to relay an update and also have an interview with Dr Eisener for your first forecast."

"I need an update now," Richard said. "It's four hours since our last. That storm could have done anything in four hours. Listen, get through to whichever technicians are on duty and tell them we have to have a link opened to the Hurricane Centre as quickly as possible, and then call Coral Gables and get that crew awake."

"For a live show? We'll need a producer and a director, and God knows who else."

"Forget that," Richard snapped.

"Company policy."

"I'll produce and direct," Richard told him. "It won't be a live telecast, anyway, just a recording. We don't have the time for any company red tape." The phone buzzed, and he grabbed it.

"I have Bognor on the line, Mr Connors."

"Hello," he said. "Mr Donnelly?"

"Speaking," said the gruff voice. "Who the hell is that?"

"Richard Connors, from NABS. I'd like to speak to Jo, please."

"To Jo? What the hell is this?"

"She asked me to call," Richard explained, patiently.

"At two o'clock in the morning? Holy shit! Anyway, she ain't here."

Richard frowned. "Hasn't she been there?"

"No, for Christ's sake."

"But . . . aren't you expecting her?"

"Sure. Tomorrow morning. This morning, for God's sake. For breakfast! Now get off the line. You've woken up the whole goddamned house."

The phone went dead, and Richard slowly replaced it. What the devil could have happened? He picked it up again. "Call Mrs Donnelly's Park Avenue number, please, Maisie."

"Right away, Mr Connors." She was back in five minutes. "There's no reply, Mr Connors. I spoke with the night porter, and he said Mrs Donnelly and her children left the building, by automobile, just after midnight."

"Thank God for that," Richard said. Just after midnight. They'd have headed straight for the Bronx, New Rochelle, and the New England Thruway. And leaving immediately after the telecast they'd have beaten the traffic build up. Presumably she had called him to explain the reason for her delayed departure, whatever that had been – but it didn't matter now. She was safe and in another hour and a half she'd be in Bognor, well away from the coast and anything more than a strong breeze: he could concentrate on the job.

The phone was buzzing again. "I have Mr White for you, Mr Connors," Maisie said.

"Oh, Christ," he muttered and wagged his eyebrows at Julian, who was still trying all sorts of internal numbers in his efforts to create a link with the Weather Centre, presently without success. But how the hell had JC got into the act so early – and yet not early enough if he had actually seen the telecast? "Good morning, JC," he said. "Well, it isn't such a good morning after all, is it?"

"Richard," JC said. He did not sound very angry, not even like a man who has recently been awakened in the small hours of the morning. But then, JC's voice never did change its timbre. "I have just been called by Assistant Commissioner McGrath, inquiring if I had authorised my station to put out an emergency warning for the evacuation of New York City. Has such a warning been issued by NABS?"

"Yes, sir, Mr White."

"Who by?"

"I made the telecast, sir."

"On whose authority did you do that, Richard? Did Waring give you authorisation?"

"I haven't seen Hal since the 10.30 forecast, sir, although I'm expecting him in at any moment for the morning update. If he can get through the traffic."

"Then on whose authority did you make that telecast? What programme did you interrupt?"

"I interrupted a movie, Mr White. I convinced the programme controller that it was necessary to do so. He wanted to call Mr Kiley, but I told him I had your authority. I take full responsibility, sir."

"You do." Still JC did not raise his voice. "You acted on your own initiative despite an express directive from me to the contrary?"

"I felt it to be necessary, sir, in view of the direction Hurricane Faith is now taking."

"Has she changed speed or track since last we spoke?"

"Not to my knowledge, sir. But . . ."

"So, she still cannot reach New York for another 24 hours at the earliest, right?"

"Well, sir . . ."

"Thus the circumstances are exactly the same as when I gave you definite instructions last night, are they not?"

"They are, sir, except that the hurricane is now that much closer, and she could quicken up. There is simply no way of telling."

"Just as there is no way of telling if she might suddenly stop, or turn away. Richard, has it occurred to you that the National American Broadcasting Service may well have to face severe censure – and withdrawal of advertising revenue as a consequence – for what you have done? You have deliberately created a panic situation without the slightest justification."

"I disagree, Mr White. I think I had every justification. In fact I think I, we, the service, had a responsibility, in view of the facts in our possession."

"Richard, I would like you to clear out your desk and be off the studio premises by seven o'clock this morning. Your employment is terminated as of this moment. I will call my lawyers on Monday and have them advise me on whether, in the circumstances, we are under any obligation to buy out your contract. I doubt, in view of the utter irresponsibility of your action, your flagrant disregard of a directive from the company president, that they will consider that a necessity. Now remember, Richard, I do not want you on any property owned or controlled by me after seven o'clock this morning. Or you will be charged with trespass, in addition to whatever other charges the police may be intending to bring against you. Have a good day." The phone went dead.

Richard looked at it, then at Julian, then at a wind-swept and rain-drenched Jayme, who had just come in and was peeling off a slippery anorak. "Hi," she said. "Do you have any idea what it's like out there?"

"I thought I told you to leave town?" Richard demanded.

"Well, I was going to do that . . . but then I decided I should be with you guys. The fact is, I abandoned my automobile. There's an eight-mile tail back through the Hudson Tunnel. They're bumper to bumper and jammed solid. I've been walking for the past hour, in the rain. You could at least seem happy to see me."

"I always thought you were a natural blonde," Julian remarked.

Jayme surveyed the black line through her dripping hair in her compact mirror. "Needs touching up, doesn't it?" she agreed, and looked over her shoulder at Richard. "What's the matter with you, then?"

"I have just been fired."

"Oh. Ah . . . I'll make some coffee."

"Silly old bastard," Julian grunted. "Let's hope Faith scores a direct hit on his part of Long Island, just as Gloria did. Only he's so goddamned lucky he probably won't even have a tree down. I don't think he lost any in Gloria, either. What are you going to do?"

"Stay right here until this thing is over."

"But . . ."

"Sure, he says he'll charge me with trespass if I'm here after seven. So let him."

The phone buzzed.

"But if that's him," Richard said, "you'd better tell him you're in charge."

"Yeah," Julian said, uncertainly, and picked it up. "Summers. Oh, hi. Yes, he's here." He handed it over. "Your friend Hammond."

"Mark!" Richard shouted, then flipped on the open speaker and returned the handset.

"I've been trying to get you for damn near an hour," Mark said. He sounded at once tired and aggrieved – but also excited.

"Well, the line's been kind of busy. What do you have?"

"What do I have," Mark said. "I got back just after midnight. Christ, I have never been in anything like that, and I sure as hell hope I am never in anything like that again. Write down these co-ordinates."

Richard grabbed a pad and pencil and wrote, then frowned. "Hold on, old buddy, that can't be right. We got a ten o'clock update from Coral Gables which placed her 280 miles south-east of us. These figures make her only 240. And you say you got them just before midnight? Faith has moved 40 miles in two hours?"

"That's what I'm telling you," Mark said. "She has suddenly put her skates on, and turned some more, and she is moving north-west at 20 knots."

"Holy shitting cows," Julian commented.

"And then some."

"But that means she'll be with us . . . Christ, at two o'clock this afternoon," Richard said.

"I reckon so," Mark said. "But that ain't all. Sustained winds are 180 miles an hour plus."

"Say again?"

"You heard me, buddy boy. I damn near lost the ship. Listen, I'm going out again at dawn. I'll call you again when I get back. Right now I'm aiming for a little sleep. Can you use the data?"

"Use it," Richard said. "God Almighty! 180 miles per hour. You ever heard of that before?"

"Can't say I have. As they say, it's gonna be a great time in the old town tonight. Or rather, this afternoon. If I were you, buddy boy, I'd head for the Catskills. See you."

The phone went dead, and the three of them stared at each other. "Tides," Richard snapped. "Holy Christ, tides!"

"Jayme," Julian snapped. "The tide tables." He snatched the booklet from her hand. "High tide 1.18 this afternoon. And it's a biggie; more than six feet."

"Hell," Richard said. "Oh, hell."

"You reckon this is the biggest storm in all history?" Jayme asked.

"I don't know," Richard said. "But I reckon that we need a new category to describe it: Category Six!"

GREENWICH VILLAGE

1.45 am

Marcia yawned. "Jees, I can hardly keep my eyes open. Where are we?" She peered through the steamed up windscreen at the deluge outside the automobile, half blinded by the oncoming headlights.

"Just coming through Stuyvesant Square headed for Houston," Benny replied briefly, frowning at the traffic.

"Why Houston? Why didn't you turn on to 14th, as usual?"

"Thought this would be quicker."

Marcia peered out again. "What the hell's going on, baby? Will you just look at all this crowd? What time is it?"

"Not two yet."

"Seems like Kitty's wasn't the only party. I'm never going to be able to get out of bed in the morning. And I'd so wanted to finish the paintwork in the lounge. It's looking pretty good, don't you think?"

"Great," was Benny's absent-minded reply. He was feeling grouchy. The more of these parties they went to, the less he liked them. They had planned to arrive early and leave early, but all the late arrivals had jammed their auto in tight and he and Marcia had realised that they couldn't get away without breaking up Kitty's entire evening – so they had returned to the mêlée, trying to look jolly while bored out of their minds.

It was 2.15 when they rolled up on to the concrete parking space and they failed to unlock the front door before they were drenched to the skin, while thunder and lightning crashed and flashed around their heads.

"Phew, this is some storm. Must be an offshoot of that hurricane people were talking about at the party. It's the same one as hit your folks' place in the Bahamas, you know.''

"I know," Marcia said, for a moment almost sober. Taking Belle out to Bognor had been the most traumatic experience of her life, and of course they were all still mourning poor Lawson . . . she hadn't been able to make herself tell Babs about the baby. But heck, life had to go on.

Benny bolted the door on the inside, leaned against it, and yawned. "What say we take the phone off the hook and sleep in, huh?"

"Hiram Korovski is calling early about that idea he had . . ."

"That's why I suggest we disconnect it. I'll be in no state to discuss Hiram's ideas till after lunch."

"True." Marcia giggled and rubbed her wet face against his. "Come on, let's take just one look before we go up." She pulled his arm towards the lounge door. Together they stood, dripping, to admire their handiwork – the fresh wallpaper which covered all the nail holes, scars left by mindless tenants over the years, the new white paint on door and window frames, and the alcove of shelves by the fireplace, which Marcia planned to finish when she woke up. The four second-hand chairs and the settee stood in the middle of the room with the pile of loose covers and matching drapes, all under an old sheet, waiting to be fixed in place as soon as the paint pots were out of the way. "Whee! Isn't it exciting?" Marcia hugged Benny's arm.

"It's the best looking lounge in the village." He kissed her nose. "And when it's finished, we start on the nursery." Benny was more excited about the baby than anything else.

Marcia patted her stomach. "Junior, you are going to have the neatest nursery in New York." Then she suddenly shivered. "Let's get out of these wet things. Either I'm catching my death of cold, or a goose just walked over my grave."

LONG ISLAND

2.00 am

"Kiley?" asked J. Calthrop White. "Is that you, Kiley?"

"For God's sake . . ." Kiley started, then realised who was on the other end of the telephone. "Oh, good morning, JC. Kind of early."

"Kiley, what the hell have you been doing?"

"I've been sleeping, JC. It's two o'clock in the morning."

"Haven't you been watching television?"

"JC, I never watch television, once I get home."

"Well, let me tell you that all hell is busting loose out there right this minute."

"Oh, you mean the storm. Yeah, I can hear it."

"I do not mean the storm. I mean New York is goddamned well running wild. It's all the fault of that goddamned protégé of yours, Connors. I've told him to quit."

"You what? JC, I do the hiring and firing." Outrage at being awakened had given Kiley unusual courage.

"Well, you weren't there, were you? And you didn't know what was going on. But that's not relevant. Listen to me, Kiley: that asshole may just for once have hit the nail on the head. Seems this storm could hit New York after all, some time this weekend. Now, Kiley, did our bid and the bank guarantee go off?"

"Well, no, JC. You told me specifically it was to go on Monday morning so no one could tell in advance what we were offering. Don't worry, JC, it'll be faxed out at six o'clock Monday morning. Bids close noon UK time, so it'll be there spot on."

"Kiley, what happens if there are no electrics on Monday morning?"

"No electrics? Now, really, JC . . ."

"According to Connors, this storm could cause a two-day outage."

"And you believe that?"

"I don't know whether I believe it or not. I know if it happened it could fuck us up. Kiley, I want you to get down to the office rightaway and put in that bid. So it'll stay cold until Monday; even if somebody does look at it and tell our competitors it'll be too late for them to do anything about it."

Kiley hesitated, then sighed. "Okay, JC. But all bids have to be supported by bank guarantees. Hunt were going to fax that Monday as well."

"Well, they'll have to do it today."

"Saturday?"

"Get them moving. Get someone down there to do it. Come to think of it . . . holy shit! I want all our funds moved out, Kiley. Personal accounts too. Get them off someplace inland."

"JC, nothing can possibly happen to Wall Street."

"Yeah? It's kind of low down, right? Again, if this asshole Connors is right it could get flooded."

"JC, the computers with your accounts in them are in the vaults. Nothing can get into those vaults."

"Kiley, those vaults are under ground. I want my money out of there, this morning. Now get on it. Have a good day." The phone went dead.

Park Avenue

2.15 am

"We might as well leave the bag in Washington's office while we change," Jo told the children as they staggered through the glass doors into the lobby of the apartment block. It had been a dreadful walk back through the rain and the strong blustering wind and the teeming streets, and she was exhausted from carrying the heavy suitcase. The children were pretty weary as well, but at least they had had six hours' sleep before setting off. Orphans of the storm! That was an apt description of them now. It was hard to decide whether to curse the ill luck of the accident or thank God it had happened so close to the apartment. Though they were all soaked to the skin, at least they would be able to change into dry clothes before trying again with Michael's Cadillac.

Washington's office was empty, and she remembered that she had advised him to leave while he could. But it was also unlocked, the light was still burning, and his pens were lying on the desk – so he was clearly still somewhere in the building. She put her suitcase in one corner, and encountered several people in the foyer, clutching bags and hurrying for the basement garage. As was usual in big apartment blocks, Jo hardly knew any of her neighbours, and so she merely summoned up a tired smile. But one of the women apparently knew her by sight, because she shouted, "Mrs Donnelly! Haven't you heard the news? We're leaving town. Aren't you?"

"I'm trying to," Jo confessed. "We've had an accident. The traffic out there is something else."

"You poor girl," the woman said. "You're not hurt?" She peered at the children."

"We're okay," Owen Michael said.

"Well, say," said the woman's husband, who was waiting impatiently for his wife to join him at the elevator, "if you want a ride with us, Mrs Donnelly, there'll be room."

"That is awfully kind of you," Jo said, "but actually I've just come back to change my clothes and pick up my husband's car. Thanks again."

She hurried Owen Michael and Tamsin into an ascending car. "Say, Mom, is this Hurricane Faith?" Owen Michael asked.

"Naw," Tamsin declared before Jo could reply. "Faith was much worse than this."

"How much worse?"

"Oh . . ." And suddenly she began to cry. She was really scared, as well as wet and miserable. And she had been scared before.

"Faith isn't going to hurt you here, darling," Jo promised her. The car

254

stopped, and they ran into the apartment. "You two change while I get the car keys." Seeing all those frightened people had increased her sense of urgency, and she had decided against wasting the time to change herself.

But the keys weren't in Michael's desk, their usual resting place. She knew he kept a spare set at the office, but where the others were . . . she hunted through every pants and jacket pocket in his closet and every drawer in the apartment, while a build-up of panic clawed at her mind, making her catch her breath.

"They must be in the pants he was wearing when he left," Owen Michael said logically, emerging from his room in dry clothes. "So we'll have to take that ride after all, I reckon."

"If they're still there," Jo muttered. The lousy, rotten bastard, she thought, leaving his car, but taking his keys with him. She called Washington's office, but there was no reply. "You two stay here," she told them, and took the elevator down again. Washington could be anywhere, and now the foyer was deserted. So was the basement garage, of people, and there were only one or two cars left as well. One of them was Michael's gleaming white Cadillac El Dorado. When she looked at it she wanted to scream. And when it slowly dawned on her that probably everyone had left the building, even Washington, she wanted to scream even louder.

She rode back up to the apartment. "We'll call a cab," she told the children, trying to appear calm and unflustered. She flicked rapidly through the yellow pages – but either the lines were busy or just not answering. Sweat was running down her face as she punched over and over at the same numbers, until at last there was a reply. Hastily she gasped her request.

"Sorry, lady, but there won't be nothing available for at least two hours, if then. If you'd like to leave your name and number we'll get back to you whenever we can."

"Forget it," she said. Two hours! Already the wind was howling outside the plate-glass window. There was only one person she could turn to, now.

"Who're you calling now, Mom?" Owen Michael yawned and sat on the settee; Tamsin had already stretched out on her bed and was fast asleep.

"Mr Connors at the TV studio," Jo explained. "Just to find out what's happening. Hello," she said. "May I speak with Richard Connors, please? I'll hold."

She looked into the street as she waited. The rain had eased temporarily, but the lightning still flashed, and the thunder was continuous, mingling with the whine of the wind. And she was totally shattered, emotionally and physically. She did not think she had ever been so frightened in her life, even if she couldn't let herself show it to the children. But Richard would be able to help; just to hear his voice would be a reassurance.

The girl came back on the line. "Mr Connors isn't available right now," she said. "Who's calling, please?"

"Ah . . . it's Mrs Donnelly. I'll call him back later," she said, and replaced the phone, feeling crushed with disappointment. But poor Richard was probably up to his ears in it, and it wasn't really fair to burden him with her troubles as well – especially as those troubles were because she hadn't taken his advice . . . or kept her promise.

If only she could find those keys. Again she looked down into the street. And having found them, go where? The traffic was worse than when they had come in, and even as she watched there was an accident right outside the apartment building, causing an immediate pile up of vehicles, and an immediate accumulation of angry drivers, shouting at each other and waving their fists.

Yet she had to get out. She had to find those keys. Not even Michael would be such an idiot as to have taken them with him without the car.

Owen Michael followed his mother from room to room, watching as she emptied drawers and fished through pockets again. Then she dialled the cab company again, but got only busy tones. She tried again and again, and simply could not get through. She wanted to weep with frustration.

"Mom, we're obviously going to be here for a while," Owen Michael said. "Why don't we go back to bed for a couple of hours. We'll make a move when it's daylight."

Jo hesitated. But bed, if only for an hour, was what she wanted more than anything else in the world. She'd been up all night, she was cold and wet and clammy, and she was additionally exhausted by the nervous strain she'd been under for several days. She knew she was no longer thinking straight. If she could just put her head down for even five minutes, she'd probably be able to remember where the keys were. Just five minutes. And by then the traffic would have eased. The storm wasn't going to hit before tomorrow morning. There was still ample time to get out of town.

SATURDAY 29 JULY

Early Morning

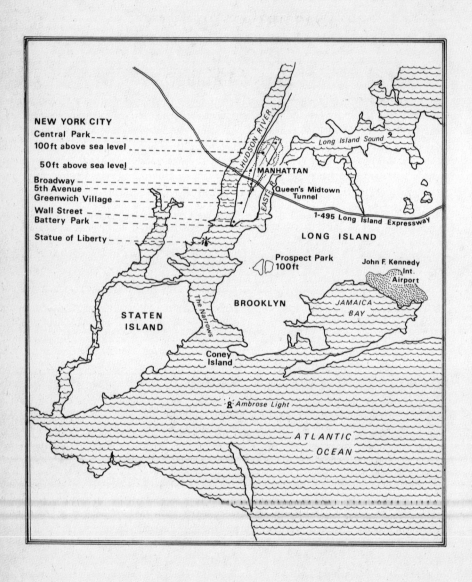

NEW YORK CITY

Central Park
100 ft above sea level

50 ft above sea level

Broadway
5th Avenue
Greenwich Village
Wall Street
Battery Park

Statue of Liberty

HUDSON RIVER

MANHATTAN

EAST R.

Queen's Midtown
Tunnel

Long Island Sound

I-495 Long Island Expressway

LONG ISLAND

Prospect Park
100 ft

John F. Kennedy
Int.
Airport

JAMAICA
BAY

BROOKLYN

STATEN
ISLAND

The Narrows

Coney
Island

Ambrose Light

ATLANTIC

OCEAN

City Hall, Park Row and Broadway

4.00 am

The helicopter dropped out of the dawn murk, swirling in the near gale force gusts as it slowly settled on to the grass. Waiting staffers ran forward with umbrellas, promptly blown inside out, and with mackintoshes to hold over Mayor Bill Naseby as he jumped from the cabin out into the rain. People tried to shout information to him, but he shook his head and ran towards the building; talking out there was a waste of time.

He got inside, shook water from his thinning hair. "You, you and you," he snapped. "Come with me."

His aides fell in behind him, delighted to be under his aegis at last; if there was one thing Bill Naseby possessed, it was the ability to make decisions.

He entered his office, where Police Commissioner Grundy and Assistant Commissioner McGrath were already waiting, and sat behind his desk. Water ran out of his hair and into the neck of his pullover; he wore an anorak – which he did not bother to remove – but no tie. He was a big man, and when sufficiently aroused, he could look formidable. He was certainly sufficiently aroused this morning. He pointed. "I've spoken with the Governor, and he's turning out the National Guard. Tom . . ." he turned to Grundy. "We have to have every man on the streets. Do you know what's going on out there?"

"It's a solid traffic jam the length and breadth of the city," Grundy confessed. "Heck, Bill, there's nothing my men can do without bulldozers. And you know what? They're getting nasty. The populace, I mean."

"I can believe that," Naseby agreed. "I saw some of it as I flew in."

"It's all the fault of that mother fucker Connors," growled Assistant Commissioner McGrath. "I sent a squad car out to bring him in, and the bastards haven't got back yet. Christ, they must be snarled up in the traffic. But when I lay hands on that asshole I am going to . . ."

"You'd better shake his hand and say, well done, boy, at least you tried to help."

McGrath scratched his head.

Naseby pointed. "Because that's what he did. Which is more than any of us, including myself, has done so far."

"Well, hell, how were we to know this goddamned thing was going

259

to keep coming straight at us?" the Commissioner complained. "She should've veered off by now. They always have in the past."

"The past doesn't always indicate the future, Tom. Connors maybe didn't go about it the right way. He may even have made matters worse. But at least he knew something had to be done. And Dr Eisener from Coral Gables confirms that it is going to be every bit as bad as Connors has claimed. He's just had a radio report from a navy plane flying into the eye, and there are sustained winds of 180 miles an hour, with gusts of over 200. You got that? 200 miles an hour. That storm is going to hit this city with the effect of an atomic explosion. And it's quickening up. It's now moving at 20 knots and it's only 200 miles away. That means the eye could reach the mainland at two o'clock this afternoon. And that means we are going to have hurricane force winds here in a couple of hours, and the sea is going to start to rise around nine this morning. And you know something else? The tide is going to start rising around then too."

The aides and the policemen exchanged glances; they had never seen the Mayor so agitated.

"Now you guys listen to me," Naseby went on. "I'm trying to persuade the Governor to declare New York a disaster area and put in martial law, right now. He's worried about doing this, because it's before the event, so to speak, so he's checking with his legal department. However, he has agreed to mobilise the National Guard. And I'm prepared to call the President if I have to. We'll get that martial law. But we can't wait for it; we have only five hours before all hell is going to bust loose. Tom, you and your men, and the guardsmen as soon as they arrive, are going to move straight in and clear those streets. Otherwise we could be looking at a massacre. Use bulldozers if you have to, but get people going: everyone who can, out of town. Everyone who can't, by noon at the outside, on to high ground. And anyone who objects, we move him, or his automobile, by force. You got it?"

"The tunnels and bridges are jammed solid," McGrath said gloomily.

"So concentrate on them first. There's time, just, if we get moving right away. It's the lower levels that have to be got out first. That means, if necessary, putting a ring of policemen and military round the areas safe from flooding, and keeping people in them until we have those most in danger cleared. I make that like taking a big loop, down West End Avenue to about 34th Street and then back up Park Avenue to say 62nd Street, and then right down to York Avenue. Anywhere south of that is liable to be flooded. By my reckoning that includes the Empire State Building, Penn Station, Madison Square Garden, Greenwich Village, Soho, Little Italy, and of course Wall Street and the UN Building."

"You really think that'll happen, Bill?" the Commissioner asked. "Surely the Narrows . . ."

"I'm told by Dr Eisener that the Narrows won't keep this dame out," Naseby said. "In fact, they might just act as a funnel and increase the volume and flow of water. With the rise of tide, he's talking about a possible 40 feet of water coming through there, and racing across the harbour like a tidal wave."

"Holy Jesus Christ!" McGrath said.

The Mayor gave a brief grin. "You guys will have noticed, I guess, that right here we'll also be below the mark – well below it. And so is the telephone exchange. In fact, situated where that is, right on the waterfront, that's going to be one of the first to go."

"Jesus," commented one of the City Hall aides. "What do we do?"

"We evacuate, Mitch," Naseby told him. "After we have got every civilian to safety."

"But the files, the records, the computers . . ."

"They go too, right away. Not the computers, just the discs. I've arranged for a helicopter fleet to lift them out. They should be here in another hour. So get packing. But no human being leaves this building until I say so. And that will be when Manhattan has been made safe."

"We'll never do it in time," Grundy said. "You're talking about two days' work."

"Sure we can."

"But where are we gonna put all these people?"

"Requisition every hotel that's above the 50-foot mark. And then use Central Park."

"You're gonna send maybe a million people to Central Park, in a hurricane? In lightning, thunder, rain, and 180-mile-an-hour winds . . ."

"So you come and tell me when you have any better ideas," Naseby snapped. "We've been caught with our pants down, but good. Now we just have to pull them up as best we can." He grabbed his phone as it buzzed. "Governor? Oh, hell. Sorry, Joe, I was expecting the Governor. Look, Joe, we have problems down here, as you know . . . You what? How the hell can you be running out of water when it's acting like a cloudburst out there? . . . Oh, sure, I know this rain can't help until it gets through the system. But what the hell are people using water for in such quantity right now? I understood everyone was leaving town. You must have a massive mains fracture someplace . . . Filling bathtubs? Jesus . . . Everyone in New York is filling a bathtub at the same time? . . . Yes . . . Yes, I see what you mean, but you can't turn anything off. Let them have it for as long as possible . . . We'll worry about a shortage later." He replaced the phone. "Joe Erskine wants immediate authority to institute water rationing. Would you believe it?" He glanced at his notepad. "Now, let's get on with it. Kennedy! Kennedy is going to be under water. Keep the planes flying as long as you can, but only out. All incoming flights are to be diverted. And by nine o'clock every last aircraft must have gone and all personnel evacuated. Same thing for La Guardia; it'll probably be flooded as well. The whole of Brooklyn looks like going . . ."

"That's another solid jam," McGrath said. "I checked with Tommy Burns, just to see if we could route some of our problems through there. He's threatening to shoot anyone coming over the bridge."

"But they're already over the bridge," Grundy commented. "As for Staten Island . . ."

Two aides hurried in. "They're reporting 150-mile-per-hour winds in Atlantic City," one gasped. "And 20-foot waves. The Boardwalk is just falling apart."

"There's a guy on the phone from Prospect Park Zoo asking if he should turn the animals loose," said the other.

"Holy Jesus! Is he mad?" the Commissioner shouted. "That's all we need, a bunch of lions and tigers running down the street."

"And snakes," McGrath put in dolefully. "They got some big ones in there."

Naseby sighed. "I'm sorry, Lou, but people have to come before animals. Anyway, Prospect Park is way above the flood line. And why is he calling me? Isn't there anyone awake down in Brooklyn? Now, shipping. All small craft should head up the rivers as far as possible."

"They're doing it," McGrath said. "The Harbour Police report there's nearly as big a crush on the water as on the street."

"The big stuff will have to sit it out," Naseby said.

"Well . . . some of them are already putting to sea."

"Out into that?"

"They reckon they have more chance riding it out at sea. They could be right. Those big ships are sitting ducks in harbour. A 40-foot tidal surge pushed by a 200-mile-an-hour wind could just land one of them in Times Square."

"Well . . . we'll have to leave that to the judgement of individual masters, but they have to understand there's going to be no coastguard assistance if they get themselves into trouble. Christ, I know we haven't thought of everything. But first, we have to get those streets cleared, and get the evacuation under control. I want a comprehensive plan to handle the situation placed on my desk just as quickly as possible."

"You will have it," promised Mitch. "By 8 am."

"8 am will be too late. I want it by 5.30. That gives you one hour." The phone buzzed again. "Yes? Oh, Governor, thank God . . . yes, from all reports it's sheer hell out there . . . Yes, everything you have . . . The President? Oh, that's great . . . Okay, we're moving into action, right now." He replaced the phone. "The President has authorised the imposition of martial law; it takes effect at 6 am. The message is being put out over all TV and radio stations now. The National Guard is being assembled now, and the army is being sent in to help. Seems there's nothing legal about what we're doing, but we're going to sort that one out afterwards. Now we have to hustle." He looked at his watch. "4.30. Mitch, arrange for me to make a broadcast at 6.00, telling people what we're trying to do. Fix coverage on all networks, and on radio."

"How do we get them here?"

"Use the helicopter. Starting now." He pointed at the Commissioner and McGrath. "I want things under control when I go on the air."

CONEY ISLAND

4.45 am

The bedroom faced south, but the buildings opposite blocked out the sea view even without the rain which was streaming down the window. Just their luck, Florence Bennett thought, to have weather like this for their annual Coney Island vacation.

"Looks pretty horrible out there," Bert mumbled through empty gums. "What're you out of bed for, anyway? Not thinking of going for a swim, are you?"

"It was the thunder woke me. Thought I'd take a look," Florence replied. "I guess this is a bit of that hurricane that hit the Donnellys' place in the Bahamas a few days ago. I wonder if it'll come up here."

They hadn't looked at a television or read a newspaper since coming to Coney Island: Bert's idea of a vacation was to forget the world existed, and if there'd been considerable discussion and agitation about the weather amongst their fellow boarders the past few days, he had ignored it with great determination.

"Hurricanes don't come this far north, girl," he pontificated. "They kick off into the Atlantic. Come on back to bed for a cuddle; it's been a long time."

"Now then, Bert," his wife scolded. "We can't have any of that first thing in the morning. Emmie's in the next room and the walls in this place are paper thin."

"So what? Don't she think we do it any more? Huh, come to think of it, it's been one hell of a long time," he finished on a note of complaint.

Florence sighed and started to remove the curling pins from her hair – but there was a smile twitching the corners of her mouth.

PARK AVENUE

5.00 am

Washington Jones took his father's silver pocket watch out of his fob pocket and peered at the Roman numerals, only vaguely readable without his spectacles. Five o'clock: Edwardes wasn't due to relieve him for another hour – if he was coming at all. He returned the watch to its pocket, rubbed his eyes, and yawned. Boy, was he weary. Quite apart from the lack of sleep involved in night duty in any event, he had been on his feet for the better part of the past five hours, ever since Mrs Donnelly had told him about the emergency. He had called all the apartments, and then he'd gone up to each floor to knock on the doors of those who hadn't answered the phone, just to check that everyone was warned about the possible dangers of this storm they called Faith. He hadn't liked leaving the foyer unattended all that time – he'd had to leave the glass doors open so that anyone who wanted could get out . . . but that had meant anyone who wanted could also get in. Not that anyone had done that, apparently, and waking the tenants had been the more important. Strange the way different folk had reacted. Some had been terrified, effusively grateful to him for contacting them, and couldn't get out fast enough, not even waiting to pack a bag, while others, like old Mr Jurgens, looked like they'd wanted to knock his head off his shoulders for waking them up, and just slammed the door in his face.

Then there had been Miss Schmitt, who was deaf as well as elderly; he had spent damned near an hour in Miss Schmitt's apartment, trying to explain exactly what was going on. Well, she had gone in the end, and so had everybody else . . . except for Mr Jurgens. If he wanted to stay that was his decision. Certainly no one, not even the agent, could expect him to hang about any longer. Mrs Donnelly had told him to get out of town, and he'd told the wife to pack. She'd be waiting.

He frowned at the suitcase placed neatly in the corner, bent to examine it. The name tag said Donnelly, which didn't make sense. Except that Mrs Donnelly must have forgotten it in the elevator when she and the children had left – they sure had been in a hurry – and some other tenant must have found it and put it where it could come to no harm. They were a real good crowd, his tenants – except for Mr Jurgens.

But that Mrs Donnelly was the best. He was truly happy she and her kids had got out so early, before the traffic had built up. She was one nice lady – and the only tenant who had given a thought to his predicament. Well, he was going to start thinking about himself, right now. He was damned sure Edwardes wasn't coming in. So the hell with it.

He took off his green uniform jacket and hung it neatly on its hanger, slid his shirt sleeves into the crumpled black plastic raincoat, and picked up the zipper bag in which he had carried his dinner, before switching off the security screens and the office light and locking the door. It went against his instincts to leave the apartment building all but empty and unguarded, but the agents should have contacted him and told him what they wanted done. Instead, he had been entirely forgotten and those guys were probably fifty miles away by now. He had a responsibility to his family just as great as to his employers.

He had turned off the automatic street doors as well, and had to push them open, to gasp in amazement. The wind was strong enough to make walking against it difficult, and the rain was slicing across the traffic in vicious, swishing gusts, carrying bits of plastic garbage into the air to hit windows several floors up. And what traffic! It was thick, and crawling, bumper to bumper, so slowly you could walk at twice the speed, while not even the howling gale could drown the noise of the horns and the shouted curses that were being hurled back and forth. There were policemen everywhere, and National Guardsmen as well, attempting to get cars to move this way or that, but they didn't seem to be having much success. Well, it wasn't his problem. He never brought his old Chevvy to work, anyway; it wasn't worth the hassle of sitting in ordinary traffic jams, and the exercise did him good. He locked the street doors, pulled a flat cap from his pocket and dragged it down over the tight grey curls, turned up his collar, and headed for home. Celestine would be packed and ready, and have the girl and the grandchild waiting at the house for him, and Robert as well, if she'd done what he told her and called the place where the boy worked nights – and she'd have a pot of coffee brewing. He looked forward to that.

"Okay, Buster, hold it right there."

Washington obeyed. He wasn't going to argue with any large young man wearing rain-soaked khaki and carrying an automatic weapon.

"Where do you think you're going?" the guardsman inquired.

"Home." They were both shouting above the whine of the wind and the roar of the traffic.

"Yeah? Home being where?"

Washington told him; he lived only a couple of blocks from Penn Station.

"You got proof of that?"

"I need a passport to get home?"

"Listen, Buster . . ."

"Hi, Washington," said a patrolman, joining them.

"Morning, officer," Washington said gratefully. "Get this kid off my back, will you?"

"Says he's going home," the guardsman explained. "Well, if he's on

48th Street he has to stay on 48th Street, right? Those are our orders: no movement south."

"He only works up here," the policeman explained. "And his home is below the 50-foot marker. I guess you're going home to collect the family and get out of town, eh, Washington?"

"You're damn right," Washington agreed.

"You'll need this." The policeman reached inside his wet gleaming cape and produced a piece of cardboard. "That gives you permission to go down to your home, and to leave the city after."

Washington scratched his head through the cap; it appeared he did need some kind of a passport to go home. But, as he had just been given one, he wasn't going to quibble. He thrust the by now very wet piece of cardboard into his pocket, and weaved across the street, through the all but stationary autos. This traffic was starting to get him worried; suppose they all got stuck in a big jam in the Chevvy, what would happen when the storm broke? In his hurricane chats, that Connors had said there might be window glass and other debris flying about all over – one wouldn't even be safe in an automobile . . . well, there was nothing for it; they'd have to get out by Subway and take a train from Jersey City.

A vivid blue light flashed at the same moment as the street rocked with the violent crack of thunder; one of the buildings nearby had been struck, and the noise bounced off the walls, echoing and re-echoing all the way across Manhattan. Fear gripped Washington Jones' chest, and his lips moved in an incoherent prayer . . . that he had not left his departure too late.

NATIONAL AMERICAN BROADCASTING SERVICE
OFFICES, FIFTH AVENUE

5.30 am

"Will you get me that Michael Donnelly number in Connecticut again, please, Maisie?" Richard said.

"Of course, Mr Connors. Say, I've been so busy I didn't tell you before, but that Mrs Donnelly called again."

Richard sighed with relief; she must have reached Bognor. "Great, Maisie. What time was that?"

"Let me see . . ." She was consulting her pad. "2.47."

She must have driven like a bat out of hell, Richard thought. Still, say two and a half hours . . . it could be done. "Okay, Maisie, but try that number anyway."

Julian had just finished putting out another update; they had a minute or two. Jayme was making coffee, part-blonde hair still straggling. It was difficult to realise that they had been on duty all night without a wink of sleep, because he did not feel the least tired. Subconsciously, he had been waiting for this day all his adult life, ever since he had taken up meteorology as a profession: that when it arrived he was being prevented from fulfilling his other ambition, to be the man who kept giving news of the storm to the nation, was just an aspect of Murphy's Law. But at least things were happening, officially; Hal Waring and a camera crew had been whisked away by the helicopter which had put down on the NABS roof, over the traffic jams and the skyscrapers, to enable the Mayor to broadcast to his people and, hopefully, begin to sort things out . . . supposing he had the time.

"Bognor, Mr Connors," Maisie said.

"For Jesus' sake, not you again?" Big Mike complained. "Don't you ever sleep?"

"I just wanted to make sure Mrs Donnelly got to you okay, Mr Donnelly."

"Look, asshole, she isn't due here until breakfast time. Right?"

"Breakfast time? She left her apartment to drive up to you just after midnight. With your grandchildren."

"The grandchildren? Goddamn! But that's nonsense. It don't take five hours to drive from New York to Bognor. Three maximum."

"Yes," Richard said. "That's what I thought. Something's happened to her."

"Happened to her? Holy shit! You mean a breakdown? In this rain? Say, is it raining in New York?"

"Yes, Mr Donnelly. It is raining in New York. And there's not a hope in hell of anyone getting out in a hurry to go look for her right now. I'm going to have to leave this one with you. But I'd be very grateful if you'd call me back and let me know what's happened to her."

"Yeah," Big Mike said. "Yeah. Holy shit! What a fuck up."

The phone went dead, and Richard gazed at it. It had to be a simple breakdown. And if it was outside of the city there would be no problem. But if it had happened on one of the bridges . . . and there was absolutely nothing he could do about it. Even if he decided to abandon the studio, he wouldn't know where to start looking . . . the door opened and he gazed at Kiley.

A very wet and angry looking Kiley. Who was gazing at him. "What the hell are you doing here?" he demanded. "JC fired you, a couple of hours ago."

"To take effect at seven o'clock, Mr Kiley," Julian chipped in. "So he's been giving me a hand. You're kind of early, ain't you?"

"Early!" Kiley exploded. "JC is going wild. I've spent the past three hours trying to get here. God knows if I'll ever see my automobile again; I've had to walk from the bridge; they're jammed solid, all lanes, all going north. Now you tell me, is this storm really going to hit us?"

"Yes, Mr Kiley, it is," Richard said. "In about five hours from now."

"Goddamn," Kiley said. "And I've got to get someone down to Hunt to make some transfers. Holy Jesus." He wandered out, closing the door behind him.

"He doesn't know what time of day it is," Jayme commented.

"I don't think he knows what day it is," Julian said.

"Well, I think he's going to find out." Richard picked up the phone again.

PARK AVENUE

6.00 am

Jo awoke with a start to the jangling of the telephone. It was broad daylight, although there was obviously a total overcast, and the rain was lashing at the windows, driven by gale force winds, while the thunder crackled continuously. She sat up, unable for a moment to grasp where she was; after a hot shower she had lain down in her bathrobe and fallen into a deep sleep. Now she gasped as she saw the time on her bedside clock – six o'clock. Immediately her brain was awake. She pushed hair from her eyes and reached for the phone. "Richard!" she gasped. "Oh, thank God!"

"Jo?" The woman's voice was high, and disconcerted.

"Oh, my God! Sally? Sally Davenport? Where are you?"

"I'm at home, Jo," Sally said, somewhat acidly. Home for Sally Davenport was ten miles outside Newport. There'd be no chaos out there . . . yet.

"Oh. Well . . . any word from the boys?"

"I was going to ask you that? I tried to raise them through the exchange here but they told me they can't handle any personal traffic right now as there's an emergency on. Have you ever heard such damned nonsense?"

"Well," Jo said, "there is a hurricane racing at us . . ."

"For Heaven's sake, Jo, you'd think in this day and age they'd be capable of coping with a hurricane," Sally complained. "Sam was supposed to call me last night; they were going to be back within radio range by then. But he hasn't. Jo, have you heard from them?"

"No. Not since . . ." For a moment Jo just could not remember when last she had spoken with Michael. "My God! Not since midnight on Thursday. I spoke to him about the hurricane and suggested he turn back to Bermuda."

"And did he?"

"No. He said he was standing on. You know what Michael is like."

"Good Lord! Aren't you worried? I mean, he has Sam with him."

"Sally," Jo said impatiently. "Of course I'm worried. But Michael was confident he could outsail the storm, and he's probably right. He usually is. Anyway, it's turned away from him. It's virtually on our doorstep down here, and it's coming straight at us. I have things to do. I'll call you later." She replaced the phone, jumped out of bed, and ran into the lounge, where Owen Michael was watching television.

"Hey, Mom," he called. "The Mayor's on."

Jo gazed at Bill Naseby, wearing his electioneering expression – he was famous for his ability to reassure – as he filled the screen.

". . . you folks out there know I've never let you down, and by golly, I'm not going to let you down now. But I'm also going to give it to you straight. We have a major crisis here, and we have got to tackle it in the best possible way. So firstly, I have placed police, National Guardsmen, and Army units on every bridge, in every tunnel, and at every intersection in or out of Manhattan, to control movement. Now I know you can look out of your windows and see that there's one heck of a snarl-up out there, or maybe you're in that snarl-up at this moment, and I know you'll have heard that the bridges and tunnels are jammed solid, but I can assure you that we are working to clear them, and we are winning. But to win, we need your co-operation. Obey the instructions given you by the men on duty. The important thing is that we firstly evacuate all persons living less than fifty feet above sea level. Those people's homes are in danger of being flooded; they have to have a number one priority. There may, I am sorry to say, be a great deal of wind damage to many houses and other buildings from this storm, but it is the surging water that can kill, and this we must deal with first. To all people living in such areas, I want to say, pack up only as much as you can carry in one suitcase, and move out on to the street. You will find policemen there, and they will direct you to the best route to take. They will also give you a ticket, just like this . . ." he held one up, "which it is very important for you to carry and present whenever you are stopped by any patrol. Only if you have one of these tickets will you be allowed to move from one location to another. Anyone, and most especially those with any automobile or other vehicle, not in possession of one of these tickets, will be stopped and pushed off the road until all those low-lying areas have been evacuated.

"Those of you living more than 50 feet above sea level, that is, all of you north of 34th Street, between Lexington and Tenth, except where you may be specifically told to evacuate by the police, must stay in your homes and apartments until instructed to move by the police. If you attempt to move without possession of one of our exit tickets – which can only be obtained from the policemen on duty – not only will your automobile be pushed off the road, but you yourself will be liable to prosecution. We will get to everyone just as soon as it is possible to do so. But until then, we ask you, in the name of common sense, in the name of humanity, not to clog the streets which are needed by those in greater peril than yourselves. You will not be flooded. Your buildings are in no real danger, and neither are your lives. However uncomfortable it may be for you during the next twenty-four hours, you will survive. Others may not unless we can get them to safety in time. I must attend to my duties now. But I will tell you this: as long as there is one life in danger in this city, I and my staff and your gallant police force will remain at our posts. And as long as there is electricity, keep your radios and televisions tuned in, to keep yourselves informed of the situation. God bless you all.''

His face disappeared, and one of the senior anchormen replaced him. ''That was the Mayor of New York, William 'Bill' Naseby,'' he said. ''And that telecast will be repeated every hour, on the hour, throughout the morning. And now, at this grave hour, we turn . . .''

Jo switched off the set.

''Hey, Mom, he said to leave it on,'' Owen Michael protested.

''I know he did. And we can put it on again later. But I have to get through to the studio.''

''The studio?''

''We're . . .'' We're trapped, she wanted to shout. Don't you understand? Because of that goddamned shit of a careless driver, and because I was careless enough to fall asleep, we're stuck here, above the 50-foot mark. She had to contact Richard; she could think of nothing else to do.

But all the studio lines were busy. She went into the bathroom to wash her face, and found only a rusty trickle coming out of the tap. The kitchen was the same. Oh, God, she thought. Oh, God! It was not possible for the water to have gone off while it was clouding past her windows in what seemed solid sheets.

She tried the studio again, and heard it ring. ''Mr Connors,'' she gasped. ''It really is urgent. My name is Donnelly.''

To her amazement, she was through in ten seconds. ''Richard!'' she shrieked. ''Oh, Richard! I've been trying to reach you forever.''

''My darling,'' he said. ''Where are you? Did your father-in-law find you?''

''My father-in-law? I haven't seen him.''

''But . . . aren't you in Bognor?''

"No," she gasped, trying to disguise her despair and misery. "No. I'm not in Bognor. I'm right here in the apartment."

"You're *where*?"

Swallowing hard, she launched into the story of their morning.

"Christ," he said when she had finished. "Look, have you food and water?"

"We have food," she said. "But there's no water. I tried the taps just now and there was nothing."

"You have nothing to drink at all?"

"Oh, there's plenty to drink. Except water." Just hearing his voice was making her feel normal again.

"Okay. Listen . . . there's no way you can leave town now."

"I know that. I just heard the mayor say so on television. Richard . . . what do we do? I have the children here with me."

"Keep calm, for a start. Move yourself, and everything you have to drink, and a good supply of canned food – stuff which doesn't need cooking, or even heating – away from your windows. Into . . . how about the bathroom."

"Which one?"

"Whichever one has the smallest window. Or better yet, one with no window at all. Move yourself and Owen Michael and Tamsin in there and sit tight. Expect the electricity to go off some time this morning, and it won't come back on again until maybe Monday. It'll be warm, but liveable. Just stay there. I'm going to try to get to you, the moment I'm of no use here."

"Richard!" she screamed. "You can't. Don't try, please. It'll be too dangerous."

"I won't take any chances," he promised. "Just make yourself and the kids safe and sit tight. I'll be there if it's humanly possible."

PARK AVENUE

6.30 am

Jo sat with drooping shoulders, arms hanging limply between her knees, staring at the phone.

Owen Michael and Tamsin, who had also now woken up, stood together, gazing at her. "What are we going to do, Mom?" Owen asked. He was smiling, trusting, and confident that Mom could be depended upon to cope with anything.

If only he knew how inadequate she felt. She looked at him and warmed with pride. He was thinner and paler since his surgery but had surely grown at least another inch – he was quickly developing into a young lion like his father, almost taller than herself. And she had failed both him and Tamsin – and Richard – and herself, by not getting them out of town in time.

She returned the boy's smile and squared her shoulders. There was no time for regrets, for backward thinking; they must prepare for their joint battle for survival. "I guess we have to get ourselves ready to ride out the hurricane, right here. Shouldn't be too much of a problem."

"Heck, no, Mommy," Tamsin said. "I wasn't scared, down in Eleuthera, not until the roof blew off. Then it was so cold and wet, and scary."

"Oh, my darling girl." Jo hugged her close. "I was so determined you wouldn't have to go through that again."

"But our roof won't blow off, will it, Mommy?"

"Of course it won't," Jo asserted, and stood up, just as lightning struck another building close by, pretending she hardly noticed. Of course it won't, she told herself . . . but Faith was now carrying winds half as strong again as those which had blown over Eleuthera.

"What do we do to make ready?" Owen Michael wanted to know.

"First we decide which bathroom to use . . ."

"Tamsin's and my bathroom," the boy interrupted. "There's no window in there to get broken."

"Good thinking." The bathroom the two children shared was between their rooms and had only an extractor fan let into the wall of the building. "Let's all go see how we'll manage it." They stood in the bathroom doorway as if seeing it for the first time. It was cream; cream marble round the bath and shower stall and across the vanity top surrounding the twin marble basins. The paintwork and rugging were cream, and by contrast the towel and bathmats were chocolate brown.

"Let's fill the vanity cupboard with food for a start," Jo said.

"How will we cook it in here?" Tamsin wanted to know.

"We won't. Cold soup. Cold ham . . ."

"We've got picnic flasks. Can't we heat the soup and some coffee now?" The little girl seemed excited at the thought of this new adventure – providing the roof wasn't going to blow off.

Her mother tried not to let her anxiety dampen her enthusiasm. "Sure. Why not? The soup, at least. We can't make any coffee because we have no water."

"Water? There's water in the bathroom . . ." Owen Michael turned on the tap while he spoke, gazed at the rusty trickle.

"You wouldn't believe it, would you, with all this rain coming down? No, what you have to do is go to the bar and collect all the mixes we have, all the orange juice and pineapple juice and ginger ale and lemonade and soda water you can find."

"Hey, Mom, we could make coffee with soda water," Tamsin cried.

Jo raised her eyebrows, but could not suppress a smile; Tamsin's suggestions were all so positive. "Why not?"

"There's bottles and bottles of soda water in here," Owen Michael shouted, dashing into the bar. "If we take the electric kettle into the bathroom . . ."

"It won't do us much good when the power goes off," Jo told him. "Anything we're going to boil has to be done right now."

Tamsin's eyes were wide. "You think there could be a power outage? In New York?"

"It could happen. I guess there was one in Eleuthera, huh?"

"Oh, yes. That was scary too."

"It's going to be pretty boring, sitting in the dark all evening," Owen Michael declared. "I know, I'll get my flashlight."

"That's a great idea. Do you have spare batteries?"

"Of course I have spare batteries, Mom. How long do you reckon we'll be without power?"

"It's a big storm and moving slowly. Could be the best part of 48 hours."

"48 hours! Heck!" Owen Michael commented.

"I'm hungry. I'm sure it's breakfast time," Tamsin complained.

"Of course it is," Jo agreed, realising that she was pretty hungry herself. "Let's make a really good, big, solid meal," she suggested. "We can eat what's left over later, even if it's cold. I'm going to put some meat in the microwave to thaw and see if we've got any fresh vegetables."

While the meal was cooking, they hauled two single mattresses into their refuge, together with pillows and blankets; there wasn't actually room for them, and Tamsin suggested putting one in the bathtub and sleeping in there herself, while Owen Michael and Jo shared the other. Jo found some fancy candles she used for dinner parties, and soon had the immaculate bathroom looking like the inside of a camping tent. By now, the howling of the wind, the roar of the thunder, the shuddering of the building in the gusts, seemed almost normal.

When they had eaten and cleared up, Owen Michael disappeared. Jo suddenly remembered the bag she had left in Washington's office. She thought she would take both Owen Michael and Tamsin down with her to collect it – she did not want to be separated from them for a moment – but when she went looking for the boy she found him standing on a chair carefully placing his beloved model aircraft in the storage cupboard over his closet. Poor kid. He obviously was far more aware of the possible extent of storm damage than she realised. But only she had the almost terrifying feeling of claustrophobia of knowing that they were, so far as she was aware, alone in this huge building.

As the lights had flickered once or twice during their breakfast she decided against using the elevators to get down to the lobby; the thought of their being trapped in one of the cars throughout the storm by a power outage was traumatic. Instead they used the stairs, hurrying down all thirty-eight floors. On the thirty-third she was sure she heard music, but the sound of the wind whistling outside was so great the noise was surrealistic, and she certainly had no intention of going to investigate; they arrived in the foyer panting as much with apprehension as exertion.

Washington's office was locked, the light off. Jo and the children could look through the glass door and see the suitcase, but there was no way they could get at it short of breaking the lock. And presumably it was safe in there anyway – at least as safe as in the apartment. Besides, Jo was suddenly obsessed with anxiety to regain the safety of her own home, nor did she think she could face the climb back. She stood in front of the silent elevators, chewing her lip for several seconds, while Tamsin held her hand, before pressing the ascent button, feeling her heart give a pit-a-pat of relief as the light glowed normally. Then she glanced round to see Owen Michael standing in front of the street door. "Hey, Mom," he called. "Come look at this."

She left Tamsin at the elevator, hurried to his side, to gaze through the glass at the street, just as jammed with vehicles as before, but now deserted by humans, save for the single lane which had been cleared and along which cars were proceeding in a steady stream, and for the police-men and National Guardsmen huddling in groups on corners and intersec-tions, only dashing forward whenever there was a hold up or a driver seemed uncertain which way to go.

"Ain't that something?" Owen Michael asked. "All those automobiles . . . what happened to all the people?"

"I guess they must live above the flood level, and the police have sent them home," she said. "Like us," wondering why the three of them had to be numbered amongst the unlucky ones who hadn't got out before the martial law went into effect. "New York," she said. "A ghost city. Now . . ." Before she could finish, a tremendous gust of wind forced open even the electrically controlled and now locked doors. "Owen!" she screamed, as she was blown back, staggering and then falling, rolling across the tiled floor. So was the boy, fortunately, because the doors had been hurled back so hard on their hinges that they had shattered against the walls – glass splinters showered the foyer, carried on the wind, but miraculously neither of them were hit by flying glass, though the soles of their shoes crushed the shards into the floor and a few small pieces had pierced their hands and knees when they fell.

Neither was Tamsin hurt, sheltered behind the square block of the elevator shaft, but she was screaming her terror.

Jo grabbed Owen Michael, bundled both children into the now waiting car, and pressed the ascent button, praying it would work. It did, and a few minutes later they reached the thirty-eighth floor, breathless and frightened, listening, and indeed feeling, the wind whistling up the stairwell, but in comparative safety, at least for the moment.

They jostled into the apartment and closed the door, looking at each other, still too breathless to speak. Jo found the First Aid box and dabbed antiseptic on their cuts, then she poured herself a drink and gave each of the children a soda. Every so often the apartment door rattled, but she didn't dare think what the wind might eventually do. Surely, if all the apartment doors, and more important, the door on to the roof, were firmly closed . . . as the minutes passed her heart settled down, and she decided it was going to be all right.

Now it was just a matter of waiting, and of restoring normalcy, as far as that could be done in the frighteningly abnormal conditions. Jo suddenly remembered that in another hour or so she was due at Pinewoods for breakfast. She picked up the phone to call them and tell them she wasn't going to make it, but it seemed all the lines even in the New York telephone exchange were busy and she could get no replies at all, although she tried Marcia's number as well – but Marcia would surely be safely in Connecticut by now. Then she tried Complaints but they were engaged too, so she gave it up for a while, and instead busied herself with removing pictures, ornaments, everything in fact for which she could find safe storage. Plants and photo albums joined them in the bathroom, along with a precious antique tea service which had belonged to her grandmother.

"Have we got a can opener in there?" Owen Michael asked.

"Yes," she called loudly, to be heard above the storm. But she didn't know where it was – or care, for the moment. She was staring at a ghost: the fearful apparition of a woman, hair matted into dishevelled points, shoulders drooping under damp crumpled clothes, while from deep, dark shadows, the terrified eyes gaped back at her through the bathroom mirror.

My God! Is that really me? Already? And Faith hasn't even got here, yet. She swallowed, took a deep breath, and squared her shoulders. What confidence could the children have, seeing her like that? She opened a drawer and pulled out a hairbrush, rushed into the dressing room for a fresh blouse, moistened a tissue in soda water and rubbed it over her face and hands. Forcing a wide smile she said, "Let's see what's on TV."

They sat in silence, half watching some filler programme being relayed between announcements, being promised a full weather update as soon as possible – Jo praying for a glimpse of Richard's face – while the picture was constantly broken up by flashes of lightning, and the building shaken by gusts of wind.

But for the children, she would actually have wanted to be here in the city, close to Richard, sharing, even at a distance, the danger with him. And suddenly she was reminded of the people she had interviewed after he started his 'hurricane chat' spots. There was that funny old girl, Lila something, from Florida. She knew all about hurricanes – they didn't frighten her, she'd said. Not even this one? She was probably huddled in her sister's bathroom, eating her words. And what about that cab driver who never stopped swearing? Muldoon? And Nancy, of course, her hairdresser? She'd have fled at the first suggestion of a storm. Washington had left early, too; she hoped he'd got all his family to safety by now.

She shuddered; Alloan. The memory of that visitation made her skin crawl. Presumably the police would have got him out of the city, along with all prisoners on remand. Ironic, in a way, that the scum of society should be saved, while possibly hundreds of decent folk could die.

And while she could do nothing but wait, trying not to wonder what was happening downstairs. Or outside in the city.

Saturday 29 July

Mid-Morning

City Hall, Broadway and Park Row

7.00 am

"Here come the choppers," Mitch said.

"About time," Naseby grunted. "Everything ready to go?"

"Just about."

"Well, get them moving."

Mitch nodded and hurried from the Mayor's office. Naseby rested his head on his hands for a moment, raised it again as the phone buzzed.

"Naseby."

"I have Mr Hatton from Hunt National, Mr Mayor," the girl said.

"On a Saturday?"

"Well, it seems he has some problems."

"Haven't we all. Put him on. Good morning, Mr Hatton. Can I help you?"

"Mr Mayor, we are facing a serious situation."

"I know that, Mr Hatton. We are doing the best we can."

"I'm talking about here on Wall Street. Mr Mayor, we are trying to transfer funds . . . I'm not just speaking of Hunt. I am speaking for all the banks . . ."

"You're transferring funds on a Saturday?"

"Our customers are uneasy about the situation should this hurricane strike New York."

"I don't think 'should' is any longer the operative word, Mr Hatton." Naseby gazed through his window into City Hall Park and watched the first helicopter lift off; the wind was now very nearly up to hurricane force, and the big chopper swayed uneasily – it had obviously been packed to the door with files and computer disks . . . all the million and one records that are required to operate a city. But then the rotors began to win, and the machine rose out of the park, immediately to be replaced by another.

"Quite," Hatton was saying. "That is the point. The wire services, the telephone system, just don't seem able to cope. Everybody and his brother must be using the phone at the same time."

"I can believe that, Mr Hatton. Just like you and me."

"Well, really, something has got to be done about it. And now we are told that Wall Street is liable to be flooded."

"The word is certain," Naseby said, with gloomy satisfaction.

"That is quite intolerable. Perhaps you do not realise this, Mr Mayor, but it is possible that water may penetrate our vaults."

"I do understand, Mr Hatton."

"Well, then, you will understand that as it is quite impossible to transfer all our accounts in time, even if we had sufficient air space, we simply must move out our computer systems."

"That's a good idea. If you can."

"We must be assisted to do so, Mr Mayor. A road must be cleared for us . . ."

"Forget it, Mr Hatton. Roads are for people. Use helicopters. That's what we're doing. Charter every chopper you can . . . Holy Christ!"

The third helicopter had been put down and loaded, and was now lifting off. But at that moment there was a stronger than average gust of wind; the entire City Hall shook, and the helicopter was whipped sideways before it was properly airborne. The pilot obviously gave it everything he had, and it rose sharply, but still being pushed sideways too fast; its belly brushed a tree and then another, and it turned over, plummeting to the ground to burst into flames with a sickening explosion.

"Did you see that?" Mitch shouted, running into the office.

"I saw it," Naseby said. "That's it, Mitch. Send the rest of those guys home. We're just risking brave men."

"But . . ."

"We'll have to think of something else."

Mitch hesitated, then left the office.

"Mr Mayor? Mr Mayor?" Hatton asked. "What's happening? What was that noise? Do you know there's a fire very close to City Hall?"

"I know, Mr Hatton," Naseby said. "It means helicopters are out. The wind is just too strong."

"But what are we to do?" His voice had become a wail.

"Organise yourselves a truck convoy. We will do the same, and we'll leave together, under police escort. But Mr Hatton, no truck leaves until I am satisfied the roads are sufficiently clear of people. They still have priority."

EAST HOUSTON STREET

7.30 am

The door phone buzzed on the wall of the tiny kitchen, barely audible above the blare of the pop music coming out of the cassette recorder. "I'll get it," Lila Vail called to her sister, lifting the handset.

"Who is it?" Tootsie called.

"Some guy called Evans. Says he's a friend of yours," Lila shouted through the bathroom door.

"Oh, Dai!" Tootsie gave a girlish giggle; she had been widowed several years longer than Lila, and was not without her admirers. "Yeah, tell him to come up."

The sisters were still in curling pins and dressing gowns when the visitor hurried in. "Say, you girls packed and ready to leave?"

"Leave? What, you planning to take us on vacation?" Tootsie dug him in the ribs with her elbow, adding, "Your old lady gone off to see your mother again?"

The arch reply she anticipated never came. Dai Evans was not his normal self, today; the short, chunky body was unusually tense, his unshaven face grey and serious, lapsing into obvious alarm when he realised they didn't know what he was talking about. Frowning, he switched off the tape so he could make himself heard without shouting. "Don't you realise the Mayor has ordered an evacuation of the city?"

"He's what?" Lila swung round, kettle in hand. "Is it a nuclear attack?"

"When did you girls last have the TV or radio on? It's this hurricane, Faith. They say it's the biggest storm in history, and it's headed straight for us. Could be here this afternoon. Can't you hear that wind?"

With the cassette off, the howling of the wind was very loud.

"Oh, shit." Lila poured water on to her tea bag. "You sure had me worried there for a moment. I thought maybe it was something serious. It's been blowing like that all night. Call that wind? You want to be in Florida when it's really gusting."

"It hasn't got here yet." Dai grabbed Tootsie's arm. "This is serious, honey. They're saying that half of Manhattan will be flooded – and we're in the wrong half."

"Jees, I guess I'd better get dressed. How do we get out?" Tootsie turned pale under her recently applied pancake make-up.

Lila threw back her head and laughed. "Oh, come on, you goddamned fool rabbits. You really should take a spell living down in Florida. We get this crap on the news stations every summer, and the hurricanes to match. Newcomers would fall all about with heart attacks, frightened to death by these panic stirrers. I bet it's that damned fool, what's his name, the good-looking boy . . . Connors, that's right, Richard Connors. I bet he started all this."

Dai looked at her, doubtfully. "Yeah, I guess he did. But it seems he's right this time. The Mayor says so."

"The Mayor says so," she mimicked. "Come on, Dai. Can't you see he's been got at?" She carried her teacup to the table and sat down, crossing her legs and lighting a cigarette. "Well, I'll tell you this; you won't catch me sitting for hours in a traffic pile-up, trying to run away from some non-existent flood waters twelve floors down. So what if the basement floods? That's the landlord's problem. I'm staying right where I am."

Tootsie looked from one to the other. If Lila hadn't been staying with her, she would have been out of the apartment by now, running like hell. Dai's news scared her to death, but . . . well, Lila had lived with hurricanes for years, and she undoubtedly knew more about them than the Mayor . . . or, probably, Richard Connors. Anyway, she wanted to finish turning up the hem of her dress, and she'd promised to make a big batch of almond cookies for the Senior Citizens' Party tomorrow. "Don't worry about us, Dai," she said. "You get your old lady out of town if she's scared, but . . ." She smiled confidently at her sister. "I guess we're staying. Like a cup of tea before you go?"

Dai wanted to argue, tell them that their lives were in danger, but he could see it would be useless. Some people would always believe only what they wanted to believe. Anyway, the wife was waiting with her bags packed, and he'd told her he was just getting the old Dodge – she didn't know about the spare time he spent with Tootsie, and he had been going to pretend he had met the sisters preparing to leave and had offered them a ride. He sighed. "Okay, girls, if that's the way you want it. I can only tell you . . . best of luck."

When he'd gone, Tootsie turned on the tape again, sat opposite her sister, and lit a cigarette. While the music had been off, the sound of the wind whistling outside of the apartment, the constant growl of the thunder, had been very loud and quite frightening. She wanted to shut it out. She also wished she could shut out the nasty niggling feeling of unease at the back of her mind, which seemed to be affecting her chest, giving it an unpleasantly tight feeling. The music would help her to relax and get rid of it, but if she couldn't, she could always take one of her pills.

EAST TWENTIETH STREET

7.50 am

"Come on, you guys, I need help with the dishes," Nancy called from the kitchen. As expected, there was no reply – they were all playing deaf as usual, and they knew she expected assistance with breakfast, even on Saturdays – the hairdressing salon opened, of course, six days a week. She went to the door and shouted, "I know you can hear me, you lazy bums. I'm going to be late for work again, and I've got an early customer who's always difficult." Christ, she thought; the kids you could under-stand, but you'd think Bill . . .

"Nance, shut up your bawling and come here," Bill called from the lounge. "They've just said the Mayor's gonna address the city in a few minutes. It's a recording of some speech he made earlier, this morning."

"What's it to do with you, Bill? You didn't vote for him last time. And I haven't got the time . . ."

"It's not an election speech," he snapped. "It's about evacuating the city. Will you shut up and listen?"

It wasn't like Bill to talk like that! Nancy hurried into the room to see what the fuss was about . . . and slowly her jaw dropped as she gaped in horror, speechless until Bill Naseby was finished. Then her knees turned to jelly. "For God's sake let's get out of here," she gasped, untying the strings of her pinafore. "Kids, quick, get your raincoats."

"Just hold on a minute," Bill suggested. "Let's just talk about it for a moment. There's your job . . ."

"Talk? Don't be a nut. We'll talk about it when we're in Yonkers. As for my job, my job can go . . ."

The phone bleeped, and Bill reached it first. "Yeah? . . . oh, hi, Ernie. What's up? . . . Yeah, we were just watching it. What are you and Marge gonna do?" There was a long pause during which Bill's ever cheerful face grew longer and more serious. "Okay," he said at last. "That sounds best. Just let me check with Nance." He turned to his wife. "Ernie says the streets really are jammed and do we want to go up-river with him and Marge and their kids on the *Glory of Liberty*? It'll mean walking down across Eleventh but he's got her moored at the end of the 54th dock, so it won't be too far."

Ernest, Bill's brother, was mate on one of the tourist pleasure boats which toured the harbour.

"But where'll we go on her?" The blonde curls were shaking with fright. "What'll we do for wheels when we get ashore? I'll bet the river's real nasty already and the storm's not due here till this afternoon. That poor old tub can't take rough weather – she'll sink." She remembered a Sunday afternoon trip on it last year, the stink of oil, the way the bulkheads creaked and groaned as the boat nosed the current back up to her berth, layer after layer of thick paint, soft as putty in the sun, covering the crumbling areas of rust.

"The *Glory*'s got to be a better bet than the streets," Bill said. "Come on, if you're worried about staying . . ."

"Worried?" Her eyes filled with tears. "Of course I'm worried, Bill. I'm shit scared. We gotta get out, quick."

"Then grab your coat, sweetheart, throw some clothes in a bag, and get the kids moving. I'll lock up."

The three children soon reappeared in cagoules and the young family huddled together on the sidewalk, heading for the docks on the Hudson River. Nancy was clutching the little silver swimming trophy she'd won fifteen years ago, before she'd ever met Bill. She'd always treasured it.

NATIONAL AMERICAN BROADCASTING SERVICE OFFICES, FIFTH AVENUE

8.30 am

"I'm standing on the Battery," Rod Kimmelman shouted into his microphone. "And boy, is it blowing out here!"

The camera moved away from the close-up of his face to show him huddled in the shelter of the huge mobile NABS camera van; even the van was trembling in the gusts.

"I reckon there are wind speeds here of well over 100 miles an hour," Kimmelman said. "Certainly no man could stand up to them. Look there . . ." Once again the camera tracked, to where trees were bending almost to the ground; one or two of the smaller ones had already been uprooted.

"This is where," Kimmelman continued, "the real brunt of the storm will first be felt here in Manhattan. It is expected that within the next few hours the wind strength will increase dramatically as the eye of the storm approaches, and the water level is going to rise even more dramatically, as the tide starts to come in. In fact, the experts say that where I am now standing may be under several feet of water. They could be right; the sea has already risen some three feet above normal for the state of tide, which is dead low at the moment." The camera tracked away to show large wavelets lapping at the shore, clearly only inches beneath the park itself.

"Over there . . ." another point, and the camera moved again, "there are the Narrows, leading out into Lower New York Bay and then the Ambrose Channel. That cut normally protects the harbour from the worst effects of gale force winds. Well, no one knows for sure what is going to happen later on this morning and this afternoon. Reports from Sandy Hook, Crookes Point, Rockaway and Coney Island already indicate considerable flooding; if the tidal surge does reach something like 40 feet, as some experts are predicting, it is going to come pouring right over there, pushed by maybe 200-mile-an-hour winds. It's already pretty rough out there." The camera focused on the Narrows; the Bridge was some six miles of water from where the van was standing, but even at that distance the surging whitecaps could be seen, and the zoom lens revealed that spray was being tossed higher than the deserted bridge itself.

"What do you think of the Grand Old Lady, then?" Kimmelman asked. Another track, to reveal the Statue of Liberty, standing as proud as ever amidst the sweeping clouds and the forked lightning. "I tell you, folks, I wouldn't want to be on top of her right this minute. This is Rod Kimmelman, reporting for the National American . . . Holy Jesus!"

The screen went blank.

"He's lost power," Jayme said, grabbing Richard's arm as they stood before the monitor.

"The van's been overturned," Richard snapped. He had warned Rod not to go out there, but Rod had his reputation, as the man who always reported the unreportable story, to protect. He picked up his phone. "Jay, Alan . . . okay, but you'd better make it quick." He put the phone down. "They're sending out a rescue team. I don't know if they'll get through. Christ, the crazy fool."

"Here's the latest update from the Hurricane Centre," Julian said, pulling the sheet of paper out of the teleprinter and handing it across the desk.

Richard looked at it. Faith was now holding an absolutely steady course and speed, north-west at 20 knots. But she was still nearly 120 miles away, and yet already the winds were strong enough to knock over a heavy television van. And Atlantic City was only just within the 100-mile arc – the normal maximum distance for hurricane winds to reach out from the centre – and they were recording 150-mile-an-hour gusts. There could no longer be any question in anyone's mind that they were on the edge of a catastrophe. Even the double-glazed windows in the office were buckling, and a variety of noises penetrated the supposedly soundproof room from the outside world. But it was the window, all the windows in the building, that were principally worrying him. He would have liked to evacuate the weather room, but it was their duty to send out the news for as long as there was power, and it would be impossible to move and re-site all the computer equipment in the windowless studios.

He stood looking down into the streets, still clogged with vehicles, scattered every which way now, but mostly abandoned by their drivers and passengers, who had sought shelter, either returning home or wherever seemed safest; scattered around the vehicles, or on top of them, was all manner of debris, from shattered billboards to television aerials and the branches of trees.

The lights flickered, went off, and came back on again.

"What the hell . . .?" Julian demanded, staring in outrage at his computer screen, which had promptly returned to the 'please wait' display.

"Power outages," Jayme announced, returning from down the corridor, where she had taken a copy of the weather update to Hal Waring. "Seems it's pooping out all over the place. Greenwich Village is blacked out."

"So thank God it's daylight," Julian said, having got his data back again.

"The whole lot is going to go before too long," Richard warned. "There doesn't seem too much point in us all staying here. Why don't you try to get home, Julian?" Julian lived in the city, and well above the 50-foot mark. "Take Jayme with you."

"And you? Who's going to do the next update?" Julian demanded.

"I'll do it." Richard grinned. "I shouldn't think JC will be watching. And if he is, there's damn all he can do about it now." He could, and should, of course, leave the updates to Julian and get out himself – and get to Jo while he could. But this hurricane was his baby, the one he had foretold, and which was behaving so much more horrifically than he had ever supposed it could. He wanted to be involved with it in more than a passive way, for as long as he could – which meant for as long as there was power.

Jayme and Julian looked at each other. "We'll stay, too," the girl decided. "Heck, I don't really want to go out into that; it was bad enough this morning."

"Okay," Richard agreed. "Just remember that the time is going to come when you won't be able to go, even if you want to."

"So we'll set up house for the duration. I'll grab us some lunch from the canteen."

"Here's your spiel." Julian tore the sheet of paper from the print-out and placed it on Richard's desk. "Not a lot to add, really. It's just . . ."

"God Almighty!" Jayme screamed. She had just opened the door and had glanced at the window as she did so, to see a television aerial, swept off the roof of one of the neighbouring buildings, come straight at them.

"Down," Richard shouted, and hurled himself across the desk at the girl, taking her round the thighs in a football tackle and sweeping her to the floor, skidding round Julian's desk as he did so. The noise of shattering plate glass was enormous. The flying metal actually only smashed the outer pane, but it also cracked the inner one; that was sufficient to give the wind a target. The room seemed to swirl around them, papers, pens, computer screens, printers, even chairs being lifted into the air. The TV monitor crashed to the floor and dissolved into flying splinters. Richard had to force Jayme and himself into the knee well of the desk to stop them being lifted too, but even the desk was moving, being driven across the floor, and the wind was searing through the open door and down the corridor, bringing a chorus of screams and shouts of alarm from the other offices.

"Get through it," Richard yelled into Jayme's ear, pushed himself off her, and shoved her towards the door. She tried to crawl, her shoes coming off, the wind seeming to inflate her trouser legs so that she looked like Michelin woman, then dropped to her stomach as a fresh gust sent furniture again whirling around the room. She rolled and screamed in sheer horror as the front of her white shirt became covered in blood.

"Oh, Jesus Christ!" Richard groaned, forcing himself up, and leapt at her again. They went rolling over and over, through the doorway, helped by the wind now. Men were running up the corridor, being checked and forced back by the enormous force thrusting at them, but grouping together in an attempt to push the door shut.

"Julian," Jayme moaned. "Julian!"

Richard dragged her to her feet against the wall, hastily checked that the blood was not hers; she was actually unhurt except for scratches and bruises. He shouted at the men to wait, hurled himself back into the stricken office. Two others came with him, and they seized Julian's arms and half pulled him, half fell with him, through the door. Then the door was slammed shut, and Richard knelt beside the injured man, his heart seeming to slow; Julian's throat had been cut by a jagged piece of flying glass.

LONG ISLAND

9.00 am

"What?" J. Calthrop White shouted into the telephone. "What? Rod Kimmelman? Disappeared? With one of our camera teams? The building damaged? How the hell? . . . A window? Who the hell was the moron opened the window? . . . Blown in? . . . Several? Whose fault was that? I want to know, by God . . . Julian Summers? Dead? Look, don't bullshit me . . . Shut up, goddamn you, and listen. What was Connors doing giving the latest update? I fired that bastard myself, this morning. And he was a disgrace to the station, hair blowing about, eyes staring, tie under his ear – who was the goddamned director? . . . Shut up, God damn you, and listen . . . Listen! . . . Okay, goddamn it, you're fired too. Give me Kiley . . .

"Kiley, what the hell is all this crap? Windows blown out, people disappearing or being killed . . . all true, is it? Well you'd better get things under control down there. Now look here, Kiley, has that fax gone off to London? And the transfer made? . . . Now you look here, Kiley, I don't give a goddamn if everyone else in New York wants his money out, I want ours out, now. You tell Hatton that if he doesn't get his ass moving he's lost my business. You tell . . . Christ Almighty!'' He stared at the phone for several seconds, then raised his head to look at his wife, his butler, his chef, and the three upstairs maids, who had gathered in the downstairs hall of the Long Island mansion. "He's hung up. The shitting bastard has hung up on me. Me!''

"James, do remember your blood pressure," his wife remonstrated.

"Hung up on me," JC screamed. "My own goddamned employee, hung up on me.''

"Ahem," remarked the butler. He had worked, briefly, for one of the royals in England, and was not prepared to acknowledge even J. Calthrop White as a god. "It is possible, sir, that the telephones have ceased to operate.''

JC stared at him. "Ceased to operate?''

"He means they may no longer be working," his wife translated.

"Oh, Jesus Christ . . . you could be right. Where's Murray?''

"Here, sir." The uniformed chauffeur, also English, had just come in; now he stood to attention, cap under his arm.

"Get out the Rolls. I'm going into town. That goddamned station is falling apart, and Kiley isn't worth a damn.''

"Now, sir?" Murray cocked his head. Even on Long Island – the house overlooked the Sound – the wind was howling and the trees in the twelve acres of landscaped garden were slashing back and forth.

"Now, you goddamned popeyed idiot," JC shouted.

"James," remonstrated his wife. "I think it will be a very tiresome drive, especially if the reports of traffic tailbacks are true.''

"It could possibly be dangerous," the butler suggested.

"In the Rolls? For Chrissake, that thing is built to keep out a bullet. I may not be back for lunch, dear. Don't wait for me; I'll grab something from the canteen." He pointed at the butler. "You're in charge should this wind get up.''

The butler bowed. "Of course, Mr White.''

The chauffeur was holding on to the door of the Rolls with both hands – inside the garage; the steel gates were open. JC climbed inside and the door was slammed shut. Murray sat behind the wheel. "I heard on the radio, sir, that all the bridges in and out of Manhattan have been closed.''

"For Christ's sake," JC snapped. "I am J. Calthrop White. Do you suppose anyone is going to close a bridge to me? Drive, man, drive.''

KENNEDY INTERNATIONAL AIRPORT

9.30 am

In the sheltered area of the taxi rank, the rain had dried off the automobile, long ago, leaving streaks of oil and dust on the windows and yellow paintwork. Albert Muldoon had actually awakened half an hour before, in a thoroughly bad temper. His recently repaired radio had failed on him the previous night, and when he had started off to drive back to Manhattan early this morning he had run into the mother and father of all traffic jams, with people shouting about the storm being about to hit the city. He had reckoned they were all nuts, but there had been no arguing with them. So he had made a U-turn and regained the comparative sanity of the airport; there had been flights enough coming in but he was off duty and so he had slept in his cab. Because of the radio failure – goddamn that asshole of a mechanic who'd said it was fixed when it wasn't – he'd been unable to call in, but he knew Carrie wasn't going to worry about him; he'd been out all night before.

But now he had overslept, with the result that he was the only cab on the rank. All those other shits had got fares and pulled out . . . but none had returned from delivering their passengers? They were probably caught in that jam. Serve the bastards right.

Well, he wasn't going anywhere without a fare. He poured the last of the coffee from his vacuum flask, debated about going into the building for a sandwich, and decided against it: he might just miss the fare. So he moved the cab to the very front of the rank, and sat there, listening to the wind howling, watching the rain hitting the road beyond the drive-through . . . and listening, too, to the familiar roaring of airplane engines; there was a lot of activity out there.

But where the hell were the passengers? He lit a cigarette while he stared at the glass doors, the empty pavements. Normally, at this hour of the morning, there'd be hordes of people spewing out of the terminal with their bags, fighting for cabs. But even the rank captain wasn't to be seen. There was probably some kind of strike on, Muldoon figured. He never doubted a fare would eventually arrive.

The noise of the aircraft taking off died, the doors opened, and people ran out. But these weren't passengers; they wore the uniforms of various airlines and they were heading for the staff car parks, totally ignoring the lone taxi cab. Muldoon rolled down his window. "Hey, you!" he bellowed. "What the hell is going on? Where are all the goddamned people?"

A ticket clerk paused beside him. "They're all going someplace else. Haven't you got a radio? The Governor has ordered the evacuation of the airport. All incoming flights have been diverted, all aircraft on the ground have left." He followed the exodus towards the parks.

"What the fucking *hell* is going on?" Muldoon shouted after him again, gazing at the other people, clerks and ground hostesses, security guards and concessionaires, cleaning women and baggage handlers, who were now pouring out of the terminal. "Someone plant a bomb in there?"

"Haven't you heard of Hurricane Faith, you dumb asshole?" a police-woman demanded. "In a couple of hours she's gonna flood this airport with forty feet of water. You get the hell out of here." She joined the rush round the corner.

Muldoon scratched his head as he again mentally cursed that god-damned mechanic; he'd been sitting here all night to no purpose. And if there really was a big storm coming, Carrie would be scared out of her wits. He switched on his ignition and pumped the gas pedal, tooting his horn to get through the crowd. Back into that fucking traffic.

LONG ISLAND

9.45 am

The Rolls-Royce slithered to and fro over the road as the wind gusts became stronger.

"What the devil is the matter with you?" J. Calthrop White demanded. "You been drinking?"

"It's the wind, Mr White. It really is getting kind of strong. I wonder if we shouldn't turn back."

"Turn back? Look, don't give me any bullshit, Murray. Put your foot down."

"I was thinking of the bridge, Mr White. It's going to be scary up there."

"So what, are you afraid of a little wind?"

Murray sighed, and rounded a corner, both hands tight on the wheel. At least there were no other vehicles around – everyone else had more sense than even to open a garage door in this weather.

The automobile slithered again, and he got it straight by using all of his strength, but lost it again when by far the strongest gust so far gripped the high body. "Hell!" Murray gasped, and pressed his foot flat to the floor, but the Rolls still continued to move sideways.

"What the devil . . ." shouted J. Calthrop White. But the Rolls was already off the road, sliding down the parapet to come to rest in a ditch, presently dry, but very muddy.

"Sorry, Mr White, I just lost her," Murray said. The engine was still running, and he put the car in low gear and revved, but there was merely an enormous upheaval of mud and a grinding noise. "I guess she's stuck."

"For Jesus' sake . . . you are fired, Murray. I am giving you 24 hours' notice. Now get out of here and raise some help."

"I don't think I can walk against that wind, Mr White."

"Goddamn it, man!" J. Calthrop White shouted. "I have given you an order. Get on with it."

Murray sighed, and opened the door.

CONEY ISLAND

10.00 am

The tremendous banging on the downstairs door made Florence sit up. It had been so lovely, lying in bed with Bert, all morning, dozing off and waking up again to listen to the howl of the wind, the distant booming of the seas on the beach, the crackle of the thunder; that was what being on holiday was all about – not having to go out in weather like this.

Eventually she had got up and fetched coffee from the vending machine in the corridor, then she had gone back to bed; it was a very long time since Bert had been so virile . . . she was feeling quite reassured that their love life – increasingly disarranged at home by his poker nights with the boys and his baseball Saturdays and her sometimes having to stay overnight at the Donnellys caring for the children – was still going strong. Maybe it was something in the violence of the storm outside had touched an elemental chord in his libido – it had certainly touched something in her.

Then they had slept again, in each other's arms. At some stage Emmie had banged on the bedroom door, and gone on banging even when they totally ignored her. Emmie didn't have a man, and her idea of fun was to go out and look at the waves. But eventually they had been left alone until this much more insistent banging . . . which was now being accompanied by the sound of shattering glass.

"What the hell . . ." Bert had heard it too, and jumped out of bed. "Somebody's breaking in!" He nearly lost his balance as the building shook, but he grabbed a towel to wrap around his waist and unlocked the bedroom door, to be driven back by the blast of air which came gushing into the room. "Shut that goddamned street door," he bawled down the stairwell; the little hotel, set well back from the Coney Island beach front, was a walk-up.

"Hey, who's there?' came a shout back. "Your name Bert Bennett?"

"Yeah. So what?" Bert demanded.

"Your sister-in-law sent us down. She thought you'd left with everybody else, but when we got to counting heads up at Prospect . . . say, you guys deaf, or what? You didn't hear everyone else leaving?"

Florence had got out of bed as well, and, wrapped in a dressing gown, stood at her husband's shoulder, gazing down the stairs at the patrolman, his cape and hat glistening wet, listened, too, to the sound of the surf, so close, closer than she had ever heard it, almost drowning out the whine of the wind. Suddenly she was gripped with a deathly fear.

"You mean . . . everybody's gone?" Bert was asking in bewilderment. "This place was full."

"All of Coney Island was evacuated two hours ago," the patrolman told him. "Christ, you guys must've been dead. Come on, we have to get the hell out of here."

"I'll just get dressed," Florence said.

"Lady," the patrolman said. "You're gonna have half the Atlantic Ocean inside that bedroom within half an hour. You coming now, or not? Because I sure as hell am leaving now, and I ain't coming back."

Florence looked at Bert, and they ran down the stairs together, gazed in horror at the street, over which several inches of water were pouring, while at the intersection . . . even as they watched, a wave came bubbling down the alleyway, sweeping before it a garbage collection of shattered deck chairs, plastic bottles and boxes, discarded sun hats and shoes, and several drowned cats and dogs. "Oh, Jesus," Florence whispered.

"The beach . . . ?" Bert asked.

"The beach ain't there any more," the patrolman said. He pointed, and they splashed round the corner, away from the sea, to where a patrol car was parked. Inside was another officer, using his radio. He stared at them in amazement. "What the hell . . .?"

"That dame was right," his partner told him. "Would you believe it, Charlie? These two were in bed. In bed!" He opened the rear door and bundled the two almost naked bodies inside.

"Well, they have to be the last," Charlie said. "We're under orders to get the hell out of here and rendezvous with the others at Prospect Park."

"Prospect?" Bert asked. "Say, we have to get home. We need some clothes."

Charlie gunned the motor and turned the patrol car; water was swirling around its axles. "Home being where?"

"We live in the Bronx," Florence told him, breathlessly, hugging her dressing-gown around herself.

"Well, you can forget that," the patrolman told her. "All the bridges and tunnels are closed. They're setting up an emergency centre at Prospect Park. They'll take care of . . . oh, Jesus Christ! Charlie!"

The patrol car had slowed through a larger than usual surge of water coming down the street, and the engine coughed and died.

"Fuck it!" Charlie opened his door and got out, throwing up the engine hood; he was knee deep in water. But the rain was falling so heavily there was no chance of anything under there drying out in a hurry.

"We're gonna have to walk it," the patrolman said.

"In this?" Florence asked.

"Like this?" Bert put in.

The patrolman grinned. "Maybe you're better off than us, at that. Let's go." He opened the door for them, and they splashed out.

"I can't," Florence protested. "I can't. I'm freezing. And I'll cut my feet to ribbons."

"Lady," the patrolman said. "Look." He pointed. "That row of houses over there is all that's standing between us and the whole goddamned ocean. You reckon . . . oh, Holy Jesus Christ!"

Even as they looked, the houses in front of them started to collapse, as if struck by a series of large bombs, windows and doors flying out beneath the impact of the sea, which was now assaulting them with 20-foot waves.

Hunt National Bank, Wall Street

10.30 am

Seth Hatton was pleased with the turnout at the bank. Despite the massive traffic jams, the appalling weather, and the complete lack of co-operation from the authorities – added to the fact that it was a Saturday morning – he and his senior staff had been able to contact almost every employee . . . and a good percentage of them had reached the office. Hatton did not think any of the other banks, or financial institutions, most of them far larger than Hunt National, had managed to obtain as good a response. He had also been first off the ground with moving records, thanks to J. Calthrop White. He didn't like the man, but he certainly was a live wire. And if JC hadn't started acting like a madman at two o'clock this morning, having his yes man, Kiley, actually ringing a bank president at home and convincing him that he had to get down to the office, they could have lost a lot of business – especially as other wealthy people had apparently awakened to the realisation that the money market was going to be in utter confusion for the next couple of days. They had even opened the Stock Exchange, but down there the chaos was indescribable. People were unloading so fast, any commodity or property share remotely connected with the New York and New Jersey seaboards, that millions were being wiped off the Dow. There would be several fortunes to be made come Monday, if the storm was gone by then and the damage not as severe as people thought; it would be a case of who could start buying first: Seth Hatton had that much in mind.

But meanwhile, business. He had all his top people on the fax machines and the computers, and everyone else on the telephones, even pool-room typists; it was a case of getting a line and keeping it until cut off, and then getting it back again. The voices ranged across the huge office, some shouting, some pleading, some speaking in low, confident tones, some almost in tears with frustration.

But a lot were getting through, despite the enormous competition for air space; the truly amazing thing was that, realising the extent of the emergency, overseas banks had also pulled staffers in to handle the enormous amount of transactions so suddenly required. "Hello! Is that Barclays, London? . . . Oh, thank God! Say, are you the person I was speaking with earlier? . . . Hi, there. That's right, Hunt National. I have another one for you . . . yeah, to open an account and effect an immediate transfer . . . The name is James Jonathan Jurgens, address Apartment 35, Park Avenue and 48th Street, New York, New York . . . Right. The amount is $687,000 . . . That's it . . . Yes, same as before. Open the account and send us the necessary documentation and signature cards . . . Oh, sure, we'll probably want it all back next week. Okay. Don't go away." Someone else, overhearing to whom the clerk was speaking, had rushed up with another batch of papers. "I have a couple more for you . . . Yeah . . . Okay, first . . . oh shit!" The clerk gazed at the phone in dismay. "I've been cut off."

"Keep trying," his senior advised him.

But the complaint was general.

"What's the trouble?" Hatton inquired, standing on the mezzanine outside his office and looking down into the well of the bank.

"All the phones are dead, Mr Hatton."

Hatton hesitated, and the lights flickered, then went out, followed by the air-conditioning. The bank's doors were naturally closed, and the gloom and heat was suddenly intense. "Well," he said. "I guess that's that. Thanks a million, everybody. We've all done the best we could. Now . . . let's get the hell out of here."

New York Police Department Headquarters, Park Row

11.00 am

"Yeah," said Assistant Commissioner McGrath into his radio. "Yeah . . . Yeah . . . Okay, that's it. You guys pull out." He put the handset down, looked at his waiting officers. "The tide's surging right over the Battery and starting to flood down Broadway. I've told them down there to get out while they can, and it's time we did the same. And the Mayor." He picked up the radio again. "City Hall, City Hall, NYPD here. City Hall, NYPD. For Christ's sake, why don't they answer? I can see the God damned building, can't I?" Not that he liked what he saw when he looked out of his window. Apart from the flying debris and the upturned trees, even as he watched a patrol car came round the corner, sideways, obviously being blown by the wind; he could see the driver fighting to regain control. "Jesus," he muttered.

The car tipped on its side, went right over, and came to rest against a wall.

"City Hall."

"The Mayor about, Mitch?"

"Right here."

"Naseby. McGrath, what's happening now?"

"This is it, Mr Mayor. The Battery's gone. Water's on Broadway. That means it's only nine blocks from us. I guess we have to get out of here."

"Is the evacuation complete?"

"Well, I guess not. We're doing the best we can, but there's been some resistance to the idea. You know what these folks are like, especially the older ones. Some of them don't even answer the door, and I just don't have the men to go through every apartment building. Mr Mayor, I want you to pull your people out."

"I promised . . ."

"Sure you did. But this city is going to need you just as much to put it back together again when this storm is finished; you can't do anything about that if you're dead, now can you?"

Naseby hesitated, then sighed. "Okay, McGrath, I guess you're right. Evacuate now. We'll be doing the same. Is your mobile headquarters set up?"

"Yeah, at the Plaza Hotel. We have an emergency generator up there too."

"Did all the Telephone Exchange people get out?"

"So far as I know."

"Okay. Keep in touch. Let's move."

McGrath replaced the handset, crammed the last mouthful of his sandwich down his throat, swallowed, stood up. "Everybody out. Those files ready?"

Captain Luther nodded.

"Okay, don't forget the cells, now. Mustn't let any of the bastards on remand drown. Let's move it now, boys, or we are going to get our feet wet, and then some. I'm going up to the Chief."

Chief Grundy stood at his window, watching the streets. "Christ," he remarked. "Listen to it howl. Look at that rain; it's coming at us horizontal."

"It's gonna be salt in five minutes," McGrath told him. "Naseby says out. So let's go."

They put on their hats and coats, headed down the stairs; the elevator had ceased functioning when the electrics had gone. Their desks had already been cleared and everything loaded into the waiting fleet of vans. Now these too started to move. The streets down here had been completely cleared, all abandoned vehicles pushed on to the sidewalks, and had been patrolled all morning to make sure they stayed clear. But now the outflow of vehicles from City Hall joined those from Police Headquarters to create a new jam.

"For Christ's sake," McGrath muttered, staring through the door. "Sort it out. I'd better get out there . . ." He checked as one of the vans, caught by a gust of wind, slewed round and crashed over on to its side; the rear doors burst open and papers flew everywhere. "Oh, hell. Well, that's it."

"Get it moved," Grundy snapped. McGrath pushed open the door, followed by a squad of policemen, and other staffers, and ran into the teeming rain to join the blue clad crowd already around the overturned vehicle. Even sheltered by the buildings standing up was next to impossible; McGrath found himself on his hands and knees, and up to his elbows in water. "Jesus Christ," he gasped, and struggled up, to be thrown down and sent rolling and splashing several feet further up the street. He realised that they might have left the evacuation just a little too late, looked up and saw an entire roof, it seemed, sailing through the air to crash into the building opposite, demolishing the front wall as if it had been cardboard. Then the wind got inside, blowing out the windows, tearing doors off their hinges, picking up desks and filing cabinets as if they had been toys and tossing them out into the street.

A police sergeant landed beside him with a splash; he carried a megaphone. "We gotta go," he bellowed. "Files or no files. Those vans don't stand a chance in this wind."

McGrath wondered how he figured human beings could stand a chance, either. But he snatched the trumpet. "Clear out!" he screamed. "Forget the vehicles. Clear out while you can. Rendezvous at the Plaza Hotel."

Nobody heard him above the shrieking of the wind, the roaring of the water, which was now racing through the streets as if they had all been rivers. But people were making their own decisions, staggering and floundering to where they supposed safety to be, or clawing their way back into the buildings in search of at least temporary shelter. Chief Grundy, on the headquarters ground floor, stamped his feet impatiently as he watched a trickle of water come in the door and make its way across the lobby. "Where the hell is Harmon?" he bawled.

"Those guys down there don't want to come out," Luther gasped at him from the stairs to the remand cells. "They reckon they're safer in the cells."

"Are they nuts?" Grundy himself ran down to the lower level. The cell doors were wide open, and the remand prisoners were free to leave – indeed, they were being implored to do so, but none of them looked anxious to take advantage of the offer. "For God's sake," Grundy bellowed. "Use force, Harmon. Throw them out."

Harmon turned to the policemen with him. "You heard the Chief," he said. "Get those guys out."

Stuart Alloan scrambled on to his bed, dragging Domingo Garcia with him; he reckoned staying close to the monster was his safest course.

"You trying to drown us?" Garcia yelled. He was a sallow little man, but he had a loud voice. "You leave us right here. You . . ." His voice trailed away as he stared at the stairs. Grundy and Harmon turned together, to watch a four-foot high wall of water rushing towards them.

PARK AVENUE

11.15 am

When the phone went dead, Jo decided it was time to take shelter. She had tried calling Marcia and Benny again, eventually asking the operator for help, only to be told that all communication with Greenwich Village was cut – as if it had been a defaulting spaceship, she thought. Then she tried Connecticut, and Richard, but with no more success. At least she had been able to see his face on TV from time to time. Amazingly, the windows in the apartment were holding – fortunately the plate glass in the lounge faced away from the worst of the storm – but judging by the noise outside, and the heavy debris she could see flying past the apartment block, added to the howling of the wind inside the building as it blew through the broken street-doors, she didn't reckon they would stand up to much more. So she herded Owen Michael and Tamsin into the bathroom, bolted the door, and they sat together on the mattress drinking hot soup out of mugs.

"I don't think I could eat a burger as well, Mom." Tamsin eyed the steaming plateful that Jo had hastily prepared while the electricity lasted.

"Do try, sweetheart. It may be a long time before I'll be able to cook again." She could see that both the children were frightened, each determined not to reveal the fact to the other.

"I wonder where Dad is now?" Owen Michael said.

"Probably in sight of Newport," Jo told him. "Having the time of his life."

"I wish I was with him."

"Well, I wish you and Tamsin were with Granpa and Granma."

"And you too, Mom," Tamsin added.

Jo wasn't sure what to reply to that. She still wanted to be near Richard, even though in the bathroom the roar of the wind and the crashes of thunder were terrifying . . . as was the thought that he might try to reach her. Oh, no, my darling Richard, don't do it, she prayed silently. Nobody can get through this.

But all the same, she realised she was constantly straining to hear his voice calling his arrival above the din, imagining that each unidentifiable crash or bang was his knock on the door.

QUEEN'S MIDTOWN TUNNEL

11.30 am

"Fucking hell," Al Muldoon remarked. "Oh, fucking hell!"

It had taken him two hours to drive from Kennedy to the entrance to Queen's Midtown Tunnel – somebody had told him all the bridges were jammed, but nobody had said anything about the tunnels. If only he had a radio; when next he saw that asshole of a mechanic he was going to wring his neck.

Two hours! It hadn't mattered that the traffic was almost all going the other way . . . they were driving on both sides of every street. He'd kept having to pull off on to the sidewalk to avoid being rammed, and even so his cab had been hit several times. The first time he'd jumped out, despite the rain which promptly poured down his neck, and wanted to beat the hell out of the stupid moron who'd sideswiped him – it was clearly the other guy's fault as he was on the wrong side of the street. But immediately he'd been grabbed by two soldiers. Fucking MPs! He could as well have been back in Vietnam.

"Cool it, buddy boy," they told him. "You're going against the stream."

Muldoon had supposed he was about to have a heart attack. "Me? Against the stream?" He had pointed at the street signs in impotent anger. These guys had to be stupid or something, or the whole world had gone mad. And who the hell were they to tell him what to do? He was a civilian now. "Look," he said, as reasonably as he could. "You guys get off my back. This ain't the goddamned army."

"It is to you," the first MP said. "Ain't you heard this city is under martial law?"

Muldoon was speechless for a moment. "On whose say so?" he demanded when he had got his breath back.

"On the say so of the Governor and the President of the United States. Now, you all finished arguing?"

Muldoon fell back on defence. "That guy was breaking the law. Driving the wrong way."

"No, you were driving the wrong way, buster," said the second MP. "All roads lead out, right now. Where the hell are you going, anyway?"

"I'm going home, that's where I'm going," Muldoon shouted, resisting with some effort the temptation to call them what he was thinking. "Where the fucking hell would I be going?"

"Where's home?"

"Manhattan. Where the hell do you think it would be?"

"Let me get this straight," the MP said. "You're out here in Queen's, and you want to go in to Manhattan?"

"Look, fella," Muldoon said. "I don't know what the shitting hell is going on, but I have a home, and I have a wife, just on the other side of that river, and if there's something happening, I aim to be with them. You guys gonna try to stop me?"

The MPs had looked at each other. One had shrugged. "We don't have orders to stop nobody going into the city," he said.

The other had nodded. "Okay, buster. You can keep going. Just keep out of the way of any vehicles coming this way; you're driving up a one-way street."

"Jesus Christ, the whole fucking world has gone mad," Muldoon commented, and got back into his cab. He was sopping wet, and the inside was all misted up. And there seemed to be automobiles coming at him from all directions. And he hadn't had any breakfast and was as hungry as hell. But he made progress, until he got to the tunnel entrance itself, having been side-swiped half a dozen times by other crazy drivers. And here, suddenly, there was a complete absence of traffic, although it continued to roar by on the next street.

Instead, there was a roadblock.

Muldoon braked, put his head out of the window. "This is the first sanity I've seen today. Now move that goddamned barrier."

"Yeah?" This time he looked at policemen, bending against the wind. "No one's allowed through that tunnel."

"Why the hell not?"

"It ain't safe, that's why not."

"Ah, for Christ's sake. Look, I've been trying to get home for two fucking hours. I have a wife waiting for me over there. I can be through that tunnel in ten minutes."

"No one is allowed through this tunnel," the policeman said again.

"Oh, Jesus . . ."

"Well, if it ain't Muldoon," the sergeant said, splashing towards him and holding on to the automobile to avoid being blown away; his cap was tightly strapped under his chin. "You crazy or what?"

"Oh, Jesus," Muldoon repeated. He'd been on the wrong side of this character before. "Listen, Mac, I gotta get home. The wife has a weak heart. You know that. I gotta get home."

The sergeant pulled his wet nose.

"Nobody . . ." the policeman repeated.

"Forget it," the sergeant said. "Look here, Muldoon, I have to tell you that tunnel ain't safe."

"It's caving in or something?"

"Nope. Not yet. But there's flooding on lower Manhattan, getting worse all the time. It'll come down that tunnel any moment now. And the electrics are out; you'll have only your headlights to see by. If you want to go through that bad I'll let you, but it has to be at your own risk."

"Sure it'll be at my own risk," Muldoon agreed. "You think I'm afraid of the dark? Or of a little flood water?"

"Okay." The sergeant stepped back, and saluted. "Good luck, fella."

He signalled his men, and the boom was raised. Muldoon put the cab into drive and dipped into the tunnel. As the sergeant had prophesied, it was pitch dark in there, but he turned his headlights up to full beam and they provided adequate illumination. Yet he drove slowly, determined not to have an accident – there was no way of telling when he might come upon abandoned vehicles. Above him he could hear the roar of the river, and he cast one or two anxious glances at the walls to see if they were standing up okay. They looked as safe as ever, and he realised that down here the turbulence up there could have little effect. His confidence began to grow.

He was half way through when he heard the other noise. He had realised only slowly that he was actually driving through water, several inches deep – the Chevrolet was sliding about, but this was something else. Muldoon instinctively braked, staring ahead to the limit of his lights, and beyond, at a foaming mass of white coming out of the darkness. "Holy fucking hell!" he shouted, and swung to the left to make a U-turn. Immediately he skidded and struck the wall of the tunnel. The taxi slewed half way round and he had not regained control when the rushing flood water smashed into the vehicle, sweeping it up towards the York side of the river as if it had been a cork.

SATURDAY 29 JULY

Afternoon

Herald Square

12.00 noon

Alloan half ran, half fell, dragging Garcia behind him, the two men carried along on the wind from alleyway to recessed doorway, from the lee of abandoned cars and through the shattered glass doors of lobbies, falling against each other in the scant shelter as they tried to catch their breaths. It was difficult to find protection anywhere, even in the cavern-like New York streets, now the wind was funnelling between the high buildings, increasing its strength. It was almost impossible to see, identify individual noise or even to think; apart from the driving rain and continuous thunder the air was full of dirt and flying debris. The young man knew it was a miracle they had survived this long, not been cut to ribbons by hurtling glass or crushed by automobiles which were being picked up and thrown through the air. They had side-stepped a number of casualties, some clawing at them for help, mouthing inaudible pleas which they ignored. They had crawled through giant tangles of fallen trees and torn power lines – if the electrics hadn't been out they'd have fried to a chip. Garcia was a helluva burden, lying wherever he fell, pleading exhaustion and having to be hauled each time to his feet. If he hadn't known that Garcia was an expert locksmith he would have abandoned him long ago; but to achieve his goal he might well need the man. He was not only driven by fear of the rising water behind them, but by anger – and an all-consuming desire . . .

Garcia had no idea why they were still together. In a way he wished they weren't, that he could be left in a doorway to rest his aching limbs and chest. But as the kid had got them out of the cells, fighting a way up the stairway through cascades of water and people screaming, gasping and being trampled underfoot to drown, subconsciously he felt obliged to force himself to keep going. He didn't know where but the kid had some place in mind. Come to think of it, he didn't even know the boy's name.

Alloan looked at Garcia, at the heaving chest and tinge of blue round his mouth. Might be wiser to show a bit more patience, he didn't want this character passing out on him. It was fairly sheltered just here and the storm would continue for hours yet; plenty time to do what he wanted.

His eyes narrowed. That weatherman he'd seen on the station box had spoken of 'an eye', a patch of calm weather in the centre of the storm. They could wait on that 'eye', then they'd get there in a fraction of the time. "Okay, Domingo. We'll rest up here a while. That's it," he nodded as Garcia slid gratefully down the wall and leaned his head back, "you have yourself a rest."

The Subway

12.30 pm

There was still electricity at Penn Station, where they were using emergency generators. Washington Jones was told there were no more trains running north, but that he could take the cross line, under the East River, to Lorimer. He held Celestine's hand, carrying two suitcases in the other, and Patsy ran behind him, the baby in her arms; they had become part of a terrified mob of people trying to get away, driven by reports that rising flood water was within a few blocks.

Washington knew that he had indeed left it too late – but the fault was not entirely his. It had taken him more than an hour to regain his house, and then he discovered that Celestine had done nothing, that she didn't really want to go. She had neither packed nor called the boy. He had convinced her that it was urgent, and she had got to work, slowly and resentfully. He had tried calling the boy's work place, over and over again, and never got through. He shouldn't have had to get through; the boy should have come home by nine. But he hadn't. So they had waited, and waited, because Patsy wouldn't leave without him, while the wind had grown stronger and the house had trembled and the phone and the electricity had gone dead. And at last they had realised the boy wasn't coming, for whatever reason, and Washington had been able to persuade the woman to leave.

Just in time, he thought. Oh, just in time, as he tried to keep his family together in the midst of the huge crowd of people, hurrying down the corridors, jamming the stairs, filling the elevators, screaming and shouting. They had left home with three suitcases, but the one Celestine had carried caught in an elevator door and Washington made her abandon it.

They reached the platform and piled into the train, which immediately started to move off, attendants shouting at people who were trying to push their way into the compartments, and then being crammed in by those behind them. "There ain't gonna be no more trains after this one," a man said to Washington. "They say Greenwich Village is almost under water. Did you hear that, man? These electrics can't last too much longer."

Obstructing bodies prevented the door from closing until the attendants started shouting that another train would be along in a minute.

"Wanna bet?" the man asked.

The train moved off very slowly, gathered speed, slowed, stopped and started again. "Holy Mother of God, we're going to be here until the middle of next week," a woman yelled. She had a little girl on her knee, who wore a straw hat with a ribbon and carried a plastic doll with long hair.

Washington saw they were all alone and took pity on them. "Don't fret. We'll all stick together. Can't be much further now." He could feel them begin the gradual ascent on the east side of the river.

Suddenly the train stopped; at the same moment the lights went out. There was a chorus of screams and shrieks, and Washington abandoned the suitcases and put both arms around Celestine and held her close. The din was tremendous as more than a thousand people all shouted together and pushed against each other and the doors, which remained firmly closed.

"We're going to die," Celestine gasped. "We're going to die."

Patsy wept, and the baby wailed, and the woman with the little girl kept shouting, "Holy Mary Mother of God, save us," over and over again.

They heard, faintly, an attendant out in the tunnel shouting for calm, but nobody was paying any attention to him, and the press was growing greater and greater. Washington felt all the air being crushed out of his body, that he was indeed going to die, when suddenly the doors against which he was being flattened opened and he almost fell out. Celestine went with him, and Patsy and the baby. And then the crowd followed, screaming and yelling, trampling over each other. He heard people shrieking in fear and agony as they were thrust into the water . . . because he realised that he was ankle deep in water. But they had been first out and could move along the track.

"The electric line," Celestine gasped.

"If that line was live, the train would be moving," Washington gasped back at her. "And if it comes live again we're all going to die anyway. Just hold on to my jacket with one hand and Patsy with the other. Careful now, mind your step. I'll lead the way."

He was worried by the water; it was rising quite quickly. They must get out, but people didn't seem to be moving in any particular direction, just floundering. Thanks to God they had been in the front carriage. He suddenly felt compelled to do something – help these terrified, braying sheep to get out in time. In his youth he had been a good baritone in the church choir. Now he stood tall and called, his voice resounding down the tunnel behind them. "Just make a line, folks, and follow behind us. We'll soon be out of here. Just keep calm, and sing to the Lord." He drew a deep breath and began: "Oh, God, our help in ages past, our hope in years to come . . . "

Celestine smiled into the darkness, and her soprano joined him. "Our shelter from the stormy blast . . ." and Patsy and the man who held her coat and the woman who held his hand all began to follow the strong baritone who was attempting to lead them away from impending peril.

Washington could feel his way because of the train, and when the train ended there was the wall of the tunnel. His fingers groped and his feet stumbled and splashed. He was aware that there were a lot of people behind him not singing, just shouting and sobbing, moaning and cursing, falling and being pushed over. His breath became short and his throat dry. The hymn ended, and he swallowed and started again. How long was it to the next station? And the water was rising every minute. It was past his knees, and his legs were feeling like lead. Once Celestine fell, and he had to drag her up again, soaking wet. He didn't know how much longer he could keep going, when he saw flashing lights ahead of him.

Several MPs were peering down from a platform, waving their powerful flashlights. "We heard there were people in here. Listen, you guys, you gotta get out, quick. This tunnel is gonna flood any moment now."

Washington helped Celestine up as one of the young men held her hand. "Son," he said, "you just show us the way."

Patsy passed the baby to another soldier and was heaved up out of the water. People stopped singing and began to clap and cheer as they realised they'd all but reached safety. By the dim glow of the flashlights, several stopped to shake the big black man's hand, and thank him as he handed them up to the platform. But that only embarrassed him. He couldn't see that he had done anything except walk, and sing.

"Washington, come on, or we'll get separated," Celestine begged.

"She's right, mister," an MP said. "It's time you were with your family. You've done your bit." He offered his hand while another MP held the other to heave together; Washington Jones was a heavy man . . . and very tired.

More MPs appeared with hand-held floodlights, linked to a portable generator, illuminating the stream of frightened humanity, flowing up the stairs ahead, along the crowded platform, and beyond them the swirling black water.

Washington, Celestine, and Patsy with the baby, were half way up the stairs to the street when frantic screaming exploded from the platform below them. They turned, and, above the heads of the crowd pressing urgently behind them, saw a great wall of water gush out of the tunnel they had just left, engulfing everyone on the platform, sweeping those on the outer edge away with it. Those nearest the wall clung together, clutching at rails, seats, anything that might keep them on their feet in the surge swirling around their chests.

The water rose over them and reached even the step on which Washington was standing . . . and there, spinning at his feet for a few moments, was a little round straw hat with a ribbon. Then it was drawn away into the main stream again, and disappeared.

LONG ISLAND

12.45 pm

An enormous gust shook the Rolls-Royce; it rose on two wheels, and then thudded back down again with a thump which drove the breath from J. Calthrop White's lungs. But he had already been breathless – for over an hour.

He was on the floor of the back seat, kneeling, heart pounding. He had never experienced anything like this, had never expected to. He was J. Calthrop White. He owned things, from huge buildings down to this car, and he owned people's opinions as well. Hell, he even owned people. He gave orders, and they were obeyed.

Why was this happening to him?

Another gust, and he nearly vomited. The rain was teeming down, now, pounding on the roof of the car; he could hear it gurgling in the ditch. My God, suppose it rose sufficiently to drown him? God, why hadn't he stayed at home? If he could get home, he'd never leave again. "I mean that, God," he whispered. "Sincerely."

Maybe God wasn't listening.

Another sound. Something against the car. My God, he thought, water, trying to push it over. "God," he whispered. "Save me."

The leeward door was clawed open. J. Calthrop White stared in horror at the apparition which climbed into the back beside him. It was capless, uniform torn and filthy, face a bloody mask – there was blood on his feet and staining his breeches, as well.

"God," the apparition said. "Oh, God." He slumped against the seat for several seconds then raised his head. "I'm sorry, Mr White. There isn't any help."

"Where have you been?" J. Calthrop White demanded.

"Not far," Murray said with a deep sigh. "Maybe a hundred yards."

"You've been gone damn near three hours."

"Yes, sir," Murray said. "I've spent all that time trying to get back. Mr White, it's death to be out there."

"It's damn near death in here too."

"Mr White," Murray said, as the car seemed to lift into the air and then thump back down again. "I think we should pray."

"What the hell do you think I've been doing?" J. Calthrop White shouted. Then his voice lowered. "But you're welcome to join in. And Murray, if we ever get out of here, you can have your job back."

Greenwich Village

1.00 pm

"Aaagh!" Marcia screamed. "Benny, I'm scared. I've never heard a noise like this. The whole house is shaking."

"Guess we're getting the edge of Faith all right," Benny agreed.

They had slept late, very late, and brunched on tinned soup, cheese and fruit at twelve o'clock. Occasionally they had been disturbed by the wind and the thunder. Once they thought they heard a police siren close at hand, and a loudspeaker blaring, but the noise had been subdued by the pounding rain. Then someone had knocked on the street door, several times, and then rung the bell, but they had ignored whoever it had been; in weather like this, with hangovers, bed had seemed the best place to be.

When they finally got dressed and went downstairs to the kitchen – they had chosen to keep the one in the basement apartment, which was actually below street level – the thunder and lightning and howling wind didn't seem so ominous, but having come upstairs again, the upper part of the house appeared to be swaying, beams and joists creaking and groaning behind the plaster, and they had to shout to be heard above the noise.

"Edge of nothing! This has to be the real thing. God!" Marcia cowered back against the door as a violent gust cracked a window pane.

"Jees! That whole window will go in a minute; the wood is rotten. We must nail something over it." Desperately Benny looked around. "What? Quick, what can we use?"

"Try the plywood back off that old bureau that fell off when we moved it." Marcia tugged at the ancient piece that had served for years as a dressing table.

"Yeah, that'll do. Look, I'll hold it over the window while you go down for a hammer and nails."

When the frail window was safely boarded up, they went round the other rooms, checking that everything was secured, and were halfway down the stairs when the lights went out.

"Damn," Benny said. "That means we can't check the weather on TV." They groped through the gloomy daylight filtering into the hallway. "Who'd believe it was one o'clock in the afternoon?"

"Benny, do you think we're safe here? Shouldn't we be in a stronger, concrete building?" She peered out at the street. "Jees, it's dead out there. Not a soul in sight."

"Sweetheart, will you just look at the bricks and tiles scattered on the road? It's dangerous outside, even if you were able to stay on your feet. I reckon we're a whole lot safer inside, and obviously everybody else thinks so too. Let's get on with the painting."

"How the hell can we paint in this light?" Marcia moaned.

"I guess they'll fix it soon," Benny said, hopefully.

"You're an optimist. They took more than a day, last time we had an outage. Well, as there's only that corner left to do, I guess we could hang the drapes and put the loose covers on the settee and chairs." Anything to occupy her mind, fight off the pangs of fear which were paralysing her movements.

A sudden tremendous crash rocked the building, scattering crockery in the kitchen. It continued to boom and rattle for several minutes.

"Oh, dear God! What was that?" Marcia was white as a sheet. She followed Benny to the window – then drew back in horror, tears starting to course down her cheeks. The old brown house across the street, loved, tended and preserved in all its traditional character by a young couple who had become good friends of theirs, was now only a heap of rubble. The roof had lifted and fallen back, breaking up as it did so, heavy tiles and supporting joists devastating the floors and walls below.

"Christ, how did that happen? Could've been struck by a bomb. I must go see if I can help them." Benny started for the door.

"No, Benny, no! They're not there. They went to Joyce's mother for the weekend. Oh, Benny . . ." Marcia flung herself into his arms. "I'm so frightened. Could . . ." she gulped. "Could that happen to us?"

"No way. I told Tom he should've had that building surveyed. We'll be okay, baby." He held her against him, patting her shoulders and displaying a confidence he was far from feeling. The only comfort was that the new joists they had put in on the second floor had to be a source of strength. Whatever happened upstairs, nothing could come through there. They'd just have to stay down here until this thing blew itself out, and worry about the roof afterwards.

But he couldn't avoid a terrible feeling that maybe that police siren and the banging on the door might have been some kind of warning. If only he had even a portable radio – but he'd never bothered; he had always preferred his collection of tapes and his own kind of music to the brainless chat which filled so much air time. And anyway, a hurricane . . . in Greenwich Village?

Yet to think of the place opposite. To see a house just collapse . . .

But he couldn't communicate any of his fear to Marcia; she was sufficiently terrified as it was. He said, "Come on and stop worrying. We've got work to do. Where are the hooks for the drapes?"

The young couple tried to concentrate, pushing the hooks into place with fumbling fingers, but they were shaken every few minutes by new bangs and crashes as lightning struck the taller buildings around them, and the ever increasing wind force carried chimney pots, tiles, and even sheets of plate glass slicing through the streets. Half an hour later, the curtains were all neatly in place – but it was hard to appreciate the full effect against the wallpaper and paint – the light was too bad.

The downstairs windows had old casement shutters, most of which Benny had securely fastened except for the two centre folds in the lounge. Now he closed these as well. "That last gust nearly took the house with it. We'll just have to sit in the gloom unless you can find some candles. There'll have to be . . ." He never finished the sentence. A deafening roaring, creaking, groaning, whirring, moaning sound thundered round their heads, and showers of ceiling plaster rained down on them.

Marcia screamed. Benny grabbed her and drew her towards the outer wall, praying that the new joists would hold, but if not, that they would only give in the centre. It was impossible to speak – but they both knew the roof had gone. Instinctively they went down the stairs to the comparative safety of the kitchen, closing and locking the door behind themselves. Marcia slid down the wall to sit on the floor, hands clasped over her abdomen in a gesture of protection for their baby. She must look after it. All this frightening experience was so bad for it; she and Benny would both be devastated if she miscarried.

Suddenly she realised that the floor was wet. "Ugh!" She jumped up and grabbed Benny's hand. "The rain's coming through the ceiling," she yelled in his ear.

But Benny knew it wasn't rain water. It was already swirling round their ankles, and it smelt . . . of sea and salt. "Upstairs," he yelled back, and started for the door, icy fingers of terror clawing at his chest, trying to drag Marcia with him.

They never reached it. With a series of massive, rapid cracks, like a barrage of artillery fire, the door was burst open, and a cascade of water, carrying nameless, stinking flotsam, converged on them in the gloom.

"Oh, my new drapes!" Marcia cried, a split second before she was swept off her feet. She struggled, lungs bursting, seeking to surface – but she didn't know which way was up. She thought she felt Benny brush by her and made a grab for him, but it was only a chair.

"Marcia!" Benny plunged this way and that, surfaced, drew breath . . . and realised his feet were not touching; the water pouring down from the street was over his height. "Marcia!" he screamed.

There was no reply.

He dived, swam desperately, reaching out in all directions, until his lungs were exploding, then he kicked for the surface again.

But this time there was no surface – his head struck the ceiling.

EAST HOUSTON STREET

1.30 pm

Every few seconds Tootsie shuddered and gazed anxiously at the lounge window. Not that she could see out of it, as heavy rain was hitting it almost like waves, streaming across it horizontally, instead of pouring down on to the sill.

"You'd think that having called four no trumps she'd have finessed the . . ." Lila Vail stared at the back of her sister's head and clicked her tongue. "You're not listening."

I am listening, but not to you, Tootsie thought. Her mind was nearly paralysed with fear that the window might blow in and her new rugging be ruined. Complaints about the inadequacies of members of their Ladies' Bridge Club was not a stimulating topic in these circumstances. But she supposed she must try to keep Lila happy; her older sister could get quite nasty when irritated. "Of courses I'm listening, sweetie. Go on. What did she play?"

Before Lila could answer there was a deafening crash from above them and even she was distracted. "Shit!" she exclaimed. "That cow upstairs must've dropped the piano. Now, as I was saying . . ."

The lights flickered and faded off, leaving them sitting in semi-darkness.

"Jees! That's the power gone. We'd better drink that coffee while it's still hot." Tootsie groped over to the coffee maker.

"To hell with coffee. Let's have some light. Flashlight? Candles? Where do you keep them?"

"I don't have either."

"Oh, shit! Are you telling me we're stuck with sitting here in darkness tonight? Sister, if you'd ever had to live in Florida you'd be better prepared than this. How'll we see to cook our dinner?"

Lila was getting tetchy, which in turn irritated Tootsie. What right had Lila to complain? They were only here because she had insisted on staying. Left to herself, Tootsie would have preferred to have left with Dai Evans. That might have been fun, even with his miserable wife along. "Cooking dinner won't be a problem." She giggled. "No power, no dinner." Let old bossy boots put that in her pipe and smoke it.

"That's not funny," Lila snapped. "What are we supposed to eat?"

"Cheese, and fruit and crisp bread – oh, and we have a tin of sardines I bought for the cat . . ."

"Catfish? For dinner! That's crazy . . ."

"Pussikins!" Tootsie called. "Where is she? Hiding under my bed, I'll bet. Scared stiff."

"Damn the cat."

"Lila! Will you stop that. Pussikins has been my little pal for years, ever since Edgar passed away . . ."

"Okay, okay. Just stop whining . . ."

"I'm not the one who's whining. You were fussing about your dinner . . ."

"Shut up!"

"No, you shut up!"

Another deafening crash interrupted the quarrel and the two women sat watching in alarm as a hail of bricks and debris fell past the window until a sudden extra gust of wind spun through the street and hurled the missiles through several windows – including theirs.

Both sisters screamed as drapes and all moveable objects in the room were hurled into a corner. The table cloth carried cups, saucers, sugar and milk bowls with it, pictures flew off the walls, and Tootsie half ran, half fell, about the room trying to rescue her treasures, wailing and moaning.

"Let's get out of here," Lila yelled. But the noise was too great and Tootsie couldn't hear her. So the older woman grabbed her arm and tried to drag her to the door. Tootsie got the message and with a last agonised glance around her room turned to help Lila, who was tugging at the door handle.

But the door wouldn't move, held solid by the pressure on its frame. Neither of them noticed the crack in the wall above their heads.

New York Harbour

2.00 pm

As the centre of the hurricane swept in towards the land, it pushed more and more water in front of it. The seas climbed, higher and higher. Fifteen miles from the Narrows, the Ambrose Lightship parted her moorings and was swept towards the beach; nearer at hand the Sandy Hook Light Tower was overwhelmed by sixty-foot waves. In Lower New York Bay, the buoys and lights were scattered, Rockaway Beach, Jones Beach and Coney Island were obliterated. Some of the surging water found its way into Jamaica Bay, and the Wildlife Sanctuary was destroyed; waves broke across the runways at Kennedy and smashed through the glass doors to batter the luggage carousels to pieces. But by far the greater volume of water was funnelled into the Narrows, from which it exploded in a mountainous fifty feet of surging sea, bursting across an already turbulent harbour to engulf the Statue of Liberty. For some minutes the recently rebuilt structure defied the waves, even as they struck at the finely chiselled face; the hand holding the torch continued to thrust itself above the water. Then the tremendous force of the storm proved too much for the foundations, and the great statue dissolved, the noise of its fall lost in the howl of the wind.

The storm surge continued on its way to smash into an already half-submerged Lower Manhattan. Staten Island disappeared beneath flying waves as part of the wave found its way down Kill van Kull into Newark Bay; the main force tore up the East and Hudson Rivers with the force of a gigantic express train.

The Hudson River

2.30 pm

Ernie turned the motor boat in alongside a pier in Yonkers. "This is far enough."

"You reckon?" Bill asked uncertainly.

"Sure. We're 15 miles from the harbour. All the experts say the danger is in the five miles nearest the sea, right? Besides, I'm starving. Hey, you guys," he bawled at some men who had just finished mooring their own boat. "Take a line."

Nancy raised her head, slowly and sadly, unable to believe that they had really come to rest at last. It had taken them more than five hours to make the journey from Lower Manhattan – fifteen miles. She, and the children, had been violently sick for most of the time, the wind had been howling, the rain had been pouring, and the waves on the river had been high enough to make her feel she was in a storm at sea. The boat had leaked like a sieve through her decks, and had been leaking through her hull as well – Ernie had had to keep the bilge pump working all the time – and the roughness had been accentuated by the myriad wakes carved back and forth, as it seemed everyone who owned a boat in New York was trying to take it to safety at the same time. Added to which, in the Upper Harbour, and alongside the docks on Hoboken, Weehawken, and on the West Street side, the big ships had their engines going as they had been swinging and heaving at their mooring warps; many had apparently already left the harbour that morning, before the full force of the storm had actually arrived, preferring to risk themselves at sea, where they could use their immense turbines at full power, to remaining trussed up like ducks for the table, with ropes and hawsers which were already beginning to part.

Nancy wished them joy. She only wanted to get ashore, and several times on the voyage she had consigned her soul to God, as boats had come perilously close, several even colliding, with much grinding of fenders and shouting and swearing from irate skippers and terrified passengers. If Ernie thought that Yonkers was safe, that was good enough for her.

Her sister-in-law, Marge, obviously felt the same way. "Just let Nance and the kids and me ashore," she begged. "You can do what you like after."

"In one minute, darling," Ernie promised. "Secure that bow warp, Bill; make it good and fast."

The pier was crowded with boats already moored or mooring up, and with their crews. There were a couple of restaurants across the street with their awnings destroyed by the wind, but their interiors could be seen to be packed with people, either having a late lunch or drowning their sorrows. The wind was powerful up here, but not half as strong as it had been down in the harbour.

As soon as the boat was secured alongside, Marge and Nancy grabbed the children, one by each hand, and staggered up the pier and on to the land. Nancy felt like kneeling down and kissing it, even in the pouring rain. The two women got the four children across the street and into the warmth and forced jollity of the bar, where there appeared to be a huge, if somewhat hysterical, party in progress; they were welcomed as if they were the two special guests for whom everyone had been waiting. A jukebox was blaring, and someone bought each of the women a beer. The children were lifted up to sit on the bar counter and given sodas – there was apparently no question of paying.

Relief flooded through Nancy's system, as she turned round to look at the boat, where Bill and Ernie were still patiently securing extra warps and springers, making sure nothing was going to damage her.

Nothing?

"Holy Mary Mother of God," said the Irishman standing beside her. People crowded against them, rubbing misted breath from the glass to see better, staring in horror at the huge wave coming up the river.

"Just like a bore," said someone who had obviously seen one of the rivers in Europe acting like a funnel for the rising tide. "What the French call the Mascaret."

Nancy abandoned the children and ran outside. "Bill!" she screamed, her voice dissipating on the wind. "Ernie! Come ashore! Hurry!"

The men, and all the others still tending their craft, had seen what was coming, and scrambled on to the pier. Ernie slipped and fell, and Bill turned back to help him. Then the tidal bore struck. It was already carrying, high on its 15-foot crest, an assortment of shattered boats and pieces of driftwood and various flotsam. Now it smashed through the pier and the moored boats like an axe through pastry, sweeping them on up the river, a foaming maelstrom of destruction, boats, animals, shore side houses . . . and men. The last Nancy saw of Bill and Ernie was them clinging desperately to pieces of the destroyed pier as they were carried out of sight. She looked up at the heavens to scream her agony and grief . . . and found herself looking at blue sky.

NATIONAL AMERICAN BROADCASTING SERVICE OFFICES, FIFTH AVENUE

3.00 pm

The lights in the NABS building had flickered several times before finally going out. By then Richard, to whom everyone left in the building had instinctively turned for leadership, had had the emergency generator started, and he had also assembled all the staff in the main studios, which had no external windows and was by far the safest place to be; all broadcasting had naturally ceased – if they still had the power to put out, they knew no one in the city still had the power to receive. They were all suffering from at least shock. In addition to Julian, several people had been badly hurt either by flying glass as more and more windows had shattered, or by falling down stairs when caught by sudden gusts of wind rampaging through the building. These had been treated and sedated as far as possible. But the building itself was a wreck; nearly all the windows had been blown in or sucked out, and the resulting to offices were shattering; that the roof had remained on was due not only to the strength of its construction but to the prompt closing of every possible door. Those doors were in fact failing, one by one, but slowly, and Richard had some hope they might just last the storm; he knew they had to be approaching the eye.

The principal horror was Julian's body, lying beneath a sheet on the studio floor, with the room around him packed with frightened people – even if the generator kept the air-conditioning going. The Mayor had said, justifiably enough, that the most acute danger was that of drowning, that those in buildings situated more than fifty feet above water level would be physically safe, whatever damage their dwellings or offices might have to suffer. Julian had been in such a building, and the storm had not even reached its height when he died. If only they had evacuated the offices a few minutes earlier – but not even Richard had envisaged such a tragedy.

The thought of that happening to Jo was unbearable. He had tried to reach her by phone several times, but without success; now the phones were all dead. Then, once he could no longer fulfil his role as a weatherman he had thought of attempting to get to her . . . it was only a few blocks. But he had known that no one could survive, much less move on those streets. So he had waited, and now . . . others had heard it too. Heads began to raise as a huge, deathly stillness overtook the afternoon; the sudden cessation of the almost intolerable racket with which they had existed for so long was stunning. People stared at each other in bewilderment, and when they spoke, they shouted, as they had had to do all morning, and then hastily dropped their voices to whispers. But they were euphoric whispers; could the catastrophe be over?

"Not quite," Richard told them. "This is the eye of the storm. It was travelling so quickly last time we had an update that it's not likely to last more than half an hour at the outside. Then the wind is going to blow again, just as hard as before, only from the other direction, west, instead of east. But we're winning. We know the storm is passing through; things can only get better from here on. And with the wind in the west that water level is going to get pushed back down to normal pretty rapidly. So just sit tight for another few hours, and we'll all be able to leave."

Reassured, they were chatting now. Richard went over to Jayme, who sat on the floor staring into space; Julian had been a special friend. "Listen," he said in her ear. "I'm leaving now. If anyone wants to know where I've gone, tell them I'm trying to find out what's happening out there, and that I'll be back. But keep convincing them they're better off here than anywhere else, at least until the wind has dropped."

For a moment she just looked at him, eyes blank. Then her head jerked. "Going out? Where?"

"I must get to Mrs Donnelly. She's alone in her apartment with her children . . . God knows what they must have gone through."

"Mrs Donnelly . . ." she blinked at him, then gave a faint smile. "You and her? Well, what do you know. But you can't go outside. When the storm comes back you'll be killed."

"I reckon I have time to make it, just. I have to go, Jayme. So, see you tomorrow."

"Tomorrow!" Her eyes were wide. That wasn't a thinkable thought.

Richard let himself out of one of the doors leading into a side corridor. The utter silence of the building outside the studio was uncanny. He didn't want to chance the elevators just in case the generator failed or the mechanism had been damaged, instead took the stone stairs, hurrying down, panting less with exertion than apprehension.

At the bottom the street doors were closed, but he leaned on the bar and stepped out, blinking in the sudden bright daylight, looking up at the blue sky above him, and then gasping at the destruction to either side. It was some hours since the breaking of the office window, and he had not looked out since. Now he gazed at automobiles tumbled one on top of the other, trees down in every direction; broken glass crackled beneath his shoes, water flowed everywhere – if the area was above any possible flooding from the sea, it had certainly been flooded by the fantastically heavy rainfall which had been unable to run off through the waterlogged sewers.

He hurried along the avenue, meaning to turn to the right when he got to 48th Street, picking his way through the debris, listening to sounds of returning life, windows being thrown open, people calling to each other . . . he hoped they knew that this respite was only going to be of the most temporary kind. But he could no longer help anyone, nor did he want to help anyone, save Jo. His mind was clouded with fear – 48th Street was only just on the 50-foot mark, and although he was certain that no sea could really have reached it, he could not stop his imagination doing its worst.

He was still several blocks short when the daylight faded, and he looked up in time to be blinded by a vivid flash of lightning, accompanied simultaneously by an ear-splitting clap of thunder. The blue sky had disappeared, and instead the black clouds were back, and with them, sudden teeming rain and the enormous roaring of the hurricane wind.

Richard knew he had to reach the nearest street, where he reckoned he would obtain a lee. But crossing the intersection was going to be no easy task as the wind picked him up and sent him sprawling. He made no attempt to rise, clung to the sidewalk and began to inch his way to a pile-up of automobiles on the corner, only to be caught by another gust and sent rolling, splashing through the water running out of the gutters. He came to rest against an uprooted tree, held on to it, and worked his way once again towards the hopeful shelter of the automobiles. These were shuddering and threatening to break loose from each other with every gust, but for the most part were so tightly crushed together they acted as a windbreak, although even as he inched his way along beside them one was picked up and hurled over his head, to land some fifty feet farther down the avenue, and the whole pile threatened to disintegrate on top of him.

He got up and made a dash for the street, and was thrown down again, battered and bruised, against a bent railing which had once surrounded a trashcan. He lay there, watching water bubbling out of a sewer hole only inches from his face. It would be damned silly to lie there and drown on Fifth Avenue, he thought, pushed himself up, and once again fought his way forward.

PARK AVENUE

3.30 pm

"What's in that box, Mom?" Owen Michael asked, indicating the heap dumped in the shower stall, topped by an old cardboard box.

"Photos, waiting to be fixed in those albums."

"Can we see well enough in this light to do them?" The power had been gone some while and they were trying to economise, using only one candle.

"Let's try." It would help occupy their minds, an alternative to racking her brain to invent children's stories: no drama could compete with the current destruction of their city.

Together they knelt on the bathroom rugging and set the photos out in neat piles.

"That's an awful one of you skiing, Mom." Tamsin held up a shot of Jo slithering down a slope, a flurry of skis and snow in the air.

"What about this one of you and Owen Michael under water, last year?"

Owen Michael grabbed it. "Heck, I don't recall that. What camera were you using?"

Every few moments they held their breaths, listening, mentally and physically shaken, even shut away in their inner sanctum.

The sudden silence took them completely by surprise. "Holy shit!" Owen Michael exclaimed. "What's happening?"

"It's the eye," Tamsin said, trying to control the quivering of her lower lip. "We had it in Eleuthera."

"You mean it's done? It's over?" Owen Michael shouted, scrambling to his feet.

"No, it's not done," Jo told him. "Don't open the door."

"It'll start again," Tamsin said, her voice containing a sob as she remembered that terrible night. "Worse than before."

"But . . ." Owen Michael looked from her to his mother. "It must mean something good."

"Sure it does. It means we're halfway through," Jo told him. "That has to be good. Now sit down and relax."

Reluctantly Owen Michael sat down again. "Do you reckon Marcia and Benny will have been flooded out?" he asked. "Greenwich Village isn't 50 feet above sea level, is it?"

"No. They may have been flooded. But they'll have left town. I think they must have gone away yesterday." Jo didn't want to think about Marcia and Benny. They had to be safe. Surely.

"What about the cottage?" Tamsin's face was screwed up with worry, looking for all the world like a little old lady.

Jo put an arm round her. "That'll be all right. It's completely shuttered up and, anyway, Bognor is twenty miles from the sea. And on a hill. No problem there."

"But they'll have a lot of wind," Owen Michael went on, pessimistically. "What if a tree falls and smashes through the roof?"

Jo gave him a warning frown over Tamsin's head; the poor child was quite upset enough. "I'm sure . . ." she began, then checked, listening.

"That was a knock on the door," he said. "I know it was."

"There it is again," Tamsin said. "There's someone there, wanting to come in."

Jo leapt to her feet. Richard! He'd come during the eye. Thank God he was safe. But she hadn't told the children he might be joining them, so she said, "I'll see who it is."

"Are you sure it's safe, Mom?" Owen Michael cautioned.

"I'll be careful. But listen, you bolt the door behind me, just in case the wind gets up before I'm back."

"Mom . . ." he said uneasily, but she had already opened the bathroom door and stepped into the corridor.

Everything was amazingly quiet. "Bolt it now," she called through the door as she closed it behind her. As soon as she heard the bolt slip into place she hurried eagerly across the lounge. It was such a relief to know Richard was here; she couldn't wait to hold him in her arms.

And he was only just in time. The lounge had seemed startlingly bright compared with the enclosed bathroom, but before she could reach the main door the room was darkening and there was a flash of lightning which made her gasp, while immediately huge drops of rain began slashing at the window again.

"Richard!" she shouted, running into the lobby to release the bolts, pull the chain free and swing open the heavy, security door . . . to gasp in horror. It wasn't Richard. It was Stuart Alloan. And another man.

"Hi, there," Alloan said with a sneer. "My lucky day. I was afraid you might've gotten away."

The wind had returned, whistling up the stairwell and into the apartment. Breathless with shock, Jo staggered back against the lobby wall, held there, momentarily, by the force of the sudden gust. If only she'd had time to slam the door in their faces . . . but they had been blown into the lobby with her.

"Let's get this goddamned door closed," the second man shouted, and it took the strength of both men to swing it back on to the latch.

It gave Jo a few moments in which to recover her breath . . . and her senses. She could see at a glance that this new man, small and dark with a vicious curl to his lip, would probably prove to be as evil as Alloan. Her legs felt weak, but she had to keep her head. "What do you want?" she asked, trying to sound calm, praying that the children would remain locked in the bathroom, no matter what happened out here.

"That depends what you have, sister," Garcia leered at her before staring about him, mentally assessing her material as well as her physical worth.

Alloan stared at her, unsmiling. "We want you, for a start," he said. "I owe you plenty, remember?"

Jo licked her lips and looked right and left. But now she was helpless; even the statuette was out of reach. And anyway, there were two of them this time.

"I'm gonna fuck the ass off you, you bitch," Alloan continued. "And I promise you, it won't be an act of love. I been dreaming of fucking you, ever since last time I was here and you turned nasty on me. You feel like fucking her, too, Domingo?"

"Sure," his friend replied from the lounge. "But I feel like a drink, more. Bring her in here."

Alloan advanced on Jo.

"All right," she said, trying to reject the blind panic clawing at her brain. She was about to be raped, twice, by these men. But she could stand that if it would save the children. As for what Alloan meant to do to her afterwards . . .

He caught her as she went through the door, slid his arms round her waist, began to squeeze and fondle her breasts. She wanted to kick him but didn't dare, watched Domingo at the bar, pouring himself neat whisky, draining the glass in two gulps. "Christ," he said, "I needed that." He turned, "You got food, sugar?"

"Yes," Jo nodded. Anything to keep them busy. "Let go of me." She tried to shake off Alloan. "Let me go."

His fingers scraped across her flesh, but he released her.

"It'll have to be cold," she told them. "There's no power."

"So it'll be cold; just get it," Garcia said, sitting down. "You watch her."

Jo went into the kitchen, Alloan at her shoulder. She opened the ice box, and he began to touch her again, at her waist now, playing with her belt. "Let's get these pants off," he said. "I want to look at your ass. I remember it, you know. The sweetest little ass in town."

"Leave me alone," she muttered, taking out ham and tomatoes and lettuce, opened the kitchen drawer to find a knife, and had her wrists seized.

"Forget it, baby," he said. "I know you. We'll eat with our fingers. You got bread?"

"In that bin. If you'll let me go . . ."

Still holding her wrist, Alloan opened the bin and took out a loaf of bread. "Take the plates," he said.

She took both plates into the lounge, and Garcia grabbed one and started cramming food into his mouth. "Christ!" he said. "I was hungry. And hell, we only just made it, kid. Listen to that."

The wind seemed even louder because now it was blowing directly at the building instead of coming from behind.

"Yeah." Alloan grinned, and finished eating. "But I told you we'd be snug here, Domingo. Right?"

"Right." Garcia stretched. "That feels better. Now what d'you say we play with the dame a little."

"Yeah," Alloan said. "Yeah."

Jo had stood between them, trying to make up her mind what to do, hoping that maybe they would fall asleep after their meal – they certainly looked sufficiently beat up, with their wet clothes torn and dishevelled, to need sleep. She was taken by surprise when Alloan threw his arms round her waist and stretched her across his knees on the settee. She cried out and struck at him, and he laughed and caught her wrists. "She's a fighter," he said.

"I like them best. You hold her arms." Garcia got up.

Jo strained and twisted, but Alloan merely moved from beneath her and then knelt, one hand on each wrist, pinning her to the settee. Her legs flopped away from it, and she kicked at Garcia, but he laughed and knelt beside her to unfasten her belt. "Let's see what you got in there," he said, and then jerked his head. "Holy shit!"

The outer door had burst open before the force of the wind, and as the lobby door had been left ajar, an almost solid mass of air rushed into the apartment. Jo heard a tremendous crack from behind her and knew that the picture window had at last gone. She also knew what was going to happen next, instinctively.

Garcia had released her and got to his feet. "Shut that goddamned . . ." he was shouting, when the wind picked him up and lifted him right over the back of the settee. He gave a despairing shriek as he was carried to the huge, empty window and gazed at nothing but space.

Alloan had released her wrists to turn and look at the door and the wind caught him in turn. He fell over the back of the settee with a shout of dismay. Jo, already half on the floor, lay against the heavy piece of furniture and felt it move, even as she flattened against it, all the breath being crushed from her body. She heard Alloan scream again and again, the last scream being a despairing wail. But now the settee was moving with increasing speed, carrying her with it as she threw her arms around as much of it as she could hold. She shrieked, and again as she left the floor, and then the gust slackened and the settee crashed into the wall beneath the window, causing her to release the springs and fall on her back, gasping and weeping.

"Mom!" Owen Michael was shouting from the bathroom. "Mom!"

"Get back inside," Jo shouted. "Bolt the door."

She struggled to her feet; the wind was still strong, but she could move against it until the next big gust. She drove herself forward, into the lobby. The outer door had only been slammed to, not bolted. The Yale lock had been torn from the wood, as had the ordinary lock. But the three bolts and the chain were still intact, and the door looked solid enough. Exerting all her strength, moaning and crying, she slowly forced it shut, shot the bolts, fixed the chain. The apartment was still a turmoil of wind, gusting in through the broken window; bottles were swept out of the bar, furniture thrown left and right, pictures torn from walls; from the kitchen she again heard the sound of shattering glass and crockery. But she could move, and regain the inner corridor, shutting every door behind her. She banged on the bathroom door, and Owen Michael let her in. She collapsed between the two children, and they gazed at her cut lip and bruised hands.

"Who was it, Mom?" Owen Michael asked.

"Nobody," Jo gasped. "He went out again."

SATURDAY 29 JULY

Evening and After

East Houston Street

7.00 pm

Tootsie and Lila sat on the kitchen floor huddled against the cooker. During the lull they had managed to crawl back from the lounge door to the archway into the kitchen where they were slightly more protected from the wind and the rain and the flying debris. Tootsie sobbed occasionally while Lila swore, complaining that she had pulled a muscle in her chest trying to open that damned door. They had draped dish towels over their shoulders but that didn't stop them from shivering. They were both soaked to the skin.

Then the wind started again, louder than before with the window gone. It was impossible to speak above the continuous deafening noise, and neither had any idea how long they had sat there – it seemed like forever.

Lila started to pant and gasp. The pain in her chest was spreading, tightening, clutching her throat and sending rivers of agony into her left shoulder and down through her elbow. She hugged Tootsie as close as she could.

The younger sister stared in horror as air rattled in Lila's throat and her back arched in agony. She gazed helplessly at the struggle for breath, put both arms round her sister and tried to comfort her.

She held her for several more hours – long after the body had gone limp and cold. Lila was her only companion, even if she was dead. Tootsie continued to hold her while the cracks, which had commenced in the basement as the tidal surge had smashed its way in, spread slowly upwards, while the already weakened building was struck time and again by lightning and the 200-mile-an-hour winds rocked it on its foundations, until, finally, it all came crashing down, disintegrating into a massive pile of rubble.

9.30 pm

Jo could hardly believe her ears. Having actually fallen into an exhausted sleep on the bathroom floor, she awoke with a start when the shrieking, howling, crashing, faded; the noise of the wind was still tremendous, but the thunder was only a distant growl, and the drumming rain had ceased.

The children were still asleep, even more exhausted than herself. Cautiously she opened the bathroom door, stepped into the corridor and made her way through the darkness into the shattered shambles that had been her lounge . . . able to see the damage because the room was fantastically illuminated by a magnificent full moon which dipped in and out of the thinning clouds racing across the sky above Manhattan. She saw that the apartment door had been blown open again, the bolts forced out of the wood, the entire structure torn from its hinges – yet in the bathroom they had survived. She clung to the lounge door, still intact, and allowed the wind, now blowing something above gale force but seeming no more than refreshingly cool, to play over her, while she looked out through the shattered picture window, shuddering as she remembered those traumatic moments only a few hours before. The flickering moonlight did not reach below the rooftops, and at this level the city appeared almost normal.

But it would never be normal again. And perhaps, for her less than anyone.

She returned to the bathroom, poured herself a cup of coffee from the last of the many vacuum flasks they had filled earlier, returned to the lounge, listening, to slowly rising sounds, as other people realised they had also survived. They were mostly unhappy sounds, wails and screams, cries for help, drifting up from the street. She even thought she heard several gunshots, to suggest the police were already having trouble with looters.

Then she heard a noise closer at hand. There was someone in the corridor outside the apartment, moving slowly, laboriously, and cautiously towards her.

Her blood seemed to freeze – there was no way she could keep an intruder out, and this time there would be no wind to save her. She ran into the kitchen to find the carving knife, any knife, but the kitchen had been gutted by the wind, and she could finding nothing in the gloom. She turned, panting, and watched a man's frame in the doorway.

"Jo?" he whispered. "Jo, are you alive? For God's sake, Jo!"

"Richard!" she screamed, and hurled herself into his arms. "Oh, Richard!"

He hugged her close. "Sorry I took so long to get here, darling," he said. "I've been trying . . . God, I've been trying."

She stood away from him, stared at him in the moonlight. His jacket had been torn off and his tie, his shirt was buttonless and open to the waist. His hair was scattered and there were cuts and bruises on his face as well as his chest; his left arm hung awkwardly where he had fallen on it. And there was blood, all over him, but mainly on his torn trouser legs. "Oh, my God!" she cried. "You're hurt!"

"Broken glass, mainly," he said. "The street is ankle deep in it. After I was blown down the avenue and knocked out, I crawled part of the way on my hands and knees – I think there's still quite a lot in there."

"Knocked out?" she cried. "But . . ."

"A long time," he said. "A couple of hours. I don't know for sure. I lost my watch. But then, this . . ." he touched his arm and winced.

"Oh, Richard! It looks broken or something."

"It sure hurts."

"Oh, Richard!" She wanted to scream and scream . . . but at least partly with joy – and pride. "Oh, darling Richard, you came through the storm . . . what a risk you took."

He gave his crooked grin. "Well, I had to wait for the old girl to say I could. Then she changed her mind. Women are like that."

"You could have been killed." She held his good arm and drew him towards the bathroom. "And I had better set that arm and patch you up before you bleed to death."

He had been taking in the damage. "But you . . . and the children . . ."

"We're okay," she said, opening the bathroom door. "We're really quite snug in here." She closed the bathroom door behind them and lit a candle. Suddenly she felt faint and weak – from exhaustion mostly, but also from sheer relief at Richard's presence. Despite his torn and ragged appearance, his legs dribbling blood into the rugging, his broken arm, he was still a tower of strength. "Hey, kids," she said, as they woke up. "You remember Mr Connors, the weatherman from NABS. He came over to see how we've been doing. Wasn't that good of him?"

"Hi, Mr Connors," Owen Michael said. "We're doing fine. We had no problems at all."

Richard looked at Jo.

"No problems at all," she echoed.

SUNDAY 30 JULY

Morning

By daybreak Faith had long turned back to the north-east, and, dying, was spending the last of her vicious energy over Cape Cod. In New York the wind was no more than fresh. The rain had stopped, the clouds had cleared, and there was blue sky to accompany the sunrise.

The flood waters had receded, and the survivors began to emerge from the hiding places they had used for eighteen hours and more, unable to believe they were alive.

Horror gripped them as they looked at the city. A jumbled mass of destroyed vehicles, uprooted trees and shrubs, shattered buildings, some totally collapsed, even the more substantial ones badly damaged. And dead bodies, choked into the most unlikely places, became too obvious.

It was time to work.

Assistant Commissioner McGrath and a handful of patrolmen had fought their way up to the emergency police headquarters in the Plaza Hotel, along with the Mayor and most of his staff, and from here McGrath assumed command of the city law and order, for Commissioner Grundy had not been seen since Police Headquarters had been flooded out. Using radio, McGrath began assembling his battered and exhausted men and women to control events, stop looting, and begin the job of clearing up and hopefully preventing disease.

He did not lack help; at dawn half the available United States Army, with their medical corps, was airlifted into the disaster area to assist.

At dawn, too, Chauffeur Murray awoke James Calthrop White; they had slept shoulder to shoulder in the back seat of the Rolls. Amazingly, although the ditch had filled with rain, the engine started first kick, and when an army helicopter landed nearby to see if they were all right, they managed to push the car back on to the road.

"You want to go into town, JC?" Murray asked.

"I want to go home, Joe," J. Calthrop White said. "And have a large Scotch. Come to think of it, we'll *each* have a large Scotch."

Which they did. Amazingly, JC's house had escaped serious damage.

And at dawn too the surviving New Yorkers, wherever they might be, gathered in church and chapel, synagogue, mosque and temple, to give thanks for their deliverance.

At 8.00 am the President of the United States arrived by helicopter, to be greeted by the Governor and Mayor Naseby, and taken on a bird's-eye tour of the stricken city and its environs. "To think that one storm could

328

do so much damage," the President mused. "It makes one wonder what we're doing, with our puny little bombs and bullets, when there is that lurking out there, waiting to strike. But do you realise how lucky we were that it happened on a Saturday? And that there was adequate warning? If all the banks and business places had been open and crowded . . . shit. Bill . . ." he turned to Naseby. "I have to hand it to you, Bill, because I reckon we were lucky in having you in charge, as well. That was some decision you took, to order the evacuation of the entire city, while the storm was still a good distance away. But by God, if you hadn't . . ."

Naseby looked down at the ruins beneath him. "Yeah," he said. "But I didn't make that decision, Mr President. At least, not until it was forced upon me. The evacuation was ordered by a television weatherman, Richard Connors, on his own initiative. Because he knew what was coming, and the rest of us wouldn't believe him."

"Then Connors is someone I'd like to meet," the President said. "Or is that confidential?"

"I think Mr President is asking, Bill, if you are going to tell that fact to the voters," the Governor put in.

Naseby grinned. "I'll have to think about that. But I sure intend to tell Mr Connors, supposing I can find him." He looked down at the city again. "And supposing he's alive."

SUNDAY 30 JULY

Afternoon

"Yeah," Mark Hammond said into his radio. "She's clear of land and heading off to Newfoundland. Winds dropping all the time. Round the centre they're 80 miles an hour. I guess by tonight you'll be able to downgrade her to a storm. That's Faith, Doctor. We're heading back to base."

He turned the aircraft, allowing it to sink lower as he did so. They left the still turbulent mass of white behind them and dipped into clear skies with only little balls of cotton wool floating gently around and above them as they descended.

"Still some sea running," Landry commented, looking down at the whitecaps and the waves, flattened by the angle but still clearly several feet high, surging up the Gulf Stream.

"Yeah," Mark agreed. "I don't give much for the chances of any ship caught out in that. Home, boys, where the sun shines all the time."

"Hold it." Mackenzie had come up to join them on the flight deck and was using binoculars. "There's something down there."

"Where?"

"I've lost it now. But there was something. Let's make a sweep, skipper."

"One sweep," Mark grunted. He, and all his crew, were suffering from exhaustion and lack of sleep. Mackenzie was probably hallucinating.

"There it is," Landry said.

"Show me." Mark swung the plane again.

"Look," Mackenzie said.

"Take her," Mark told Landry, and levelled the binoculars. By now they were only 500 feet above the waves, and following Mackenzie's pointing finger he saw the sudden spurt of orange amidst the blue and white. "That's a life raft."

"And there are men in it," Mackenzie said.

Landry had dropped to 300 feet, and now they could clearly see the bodies draped across the half collapsed raft – the canopy had blown away and one of the compartments had deflated.

"Shit, what a position to be in," Mackenzie commented. "You reckon those guys can be alive?"

"I reckon we'd better get a helicopter out here to find out," Mark said, and thumbed his handset again.

Afterwards

In a remarkable two days life was heading back to normal. It would take months, years, completely to restore the city to its old, sleazy, greatness, but as soon as the debris was cleared away from the streets, tunnels and subways and all the bodies that were going to be recovered had been found, services were working again on a limited scale, and the airport runways repaired and re-opened. People began to pick up their lives again. With massive help pouring in, not only from the rest of the United States but from all over the world, disease was averted and the job of cleaning away the demolished buildings was facilitated.

As soon as it was safe to leave Park Avenue, Richard took Jo and the children to his apartment, which had remained undamaged, and there they spent the next few days, while the roads were being cleared and the clean-up got under way. The city was supplied with food and drinking water by the army, using great trucks and containers; it was rather like being under siege, but at least there was no danger involved. Jo did not attempt to explain her situation to Owen Michael and Tamsin, who did not question it. In the aftermath of such a catastrophe questions about personal relationships seemed for the moment irrelevant.

But once power was restored Richard felt it his duty to go back to work – broken arm in a sling – nothing further having been said about his dismissal, or indeed heard from JC at all. With the NABS building a shambles, news and weather reporting was to say the least, primitive, but a service was provided.

Jo knew she had to regain contact with the family, but the telephones were still out. She and the children returned to Park Avenue, and were overwhelmed with joy to find Washington back on duty, even if the place was more of a wreck than they remembered – but the building itself remained sound, and the repairmen were already at work. While the Cadillac was still in the garage, into which, miraculously, only a trickle of water had penetrated. Jo now discovered that Washington had a spare set of keys for it. She kissed him with relief. Sadly, he had no news of Florence, and in view of the total destruction of Coney Island the worst had to be supposed.

Nor was there any news to be had from Greenwich Village, where the destruction and loss of life had been massive; the entire area had been cordoned off by the army because bodies were still being recovered from the wreckage of houses and there the risk of disease had not yet been eradicated. "Next of kin will be informed as soon as identification can be made," the major in charge told Jo. "If your sister-in-law is here, we'll find her. But . . . you'd better pray she ain't."

Jo and the children called at the *Profiles* office and found it gutted and deserted, so they drove up to New Rochelle to collect Nana, then went on out to Bognor, which had been sideswiped by the storm but suffered no real damage; Faith, having turned north-east, had been losing force when she swept over Connecticut. The cottage was untouched save for fallen trees. It was a tremendous relief to find real normalcy at last. To walk from room to room opening doors and windows to sunshine, to look at each room prettily arranged with pictures, and ornaments and undamaged furniture – drapes moving gently in the warm air. And clothes! Jo wanted to touch everything, flick electric switches to be sure they worked, check out the fridge and freezer . . .

She lifted the phone – and heard the dialling tone. She wanted to scream with joy . . . then hesitated. But she had to find out. So she dialled.

Sally Davenport said, "Oh! Jo! Yes. I'll just get Sam." Her voice sounded quite odd.

But if Sam was back . . . Jo frowned, and waited.

"Jo? Are you at the cottage?" His voice sounded funny too.

"Yes."

"Have you seen the folks?"

"No. I'm on my way over now."

"Heck," he said. "We've been trying to contact you for two days, but there was no way. Jo . . ."

"Who got ashore?" she asked in a low voice; the children were outside.

"It was a monster wave, Jo. I swear it must've been 60 feet high. We never stood a chance. Michael never stood a chance. He was on the helm and went overboard. Jo . . . he was great. To the very end he was great. A real hero. Without him, we'd have been done far sooner."

"How many?" she asked again.

"The ship broke up. We couldn't get Pete up in time . . . he had a broken shoulder. And I think Jon had already died; he'd been flung on the deck and hit his head. Larry, Mark and I got the liferaft over, but it was torn apart by the wind and the sea, kept capsizing. We hung on, somehow, and gradually the seas started going down. We thought we were dead . . ."

"But you got ashore."

"A helicopter came and winched us up. Seems we were spotted by a navy weather plane. Larry . . . Larry didn't make it. Exposure, I guess. Mark's okay . . ."

"And so are you, Sam. Thank God for that," Jo said.

"Listen, Michael was a hero, Jo. I told you, if it hadn't been for him we'd have gone down much sooner."

"Yes," Jo said, and thought, if it hadn't been for him you wouldn't have gone down at all – you would have been snugly moored in Hamilton, Bermuda. But that was a thought she would have to keep to herself.

She put the children in the Cadillac and drove over to Pinewoods. One look at the faces of Big Mike and Babs told her that they knew . . . much more than she.

Babs embraced her. "Oh, Jo," she said. "We've been hunting for you everywhere. Mike drove into town and went to the apartment, but you weren't there, and the place was wrecked . . . we were so worried."

"When was this?" Jo asked.

"Yesterday."

"Oh. We were . . . staying with a friend."

They went on to the patio; Pinewoods had suffered even less damage than the cottage, and the children immediately rushed off to change for the pool. Jo and Big Mike and Babs sat on the loungers, silently for several moments, their brains teeming with things which had to be said, questions which had to be asked . . . each afraid to start.

"Have you told the children?" Babs asked at last, watching Owen Michael and Tamsin diving into the pool.

"No. I only found out an hour ago, from Sam Davenport. I'm not quite sure how to do it."

Babs nodded. "We haven't told Belle yet. About either of them."

"Either . . ." Jo's heart sank into her stomach; the absence of Marcia had been one of the questions she had been afraid to raise. "Marcia? I tried to contact them . . . Friday night. I even went there . . . but they weren't home."

"They were home Saturday," Big Mike said. "I drove down there yesterday, when I was looking for you, as well."

"And?" Jo prompted in a whisper.

"When I told them I was her father, they let me in to the Village," Big Mike said, his voice toneless. "Two army boys came with me." His head bent, and he covered his face with his hands, shoulders heaving. "They were in the kitchen, in the basement. The whole goddamned building was on top of them. But . . . they had drowned. Would you believe it? Drowned, in their own kitchen."

"Oh, God!" Jo gasped, the breath knocked out of her body. She remembered her last visit to them, their excitement, their pride in the transformation of their house – and the baby.

"And then, you," Babs said. "We didn't know . . . that man Connors kept telephoning . . ."

"Oh," Jo said. "I'd told him I was leaving town. I guess he was worried."

"But you didn't leave town," Big Mike said.

"No. We had an accident, so we went back to the apartment."

"And sat it out there," Babs said. "Was it very terrible?"

"We sat it out," Jo said, very carefully.

"Tamsin . . ."

"She's okay. I guess having Owen Michael with her helped."

"You have to tell them," Big Mike said. "They'll cry, but they have a lot to be proud of." Tears were streaming down his own face. "Their daddy died a hero, and he died doing what he liked best. He'd have defied that fucking storm to the end. He was a hero."

"Yes," Jo said. "He was a hero. I won't let them forget that."

She went inside, and after a moment Babs followed her. "It was all over between you two, wasn't it?"

Jo's shoulders rose and fell. "That doesn't mean I don't grieve for him, Babs. I guess the shock hasn't quite got through to me, yet. He was a great guy, in his own way. Just . . . not a great husband."

"I know." Babs put her arms round her daughter-in-law, and the two women wept together. "What are you going to do?" Babs asked, when she was able to control her voice.

"Oh, pick up the pieces, I guess." She attempted a smile. "There are an awful lot of pieces to be picked up. I don't even know if I still have a job."

"You're still our daughter, you know."

Jo wanted to weep afresh. She had no idea how to go about telling

Babs about Richard – that would have to wait, for a while at least. And the children had to come first – although she had an idea Owen Michael already understood the situation. He and Richard had appeared to like each other . . . but Owen Michael had thought his father was still alive. Now . . . there were crises ahead. But she would face them, with Richard.

After Jo left, Big Mike gazed at the pool, shoulders hunched. "Jees," he said. "All gone. Just like that. Michael, Marcia and Benny, Lawson, Eleuthera . . . Palmer tells me the office is wiped out . . . God Almighty, it'll be like starting from scratch, all over again."

"Would you like a hand, Dad?" Dale asked, quietly.

Big Mike glanced at him; the boy had hardly said a word since hearing of his brother's death.

Dale flushed. "So I don't have a college degree. But I can learn. If you'll have me."

"Have you? Christ Almighty, boy, if I thought you'd settle down . . . It's going to be tough," Big Mike said. "We'll still have our clients, I guess. But sorting out the mess . . . but hell, I reckon that with all of Wall Street hit, and the Stock Exchange under several feet of water, we're all in the same boat. If you're serious . . ."

"Try me," Dale said.

Big Mike held out his hand, and his son grasped it.

NATIONAL AMERICAN BROADCASTING SERVICE OFFICES, FIFTH AVENUE

Six Months Later

"I want you to know, Richard," said J. Calthrop White, "that when you were publicly commended by the Mayor of this city for what you did, I felt as proud as if I'd done it myself. I was additionally proud because I knew you had taken such action in the certain knowledge that I would back you to the hilt, regardless of the consequences." He did not even flush as he spoke, and allowed his gaze to drift over his massed employees in the main studio of the rebuilt NABS building. "But I also felt pride in my entire network, in all my employees, who remained at their posts throughout the ordeal, and who like that gallant man, Julian Summers, were prepared to die at their posts."

He paused, and there was a ripple of applause from the assembled staffers, and a loud sniff from Jayme.

"But I know," JC went on, "that Julian would have wanted the station to continue on its glorious way, bringing to the people of this great nation the best in television, regardless of the forces of nature that may be gathered against it. And that he, and all of you, will be as proud as myself when I have to tell you that NABS has been granted a franchise to operate a television company in the United Kingdom. The news came through today."

He paused to allow another ripple of applause.

"Yes, folks," he went on, "the news of the acceptance of our bid has only just been received, but, and many of you will not know this, the bid was made on that fateful Saturday last July, and our success is at least partly due to the unremitting efforts of your Vice-President, Derek Kiley." He beamed at Kiley. "It was Mr Kiley who commanded the ship, if I may say so, during my absence, and it was Mr Kiley who brought her safely through."

More applause, and Kiley gazed at Richard, who gazed back – Kiley had been in a state of collapse throughout the day.

"My only regret," JC continued, "is that I was unable to be here with you during those terrible hours, to share your burden. You all know how hard I tried to get to you, and how I was nearly killed. Yet I bitterly regret my absence. So now, Richard, it gives me great pleasure to present you with this scroll, signed by all the civic authorities and business organisations in this city, and by myself, as a small token of our appreciation of your actions during the approach of Hurricane Faith. And to offer you a new life-time contract with NABS. I believe you have already seen the terms."

"Yes," Richard said.

"And do you accept?"

Although his decision had already been taken, and JC knew it, Richard hesitated before replying. He had been very tempted to tear the contract into little pieces. But he had discussed it with Jo, and realised that would be stupid. He was a weatherman. If he didn't work for NABS he would have to work for some other company – and the odds were he would discover another J. Calthrop White there too. At least, here, he would be listened to in the future. "I accept, JC," he said.

JC shook hands. "Now, finally, ladies and gentlemen," he said. "It gives me great pleasure to announce to everyone here your engagement to Mrs Josephine Donnelly. I guess everyone here knows that Mrs Donnelly's husband perished heroically in the storm. So did two other members of her family, her brother-in-law and her sister-in-law. The Donnellys were my friends . . ." he paused to blow his nose. "That they could have suffered such grievous losses and come up fighting is a fitting testimony to their characters. Richard, Jo . . ." he shook Richard's hand again, gave Jo a kiss on the cheek, looked uncertainly at Owen Michael and Tamsin, standing together beside their mother.

"Thank you, JC," Jo said, keeping her face straight with an effort.

"So now I guess you'll need time off for a honeymoon, Richard."

"I would appreciate that, sir."

JC smiled as he wagged his finger. "Just be sure you're back before the hurricane season. And right now, I would like to ask you a very important question."

Richard waited.

"Is there going to be another Faith, ever again?"

Richard looked into his eyes, while his hand stole out to hold Jo's. "There could be another Faith this year, JC. Until we know a lot more about hurricanes, and their movement and development patterns, every time there is a disturbance out there in the Atlantic, it could be the ultimate storm. That's something we all need to remember."

MAY

The End?

The big amphibian droned through a cloudless sky, her crew looking down on the quiet blue of an untroubled ocean.

"You reckon this has to be the most boring job ever created?" Bob Landry asked. "Day after goddamned day, just looking at sea and sky."

"Yeah," Mark Hammond agreed. "Well, I guess that's it for today, at least." He thumbed his intercom. "You ready to turn for home, Doc? There sure ain't anything to worry about down there."

"I'd like to stand on a little further, Mark," Eisener replied. "There's a report just coming in about a large stationary cloud mass off Cape Verdes. I think we should take a look. Don't you?"

Mark looked at Landry, who looked back. "Yeah," the two pilots said together. "We should take a look."

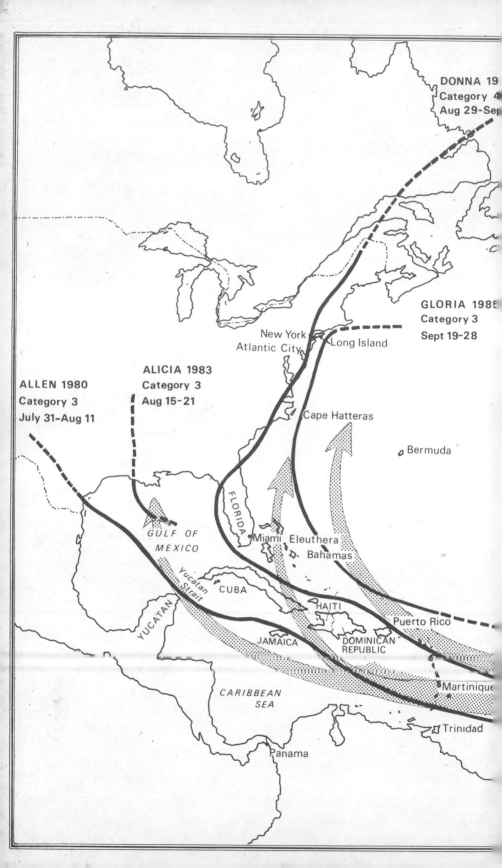

DONNA 19
Category 4
Aug 29–Sep

GLORIA 1985
Category 3
Sept 19–28

ALLEN 1980
Category 3
July 31–Aug 11

ALICIA 1983
Category 3
Aug 15–21

New York
Atlantic City
Long Island

Cape Hatteras

Bermuda

FLORIDA

GULF OF
MEXICO

Miami
Eleuthera
Bahamas

Yucatan
Strait

CUBA

HAITI

Puerto Rico

YUCATAN

JAMAICA

DOMINICAN
REPUBLIC

Martinique

CARIBBEAN
SEA

Trinidad

Panama